A Walk Through Fire

Felice Stevens

A Walk through Fire
Revised Edition: November 2016

Print Edition

Cover Art by Reese Dante
www.reesedante.com
Cover Photography by Alejandro Caspe
Edited by: Flat Earth Editing
www.flatearthediting.com

Published in the United States of America

Years after running away from an abusive foster family, Asher Davis still struggles with the guilt of leaving his foster brothers behind. He's climbed to unimaginable heights as a ruthless, high-powered attorney, creating a life of power and control and takes whatever and whomever he wants.

Blaming himself for the death of his parents, Dr. Drew Klein retreats into a shell of loneliness, merely going through the motions of life. After a disastrous, short-lived marriage, Drew leaves his lucrative medical practice to set up a clinic for abused young men and women. The decision has more repercussions than Drew could ever imagine when the dark and sensual Ash Davis volunteers to help.

Although Drew isn't gay, Ash is inexplicably drawn to him. He vows to simply bed him and forget him like he's done with every other man. However Drew's sweet and caring nature and unexpected passion both stun and frighten Ash, who questions his right to any happiness at all. And when Ash befriends an abused young man who unwittingly draws the clinic into danger, threatening Drew's safety and that of his beloved grandmother, Ash discovers there is nothing he won't sacrifice to protect the love he never thought he'd find.

Dedication

To my children. Don't let anyone ever kid you. Going to work every day is the easy part. Being your parent is the toughest job I'll ever love. I'm proud of the adults you are growing up to be and happy you want to share your joys and sorrows with me still. I love you to the moon and back.

To Marcia Miller-Rogers. Here is your Ash—I hope I did him proud for you. Thank you for loving him as much as I do and always brightening up my day whenever you speak of him. I will always think of you whenever I pick up this book.

Acknowledgments

To my editors, Hope and Jessica from Flat Earth Editing, thank you for polishing up Ash and Drew's story to its best. You guys are the best, I loved re-visiting this group of guys and hope you all enjoy their revised stories. They always reveal something new every time I revisit them.

To all the readers out there who I've met on line and in person, you are amazing. I love you all.

If you, or anyone you know is suffering please contact the Trevor Project at 866-488-7386 or go to www.thetrevorproject.org for help. The Trevor Project provides intervention and crisis counseling for LGBTQ youth ages 13-24.

Chapter One

DEATH COMES IN *all forms.* Reviewing divorce or separation agreements rarely caused Asher Davis to be this morbid or pensive, but the dissolution of a marriage after only six months seemed depressing even to a cynic such as himself. All the dreams the happy couple had planned for the rest of their lives must have crashed and burned in an inferno of pain and anger so devastating, any thought of repair was impossible. Ash gazed out the window of his office, the unending blue horizon punctuated by only a few fluffy white clouds. The bright sunlight and crispness of a clear April morning should have lifted his spirits, but this time of year never did. The beauty of this early Spring morning only served to remind him of all he'd lost and left behind.

"Let this be a lesson to you, Walker." Ash slid the file to the associate sitting across from him at the conference table. "It probably would've happened sooner or later. For some reason, men and women insist on pairing off and remaining faithful, despite evidence to the contrary that it isn't normal to do so."

The newest member of Frank and Davis shot him an uneasy smile, and Ash suddenly remembered Walker himself was a recently engaged man.

Even though he'd never been married, never even come close to a relationship with anyone for that matter, Ash had seen and heard enough gruesome stories to know how hard people had to work to make a marriage successful. Compromise, trust, and that thing called love. He shuddered, swallowing hard.

Not his problem. He was there to make sure his client, the young and lovely Jackie Klein, got out of her marriage with everything she had coming to her so her rich daddy could pay the firm's retainer. The rumor of her immediate post marital infidelity didn't trouble him in the least. He wasn't being paid to care about anything at all.

"Have you finished reviewing the file?"

"Yes, Mr. Davis. It appears Mrs. Klein was seen on numerous occasions leaving the brownstone of David Westlake. These appointments would take place at random times of the day, while her husband was at work."

"Walker." The associate's gaze met his over the table. "Mrs. Klein is our client. I'm not interested in who she was fucking."

Walker's face flushed, and he gulped. "Um, right. So, Drew Klein, from everything we can see, went to work at the same time every morning, came home at the same time each evening, and aside from a weekly night out with his friends, stayed home every night."

"Sounds like a crashing bore," drawled Ash. "No wonder she cheated on him." He flicked his fingers over the papers in the file. "Go on. Please tell me something interesting. Anything."

"I'm afraid that's it, sir."

"So it's basically a no-fault. They've passed that magic six-month period, and now we, the greedy legal team, get to hammer out all the goodies in the divorce agreement. At the end of the day, she gets her freedom to screw her way through the city if she wants, he gets his freedom from a cheating bitch, and we get our money." He stood and smiled down at Walker, who closed and stacked the files in preparation for the client meeting. "Let's go and end this farce. I'll meet you at the conference room in five."

He watched Walker stride down the hallway to the conference room where the parties were set to meet. As he did before every meeting, Ash took a moment inside his office's private restroom to check his reflection in the mirror. Navy-blue suit, white shirt, and bright green tie, all sharp, clean, and fresh. No matter that this was his firm and his name now joined Jacob Frank's on the door, he still had something to prove to himself, that he wasn't that poor little gay kid from the wrong side of the tracks. The one whose parents had abandoned him.

He was Asher Davis, and he mattered.

From his wallet he pulled out the only snapshot he'd ever possessed. It was taken on his law-school graduation day, of him and the firm's founder, Jacob Frank. He towered over the tiny man, but only physically did he best Mr. Frank. The man was his better in every way possible. Asher had managed to secure the scholarship Mr. Frank set up at his law school, and had worked like a dog to make sure he would have a place at the law firm of Jacob Frank upon graduation. No attorney bested Jacob Frank in negotiations or litigation, and there was no one he'd wanted to work for more.

Why Jacob Frank took to him, Ash would never know. Mr. Frank often joked that Asher was the son he'd never wanted, but it was said with such fondness in his warm brown eyes that Ash experienced an unfamiliar pain in his chest. Then Mr. Frank would brusquely ask him to recite the facts of his next case and drill him to make sure he was always prepared for class.

Looking down at the picture in his hand, Asher blinked against the surprising wetness in his eyes. Though he'd been gone two years now, Jacob Frank's presence remained as strong as if he'd risen from his chair a moment before. And Ash would never forget Mr. Frank's final words to him.

"Asher, my son. Let go of your past. It's the only way you can take control of your future. Rise above your pain. Don't grow old, alone and unloved like me. Find someone to share your life with. You've been the greatest source of comfort and joy to me. I wish you love and peace in your heart."

"I'll always try to make you proud, Mr. Frank."

The pad of his thumb grazed over the worn photo, tracing his mentor's face. "But you did fine on your own, and so will I."

Replacing the picture carefully, he smoothed his hair back, and like a chameleon, wiped away any evidence of sorrow and loneliness, replacing it instead with his confident, devil-may-care smile. He left his office, closed the door behind him and strode down the hall.

As he pushed open the doors of the conference room, Ash scanned the faces of the people sitting. Of course, he'd already met his client and her father, Richard Sachs. "Hello Jackie, Richard." He kissed Jackie Klein's cheek and shook her father's hand, then turned to greet her soon-to-be ex-husband, Dr. Drew Klein, and Klein's attorney, Peter Dent.

"Peter, how the hell have you been?" The two shook hands, and Ash allowed his first real smile of the day. He and Peter had been inseparable in law school; they'd sat next to one another in their section, and neither would've made it past that horrific first year without the other's help. "It's been way too long." The son of one of the premier family lawyers in the city, Peter had a job waiting for him in his father's firm upon graduation. Having no such luxury, Ash had needed to keep his grades high enough to hold his scholarship and remain in school.

"Ash, my man, I've been meaning to call, but you know how it is with the wife and kids." A faint tinge of red crossed Peter's cheeks, but Ash let it ride. He didn't begrudge Peter his family life; heck, he actually liked his wife, Lisa, even if she did think she was the gay man's answer to matchmaking.

Ash's gaze slid to the pale, dejected man at Peter's side, and extended his hand. "Dr. Klein, I presume? I'm Asher Davis."

Drew Klein met his gaze, and an iron fist punched Ash in the stomach. *Holy fuck*. The man was gorgeous. Too thin and too pale, but even that couldn't hide the high cheekbones, straight nose, and strong chin of a perfectly sculpted face. Sadness and defeat rolled off him in waves. Klein's dry palm, however, rested warm and solid within his and for some inexplicable reason, Ash's heart beat a bit faster as they shook hands.

"Hello, Mr. Davis." No friendly smile resided on Klein's lips, nor did his green eyes radiate any spark of life. His well-modulated voice sounded weary, as if he had neither the strength nor desire to expend any effort. Obviously the dissolution of his marriage weighed much more heavily on his mind than on his soon-to-be ex-wife's, who chatted busily with her father while simultaneously texting on her phone.

Somewhat taken aback by his unorthodox response to this man, this *obviously straight* man, Ash cleared his throat and backed away. "Shall we get on with the meeting?" His voice shook and he strode to the side table and poured himself a glass of water. After gulping down the cold liquid, his throat loosened, and he felt more like himself. Perhaps that third cup of coffee had messed with his equilibrium.

"This should all go quite seamlessly, as I see it. Mrs. Klein is not contesting the divorce, and Peter, I think your client is aware that under the terms of the prenup, the parties will be leaving the marriage in the same position as when they entered it."

Dr. Klein snorted, and Ash caught his eye. He cocked his head. "Dr. Klein?"

Klein arched a black brow. Damn, the man was too sexy for words. "What of our wedding gifts? We've barely unpacked and set up our joint account. I presume everything is fifty-fifty?"

For the first time Jackie Klein showed an interest. "No way. My friends gave us better gifts than your lousy friends and family. All that cheap crap we have is from your relations." Her sneer had Ash cringing and not for the first time he wondered if dealing with spoiled brat clients like this was worth the fee he charged.

"You're not getting a penny of my daddy's money to waste on your stupid clinic. You're a doctor; make it yourself. I want out." She grabbed at Ash's sleeve. "I thought this was going to be easy, but he's making it difficult like he does everything."

Instinctively, he patted her hand. "Don't worry, Jackie. That's what I'm here for; to make sure everything is taken care of properly." He turned back to Dr. Klein, who listened with a quiet intensity to whatever Peter murmured in his ear. When they finished, Ash smiled at both of them.

"The gifts will be split by the giver. The groom's

side back to you, Dr. Klein, the bride's side back to her. For mutual friends, it will be split fifty-fifty. That should be agreeable, correct?"

At Klein's nod, Ash continued. "The apartment is in Jackie's name, so you'll have six months to find a new place to live. I presume, Dr. Klein, you haven't been living there since the petition was filed?"

Dr. Klein gave a brief shake of his head, and Peter squeezed his shoulder, Ash noted. He reminded himself to make a lunch date with Peter and get the story on this guy.

They spent the rest of the afternoon going through the couple's securities and stocks, matching them up with the formal paperwork. At the end of a grueling two hours, the papers were drawn up, and the marriage of Jackie Klein and Drew Klein would be officially and legally dissolved no later than six months from this date.

Jackie and her father had already left the office; she breezed out with a wave, loudly stating her plans with her new boyfriend, which included dinner and the theater, necessitating a trip to a trendy, high-end boutique on the Upper East Side and the hair salon.

Peter hung around with his client, talking to him in that friendly, brotherly tone he always used for comfort. Ash remembered it all too well from law school. On those rare occasions when he'd become overwhelmed with work and loneliness, his tongue loosened more than it should by heartache and vodka, Peter had been the one Ash unwittingly spilled some of his past to. If anyone could lift Dr. Drew Klein out of his misery, Ash bet on Peter. He left them alone, and attended to some phone calls.

Half an hour later, Ash strolled back into the conference room, on the pretext of a forgotten file, but mainly to see if Peter had worked his magic on his client. Once again, his friend did not disappoint. The transformation in Dr. Klein proved miraculous. Instead of the subdued, morose specter from their earlier encounter, Ash came face-to-face with a handsome, charming, though still somewhat serious man. Klein's face flushed pink with good humor, and his green eyes glowed as he and Peter shared a laugh. Staring in amazement at the total transformation in the man, Ash's blood quickened, his body swept away by desire.

Shit. This had never happened before. Certainly he'd lusted after men, men with far more sexual sophistication than the quiet Dr. Drew Klein. But the need pounding through him surpassed any physical reaction he'd ever had toward any man. What made matters worse was that Peter, goddamn him, knew. He could tell by the fucking little smirk the bastard made no attempt to hide.

"Oh, Ash, could you come here?" Peter the innocent, his big baby blues so wide and bright, waved at him from across the conference table.

Shaking his head, Ash dropped down into a chair to hide the sudden tightness in his pants. "What is it, Dent?" He scowled at his friend, wishing all sorts of evil stomach maladies to happen to him on a packed subway car. In the dead of summer. "I have other meetings today, and I'm not renting you my conference room. Don't you have your own office anymore?"

Peter stopped laughing and left Dr. Klein's side to come sit by him. "Ash, settle down. I wanted to talk to you about a project Drew is spearheading."

Against his better judgment, he glanced over at Dr. Klein, but the man was busy checking his phone. With an aggravated huff, he returned his attention to his friend. "What is it, and why should I be interested?" He knew he sounded like a growly, petulant child, but didn't care. It had been too long since he'd gotten laid, and as it wasn't happening with Dr. Straight and Miserable, he needed to have his itch scratched.

Serious for once, Peter kicked his foot. "Asher. Come on. It's me. Give over and stop acting like a prick. Drew is starting a clinic for underprivileged kids, and I'm helping him. He's seen too many who've been on the wrong side of a fist wind up with permanent damage to their faces. He's donating his services to treat them, and he's gotten his friends, one of whom is a dentist, the other an orthopedist, to help as well." The two friends locked gazes.

Fuck.

What he really wanted to do was punch Peter Dent in his nice square jaw and tell him to go to hell, because he knew what Peter wanted. But that was the thing about Peter. Ash wouldn't treat him like everyone else. Peter knew Ash—or knew the small part Ash let him see.

Ash's body stilled. His fingers dug so deep into the fabric of the chair it shredded under his nails. "What..." He cleared his throat, his mouth suddenly dry as chalk. "What do you want from me?" Stupid question. He knew what Peter wanted. And goddamn him, Peter knew there was no way Ash could refuse him or those kids.

Because he too had seen kids who had been on the wrong side of an adult's rage and fists. Adults who were supposed to protect children and, if not love them, at least make sure no harm would come to them. Too many adults took in children to care for, not because they loved them or wanted to give them a better life, but because of the money they received from the state. And God help the children who ended up with those people, if they didn't clean their rooms or cook the meals or...

Ash shook his head free from his nightmarish thoughts, focusing on his friend's sympathetic face. His stomach roiled at the sight of all that compassion in Peter's knowing eyes. "Yeah, damn you. You know I'll help him. Tell me what you need me to do."

Why did he have a feeling he'd made the biggest mistake of his life?

Chapter Two

THANK GOD HE was home, with this miserable bitch of a day behind him. After their last bitter confrontation, Drew had dreaded facing Jackie again.

Who could blame him? The last time he'd seen her, she'd been on her knees, giving his former friend and one of his Wednesday night poker buddies what looked to be a spectacular blowjob.

The familiar sense of nausea rose in Drew's throat, but he fought it down as he entered his apartment. Throwing his keys in the bowl on the table by the door, he paused and surveyed the spartan one-bedroom apartment he'd rented in Brooklyn Heights after leaving Jackie's luxurious loft in Tribeca. He'd never felt comfortable there. It was always her place, never theirs.

Out of the corner of his eye he caught sight of his cat hopping off his perch by the window, coming to greet him with a loud, rumbling purr. Black-and-white with big yellow eyes, Domino had proven to be a much more loving family member in the two months since he'd rescued him from Animal Care and Control than his wife had ever been. After letting the furry creature rub against his legs for a moment, Drew picked Domino up and carried him into the bedroom, where he deposited him on his bed.

"What'd you shred today, buddy?" When he scratched under Domino's chin, he was rewarded with even louder purring and demanding, "pet me, scratch my chin," head butts. He begrudged the animal nothing. The workers had told him when the cat was brought in, he'd been half-starved, spray-painted pink, and so flea-bitten they didn't think he'd make it. Running his hands through Domino's now-thick, glossy fur, he could barely feel the animal's ribs. "Maybe you need to go on a diet, huh, buddy?"

As if he understood, the purring abruptly stopped, and Domino gently swatted Drew's hand. "Okay, okay, kidding." After spending a few moments giving the cat more chin scratches, Drew changed into jeans and a T-shirt, hung up his suit, then went into the kitchen to get a beer from the fridge. Luckily, he'd stocked up earlier in the week, as he knew after today's meeting his friends would come over to help him commiserate.

As if on cue, the phone rang. It wasn't one of his friends, though. "Hey, D. How's my big brother?"

His sister Rachel had called him by the first letter of his name since she was a baby, and it stuck with everyone close to him. Although younger than him, in the dating world she'd always watched over him like a mama bear, offering advice whether or not he asked.

"Did you see her today? She have the nerve to show up?"

He couldn't help but smile. "Yes, Rach. She was there. It's fine, and in six months I'll be free again. All done." He drank down his beer, then flopped on the couch, picked up the remote, and switched on the TV, looking for the Yankee game.

"Was it awful?"

His stomach clenched at the concern in her voice. He so didn't want his little sister worried about him. "I'm an adult. I think I can handle it. I never should've married her. You were right."

Rachel, who was finishing up her PhD in child psychology, had the grace not to tell him *I told you so*.

"So listen to me now. Don't rush back into the dating scene again. I think you need your friends and family more than anything."

"Don't worry. The last thing on my mind is getting involved with another woman. I'll see you at Nana's this weekend though, right?" They went together to visit their grandmother every Sunday. When he was a senior and Rachel a freshman in college, their parents were killed in a head-on collision by a drunken truck driver on the New York State Thruway. From that day forward their grandmother had taken care of them. Now well over eighty years old, her fiercely independent nature allowed them to do only the littlest things for her. But they never missed a Sunday visit. Another thing Jackie had complained about having to do with him.

"Of course. Love you."

"Love you too." He clicked off and was about to settle in to watch the Yankees take their turn at bat when his doorbell rang. Before answering, Drew braced himself, knowing this would be the beginning of a long night of companionship with his buddies, whether he wanted it or not.

Standing at the door were his best friends. One had two boxes of pizza from Grimaldi's. The other had a case of beer with bags resting on top that smelled like meatball heroes from their favorite place in Carroll Gardens.

"Holy shit, guys. There's only three of us." He gestured them inside, and Mike, the one holding the sandwiches and beer, made a beeline for the kitchen.

"Listen, D, we were so happy you were getting rid of that cheating bitch, we didn't know what to do first." Mike shoved the case of beer into the fridge alongside the bottles already there. "But beer, pizza, and heroes work, right?" He flashed a grin.

"Thanks, man." Drew grabbed him around the neck for a quick hug, speaking into his good ear. Mike Levin had lost almost all the hearing in his left ear after being wounded during his tour in Iraq.

Drew cast a fond glance at Jordan, busy opening pizza boxes and arranging the heroes on paper plates. The three of them had been best friends all their lives, ever since their moms met at the playground when they were children. They'd stuck through everything together: his disastrous marriage, Mike almost getting killed in Iraq and his long road to recovery, and Jordan's coming out as a teenager. Nothing could ever separate them.

"Thanks to both you guys for being there for me. It actually went a lot easier than I thought. Yeah, she was there with her father, of course, but my lawyer and hers are really good friends so they worked it out. Six months from today I'll be a free man, and now I can concentrate on getting the clinic off the ground."

They gathered their food and sat on either the sofa or the floor. After watching the Yankees kick the Red Sox's asses for a while, Drew muted the set. "So you guys are all still on board with me, right? It's going to make such a big difference in these kids' lives, knowing that they can get the medical and dental care for all the issues they face."

Jordan finished the last of his slice of pizza, washing it down with beer before he answered. "Are we dealing with mostly teens? And you said many of them are gay?" Jordan Peterson was a highly respected up-and-coming orthopedic surgeon in the city. He and his partner, Keith Hart, an NYPD detective, spent many hours at local LGBT programs helping teens with bullying and family problems. Jordan's parents had never been anything less than fully supportive of their son and welcomed his partner Keith like another one of their children. Keith's parents, devout, Bible Belt Christians, had cut him off when he'd told them he was gay. He'd neither seen nor spoken to them in years.

"Teens, young adults—many identify as being

LGBTQ, but some are still too scared to come out. I think that's why they're being abused. Either at school or at home, they're bearing the brunt of someone's anger and abuse. Rachel said she'll come by and talk to any of the kids who want to, giving them a way to ask for help if they need it."

"And I have the mobile dental clinic ready to help with chipped and broken teeth, as well as crowns and bridges," said Mike. "Whatever they need. This is a great thing you're doing."

Drew popped some chips in his mouth. "I'll never forget the show I saw on TV about kids who lived in foster care in this one home, and instead of being taken care of by their foster parents, they were made to work almost like slaves."

He glanced at the food he'd left on his plate, remembering how one boy interviewed said he'd sometimes only been fed bread and water for days at a time. But that had been the least of the boy's problems. "Many of them had suffered sexual abuse as well. It upset me so much I called Rachel and told her this is what I planned on doing with some of my settlement from the lawsuit from our parents' case."

"That's great, man. I feel sorry for these kids, you know? It's bad enough to have no family and be part of the system." Jordan stroked Domino, who'd come to lie on his lap. "They should have some kind of legal recourse to get these bastards who abuse them."

"Jordy, I spoke with Keith, and he said if the kids are willing to make statements, the police department would be more than happy to work toward arresting these bastards." Drew liked Jordan's partner, Keith, a blond, blue-eyed giant of a guy with a wicked sense of humor. The one thing Keith never found funny, however, was the abuse of children—something he constantly came across on his job.

"What's also really good is that I talked to my lawyer today, Peter Dent? You guys met him." They both answered with nods. "Well, he and his friend, the lawyer on the other side, have agreed to give legal advice to the clinic and kids on a pro bono basis. That'll be a huge help to anyone who wants to press charges."

"Who's the other lawyer?" Jordan had his hands buried in Domino's fur as he watched the Yankees' pitcher give up a grand slam home run. "No, goddamn it. You gotta be kidding me. Fucking Sox."

Drew shook his head in disgust at the television. "Uh, I think his name is Davis? Let me get his card." He picked up his wallet from the table and dug out the business card Peter had handed him with the man's cell phone number written on the back. "Yeah, it's Asher Davis."

Domino meowed loudly in protest as Jordan's hands dug into his fur. "Shit, ow, sorry, Dom." He lifted the cat off his lap, extracting the cat's claws from his thighs, and placed him on the sofa. "Fuck 'Em and Duck 'Em Davis? Oh man, you must be joking."

Drew looked at him in surprise. "You know him?" He'd paid only slight attention to the other lawyer, not recalling anything about the man which would've elicited such a strong reaction from his friend.

Snorting, Jordan accepted another beer from Mike, who sat on the sofa next to the cat. Domino transferred his affection to Mike, stretching his length across his chest.

He groaned. "Man, this cat's getting huge. You gotta stop feeding him."

Drew threw a chip at him. "He's not big; he's healthy." He prodded Jordan with his foot, wanting to hear his story about the other lawyer. "Now finish telling me why the guy has that rep."

Jordan rubbed his thighs with his hands, then cracked his knuckles. "Uh, yeah, you could say I kind of know him."

"Sounds like a story. Spill it," Drew ordered.

Jordan grimaced. "Before I met Keith, while I was a resident, I had to give a deposition on a malpractice case. Davis was with the attorney on the other side. He was good-looking." Jordan's pale blue eyes glinted. "And I was interested at first, but something about him rubbed me the wrong way, so when he asked me out, I turned him down."

"Oh man, that must've pissed him off." Drew chuckled and helped himself to another slice of pizza. "He seems pretty full of himself. Kind of arrogant and cocky." Abandoning Mike, Domino appeared at his side and he slipped the cat some cheese from his pizza.

"Ahh, you could say that." Jordan picked at the label of his beer bottle. "He's wickedly sharp and never takes no for an answer. It makes for a good lawyer, I guess, but not what I was looking for in a lover."

"So what was the problem, then?" Mike questioned. "You said no and that was that, right?"

Jordan shifted in his seat, intriguing Drew further. One thing about Jordan, he never let anyone get the better of him.

"Uh, not quite. Later that night I went out to a club with some of the other residents, and Davis was there as well. He insisted on buying me a drink, and I refused, which pissed him off even more."

"Christ, did he stalk you?" Drew leaned closer to Jordan. "He sounds like a predator."

Jordan shrugged. "Somehow he got my number, and he'd call me every few days or show up where I was hanging out after work to ask me out. I knew some of the guys he did go out with during that time, and all he did was screw their brains out and leave." He took a deep swallow of his beer. "He never called them for another date or even stayed the night with them. You know that's not my scene."

Pushing Domino away with his foot, Drew took another slice of pizza. Perhaps he did need to cut down on slipping the cat extra food. "Maybe he's calmed down since then. He seemed pretty quiet today at the meeting."

Jordan snorted into his beer bottle. "Doubtful. A few years ago I caught him getting a blowjob from one of the panelists at some dinner function we were both attending. I'd forgotten my jacket in the banquet room and went back inside. There was Asher Davis, up against the wall, pants down at his knees, having his dick sucked by the chief of surgery of one the finest hospitals in the Midwest." He chuckled. "Guys must've thought they'd be hidden by the tall, potted plants, but that's not something one can hide, know what I mean?"

Holy crap.

Mike groaned, but Drew was interested in the rest of the story. "What happened? Did he see you? He must've been a little embarrassed." To think he used to be too shy to even kiss a girl in public, and this guy. Wow. A sudden image popped up in his mind of the man he saw today, his head flung back in the throes of an orgasm. He rubbed his eyes hard, willing that picture out of his head.

"Not at all. He stared me straight in the eyes and grinned." Disgusted with the outcome of the game, Jordan changed to the Met game, where the score showed they were also losing. "If I remember, I think he even winked at me."

Drew couldn't stop himself from asking the next question. "Jesus, Jordy, did you really stand there and watch?" Mike looked at both of them, his mouth open in amazement.

At least Jordan had the grace to look a little embarrassed. "Yeah, I'll admit, I did for a few minutes." He shrugged, a defensive tone creeping into his voice. "Hey, it was hot; what can I say? I was younger and hadn't met Keith yet. But anyway, that's Davis's rep. From what I've heard about him, he came out of nowhere as a scholarship student, and Jacob Frank took him in and made him who he is. Even left him the partnership to his law firm in his will when he died. The guy's smart as a whip and hard as nails in the courtroom, but a complete asshole in his personal life." He reached over and grabbed the last of the meatball hero. "He's drop-dead gorgeous, but only after as much cock as he can get. There's never been a steady partner I've seen him with at any function. As far as I know, he lives and breathes his work."

Mike laughed. "Except when he has some random guy sucking his dick."

They all laughed. Drew loved his friends. There was never any holding back or nervousness about saying the wrong thing in front of one another.

His cell phone buzzed. Scrolling to read the message, he chuckled.

"Well, speaking of the proverbial devil, it's Mr. Asher Davis. He wants to meet tomorrow evening to discuss the clinic and the role I see for him." It took a minute of silence before he looked up from his phone's screen to see two sets of worried eyes trained on him. "What's with the looks?"

Mike looked to Jordan, and Drew's eyes narrowed. "What the fuck is going on?"

"Uh, look, don't take this the wrong way, but you just broke up with Jackie, and you're kind of vulnerable now." Jordan played with Domino's tail. "In my opinion, Asher Davis hasn't changed. When he decides he wants something, he stops at nothing until he gets it.

Then once he uses it, he's done."

Drew sat with his mouth open. This was too fucking crazy. "Are you trying to tell me Davis would hit on me? Like, he'd want to screw me?" Sputtering, he waited for his friends to correct him and tell him how wrong he was.

They didn't.

"You're insane. First of all, I'm not gay. Second of all, I don't sleep with men, and third of all, what the fuck?" Were these guys actually serious? Him and a man? "Why would you even think that was an option?"

"Let's face it, you aren't me. I'm stronger than you are. The man is a relentless pursuer when he wants something. He can sniff out the slightest vulnerability in a person; I've seen him in action in the courtroom. And if he thinks he's got you for even the briefest second, he'll pounce." Jordan turned off the game and tossed the remote. All the laughter had fled from his voice. "I don't want you in his crosshairs."

Once again, like he'd done all his life, Jordan tried to protect him. "Jordan, you're making no fucking sense. You're the one who always says you can't make someone gay, that they're born to it. So how can meeting with him make me vulnerable if I don't have those feelings?"

Drew faced his friend and saw actual fear in Jordan's eyes. "Because, and don't get mad at me, for a few seconds earlier when we were talking about Ash getting the blowjob, you got a look on your face, like, I don't know." Drew froze and continued to listen. "It looked like you were imagining what it might be like."

His face flamed, and denial sprang to his lips. "Come on, you guys, that's ridiculous. Peter Dent is my friend and Ash's as well. He's also going to be there, so there's nothing for you to worry about." Silence reigned for a few moments.

"Okay, look. If you don't have any plans, why don't you come to dinner tomorrow night too? That way you can see how wrong you are about everything."

Jordan agreed and with that, his friends relaxed, but Drew's mind continued to whirl. Jordan's comment had hit too close to home; Drew *had* been imagining Asher Davis having sex. He'd better learn to hide his thoughts from everyone.

Chapter Three

"CHRIST, ASHER, WHAT'S your problem?" Peter tossed his car keys to the valet outside the restaurant. "Slow down and relax."

Ash flipped his friend off and strode into the bar, his eyes adjusting to the dimness. A smile teased his lips, but quickly faded. "Ouch." He rubbed his side where Peter had poked him from behind. "What's wrong with you?"

With a surprisingly firm hand and an equally surprising stern face, Peter pushed him into a chair at a nearby table in the front lounge. "Now listen to me. I know you better than anyone, and that's still not a whole lot. But you like to play games—you chew guys up and spit them out once you've had your fun."

"Hey, thanks for the high opinion, friend," Ash protested, albeit not that strongly. It wouldn't be the first time Peter had called him out on his bullshit. And he happened to be right.

"Shut up and listen, Ash. Drew's a friend, and he's been fucked over badly. He's at his most vulnerable right now, and I won't allow you to do to him whatever's in that sex-crazed mind of yours."

Peter's uncharacteristically harsh tone and expression outraged Ash. "Who the fuck are you?" Furious, he spat out his words in angry bullets. "What the hell are you thinking talking to me this way? You ask me to do a favor, and here I am. Other than that, you don't run my fucking life, so back off." Unwilling to meet Peter's eyes, Ash stared at the door, knowing deep down his friend was right.

After a few minutes of uncomfortable silence, Ash raked his hand through his hair and faced Peter with a sheepish grin. "Okay, look, even if I was maybe thinking of something like that, out of deference to you, I'll pull back." He didn't mind conceding the argument to Peter; Ash knew he could find an easy lay anywhere in the city. He couldn't find another friend like Peter, and it wasn't worth risking their friendship. Besides, Klein most likely was a boring straight guy who wouldn't think of stepping outside his comfort zone.

Vanilla. And vanilla was his least favorite flavor, unless some interesting special mix-ins were added to spice it up.

Peter grinned, his good humor restored. "I'm glad I can count on you. Ah, there he is." He waved at the man standing by the entrance to the room, searching the crowd.

Ash paid little attention to Peter as he focused on the lean form of Dr. Klein crossing the room. If Ash thought Drew good-looking when they first met, tonight he was nothing short of mouthwatering. Seeing Drew Klein in a green shirt that brought out the glow in his eyes and tailored black trousers that hugged a fine-looking tight ass, Ash couldn't hold back his admiration. "Damn."

Peter squeezed his shoulder hard and shot him a warning glare. "Behave." He left to meet Klein halfway. When Ash saw who was with him, both his grin and good thoughts fled. Shit. Jordan Peterson. Ash remembered the handsome man from their first meeting years earlier. Peterson had been a medical resident; Ash had been working a malpractice case and sat in on the depositions, assisting Mr. Frank. He'd been instantly attracted to the self-assured blond-haired, blue-eyed doctor giving his testimony, and tried everything he could to get the man in his bed, but got rebuffed at each turn. It was the first time he could remember not being able to seduce the man he wanted.

As he watched the three men, he recalled that not only had Dr. Peterson not reciprocated, he'd made it a point to tell Ash how he felt about him.

"You're a player, Davis. I spotted you a mile away. I'm not interested in a quick fuck, and I'm not easy. I value myself too much."

Ash rubbed his chin, that conversation still rankling after so many years. So this was one of Klein's friends who'd be working with him on the project. Interesting. He wondered if the sanctimonious doctor would even remember him. As they approached him, he stood, an easygoing smile on his face, never alerting anyone to the turmoil of his inner thoughts.

"Dr. Klein, good to see you again outside the confines of the conference room."

"Yes, I'm glad to have put that behind me and don't hold any grudges against you, Davis. You were doing what you were paid to do." He turned to his friend. "I'd like to introduce you to one of my best friends, Dr. Jordan Peterson, who'll also be working with us on the clinic project."

The obvious look of distaste on Peterson's handsome face left no doubt in Ash's mind that the good doctor remembered him all too well. "Dr. Peterson."

"Davis. It's been years, hasn't it?" Their gazes met, and Ash couldn't tell what the man had going on behind his sneer. Had he mentioned their brief acquaintance to Klein? Did he tell Klein how Ash tried to seduce him?

Why the fuck did Ash even care?

Before he could answer, the hostess came to seat them and they followed her into the dining area of the restaurant, where they were shown to a round table in the corner.

Once they all took their menus, Ash, brushing aside his annoyance, plastered a wide smile on his face. "It has been quite a few years, yes. Good to see you."

"I was surprised to hear you were involved with this project. Didn't really seem like your speed."

He caught the warning look that passed between the two men, and yep, Peterson had spoken to Klein about him and that pissed him off.

"Peterson, you know nothing about me and let's keep it that way. Suffice it to say I have my own reasons and motivation for becoming involved here, and I don't owe any explanation to you. If you have a problem with me working at the clinic, that's too fucking bad. Get over it. I'm not pulling out because you're carrying a years-old grudge." He called the waiter over and ordered a vodka on the rocks. Ordinarily he would flirt with the handsome, slim-hipped young man, but he was too pissed at the moment. "Now, are we ready to talk business or is everyone at this table going to continue to obsess about my sex life?"

Peter laughed out loud, Peterson rolled his eyes, and Klein merely looked confused for a moment before giving the blushing waiter his drink order. They sat in uncomfortable silence until their drinks arrived.

Klein took a sip of his beer and then pulled some papers out of the thin leather portfolio he'd laid on the table. "So here is my vision. Obviously I'm not up on the legal ramifications, so that's what you and Davis are here for, Peter." He passed out several typed sheets of paper for them to look over. "We need to make sure we have all the legalities in place, as well as having you both on board to help these kids in case they want to press charges for abuse, discrimination, or sexual harassment."

Ash studied the papers. It looked like a solid proposal—one that had taken a tremendous amount of thought. If only he, Luke, and Brandon had someone who cared, and a place to run to when it all turned to shit.

Taking another gulp of his drink, he waited for the burning in his chest to subside before he continued. "Can I ask why you're doing this? I mean, you're a successful plastic surgeon who could make tons of money doing face-lifts and boob jobs. What made you want to help these kids?" Genuinely curious, he wanted to know why someone like Dr. Klein—young, obviously wealthy, and seemingly untouched by any of the ugliness the world had to offer—cared about the unwanted kids society had no trouble throwing in the trash heap.

"Because everyone matters, that's why. And everyone's life should have some kind of meaning; otherwise what's the point in getting up in the morning? When my parents were killed, I didn't want to live, but after a while I realized I was only punishing myself." Klein rubbed his thumb over the rim of his glass, and Ash couldn't take his eyes off that sensuous stroking motion. "They would have been horrified if I gave up my life to mourn their deaths. I was lucky enough to have my grandmother to look after both my sister and myself. These kids have no one to make sure they get up in the morning and have something to look forward to."

Ash's gaze remained transfixed on Klein's long fingers as they gripped the glass and brought it to his lips. Yeah, these kids were lucky to have someone, even a stranger, care about them. Most of them didn't have that reason to want to get up in the morning.

As he cleared his throat, Peterson's harsh voice broke Ash's internal musing. "Can you make time in your schedule, Davis, or is this going to cut into your busy social life? We need people who are dedicated to these kids and willing to give of their time. Peter's generously giving us legal advice, but he also said you have knowledge of family court and the intricacies of the system?" He cocked a blond brow as if challenging that statement.

"I do, yes." Without any need to further that conversation, he turned his attention back to Klein. "Dr. Klein, I commend you on this project. I'm more than willing to help in any way possible. Have you thought about setting up a help line for the kids to call? Sometimes knowing there's a person who cares, even if it's an anonymous person on the other side of the telephone might be the lifeline they need."

"Please call me Drew. And yes. My sister is finishing up her PhD in child psychology and has arranged for volunteers to man phones on a twenty-four-hour basis. She's trying to get it hooked into the school's counseling system for us." He scribbled down some notes, then smiled at Ash. "That was a great question, Davis."

"If I'm calling you Drew, then call me Ash, please." He smiled back at the man, ignoring the disgusted "You've got to be fucking kidding me" from Peterson. "Where's the clinic going to be located? I'm not familiar with Brooklyn."

"It's in Red Hook. A family court operates nearby so we can work with the kids who come through the system there. The construction on the clinic is scheduled for completion very soon. We'll have two examining rooms, an outpatient operating facility for simple procedures, and a room set aside for counseling. Our other friend, Mike, is a dentist, and he'll have a mobile dental van set up to take care of any oral problems that may present."

Ash knew only too well how teeth could be loosened or knocked out and jaws broken. Not to mention the infections and other diseases the kids might pick up from lack of oral hygiene or other, more troubling situations. His hand tightened on his glass as unbidden memories, ones he thought he'd managed to bury, stormed to the surface. A wave of dizziness and nausea hit him, and his vision wavered.

Shit.

"You all right?" Peter murmured in his ear. "Maybe you want to take a minute."

Sweat beaded on his brow. "Yeah." He managed to grit that one word out as he stood and pushed his chair back. Without any explanation, Ash fled to the back, managing to lock himself into a stall before he further humiliated himself in public. He slid down to the floor, heedless of the fact that it was a bathroom, and pressed his head against the coolness of the tile wall.

After several moments the nausea and trembling passed; he wiped his face with some tissue and stood on shaking knees. It had been months since he'd experienced panic such as this. Mortified at what the others at the table must think of him, he unlocked the stall door and came face-to-face with Peter.

"Better now?" Peter handed him a bottle of cold water, which he gratefully accepted. After drinking down half of it, Ash placed it on the shelf and braced his hands on the sink.

"Yeah. Thanks." He closed his eyes for a moment, then met Peter's somber reflection in the mirror. "What are they saying out there? You can tell me." His bitter laugh rang loud within the confines of the small restroom. "I'm sure Peterson's having a field day bashing me."

Peter looked uncomfortable. "He isn't your biggest fan, but I don't think Drew is paying him too much attention. I suggest you go back and pretend like nothing happened."

After another drink of water and a few deep breaths, Ash felt steady enough to return. He squeezed Peter's shoulder. "Thanks. At least I know I have one friend."

"Always, man."

After they returned to the table, Drew simply handed him a fresh drink and picked up the conversation as if it was perfectly natural for a man to break out in a sweat and bolt from the table, only to reappear after several minutes with no explanation.

"I took the liberty of ordering some food." Drew handed him a menu, meeting his eyes over the top of the heavy booklet. "We haven't ordered our main courses yet."

No damage done, and with confidence running warm through his blood once again, Ash resorted once more to his cocky, self-assured persona. "Thanks, Drew. Guess I forgot to eat lunch today, and it all got to me suddenly."

"No worries. Happens to all of us."

The same cute waiter returned with the appetizers previously ordered, and Ash's interest perked up for more than the food. When it was Ash's turn to order dinner, he chose the house chili, extra spicy. The waiter's eyes widened.

"Ah, sir, just to let you know, our chef already makes his chili quite hot."

Ash chuckled and winked at the waiter, bringing a blush to his fair cheeks. How adorable. A ripple of lust flowed through Ash. "I like things extra hot and spicy." He licked his lips and watched the eyes of the man widen, then grow dark with unmistakable desire. Perfect. His evening entertainment was now guaranteed. "Thank you for your concern, however."

When it came time for the waiter to take his menu, Ash made sure to brush his fingers over the waiter's hand and watched him bite his lip, imagining that full mouth wrapped around his cock. If he had anything to say about it, he wouldn't be leaving the restaurant until he paid the waiter a personal visit to show him appreciation for a job well done.

Dinner progressed without further incident, and

Ash remained impressed with how quickly Drew had set up the clinic. Peterson continued to be a thorn in his side making snide comments or simply shooting him glowering looks, all of which Ash ignored completely.

Before he knew it, it was past midnight and the restaurant had emptied out. Peter had made his farewells about an hour earlier, needing to get home to his wife and kids. Ash caught the eyes of the sweet-faced waiter, hovering near the bar, and grinned to himself.

Showtime.

"Well, gentlemen, it's been fun, and I look forward to working with you both and meeting your other friend." He shook their hands. "I'd better get going as I have an early morning client."

Peterson nodded, distracted by a text he was responding to, while Drew shook his hand. Once again, Ash enjoyed the strength and warmth of the man's hand in his, but he'd moved on to his planned rendezvous with the adorable waiter, who'd given him a signal with his pretty eyes to follow him down the darkened hallway leading to the restrooms. "Good night, Drew. Talk to you soon."

He pushed open the swinging doors, then walked down the dimly lit corridor. Upon turning the corner, he spied the young man. "Why, hello there. Waiting for me?" In two long strides, Ash pinned him against the wall, loving the feel of the man's slim body curving to fit his. The soft exhalation of breath in his ear stoked his fire.

"Yes. I don't even know your name, though."

Ash clasped the waiter around the waist, listening to his groan of desire. Their erections rubbed through their pants as Ash rocked his hips. The waiter tried to kiss Ash on the lips.

"You don't need to know anything except how to unzip my pants and suck me." Ash pulled away, placing his hands hard on the man's shoulders. He never kissed anyone. Ever. "Are you up for that?" Trading places with the waiter, Ash flattened out against the wall and pulled the young man close, rolling his hips again. The waiter's eyes glazed over with undisguised lust and his hands reached for Ash's pants.

"Oh God, yeah."

With shaking fingers, the waiter undid Ash's belt, popped open the pants button and pulled down his fly. His erection tented his boxers out, hard and hot.

"This is what you kiss. Not my mouth. This." He palmed his cock and stroked it as his pants sagged to his ankles. Ash leaned against the wall, legs spread, and waited.

The waiter sank to the floor before him and with impatient, fumbling fingers, pulled down Ash's boxers. The rush of heat, the fact that they were out in the open only added to the excitement and spurred Ash on. The man had zero gag reflex and he swallowed Ash's cock to the root.

Shit. Nothing felt as good as someone's mouth on him. Ash leaned his head against the wall, hips pumping as the eager mouth swirled, licked, and sucked at him like he was a fucking ice-cream cone. Gasping for air, he clutched the man's hair. "Fuuuck me, man. You were made for this."

Too long, too long. Ash couldn't remember the last time he'd had sex, with all the work he'd piled on. But now, with the wet warmth of a talented mouth on his cock, he wondered how he'd ever lived without it. He fucked the waiter's mouth harder. "Oh God, yes, that's it." The words of encouragement were a precursor to one hell of an orgasm he sensed building within his body. "Right there, don't stop." Fascinated, he watched his dick slide in and out of the waiter's mouth.

The man on his knees before him moaned as he sucked Ash deeper while stroking his own cock. Within moments, Ash knew he was there, coming with a blinding intensity that had him stifling his own shout of ecstasy by shoving his fist in his mouth. Shuddering with the aftereffects, he pulsed a few more times before slipping out of the man's mouth. The waiter stiffened, then groaned, coming in spurts on the floor in front of Ash, narrowly missing his shoes.

Minutes passed before Ash could catch his breath. He pulled up his pants, tucked in his shirt, then zipped himself up. Standing, the young man breathed heavily, lips pouting and gleaming wet in the hazy lighting of the hallway. With the pad of his thumb, Ash traced the seam of the man's full mouth. "You were amazing. Thank you."

"Will I see you again?" The hopeful note in the

young man's voice gave Ash a momentary twinge of regret as the kid licked Ash's thumb, then sucked it into his hot mouth. The guy had a very talented tongue.

"If I come by and eat here again, I'll make sure to look you up." It was only fair of him not to string the kid along. He wasn't made for relationships.

A sound from farther down the hallway snapped Ash out of post-orgasmic bliss to full awareness of how open and foolhardy they had been. Although his table was the last one occupied in the restaurant, waitstaff still lingered about, and Ash hardly thought the management would appreciate one of their employees blowing a patron in full view of anyone who might walk by. He didn't care who saw him, but he didn't want to get the kid fired. Contrary to what people might think of him, he did have a conscience.

"Well, see you around." He rubbed the young man's shoulder, then walked away. As he approached the entrance, he noticed the movement of the swinging doors to the hallway, as if someone had recently passed through them.

Did someone see him with the waiter?

Chapter Four

AFTER JORDAN LEFT the restaurant, Drew sat for a few moments, sipping his coffee, reviewing what they'd discussed. The night had been a success as far as he could tell, and now everyone was in place with their job to do. For a brief moment he wondered about Ash and his disappearance from the table, but Peter had been quite closemouthed about it, and Drew didn't want to press the issue in case it was something deeply personal. Besides, he'd seemed back to his normal self when he'd returned, even so much as to flirt with the waiter. That hadn't gone unnoticed, at least by him. Jordan was right. The man was an incorrigible tease.

Time to head back home. Needing to make a stop at the restroom before he hopped on the subway, Drew headed to the back where he'd seen Ash disappear to earlier. He used the urinal and washed up. As he exited the restroom, he heard a noise behind him that sounded like a groan of pain. Drew stood still, his ear trained. Someone might be hurt and need medical help. Once again he heard the sound, like a drawn-out moan, then it cut off abruptly.

Concerned as to what he might find, Drew hurried down the darkened hallway and turned the corner. His eyes widened in shock as he took in the scene before him. Instead of a potential medical emergency lying on the ground in pain, Ash Davis stood flat against the wall receiving an impressive-looking blowjob from the waiter he'd been flirting with earlier.

Drew remained frozen in place. The air seemed to thicken, and the small gasps, moans, and pants echoed in the dark, all magnifying the illicit nature of the encounter. His eyes were drawn to the act, specifically the waiter's mouth on Ash's cock. He could see it gliding wet and hard between the man's lips, and Drew's response to the explicit picture before his eyes stunned him.

Holy shit. This was what Jordan mentioned he'd seen. And damned if Jordan wasn't right. Hell, Drew might be straight, but watching the erotic scene unfold before his eyes was sexy as hell and a turn-on. Gone was the man who'd bolted from the table, a pale, sweating mess. In his place stood a man in the midst of a sexual encounter that, from the sounds he made and the look on his face, had him hovering on the brink of a violent orgasm.

Drew shook his head. What the hell was he doing standing here? He had to get out before Ash opened his eyes and caught him watching. Tearing his gaze from the scene, he turned on his heel and hastened back down the hallway and out of the restaurant. In no mood now to wait for the train, he hailed a cab and soon found himself speeding down Broadway. A sudden rainstorm splatted fat drops against the windows, steaming them a misty gray, cocooning him inside the cab, alone with his thoughts.

Thoughts that revolved around Ash. Who was he? What kind of man had random sex in a hallway? He might have been impressed with his sharp business sense, but Ash's personal life appalled Drew. And yet he couldn't help wonder more about what made Ash tick, especially after he'd fled the table at dinner in an obvious state of anxiety. Ash might want to help, but he needed to work on fixing himself before he could think of assisting anyone else.

The closer he got to home, the stronger his resolve grew. For this project, the focus needed to be solely on the center and Ash's personal issues seemed in clear conflict with the clinic's mission. What if the only reason he wanted to help was to meet people and have sex with them? Drew pulled out the business card from his wallet and, knowing it was the coward's way out, dialed the office number rather than Ash's personal cell.

"Um, hello. This is Drew Klein. I was thinking, and I'm not sure you're a good fit for the clinic, so I'm releasing you from your offer. I appreciate your willingness to help, though. So, uh, thanks and bye."

Smooth, Drew. Well, he never was great with words. It's why he became a doctor. He paid the cabbie and ran into his building, only getting slightly wet. As soon as he opened the door, Domino greeted him, weaving his furry body between Drew's legs.

"Hey, big boy, miss me?" He picked up the cat, who head-butted him on his chin. Funny how he enjoyed having a pet to come home to. Despite the lousy start he'd had in life, Domino was a loving creature, always happy to see him come through the door.

Drew gave the cat one more cuddle and placed him on the floor. Domino, proclaiming his displeasure, meowed loudly. Drew, who could deny the cat nothing, gave the cat a few more scratches, then stood and tossed his keys into the bowl on the table by the front door. As he passed through the living room to his bedroom, he dropped his jacket on the sofa. He couldn't wait to get out of his suit and tie. Comfortable at last after changing into a T-shirt and sweats, Drew logged on to his laptop to check his e-mails. The first one that caught his eye was from Mallory Construction. Jason Mallory had e-mailed him to let him know the job would be finished Monday, and he would meet Drew at the site for a walk-through.

Drew was thrilled. Not only was the job finished ahead of schedule, but it exceeded what he'd originally planned. Mallory had gone the extra mile to make sure the clinic looked welcoming and would be a place where disenfranchised young adults would want to come for help.

Once Drew discussed the reason behind the clinic with Mallory, the man had confided he was bisexual and that he'd had a difficult time with some members of his family during his coming out. All that seemed to be behind him, though, as he introduced Drew to his partner, Ryder, whom he planned on marrying this summer.

Closing down his e-mail, Drew rested his head against the pillows of his sofa and closed his eyes. Had he really loved Jackie, or was it his desperate need to have someone to come home to, someone to touch, to hold? Losing his parents so unexpectedly had left a hole in his heart he'd never been able to fill. He'd drifted through relationships, allowing his friends to set him up with woman after woman, but he'd never found that attraction or spark to take any of them seriously. Their main interest in him had been his profession. As he grew older and reverted back into his shell of loneliness, it became all too easy to let his friends and sister direct his personal life.

Jordan had Keith, Mike was a party animal with more women than sense, and Rachel…well, Rachel was a mother hen who insisted she knew what was best for him. And Drew had simply stopped caring.

When he'd ventured out and met Jackie, he'd thought she was the one, not heeding his friends' and family's warning that her only desire was to be married to a plastic surgeon with a lucrative career path. She'd been loving and supportive while they'd dated. Everything had been fine before they'd gotten married. He fell for her hard and fast, proposing marriage after only dating six months. But things changed soon after their honeymoon, swiftly going downhill. Once he'd told her of his plans to open a clinic for abused teens and young adults, she'd pulled away, uninterested in that or any other topic he brought up for discussion. Eventually she withdrew from their marriage altogether.

It hadn't even taken him three months of living with Jackie to realize what a vain, self-centered person she truly was. Shit, he'd obviously been a very poor judge of character, because seeing her on her knees blowing his friend had come as a total surprise to him. Once again, he thanked God the marriage was as short-lived as it was and they'd never had kids.

Well, no matter, as he wasn't ready for a new relationship or even to date right now. His sister was right. He had the clinic and those kids to think about. Hopefully they could find another lawyer to replace Davis. Jason Mallory had mentioned a Legal Aid attorney he was friends with who might be willing to help. Maybe Drew would give that attorney a call, as the legal work would likely be too much for Peter to handle on his own.

His phone buzzed with a call. "Hey, Rach. What's up? I was thinking of you."

"Great minds, big brother. Wanna meet for coffee Saturday? I haven't seen you in a while since I was out of town and couldn't come to Nana's last week. We need a hang-out day."

Drew's chest tightened. No matter how shitty he felt, talking to his sister always made him feel better. Not that he'd ever admit it to her. "Sure. Where and when?"

"How about the new coffeehouse by Union Square? The one on 18th St. by the park? We can walk around the farmer's market afterward."

An idea popped into his head. "Sounds perfect. I'll get some fresh fruit and make Nana a cobbler for Sunday." He hadn't indulged in his love of cooking since his marriage, as Jackie barely ate anything. She'd always been on some diet or another.

"Ooh yumm." Her moan was long and drawn out. "I love your cobbler. Maybe you'll be a nice big brother and make an extra one for me? Pretty please?"

"You'll have to help me carry the fruit home." Who was he kidding? She knew he'd make it for her.

"Not a problem. Gives me a chance to come over and see Domino. How fat has he gotten?"

"He isn't fat; he's healthy."

After she stopped laughing, they agreed to meet at noon. "Save me a seat and get me a hazelnut latte if you get there first."

"If? If I'm there first? When have you ever been on time for anything?" He chuckled, even when she blew a raspberry in his ear and hung up on him.

Swallowing the last of his beer, he closed his laptop and put it on the couch. When he got up, the cat followed him, waiting outside the bathroom until he finished and then trailing him back into the bedroom. No use in pushing Domino off the bed; he'd hop right back on.

"Well, come on. Up you go." Domino regarded

him with those big yellow eyes, swished his tail, and jumped, stalking over to the foot of the bed and curling up. Feeling happier than he had in a while, Drew slipped into the bed, allowing his body to unfold. Toes curling, hamstrings tightening, and arms over his head, he enjoyed a full-body stretch before relaxing. It had been a long day of patients, then that bizarre dinner meeting. The back of his neck cracked. Well, he sure wasn't twenty anymore. After he'd hit thirty, he'd taken up running to make sure he could stay in shape with his long hours and infrequent meals.

His phone buzzed on the night table. *Oh, Christ.* Hopefully it wasn't some emergency. He picked it up, his eyes squinting at the bright light in the dark of his room. *Crap*. Asher Davis.

What the hell was that message about, Klein? Call me back.

Screw him. He didn't owe Ash Davis anything. He threw the phone on the opposite side of the bed and buried his head under the pillow. Of course, now that the guy had texted him, Drew couldn't get that scene of Ash getting sucked off out of his mind. He understood what Jordan meant when he said it was hot to watch. He'd never admit it to anyone, but for just a moment while he was watching it…damned if it didn't turn him on. Just a bit.

Shit. There went his dick again. *Fuck.* This wasn't supposed to happen. He liked women, for God's sake.

Even though there was no one else in the room, his gaze darted furtively from side to side. Drew touched himself through his thin sweatpants, groaning at the feel of his swollen cock twitching beneath his hand.

A vision of the dark-haired Ash with the face of a wicked angel, head thrown back and gasping for breath, stirred a fantasy Drew didn't know existed in the deepest recesses of his mind. Recalling the slick, liquid sound of the waiter's mouth on Ash's cock, as well as Ash's harsh groans served as the impetus Drew needed to push himself over the edge. To his disbelief, he reached under his sweats, grabbed his cock, and pulled at the leaking head, stroking hard down the shaft. After only a few moments and several strong tugs, he stiffened and came, spurting into his hand, his rough, choked cry echoing against the walls of his bedroom.

Unable to catch his breath for a moment, he reeled from what had occurred in his bed. Did he really jerk off, thinking of another man? *Un-fucking-believable.* What the hell was going on with him?

His phone rang. Shit, nighttime calls were always bad news. What if something had happened to Nana? Without looking at the screen, he connected. "Hello? Who is this?"

"Klein? It's Davis. Asher Davis. You owe me an explanation for why you summarily dismissed me from the project."

"It's almost two a.m. I don't owe anyone explanations at two in the morning. Least of all you." Yeah, he knew that sounded rude, but the fact that he'd jerked off to the vision in his mind of Ash getting a blowjob embarrassed him enough that he didn't give a shit.

A long expulsion of breath indicated how pissed off Ash was. "Why are you being such a bastard?" Now he merely sounded confused. "Can't we talk about it?"

Did he owe the guy an explanation? Not really. But maybe he owed it to Peter, since Peter had involved Ash. "Okay. Meet me at eleven thirty Saturday morning at the new coffeehouse on 18th and Broadway." He clicked off and muted the phone. After cleaning himself up in the bathroom, Drew returned to bed and huddled under the covers, willing himself to go to sleep.

ON SATURDAY, A few minutes before he was to meet Ash, Drew entered the coffeehouse, ordered himself an iced coffee, and found a seat. Stretching his legs under the tiny table, he wondered why he'd made this appointment. He wanted this clinic to safeguard the kids from predators. While Ash wasn't that bad, Drew didn't need the distraction of wondering whether or not Asher Davis was behaving himself and not seducing the very people they were trying to protect.

A shadow fell across his eyes. "Okay, Klein." Ash dropped into the seat across from him, his silver eyes glittering like ice chips. "What the fuck happened between dinner and you coming home that made it so imperative for you to call my office at one thirty in the morning and dump me from the project?"

Drew toyed with the lid to his coffee cup before answering, his gaze taking in Ash's agitated state. "For the life of me, I can't understand why you're so upset. I had a change of heart." He shrugged. "Maybe I don't want to work with my ex-wife's lawyer."

"I'm calling bullshit on that. You had no problem when we talked about it. You even liked my ideas."

Why would a man like this care so much about this project? Did he still have a thing for Jordan and hope to get through to him this way? "You are aware that Jordan's in a committed relationship now."

A look of confusion crossed Ash's face, before his lips drew up in a sneer. "You think I want to do this because of Peterson? Did he tell you that?"

Nervous, Drew leaned away from Ash, craning his neck to catch the people walking in the doorway. For once in her life couldn't his sister be early for something? His gaze returned to the angry man before him. "No, but I know you had a thing for him once."

Ash snorted. "Listen. Tell your friend with the overinflated opinion of himself that because I hit on him four or five years ago doesn't mean I'm still interested. Tastes change."

Rachel walked in and waved to him, then gave him a questioning look. *Hallelujah.* Before he could stop himself, the snarky comment burst out of his mouth. "Yeah, I know. You're into waiters now, right? Or, I should say, they're into *you*." Getting up from his seat, he greeted his sister. "Hey, Rach, how are you?"

Her eyes flickered from him to Ash, who sat stunned, frozen in place. "Um, do you want to introduce me to your friend?"

"I don't think so. We're not friends, merely acquaintances. I don't think we'll be seeing each other after today." When he looked at Ash over his shoulder, a momentary twinge of regret pricked him. "So long, Davis. See you around." With his hand on Rachel's back, he steered her toward the door, hardly paying attention to her complaining that she didn't have a chance to get her coffee.

"Forget it, Rachel. I'll buy you lemonade. Now let's go. I need to buy the fruit to make the cobbler for Nana tomorrow and don't want to get stuck with all the bruised left-overs."

As he passed by the windows of the coffeehouse, he looked through and saw the empty table where he and Ash had sat. Guess he got the message.

"Drew."

Or not. He turned to find Asher Davis right on his heels, a sheepish expression on his face.

"Can we talk about it?"

"There really isn't anything to talk about."

Of course Miss Nosy Pants couldn't be left out of the conversation. "Hi, I'm Rachel, his much more well-mannered sister."

In a surprising, old-fashioned gesture, Ash picked up Rachel's hand and kissed it. "Lovely to meet you. Maybe you can convince your brother that I honestly want to help at the center he's setting up."

Drew stood observing the exchange between his sister and Ash. He decided to let her form her own opinion of the man. Next to his grandmother, she had the best sense of anyone he knew, not that he'd ever tell her that. Some things a brother never told his sister.

They continued walking down Broadway to the corner of 18th St. then crossed to enter the park and the crowded farmer's market. Drew dropped back, letting Rachel talk to Ash. Later he'd press her for details, but for now he remained content to sit back and study the guy.

Was Ash honestly interested in the project like he insisted, or was he using it as a way to meet men? It appalled him to think this way about another person, but Jordan's comments, plus the sexual encounter he'd caught the man in and now outed him about, made him wonder. His face heated as he again recalled the blowjob in the darkened hallway of the restaurant. All the years he and Jordan had been friends, he'd never had any sexual feelings toward him, and merely listened and offered advice whenever his friend began or ended a relationship. Jordan was a buddy, a friend. Nothing sexual with him at all.

Not so with Ash Davis. Drew couldn't get the memory of Ash's blissful face out of his mind. Nor could he, if he confessed to himself, forget the sight of Ash's cock sliding in and out of the mouth of the man sucking him off.

He stumbled. Shit. When was the last time he'd gotten laid? He couldn't even remember. Months and months. That had to be it, the reason for his strange fascination with Ash's sex life. Snapping out of his head fog, he heard Rachel laughing at something Ash whispered to her.

"Rach. We need to get the fruit." Her smile faded at his unusually hard tone.

"Um, okay." She gave him a frown and a side-eyed glare. "It was nice to meet you, Ash. Maybe I'll see you around." She shook his hand.

"That all depends on your brother, I think."

Drew scowled. "We'll see. I'll get back to you this week and let you know my final decision."

"Can we talk for one second?" Ash gestured with his head to an empty bench. "Rachel, would you excuse us?"

"Sure." Her uncertain smile flashed for a brief moment. "I'll, uh, go start picking out the fruit for you, D."

He nodded and followed Ash to the bench, choosing to sit as far away from him as possible without looking too obvious. "You've charmed my sister, which is no easy feat. But—"

"But you still think I'm nothing more than the guy you saw in a hallway getting a blowjob from a waiter, right?"

Ash's glittering eyes captured the green of the leaves, the blue of the sky, and the brown of the trees, reflecting back at Drew the emotion he held inside. Making it impossible for Drew to look away.

"Are you?" Drew held his breath. Footsteps pounded past them, and laughter drifted through the sweet, late spring air as the crowds in Union Square Park walked by. No one paid them much attention, but for Drew, for whatever reason he couldn't fathom, this conversation became as imperative as breathing.

"Look, we barely know each other, and you've already been prejudiced, not only by your friend but by what you saw the other night. I want you to know, though, that I have my own reason for helping those kids." He shifted his gaze, focusing on the sidewalk. His sleek hair swung forward, hiding the expression in his eyes from view. "It's, uh, too personal to get into now, but I would never, ever do anything to hurt those kids." He swept his hair back, revealing his anguished face. "They deserve every opportunity for a better life."

The raw pain in the man's voice struck Drew hard, lending credence to Ash's words. Whether or not Ash revealed his past to him now, it was clear to Drew this man had suffered alone, locking his grief inside. Everything made sense now—the grasping anonymous sex with men he barely knew, the need for people to like him, and the air of ineffable loneliness he carried with him.

"Hey." Drew placed his hand on Ash's shoulder, but to his surprise Ash quickly pulled away. That brief touch, however, gave rise to emotions so intense it rattled Drew to his core.

What the hell?

"It's okay. You don't need to talk about it. I'm willing to admit I was wrong to make a hasty decision without giving you a chance to defend yourself. I have to get back to Rachel, but I'm going to take some time to rethink everything. Can I call you?"

His question hung in the air as Ash continued his study of the ground beneath his feet. After a moment, Drew noted the slight jerk of Ash's head, an acceptance of his words. "Good. We'll talk. So long, Ash."

Without waiting for a reply, he left Ash sitting on the bench, alone in a sea of strangers.

Chapter Five

"LET'S RAISE OUR glasses to my parents and the realization of a dream come true." Drew held up his glass and, with his arm around Rachel, smiled at the group of people who'd made this night possible. "To the Audrey and Maxwell Klein Home Away from Home Clinic." He drained his glass of champagne and immediately poured another. His apartment might be small and lonely with just him, but tonight the people he cared most about in the world filled it with their loving presence. His sister; their grandmother who sat, wiping the tears from her eyes and smiling her sweet smile at him; his two best friends, Mike and Jordan—who was, of course, with his partner, Keith. Also included in their circle now was Peter and his wife, Lisa, as well as Asher Davis. For the past two months, Peter and Ash had helped with all the legalities, and Peter's father's influence had granted them speedy approval of all the necessary permits. His contractor, Jason Mallory, and Jason's partner, Ryder Daniels, had shown up at the party as well.

Drew moved past the groups of his friends, trying to get through them to speak with his grandmother, but to his amazement, when he got to her chair, she sat laughing with none other than Ash.

"Drew, darling, why haven't you ever introduced me to this handsome young man before?" Her blue eyes twinkled as her lips curved in a smile. "He's been so sweet to sit here with me, telling me naughty jokes."

Ash took her hand and kissed it, then placed a finger to his lips. "Shh, Esther. That was supposed to be between us." He winked, and she laughed out loud.

"You, young man, are what was known as a rogue in my day." She winked back at him. "I've always had a thing for the bad boys."

"Nana?" Drew stood, dumbfounded by the scene in front of him. Was this his fierce, independent grandmother, flirting with a man over fifty years her junior?

"Yes, dear. Can I help you with something?" She didn't take her eyes off Ash, and for some reason that irked him. He set his glass down and crossed his arms.

"Well, no, I wanted to say hello to you and invite you down to the clinic to give you a tour."

That got her attention. She took his hands into her little ones and squeezed. "Your parents would've been so proud of you, and I know that they are looking down at you and your sister with all their love."

His heart hurt. Physically. He coughed to try and relieve the pressure in his chest, but it didn't help. The second glass of champagne slid down his swollen, dry throat. "Thank you, Nana. I still miss them. Every single day." Hanging his head, her hand stroked his face.

"I do too. But they are here with us, giving us strength. If I didn't believe that, I couldn't get up in the morning."

Ash handed him another drink. "Go on, take it. Seems like you need it. Let go for once."

Drew held his silvery gaze and smiled. "Thanks, man. I think I do need it, and I'll take my lawyer's advice."

"Is it true that you're actually the lawyer for that horrible woman? The one who broke my grandson's heart?" She shot Ash a stern look, and Drew had to laugh. He patted her hand.

"Don't worry, Nana; she hardly broke my heart. It was a simple agreement, no fighting, and in a few months we'll be finished."

"She was a horrible person, wasn't she?" Nana whispered to Ash, who surprisingly, nodded his head.

"She was indeed. Not nearly good enough for Drew in my opinion."

A speculative gleam appeared his grandmother's eyes. "Do you have any nice girls for him to date, Mr. Davis? Maybe your girlfriend knows someone."

Oh brother. The last thing he wanted to do was talk about Ash's sexuality with his grandmother, for God's sake. He took a big gulp of his drink. Ash, however, came to his rescue.

"Mrs. Klein, I don't have a girlfriend. I'm gay. That's why I was so anxious to help Drew with this project, so that no one would ever have to suffer for being different."

Nana sat for a moment, her gaze shifting from Ash to him. An unreadable look crossed her face. "I see. Well, I could never understand the fuss people make about it. I mean, why is it anyone's business who you love? Look at those husbands and wives who kill their children. That's who society should shame, not someone like you."

To Drew's shock, she leaned over and kissed Ash's cheek. "If one of my grandchildren came and told me they were gay, I could never love them any less. Let that be a lesson to you both. Never settle for anything other than true love." She stood, brushing off their helping hands. "Now I'm going to get a snack. Drew, don't hover over me. Mr. Davis, I hope you won't be a stranger."

Ash, who'd sat frozen to his seat after her brief kiss, briefly touched his cheek. He shook himself out of his reverie, took her hand and kissed it again. "You must call me Ash, then."

She squeezed his arm and walked away. Drew finished his drink, realizing he was a little light-headed and not caring a bit. "She's a firecracker. And she took a real shine to you. That says a lot. My grandmother is the best judge of character." He tracked her progress across the room as she stopped to socialize with people. Too bad he didn't pay attention to her opinion about Jackie instead of stubbornly insisting on doing what he wanted.

Jordan and Keith pulled him away to talk to some other people. He glanced back over his shoulder and mouthed, *Thanks* to Ash, who stayed where he was, drink in hand.

ASH LOVED LISA, he really did, but before this party was over, he'd have to tell Peter he was not interested in his wife's gay hairdresser or decorator. There was only one man he wanted, and that hadn't changed since they'd first met over a conference table in his office. He wanted Drew Klein in his bed and under his body. He wanted to slide into the man and bury himself, balls to the wall, so to speak. Instead he was stuck listening to her extol the virtue of her decorator's blond hair and perfect tan, when all he wanted to touch was pale skin and soft, dark curls.

"Lisa, sweetheart. I know you mean well, but I'm not interested. I'm not into dating or relationships." He smiled down at the pretty redhead. Her green eyes narrowed, and he braced himself for her lecture.

"Oh come on. You can't go through life having one-night stands. I'm afraid for your health. Besides, you need someone to love. Everyone does."

He barked out a laugh. "Oh please. Look at Peter's friends. These men aren't tied down. Well, except for Peterson. But you know what I mean."

She scowled at him. "You're laughing at me, but one day you'll understand what I'm talking about, and you'll want to stop this drifting through life with no meaning."

He kissed her cheek. "I've been told I'm very meaningful, sweetheart—where it counts. If you want, I'll get you references. Now I'm getting another drink; catch you later." Ignoring her gasp of outrage, he walked away. Conversations ebbed and flowed around him, and he listened with only half an ear as he poured another vodka. Drew, he noticed, looked to be flying high and in a silly, playful mood with his friends. His lips curved in a smile. Perhaps he could end this celebration with a bang after all. Casually, he walked over to a small table by the window and slid his sunglasses behind a grouping of pots holding various cacti.

By the end of the evening, only a few people remained. Rachel had taken her grandmother home. That lady was truly a sweetheart, and she surprised him when she kissed him good-bye. *"Don't be a stranger, young man. My grandchildren and their friends stop by every Sunday to see me. I expect to see you one day."* She fixed him with a pointed look, and before he could stop himself he'd nodded in agreement.

Peter and Lisa had left an hour before to relieve their sitter, and Mike left, claiming plans for the evening. Right now the only people who remained were Drew—who was a bit drunk—Jordan, and Keith. Ash knew Jordan still didn't trust him fully and he gave the good doctor credit for being as perceptive as he was. For a moment guilt pricked his newly discovered conscience, but Ash ignored it. All he wanted was one taste of Drew Klein, and then he'd be satisfied.

"Well, Drew, looks like you need to sleep it off, so we're gonna go, right, Davis?" Peterson jerked his head toward he door. "Drew needs to take some aspirin and go to bed."

He'd make sure Drew would go to bed, but if Ash had anything to say about it, the man wouldn't be alone. "Sure. Drink lots of water, Drew, and we'll see you Monday for the grand opening."

Drew threw his arm around Ash's waist. "Yeah. Thanks for all your help. And boy does my grandmother love you, Ash. Couldn't stop talking about you." He pushed back the dark curls that fell over his forehead, a crooked smile transforming his face into someone young and vulnerable. Sweet. Ash swallowed hard. An unaccustomed wave of both protectiveness and lust coursed through him. He clapped Drew on the back.

"She's very cute. Well, everyone, I'll see you at the center. Have a great night." He left and, after exiting the building, hung around the little grocery store across the street buying mints and gum, until he saw Jordan and Keith leave the building, get into their car and drive away.

He paid for his items, slipped them into his pocket, then left the store and hurried back across the street. He buzzed Drew's apartment.

"Yeah?"

"Hey, it's Ash. I think I left my sunglasses there. Can I come up and look for them?"

"Sure." A second later the buzzer rang, and he opened the security door and took the stairs, two at a time. Within a minute he was at Drew's door. It stood partially open and Ash pushed it wider, catching sight of Drew standing in the hallway weaving a bit.

"Come on in." Drew extended his hand. "Look around, wherever. I'm a little wasted, so I wouldn't be that much help in looking."

That sweet crooked smile appeared again, sending the blood racing straight to Ash's cock. He needed to touch this man. Soon. Ash entered the apartment and closed the door behind them both. "Why don't I get you some cold water, then I'll look for my glasses?"

"Sure." Drew wandered off into the apartment, yawning and scratching his head. After getting some ice from the freezer, Ash poured Drew a glass of water. His pulse raced in anticipation.

When he returned to the living room, Ash found him lying on the sofa, eyes closed.

"Hey, Drew? I have your water."

"Mmm, thanks." He kept his eyes closed but smiled.

"Do you need some help sitting up?"

"Sure, yeah."

Drew's cat, who'd done little more than glare at him, was nowhere to be found. The air stilled as if in anticipation. Ash lowered himself to the couch and slipped his arm around Drew's shoulders and pulled him close. He froze in shock as Drew opened his eyes and laid his head on Ash's shoulder. "Wanna know something weird?" Drew's mouth hovered close enough that if Ash turned his face, their lips would touch.

He swallowed, fighting the unaccustomed urge to press his mouth to Drew's. "Sure, tell me."

Drew's slightly unfocused eyes met his, the sweet, irresistible smile never wavering. "When I saw you that night with the waiter, it was the hottest thing I'd ever seen."

Oh shit.

It took all his strength of will to keep his voice calm and steady. "Really? I'd have thought you'd be shocked."

Drew chuckled and like a cat, rubbed his face against Ash's shoulder. Ash half expected the man to purr his contentment and he tightened his arm around him.

"Nah. Jordan was right. It was hot. You were hot. I came home and jerked off, so I guess I liked it, huh?" The rubbing turned into nuzzling, and Ash's blood warmed in response. Drew continued to laugh. "A little too much information, huh?" He hiccupped, closed his eyes, and settled back against Ash's chest with a sigh.

Ash gazed down at the man virtually cuddled in his arms. What the hell was he doing? With shaking fingers, he brushed back those damp, curling dark waves off Drew's face. Drew's eyes opened, and though reddened and heavy-lidded, their focus remained steady on his face.

"I'm so lonely." The green eyes closed, and Drew's head fell back to rest upon Ash's shoulder once again.

His murmur was almost lost against the roaring in Ash's head. "I don' think you're as bad as Jordan says you are. Jus' lonely too, like me."

Hell, he couldn't take advantage of a man when he was so drunk. Even he wasn't that calculating. When it came to having sex, he'd made mistakes too numerous to keep track of. More likely than not, he could fuck Drew, and they'd both enjoy it, but for the first time in Ash's life, he stepped back and refused to take advantage of the situation. It didn't seem right.

What the hell was he thinking?

A soft snore rent the air. With regret he looked down at the sleeping man, wishing he could stretch out and join him. For the second time that day he shocked himself. He'd never spent the night with anyone. He'd never spent more than the time it took afterward to zip up his pants and button his shirt with anyone he fucked. A yowl came from the doorway as Drew's big black-and-white cat stalked into the room. After some growling and warning sounds, the cat jumped on the sofa, stretching out at its head, his baleful yellow eyes glaring at Ash as if he knew Ash had taken advantage of the situation.

Watchcat on duty.

Shame flooded though him as Drew turned and settled in his arms. How could he have thought to take advantage of the man? Besides, this cuddling with Drew was kind of nice, now that he thought about it. Another first. He didn't do cuddling. By this time he would normally be dressed and out the door, the man's face forgotten.

Now he didn't want to leave. This emotion, the flare of unexpected protectiveness fucking scared him—where had it all come from? Before he knew what he was doing, Ash touched his lips to his fingers, then pressed them to Drew's lips.

"Good night, Dr. Klein."

There was no throw on the couch, and Drew looked sweet and vulnerable lying there, so Ash looked around and found one in the bedroom and covered the sleeping man. He rubbed his hands over his face and on silent feet left the apartment, the weight of the cat's evil, accusing stare boring into his back.

Chapter Six

THE END OF the world had arrived, heralded by a head about to explode like a melon blasted by a bazooka and a churning stomach that would likely never be normal again. Even the gleeful chirping of the birds outside his window grated. Why wasn't Domino out there making Happy Meals out of them? Drew tried to think of who would be willing to shoot him and put him out of his misery.

What on earth possessed him to drink so much yesterday? He usually never drank more than two beers. Something had goaded him from within, to let loose after all the years of holding himself back. To feel something new and different.

Maybe to feel anything at all.

A nudge to his chin accompanied by a deep, rumbling purr brought him back to the painful reality that it wasn't only him anymore. Domino relied on him for survival now, and as corny as that might sound, it felt good to be needed by someone, even if that someone had four legs and fur.

"Okay, buddy." The effort to open his eyes proved monumental, involving several aborted attempts and failures, but when his vision focused, Drew's gaze landed on the large yellow eyes of his cat sitting not so patiently by his side.

"Meow." Domino swished his tail and licked his hand with a small raspy tongue.

"I know. I'm getting up now." *Shit.* He hadn't even realized until now that he'd fallen asleep on his couch, let alone covered himself with a blanket. That seemed bizarre to him, but yesterday was a bizarre day—full of emotion, sentiment, and the inevitable guilt at seeing his parents' names up on the wall of the center. Normally, he tried not to think about them too often, for the pain and guilt over their loss, even after all these years, still tore him apart.

Scrubbing his face with his hands, he took a deep breath and pushed himself to an upright position. He didn't feel like throwing up, which he considered a good thing. When he glanced at his watch, he saw it was only ten in the morning. At least he hadn't slept away the entire day, especially since he had so much to do to get ready for the grand opening of the clinic.

It looked to be a warm day, as the sun already shone bright overhead, and the blue of the sky stretched out endlessly when he stuck his head out of the window to get some fresh air into his lungs. That and coffee would kick-start his day. After feeding Domino, he made a pot, then stood in the kitchen, gulping down a cup of hot, rich coffee. The rest of the carafe he put in the refrigerator to cool down for later on.

He popped two aspirin in his mouth and swallowed them down with the coffee. Not exactly the right way to take medicine, but desperate times and all that. Still working through the fog in his mind, he padded his way through the living room, straight into the bathroom. He turned on the taps to the shower and, after shucking off his clothes, stood with his eyes closed under the stream of heated water. For some reason, as it had been for weeks now, his mind fixated on Asher Davis with a stubbornness he couldn't push away.

Ever since they'd met, that man had gotten under his skin. There was more to him than Jordan had initially said, he didn't care what his friend thought. It wasn't only sex and fucking. Call it what you will, but he'd formed a kind of camaraderie with the man. Drew sensed Ash's loneliness and could relate. There could've been a hundred people in his apartment yesterday, yet Drew still would have felt alone. Nothing broke the emptiness inside of him, no matter how he filled his life with friends and family.

Yesterday, though…his mind strained to hold on to a memory that teased at the corner of recollection. With his eyes still shut, Drew fumbled for the soap. He lathered and stroked himself, wondering if he should start dating casually. Maybe Peter's wife could set him up with a friend. But instead of a beautiful blonde or brunette woman, the memory of Ash Davis in the hallway with that waiter had taken up residence in his head. His cock hardened, and the sound of his rough breathing echoed in the small, tiled shower. With one hand braced on the wall, he slid the other, slick with suds, up and down his erection. Why did that scene, and nothing else, cause him to swell even thicker, until all he could visualize was Ash's back up against the wall, his thick, gleaming cock sliding in and out of the waiter's mouth?

What the hell? Damn Ash Davis. The man was a notorious tomcat, a living, breathing erection on demand who probably fucked any man who gave him the side eye of interest. Cursing him was of no use, however, as Drew's body had a mind of its own and his orgasm hurtled upon him. Spots danced before his eyes as he came, spurting against the tiles of the shower wall, his essence swirling its way down the drain. He turned off the shower and wrapped himself in a towel, all the while his mind racing, splintering off in a thousand possible directions.

Holy hell. What was going on in his fucked-up psyche that all of a sudden he lusted after a man? He wasn't gay. Was he? People didn't become gay or bi. They were born that way. He'd never thought of being with a man before. Even those wild times in college after his parent's deaths were a blur of names and faces. He might've ended up in threesomes with both women and men, but none of them mattered. Nothing did. All he'd wanted was to forget the pain for a little while. He didn't care how it happened.

But now. Did he want to be with a man? Be with

Ash? He might've laughed at the thought, but standing in his bathroom, contemplating these questions freaked him out. Yeah, the fact that he'd jerked himself off thinking about Ash Davis totally freaked him out. Shit, his head hurt.

He pulled on jeans and a faded Stones T-shirt. Maybe he'd bake his grandmother some cookies, visit her later in the afternoon, and everything would be fine. Since his parents' deaths he'd trained himself to compartmentalize and push off things he didn't want to think about or discuss. Like jerking off to images of a man.

Feeling better now that he'd swept his emotions under the proverbial rug, he puttered around his apartment a bit, trying to straighten up after the party last night. While watering his plants, he stopped by the arrangement of cacti he had grouped on the table and tested the dirt. Dry as a bone, so he gave each pot a small dollop of water. Something caught his eye in the grouping of the pots. He reached in and pulled out a pair of expensive sunglasses. It took him a second to recognize them as belonging to Ash.

Slipping them into his back pocket, he returned to the kitchen and pulled out his baking pans, along with everything else he needed to bake his grandmother's favorite cookies. He mixed the batter and added in extra-large chocolate chips, and put some butterscotch chips in as well. He washed his hands as he waited for the oven to preheat. When the oven beeped, he slid the pans inside and set the timer for fifteen minutes.

He drank another cup of coffee, now cool and refreshing, and wandered back into his living room. With nothing to do except wait for his cookies to bake, then cool, he stretched out on the couch and flipped on the TV. For an early Sunday afternoon, it was quiet on his block. There were no screams from playful toddlers running down the block or cars revving in the street. The silence unnerved him. He shook his head at the strange thoughts in his mind. Maybe he was still a little drunk.

He roamed the channels and found a repeat of last night's Yankee game. As he settled back to watch, once again he had the strangest feeling someone else had been there with him yesterday after the party. The sunglasses in his back pocket dug into his ass, and not wanting to break them, he took them out and left them on the table. A thought popped into his head, and he opened his laptop, then logged on to that dating site he'd seen on TV: Big Apple Meet Ups. They advertised a free seven-day trial, so he created an account and the faces of hundreds of women, all dying to meet him, filled his screen.

After three pages his eyes glazed over. So many women. Christ. Each one seemed perfect for him. But then again, he'd thought Jackie was perfect too, although if he'd looked closer, maybe he would've seen the warning signs his family and friends tried to point out. Hindsight was easy after the fact. What a waste. Yeah, the sex had been okay, but he couldn't forgive himself for being so easily duped. Guess he wasn't as great a judge of character as he thought. Either that or she was a damn good actress when she wanted something, which was more likely the truth.

He wanted to prove to them all—his sister and his friends—that he could make his own decisions about his life without the need for their well-meaning intervention, or, in the case of Jordan, his arrogant opinions.

Jackie had made no secret from the moment they'd met at the rooftop bar of Tribeca Grand that she'd wanted him. Badly. If he were the type of guy to score on the first date, he could've had her in his bed that night. And she was more than willing, he realized as he recalled her attempts in the cab they'd shared, to get him to come home with her. Maybe that was his problem. He took sex seriously and couldn't understand people like Jackie and Asher Davis, who threw it around like it meant nothing at all.

No more thinking about the past. He'd extricated himself quickly and painlessly, with nothing more than a bruised but not broken heart. Luckily, Jackie hadn't gotten pregnant. She didn't want to have any children, and he'd always expressed a desire to adopt. He didn't need to have his own children, not when there were way too many kids who suffered abuse and neglect in the foster care system. Most of the people who wanted to help were good, decent people, but like anything else, when the systems failed, the consequences could be devastating. Maybe he'd think about becoming a single dad in the near future.

The oven timer dinged, and he returned to the kitchen to pull the cookies out. They smelled wonderful as he set the pans on the counter to cool. Domino sniffed at his toes and swatted his ankles. *Looks like someone wants a treat.* Drew took out one of the bowls he kept on the counter specifically for that purpose and bent down to feed and pet the purring cat.

A beep sounded from the living room. "Come on, kitty. Let's go and see who wants what from me." He plopped down on the sofa and peered at the slightly blurry computer screen. Damn. Maybe he did need to start wearing those glasses the ophthalmologist said he needed. Until then, he'd make do with squinting.

Oh wow. Turned out he had an IM from a woman. That was quicker than he'd expected.

Hi. I'm Alyssa. How are you?

Hmm. A little strange to do it this way, but he shrugged. Technology was the way of the world now, so here went nothing.

I'm good, thanks. How are you?

Great. I saw your profile, and live near you so I wondered if you'd want to get together for a coffee or a drink this week.

Just then the downstairs buzzer rang. He wasn't expecting anyone. Domino jumped off the couch and ran into the bedroom.

Hold on for a few? My doorbell rang.

Sure. Not a problem.

He spoke into the little speaker box. “Who is it?”

“It’s Ash. May I come up?”

Funny, he’d never noticed the slight Southern drawl in Ash’s voice. An unexpected shiver raced through him. “Sure,” he said and pushed the button to release the door lock.

Within seconds, footsteps pounded up the stairs, and he opened the door to watch Ash climbing the last few steps. Ash pushed his hair off his forehead, then met Drew’s gaze and grinned. “Damn. You couldn’t live on the first floor?”

An image floated into his head and out just as quickly, of Ash bending over him on the couch. Since that made no sense, he blinked once or twice to clear his head and held the door open wide. “Come on in. Are you going somewhere?”

Ash cocked his brow and followed him into the apartment. “No, why?”

Drew gestured with his chin. “I dunno, you’re kinda dressed up for a Sunday morning.” His gaze raked over the man in a white button-down shirt and black pants. “I’m like a slob compared to you.” He laughed and rubbed his chin.

Like a breath being held, an anticipatory waiting for something to drop and cause havoc and mayhem, a heavy silence hung in the air. Ash’s glittering eyes scrutinized him, traveling with slow precision up his body. It was as if Drew could feel the press of Ash’s fingers on his back and the hush of Ash's breath against his face. His skin prickled with the heat flooding his body. He never could control his blushing. It drove him crazy.

"Don't be a fool. You're perfect."

That slight Southern drawl made every word sound like a sexual invitation. Drew let out a self-conscious laugh. "Ah, yes. Must be why the women are beating down my door."

Ash's face shuttered, closed and dark. "Perhaps you're looking for the wrong person."

Their eyes met, and once again the air vibrated with tension. Drew licked his lips. "Um, go ahead and sit down. You want some iced coffee or a beer or something?"

"The coffee sounds great, thanks." Ash strolled into the living room while Drew fixed the coffee. He brought the cups in, but there was nowhere for both of them to sit, as the blanket still lay on the sofa.

Ash placed his cup on the table, took the blanket, and folded it. "I can put this back in the bedroom if you want."

Puzzled, Drew looked from the blanket to Ash, who headed toward the bedroom. "How did you know where it came from?"

Ash froze at the entrance to Drew's bedroom, a guilty expression coloring his face red. "I, uh…" He looked up, down, and everywhere but at Drew's face.

"You *did* come back here, didn't you? I thought I was going crazy with the thoughts in my head." Drew pressed the heel of his palm hard into his eyes. "Shit. I really have no recollection of what happened. I'm no drinker."

Re-entering the living room, Ash flashed a surprisingly charming smile. "Yeah, that was obvious. You were trashed."

It made no sense to pretend to be affronted; instead Drew broke out in a grin. "Yeah, I'm kind of a lightweight when it comes to booze." He licked his lips, nerves skittering inside him at the question he was about to ask. "Um, so what happened when you were here?"

Ash returned to the couch and sat next to him. His soft voice sparked a confusing, heated response in Drew's blood. "What makes you think somethin' happened?"

If a fire truck plowed into his apartment right now, it couldn't have pulled his attention away from Ash's strong jaw and firm lips. Or that little wedge of skin, so soft looking even with the dark curl of chest hair peeking through. The man smelled like warm sunshine and coffee. Heaven and desire.

"I, um, I had some weird dreams," Drew choked out, embarrassed now that Ash sat before him. But the man wasn't smiling. In fact, he looked terrifyingly serious.

"Did you, now?" It didn't seem strange at all for Ash to reach over and brush back the curls that insisted on falling into his eyes. "Why don't you tell me about 'em?"

He shook his head, unsure where to begin, afraid he might reveal too much of the confusion inside.

A ding from the computer broke the mesmerizing spell between them. “Shit. I forgot about her.” With reluctance, he turned his attention to the computer and the series of chat messages with the woman he’d been talking to. What was her name again? Alyssa, right. Wow she had a lot to say.

Hello, hello?

Are you still there?

I guess you aren’t that interested.

A warm breath teased his ear, sending chills rippling down his spine. “Are you? Interested in her?”

Drew found it hard to swallow. Ash’s lips, his mouth, were a mere breath away from touching his hair. Much as his mind sought to ignore it, his body responded. If he chose to turn only a bit…with supreme strength, Drew wrenched away from Ash’s magnetic pull and shut the laptop, effectively ending the conversation with poor Alyssa.

“I, um, don’t know. It’s only the first time I’ve done that.” For the life of him he didn’t know why he sounded so defensive. It wasn’t as if he owed Ash an explanation. And speaking of explanations…

“You never did say why you came by yesterday after the party.”

Ash frowned, staring off into the distance. “To pick up my sunglasses, of course.”

On inspiration, Drew blurted out, "Do you want to come with me to my grandmother's today? I have to bring her the cookies I baked...." His voice trailed off as Ash cast him a look of disbelief. "Oh, sorry. That was stupid of me. I'm sure you have better things to do than hang around with my family all day long."

But to his utter shock and surprise, a wide smile brightened Ash's face. It was as if a switch had flicked on from the inside. "I couldn't think of a better way to spend my Sunday than to see Esther again. I enjoyed meeting her." His smile faded for a moment. "Are you sure she wouldn't mind me butting in?"

"Mind? You remember what she said. She'll be thrilled. Someone new to flirt with." He punched Ash on the shoulder. "Help me wrap the cookies up, and we can take off. I usually get there by one o'clock. First I have to stop at the deli and pick her up a corned beef sandwich."

Ash's eyes lit up. "Nothing like a good corned beef sandwich. Mr. Frank used to bring them in whenever we worked late on a case." And as quickly as his face had flushed with happiness, it drained of joy.

"You miss him, don't you?" The bleak expression on Ash's face hurt Drew's heart. It was obvious the man had meant the world to Ash.

"Every fucking day." The pain in Ash's voice was pitiful to hear.

Drew gave Ash's arm a sympathetic squeeze. "Then spending a day with my grandmother will help." He patted Ash on his back, noting the flex and play of muscle under the fine cotton of his shirt. Why, all of a sudden did he notice these little, intimate details about Ash's body?

Ash stilled under his touch, and Drew found he couldn't pull away. Their gazes locked. Drew stepped back quickly, withdrawing his hand. Disconcerted, he frowned to himself. What the hell was happening here? "Uh. Let's get going." They wrapped up the cooled-down cookies and left the apartment. Drew drove, the silence between them speaking louder than any words could.

Chapter Seven

THE DRIVE INTO an unfamiliar part of the city gave Ash time to contemplate what the hell he was doing here. If he had any brain, he'd tell Drew to stop the car and he'd get out, tell him, "See ya, have a nice visit with your grandmother," and be on his way. His usual Sundays were spent sleeping off the hangover he'd acquired on Saturday night. It was rare to find him up before 2:00 or 3:00 pm. He'd laze about his apartment, read the paper then go to a restaurant to find something to eat for dinner. Later on he might head to one of the clubs he knew where he'd have a private room with whomever he wanted, or he might choose to have quick, hot sex in a bathroom stall with someone who caught his eye.

None of it mattered, not the men nor the sex. He had no idea if they were good people like Drew or bad, like himself. He didn't care. When he did come home, he'd drown his pain and despair in enough vodka that the bleakness of the night faded into a beautiful oblivion.

Now he sat in a car with a man who'd confounded him from first sight, a box full of cookies in his lap, actually anticipating spending his afternoon with an elderly lady. His opponents in the courtroom would laugh at him and his night-time playmates wouldn't recognize him. For the first time in his life, Ash didn't worry what someone else might think of him. Meeting Drew's grandmother last night had struck something deep inside him he'd thought lost forever. In Esther he'd seen a person full of purity and love, and for a fleeting moment, he'd remembered what it felt like to be young and innocent again.

What the hell was happening to him?

"You're very quiet."

Drew navigated the twists and turns onto the highway and eventually Ash became totally lost. He saw high rises and then apartment buildings with children playing out front.

"I'm taking in the scenery. Aside from coming to the clinic, I never go to Brooklyn—most of my time is spent in the city."

"But you're not from here."

Ash stiffened. "Why do you say that?"

Drew shot him a quick frown. "Don't get all defensive, I wasn't snooping into your past. You have a slight Southern accent, that's all."

"Oh." He thought he'd trained himself to speak more "Northern" but conceded he might slip occasionally. "I've been here a long time."

"Why are you here with me now? I'm really curious. I can't imagine a man like you would be interested in spending one of his days off with an elderly lady, even if she is my grandmother."

"A man like me? Why is it," he shot right back, "that you and your friends think you know who or what I like or what I'm interested in?"

Curious, he waited to see if Drew would respond. Ash noticed his red face and enjoyed discomfiting him. Served him right for being so judgmental. They rode in silence for a little while, and Ash recalled what Drew confessed last night to him when he came back to his apartment. How lonely he was and how he believed Ash might be lonely too. Drew had no idea how close to Ash's secret truth he'd come. He'd walked with loneliness at his shoulder, a constant companion his entire life, except those years with Luke and Brandon and then Mr. Frank. Could the two of them be more alike than he thought? Why would Drew feel isolated with a loving family and a circle of friends always by his side?

"I'm sorry, I didn't mean it to sound the way it came out. And you're right, I don't know you well enough to insinuate that. Maybe we could start fresh, you know? I'm willing to wipe away my preconceived ideas I got of you from Jordan and that night at dinner. What you do on your own time has nothing to do with our friendship."

Friendship? Ash didn't think he and Drew were friends, but hearing him say it gave Ash a warm feeling inside. Like he was part of something special. Which, now that he knew a little more about Drew from the first time they met, he realized he was. Drew was a special man who put the needs of others before himself. Ash had never met anyone quite like him. Being included in his circle of friends was something Ash hadn't known he'd desired until now.

"Yeah, I'm willing. For friendship's sake and all that."

Drew pulled into the driveway of a small wood-frame and brick house and cut the engine. "No one can ever have enough friends, you know?" He opened the door and took the box of cookies and gestured to the back. "Can you hand me the sandwiches?" He slammed the car door shut.

No, he didn't know. Peter remained the only man he'd ever allowed close enough to see a fraction of who he was, but even that friendship he kept at arm's length, like almost everyone else. Being friends with Drew wouldn't allow for that, Ash suspected. Drew was a man who expected give and take, where Ash lived his life taking. He'd already given up everything years ago.

"Sure." Ash gave the bag to Drew and followed him up the red-bricked walkway. Inexplicably nervous, he remained a step or two behind Drew, ready to bolt. Family and everything that went along with it unnerved and confounded him. He made up his mind to say hello to Esther, stay a few minutes, then beat a hasty retreat, using his big caseload as an excuse.

The glass-front door rattled, then opened wide, and Esther greeted Drew.

"Hello, sweetheart. Come inside."

"Nana, I brought you a surprise besides the cookies." Drew opened the door wider and Ash watched Esther register something he'd rarely seen in another person's eyes when meeting him—genuine happiness.

"Asher? Oh, I'm so happy to see you, dear boy. Come inside. Drew, don't keep him waiting on the porch like a stranger."

Drew walked in and Ash passed in front of Esther, feeling awkward for the very first time in his life. Did he kiss her cheek or simply smile a greeting? He had no clue about propriety when it came to old ladies.

"Hello, Esther." He decided to treat her as the great lady she was and picked up her hand and kissed it. She blushed but kept her hand in his, giving it a gentle squeeze as they walked to the back of the house. He listened to her soft voice, so quiet only he could hear. Drew had already entered the kitchen with the food.

"I'm so happy you came for a visit. I knew as soon as I met you what a special man you were."

"Me?" He laughed nervously, running a hand through his hair. "I'm nothing. Nobody special."

She stooped and turned to him putting her hand on his arm. He shook slightly but didn't pull away.

"Don't ever say that about yourself. You're not a nobody. Look at all the good you're doing. Working with Drew, helping those poor people. Would a nobody do that?"

Admiring the tenacity in her voice, Ash still didn't buy it. Years spent listening to his foster father hurl insults, telling him how worthless he was had ingrained a sense of self he could hide from others but not himself. He could pretend from daybreak until nightfall, but when he was alone with only the scars of his past, Ash knew the truth.

"I'd have to be a heartless person not to help. I do what I can."

Huffing out a disapproving breath, Esther gave his hand another squeeze. "I know what I see. And I've never been wrong."

With those enigmatic words, she led him into a kitchen, fragrant with the smells of fried onions, garlic and delicious cooking. Ash's stomach growled and he started, embarrassed by the sound.

"Don't worry, that sound is music to my grandmother's ears, right, Nana?

Ash shot Drew a look. "I'm not hungry."

Drew snorted. "Three words you're never allowed to utter in this house."

Having tied an apron over her dress, Esther bustled over to him and pointed at the table. "Sit down and I'll bring you over a plate. I have a roast that I took out of the oven a little while ago and some mashed potatoes."

This was all too homey for him; the loving family togetherness made him antsy. It reminded Ash of the great, yawning divide between himself and Drew. Ash could play pretend in this world for only so long, before he grew tired of beating down the devil and gave in to the darkness inside him.

"I think I should go. You and Drew can have a nice

visit. You don't need a stranger intruding."

"I read somewhere that strangers are friends you haven't met yet. I've lived too long and lost too much already to let people disappear from my life." Once again Esther touched him, placing a hand on his arm. He struggled not to break out in a sweat or shake her off, and bit down hard on the inside of his cheek to feel the pain, welcoming it as he always did to ground him.

"Please, Asher. Join us. You can never have too many friends."

She echoed Drew's earlier words. Now Ash saw where Drew's innate goodness came from. And where he might have been able to brush off Drew, he couldn't refuse Esther's plea. Something about her touched a part of him he thought had shriveled up and died years ago.

"Okay. For a little while." He sat, Drew taking a chair directly across from him at the round wooden table.

While Esther busied herself, Ash studied the pictures on the shelf on the wall behind Drew. He saw a much younger Esther and a handsome man—most likely her husband—big and broad in the shoulders, holding her hand. He stared at her with a tender expression visible to Ash even in the more-than-half-century-old photograph. There were assorted pictures of them with a baby, then a young woman getting married, whom Ash presumed was Drew's mother. Recalling Drew's sister from their brief meeting, she favored her mother in the shape of her face and tilt of her brows, where Drew took after their father. Both inherited their father's light green eyes.

Drew caught him gazing at the photographs. "It took years for me to be able to look at their pictures after they died. I couldn't bear to see them smiling back at me after—" He stopped and shook his head. Fascinated, Ash watched Drew compose himself, wanting to know more of the story but sensing it was neither the time nor place to discuss the tragedy.

Esther came to the table holding two plates that gave off the most delicious aroma of roast beef. This time when his stomach growled, he felt no embarrassment. She set the plates before each of them. Slices of fresh rare roast beef lay thinly cut alongside a heaping scoop of fluffy mashed potatoes with bits of fried onion mixed in.

"Your parents would be so proud of you, darling. So many people talk about helping others. *You* are doing something about it. I'm proud of both of you."

She handed him cutlery and gestured to them. "Go eat. Don't wait for me. I'm not eating this."

Puzzled, Ash didn't understand. "But you made all this food. Who else is coming?"

She laughed. "Oh I make a big meal every Sunday; one of the children always stops by and I make sure to have enough food for everyone. But I still look forward to the corned beef sandwich Drew brings me every week."

"I have it right here for you, Nana." Drew handed it to her, speaking through a mouthful of food. "Ash and I stopped along the way."

"Here, Esther. Let me get you a plate."

A stack of heavy-duty paper plates sat on the table and Ash separated one and handed it over to her, along with a plastic knife and fork. "Wouldn't you rather eat off of a regular plate?"

"I learned after the kids started coming over that I didn't want to be stuck washing dishes; I never bothered with a dishwasher since it's only me in the house. This serves very nicely, but thank you."

"How long have you been alone?" Ash froze, his face on fire. In asking Esther that question, hell, in coming here at all, he'd broken his cardinal rule of never getting too close or personal. "I'm sorry, I didn't mean to pry."

"Don't be silly. You didn't. My Sy died seventeen years ago and I miss him every day. But I never once thought of myself as being alone, or lonely."

Sitting in this fragrant kitchen as far removed from his youth as he could possibly have gotten, the ghosts of his past brushed their ephemeral fingers against Ash's cheeks as if to remind him they hadn't left. No matter how many people he surrounded himself with, Ash remained alone, locked in his own personal hell.

"My grandmother is the strongest person I know, man or woman," said Drew, his gaze fixated on the picture of his parents. "For weeks after my parents died, I couldn't function, yet she pushed me to get up every morning and go back to school. And when I had problems dealing with it, I turned to her for help. I wouldn't have made it without her."

Esther put down the half of the sandwich she was about to bite into. "You're stronger than you give yourself credit for. I think you could face anything now that came your way and not back down."

Drew shrugged but didn't answer. He also failed to eat anything further, despite his previous enjoyment of the food. Instead he sat and pushed the meat around on his plate and toyed with the mound of mashed potatoes. Every few minutes Ash noticed Drew glancing over his shoulder, his eyes darting to the pictures of his parents. His lips trembled and his eyes shone bright with unshed tears.

Deep in thought, Ash chewed his food, wondering what truth Drew hid from his beloved grandmother. The subtle signs he'd noticed gave Ash pause to think Drew might be almost as adept at hiding his emotions as Ash himself. It was the nervous, not-quite-there smile and the way he couldn't look Esther straight in the eye. Chameleon that Ash was, it had become second nature for him to easily transfer between the personas of high-powered attorney and man seeking sexual satisfaction. Drew wasn't like him; he hadn't perfected the art of living in a protective shell, letting the world see only what you wanted them to. His face revealed every emotion, highlighting his incredible vulnerability. Ash wanted to shake him and tell him all the bad things in the world that could happen to people like him. People who cared.

Holding Drew last night and learning of his secret

pain gave Ash insight to a side of Drew he instinctively knew none of Drew's friends had ever seen. Immersed in an alcoholic haze, Drew unwittingly revealed his inner turmoil with the painful admission of loneliness and it pieced together a man Ash initially believed was nothing more than a rich person unsullied by life's pain.

Drew's pain caught him short, surprising Ash with the revelation that no one sailed through life untouched, despite the untroubled façade they showed the world. Ash lived his life as a loner, but not by choice, as he desperately wished to have his brothers with him. Drew, though lucky enough to have had a family and an amazing support system around him, remained locked in a solitary confinement of his own, a punishment for something Ash couldn't understand.

"Do you like the food, Asher? You had the strangest look on your face just now."

Esther's concerned voice broke him out of his mental study. He wanted Drew still, but his desire had shifted from the pure physical itch of sex to something on a deeper level. He needed to know what made Drew tick, what he hid from everyone—his family, his closest friends—and why. *Who was the man behind the mirror?* Afraid to delve too deeply as to the underlying reason why Drew piqued his interest after all the years of nameless, emotionless sex, Ash put on his own game face, flashing the smile he reserved for judges, or used to secure new clients.

"It's delicious; I can't remember when I've had a

better meal. I was thinking of something I had to do is all."

Peering at him over her glasses, Esther gave him a troubled smile, then returned to her massive corned beef sandwich, which she'd already split into four separate sandwiches. Drew shot him a disbelieving look, then shook his head and picked a bit at his food, answering questions from his grandmother about the clinic.

If there was anything Ash enjoyed it was a challenge, and working in such close proximity with Drew would be the challenge of his life. He'd never met anyone he'd wanted to touch more and walk away from less and it left him in the unaccustomed position of not knowing what his next move was. All he did know was he'd make sure to see as much of Dr. Drew Klein as he could.

Chapter Eight

AFTER EXITING THE cab, Ash stood on the sidewalk outside the clinic, surveying the activity. Young men and women in their teens and early twenties entered and departed the building. Those who left, more often than not, wore a relaxed, hopeful look, as if they'd found the secret answer to the problem troubling them. With any luck, the clinic had done its job.

He sipped his coffee, and as they had done so very often since he met Drew Klein his thoughts wandered to the doctor. For the life of him, he couldn't figure out why. The man's dark curls, light green eyes, and sweet smile didn't hurt, but then Ash had never lacked for good-looking men in his bed.

It was more than Drew's tight ass and lean build, though Ash readily admitted his shallow criteria in choice of bedmates, often only caring if the man had visual appeal. With Drew, his innate goodness plus the dedication he showed to his mission to create the center trumped his outward appearance. Ash had never known anyone so damn nice before and didn't know what to make of him.

Ash pushed open the glass front door, greeting Marly, a teenager with so many facial piercings it hurt to look at her. He slipped a small bakery bag on her desk. "Good morning."

"Hi, Mr. Davis." Her gaze landed on the bag. "What did you bring me today?" A gleam in her pale blue eyes indicated she already knew it would be something she would like.

Ash leaned over the top of the counter and ruffled her hair. "I know you're going to want to taste it." His eyes held hers, willing her to agree. Sixteen-year-old Marly had been at the center from the beginning, coming to them half-starved and sexually abused. Without saying a word, Ash had taken it upon himself to make sure he did everything legally possible to put her father behind bars for a long time. The case was still winding its way through the system. Thank God they had gotten her out of her abusive household and in with a wonderful foster care family.

Still somewhat mistrustful of strangers, she'd taken to him—kindred lost souls recognized each other. No one in the clinic could understand the unusual friendship between him and the frightened, bedraggled teenager, but it wasn't any of their goddamn business. He had his reasons, and one of them was the way her lips now curved in a smile and her pale eyes shone with laughter, not fear, as she peered inside the bag to see her double-fudge cupcake.

Fear was another companion he'd grown up with

and lived with each night of his life until he'd turned eighteen and escaped his foster home for good. He'd made sure he got away and could only hope his foster brothers Luke and Brandon—the boys he'd left behind who were too young and scared to leave with him—had made it out as well. He'd never stopped trying to find them, but the private investigator he had on their trail for years kept running up against dead ends.

"Oooh, Mr. Davis, you shouldn't have." But her finger sank into the two-inch topping of fudge and came away with a big glob to stick in her mouth. Her eyes rolled back in her head with undisguised ecstasy. "Yumm. It's so good. Thank you."

"Make sure you finish it, and don't let anyone sneak a bite." He jerked his head at Javier, the other teenager manning the reception desk. The teenage boy snorted, shaking his head.

"Man, I'm not gonna steal her food. Especially when her nasty finger's already touched it."

Outraged, Marly took a huge bite, leaving a glob of frosting on her nose. "My hands are clean, buddy boy. As opposed to yours, which were probably down some guy's pants this morning."

Javier's face flamed. "Not true. Marquez and I broke up."

Instantly, Marly turned from teaser to comforter, and Ash enjoyed seeing how the two formerly wary, friendless teens had bonded as she consoled him. "Bastard. You'll find someone better than him; don't worry, baby."

"Okay, kids, do I have anyone scheduled this morning?" Ash reached for the printed schedule in Marly's hand.

"Um, yeah, but not until later. It's the kid who came in last week, pretty bad off."

Stevie North. Ash's gut tightened. "Thanks." With what he hoped was a casual tone, he asked, "Boss man here?"

Too busy cutting off a slice of her cupcake for Javier, Marly didn't pay much attention to him. "Uh yeah, Dr. Drew came in about an hour ago and Dr. Rachel's here too."

Inwardly Ash groaned. While he thought Drew's sister cute and funny, she loved to psychoanalyze the shit out of him, coming uncomfortably close to the truth too many times. More often than not, he avoided her and her good-natured, nosy questioning.

"Thanks. See you two later."

Neither answered, their mouths full of cupcake.

As he walked down the hallway, he greeted the other volunteers who came every Saturday and Sunday to meet with the kids who stopped by. They had Rachel to thank for them. Ten of her fellow psychology classmates volunteered to sit with the people who came in for guidance or help and talk to them. Their problems didn't always require counseling or intervention. More often than not it came down to a simple miscommunication with their parents or siblings or a teenager being a teenager. They talked for a while and went on their way with a better understanding of how to handle a parent or a brother or sister.

Those were the lucky ones which fortunately constituted most of their cases.

But then there were cases like Marly, or fifteen-year-old Stevie, that made what Drew had set up here so extraordinary.

Immersed in his thoughts and not watching where he was going, he ran straight into the man who'd taken up residence in his mind most of the time.

Ooof. Their bodies collided, and Ash's head made painful contact with Drew's, a hard edge slicing into his cheekbone as their bodies flattened against one another. For a moment he saw stars.

A warm trickle of blood ran down his cheek. "Ow." He touched his cheek, and it came away bloodstained. "What the hell?" The words died on his lips as he saw Drew, a concerned look on his face, wearing glasses that made him look hot as shit. The pain in his head forgotten, he wanted nothing more than to flatten the man against the wall and kiss him senseless.

"When did you get the glasses, Doc?" The man looked like a sexy professor, except no professor he ever had in law school had a face or body like Drew's. Desire prickled through him, hardening his cock even as the blood dripped down his face.

Drew stopped rubbing his head. "Shit, Ash. Come on to the examining room. I have to see if you need stitches." He pointed to the door on his right. "This one is free."

Ash entered and hopped up on the table, forcing

himself to face Drew, who stood over him with a wet gauze pad, cleaning up the blood. "I'm sure it's nothing."

Drew's lips twitched. "Last time I checked, you went to law school, not medical school, so shut up and let me look." He took off those sexy professor glasses and came close to Ash's face.

Warning bells dinged in his head. *Shit.* The reality of being this close to Drew was so much better than his X-rated dreams. His deft touch soothed Ash and a clean fresh scent emanated from his skin, as if he'd stepped out of the shower only a minute before. Unwittingly, Ash groaned out loud.

Responding to Ash's pained outcry, Drew's expression changed to one of concern. "Does it hurt very badly? I might need to put in a stitch or two near your eye. That's where the cut is the deepest." The tips of his fingers touched Ash's cheek, and his eyes clouded with obvious distress. "Shit, I'm so sorry. I really didn't see or hear you."

Without thinking, Ash covered Drew's hand. "Not your fault. I was the one not paying attention."

Neither of them moved; then Ash watched as Drew's gaze flickered over to their joined hands. A sweet blush colored Drew's cheeks as he pulled his fingers away. "Uh, anyway, let me see if we can get away with a butterfly bandage on this and maybe you won't need the stitches, 'kay?"

Shit. He didn't mean for that to happen. Sure he lusted over the guy, but Drew was straight and never gave any indication he'd be interested in crossing the line. The drunken confession about jerking off while thinking about him was nothing. Everyone had weird dreams; his own happened to be full of Drew naked and in his bed, riding his dick.

"Sure. Have at it." He closed his eyes and relaxed as Drew cleaned and dressed the cut.

"Not as bad as I initially thought. The skin's so thin in that area it bleeds a lot, but it wasn't too deep. Keep it covered, and in a few days I'll check it to make sure it doesn't get infected."

Ash opened his eyes to Drew's back as he cleaned up and rinsed his hands. It gave him a chance to appreciate the man from behind. "Thanks, Drew."

"No problem. Always good to have a doctor in the house, right?" Drew winked over his shoulder at Ash, not realizing the torment he put Ash through. In the past, there would've been no question of him going after Drew and getting him into bed. The men never mattered to him. Ultimately they almost all gave in, but for Ash, the void remained—the aching, dark part of him that never went away no matter how many men he had.

Not so with Drew. Now, though he'd only known the man a few months, Ash respected Drew and wouldn't think of jeopardizing their friendship, including inappropriately touching or kissing him.

Friendship. An alien term to him, until now. Until Drew with his honesty and kindness brought Ash into his inner circle making him a part of something he never thought he'd want. Having Drew as a friend was as important as having him as a lover. And someone like Drew would insist on being both.

As he continued to watch Drew clean up, Ash focused on the part of his neck between where his hair curled at the edges and his T-shirt ended. All he wanted to do was lick that teasing bit of flesh. Lost in the fantasy of him driving into Drew on the examining room table, gripping the man's hips as he pushed into Drew over and over again, he almost jumped a foot when Drew tapped him on the shoulder.

"Whoa, what's up with you today? You're jumpy as all hell." Drew laughed and stepped back with his hands up. "You almost clocked me again."

It took every effort of Ash's will not to grab Drew and drag him up against his hard-on. The last thing he needed, however, was Drew finding out the depth of his feelings, considering his confused state of mind. "Restless night. I have a nasty case coming up I'm not looking forward to." *Big fucking lie.* He never let any of his cases get to him, approaching them as a means to an end. Helping the kids here had become his reality now, the only thing that really mattered aside from finding out where Luke and Brandon were. That was paramount and what made him get up every morning.

He slid off the examining table. "Thanks, Doc." Drew had put those sexy glasses back on again and Ash touched the rim of them with a fingertip. "You never answered me. When did you get those?"

Drew reddened. "I went to the eye doctor since my

vision started getting a little blurry close up. He said I should wear them."

"They look good. Make you look like a professor. Women will love them." Ash gave him a two-fingered salute and walked out the door, not waiting for an answer. He didn't want to think about Drew dating women. He didn't want to think about Drew at all, yet the rest of the day found his thoughts back again to Esther's kitchen and the hidden pain he'd seen in Drew's eyes. Over the years, Ash had become an expert in detecting subterfuge; whether in a witness on the stand or in a potential bed partner, he managed to ferret out their weakness and drive home for the kill.

Not so with Drew. Ash rubbed his eyes and paced his small office, wrangling with the disturbing thoughts racing through his mind. The lust to fuck Drew still remained but now something else, indefinable and somewhat frightening, cropped up to join his physical need.

The day flew, and by five o'clock he was on his last appointment. His heart squeezed at the sight of Stevie's name on the list. One of the unlucky ones, Stevie was a target for every homophobic bully he came into contact with. Small, thin, and pale, he was almost pretty enough to pass for a young girl. Two neighborhood kids constantly harassed him, pushing him around, occasionally grabbing his genitals and taunting him as he walked to and from the bus stop. It never mattered that Stevie didn't answer back. They heaped threats on him, vowing to cut off his balls and stuff them in his mouth should he ever breathe a word to anyone about what they did or said. A few times they'd dragged him into an alley where one boy held Stevie down while the other hit him and touched him inappropriately. The bruises they inflicted were crafted to remain hidden under his clothing, but from years of experience, it didn't fool Ash. He knew where to look.

At their first meeting, Stevie's nervousness almost caused him to vomit. He kept glancing at the door, later confessing he'd thought someone would burst through it to drag him out and kill him. Several weeks passed before he could relax enough to confide his painful story. But only to Ash. When Ash told him he would go to the police to report what Stevie told him, the boy freaked out. He liked his foster parents and was deathly afraid if he said anything they'd move him to a different home. There was comfort in knowing the devil you had.

"I'll run away and never come back if you do that. Please. Let me come here and talk to you for now."

Sitting behind his desk, Ash's fingers tightened on the folder that held the details of all of Stevie's personal sessions. He understood what the boy lived through. The only hope was for Stevie to gain strength and report the abuse. As of today, he was too scared. Ash could hardly blame him for his very real fear.

For over an hour Ash waited for Stevie to show, but by six o'clock he finally admitted defeat. Stevie wasn't coming. Fear gripped him; in his experience it was as easy to imagine Stevie lying beaten in a gutter somewhere than him sitting at home. Having seen the worst of what could happen to a boy like Stevie; vulnerable and defeated before he had a chance to succeed, Ash thought back to his brothers and how he let them down. At eighteen he'd no choice but to save himself or die. Now, he would use the money and power he strived all these years to attain to help Stevie and people like him to believe in themselves and a future they never dreamed possible.

But Stevie had to come to him; Ash couldn't chase him down in the mean streets of his neighborhood. And as he waited with growing frustration, watching the clock tick past six, Ash knew when to call it quits. Something had happened to spook Stevie. The last time they'd spoken he'd been full of plans to make the center a regular part of his routine. Ash surmised he might want to hang out because it kept him off the streets and out of sight as a target for the neighborhood bullies.

Once he'd shut down the computer and locked up the office, Ash turned out the light and headed to the front of the center. His shoes made no sound on the shining, laminate floors and again he marveled at Drew's fierce dedication. In his life, Ash hadn't had much to be proud of; he'd lied as a young man to make his way up north and knew how poorly he treated most men when it came to sex. But being surrounded by Drew and his friends cut through the grayness surrounding his life all these years. Being here, spending time at the center not only with Drew but with the young people who only sought acceptance and to be treated with common decency made him wonder of the possibility of his own redemption.

The two teens sat at the front desk, looking tired and anxious to leave.

"I'm sorry I kept you guys. I'd hoped Stevie would show today, but looks like that's not happening."

Javier's face darkened. "Don't you worry, Ash. I'm gonna go make sure he's okay. I know where to look." He pulled on his jacket.

Something tight unfurled in Ash's chest then, seeing the support Stevie had gained from people who hardly knew him, yet cared about his welfare. Kindness did exist if it was nurtured and given a home. Ash wondered if Luke and Brandon had managed to gain a circle of trust and friendship such as this, but doubted it. A man like Drew, selfless and giving, was a rarity.

His head ached at the point where Drew tended to it earlier and a fog of weariness enveloped him, but that didn't quell Ash's fear for Javier. He might be eighteen but terrible things could and did happen to young men at that age. Ash couldn't live with himself if anything happened to the boy.

"Don't go chasing after trouble, Javier. We don't need you hurt."

Javier flashed a smile. "Don't worry. I know the streets; I lived on them for a while. I'll be careful." The smile faded when he reached the front door. "I won't let no one hurt Stevie." Before Ash or Marly could respond, he fled.

Who would care about *him* if he disappeared? Would anyone? Would Drew?

"Are you okay Ash? You look kinda funny."

Marly's voice penetrated the fog in his head and Ash focused on her anxious face.

"I'm fine. I'll see you tomorrow and hopefully Stevie will come then. Do you have someone to walk you home?"

"It's okay; it's still light out. I only live a few blocks away."

Over his dead body would he send a young girl—especially Marly, who'd seen enough terror in the world—out on these streets if he didn't have to.

"Don't be ridiculous. I'll send you home in a car."

"But—"

Two taps on his phone and it was done. He cut her protest short. "It's all arranged. A car will be here in ten minutes to take you home. I'll wait with you."

"You don't have to do that. I'll be fine waiting here by myself."

Was anyone ever okay alone? Ash hated it; it was why he filled his nights with anonymous men and too much alcohol.

"I'm staying. No one else is here? Everyone left?"

Marly nodded. "Dr. Drew went home about half an hour ago. He left with Dr. Jordan."

Great. No doubt Jordan took tremendous delight in talking shit about him. Bastard. It didn't help that most of the things Jordan said about him were correct.

"So I'll be here with you until the car comes. And

I'm going to talk to Dr. Drew about arranging for you to have a car take you home every day."

"Really?" Marly bit her lip. "Thanks. It'll be good when the winter comes and it's dark early. But I could get someone to walk me home."

Ash made a mental note to speak to Drew about it. Marly was an at-risk girl and God knows he had enough regrets in his life; he didn't need anything happening to Marly to add to the pile of guilt he carried with him.

"Like I said. Don't worry about it." The sound of a car pulling up in front cut her protests short. "See? It's here already. Let's go."

They walked out together and Marly locked the door, setting the alarm system. Ash walked her to the black car idling at the curb and waited while she buckled her seatbelt. She opened the window and waved.

"Bye, Ash. I'll see you tomorrow."

He gave her a slight wave and called for his own car. Waiting in the early evening twilight Ash had time to reflect on the changes in his life lately and he wasn't sure they were all for the better. He wondered whether Drew had gone home or if he had started dating yet. Even more, he wondered why he cared.

Chapter Nine

"HEY, IT'S DREW. How's your head?"

Silly for him to be nervous calling, but Drew wanted to check on Ash to make sure the cut near his eye hadn't started seeping.

"What? Oh yeah. It's fine. I'd almost forgotten about it to be honest."

"Must've been the great medical care you received."

Ash chuckled, a low, comforting sound in Drew's ear. "Of course. What else could it be?"

Drew stretched out on his sofa, a cooking show playing on the television as background noise. Domino lay curled up at his feet. Just another thrilling night at Chez Klein.

"Well if you're satisfied with our service, please tip your doctor. Seriously, though, I'm glad it's okay." He was about to say goodbye, when Ash interrupted.

"Stevie North never showed up today. I waited until six tonight hoping but…"

Alarmed, Drew sat up. "Do you think something happened to him? Should we call someone?" He feared for that boy and knew Ash had taken a personal interest in his welfare.

"Javier went to look for him; he thought he knew where to look. I think he feels protective of Stevie. Not too long ago, Javier was in the same position as Stevie, but Javier could take care of himself. Stevie is more at risk."

Recklessly, Drew asked, "Is that how you feel? Protective of Stevie? Does he remind you of someone from your past?" He held his breath, expecting Ash to curse him out and hang up.

"My past is something best forgotten. I try not to think about it."

With the phone tucked under his ear, Drew lay back down on the sofa. "I know the feeling. I try not to think too hard about my parents because it makes me sad. But then I remember good times we had. Like my father taking me to the Rockaways to fish off the piers..." His eyes burned. "If I stop remembering I'll forget they ever existed. I can't let myself do that."

"We used to go fishing in the pond down the road from us," Ash blurted out.

The elusive Southern drawl that came and went like the ebb and flow of the ocean intrigued Drew. "You lived in the country?"

"Yeah. A real small town with even smaller minds. The only times we had to call our own was during the summer when we could spend the whole day fishing and swimming and picking berries. I'd catch the fish and we'd clean it then cook it along with the corn on the cob we'd swipe from the McAllisters' farm. Damn. I haven't thought about that in years."

To Drew it sounded idyllic.

"We'd grill our fish, too." Drew remembered his mother protesting having to clean and gut the fish but she didn't mean it. It was all done in their good-natured teasing way. "My dad would put on a big white chef's hat and stand over the barbecue pretending to swat at us if we tried to open it up to see it cooking."

"I never knew my father, or my mother for that matter. When I was little, I hoped they'd show up and say it was all a mistake and bring me home to stay with them. When I finally realized that wouldn't be happening, I'd grown old enough not to care."

Talking to Ash tonight gave Drew insight into his life before he came to New York and without asking, Drew knew Ash had never told anyone else these stories before. The trust Ash gave him in speaking from the heart was a gift Drew would hold close and cherish.

"It doesn't sound like you had much fun growing up." Drew chose his words with caution.

"Fun wasn't a word heard often in my house." The cold hard tone of Ash's voice sent a shiver through Drew.

"It's why you relate so well to Stevie isn't it? You see a little bit of yourself in him. Am I right?"

He held in a breath, shocked at himself for daring to ask Ash such a personal question. Not surprisingly, he and Ash had grown closer working at the clinic over the past few weeks, but Drew knew little more about

Ash than when they'd first met.

"This isn't about me. It's about these kids. And there's something I need to talk to you about that I found out tonight when I stayed late waiting for Stevie to show up."

Not surprised at how deftly Ash shifted the discussion away from his personal life, Drew found himself curious as to what Ash had to say. "What is it?"

"Did you know Marly has to walk home by herself every night? She says she doesn't mind, but if Javier isn't there to walk with her, she does it alone. That's unacceptable, Drew."

Appalled, Drew jumped off the sofa to pace the living room. "I had no idea; you're right, that's awful. Of course she shouldn't walk home by herself. I'll go with her."

"That's not the best solution either. Both of you will be easy targets. I think you should send her home in a car and have the clinic pick up the tab."

Drew considered Ash's suggestion and decided it had merit. "That's a wonderful idea. I don't know why we didn't think of it. He stopped and leaned against the wall. "Thanks, we'll put it in place immediately."

"Good. I'll be in tomorrow to see if Stevie shows up. Night, Drew."

Ash hung up, leaving Drew staring at the dead phone, once again, no closer to understanding him than before. Who was Ash Davis and why did Drew need to know?

FIVE O'CLOCK ARRIVED and Ash once again sat in his office at the clinic waiting for Stevie North to arrive. All day he played the game of "Will he or won't he?" and he decided if Stevie failed to show again today, he'd go to his house and make sure everything was all right. He heard a hesitant tap on the door. "Come on in." The door opened, framing Stevie's slender body. At fifteen he had yet to acquire any height, bulk, or facial hair. He looked as smooth as a twelve-year-old.

"Hey, kiddo, come on in." He smiled at the young boy, noting with a fury he'd learned to keep well hidden, the boy's swollen lips and the bruises that peeked out on his neck from underneath his longish brown hair. "You had a rough time of it?"

Stevie's face reddened as he stared at the floor and nodded. "I tried, Mr. Davis. I tried to tell them no, and that I would call the police, but they laughed at me. Said all faggots wanted it, even when we said no."

"Stevie, this can't go on. Those boys have to be stopped, or they're going to hurt you worse each time." Ash came from around the desk to sit in the chair next to Stevie.

"I can't tell no one. Don't you understand?" Stevie raised his big brown eyes to Ash, whose heart was breaking. "They'll hurt me even more. Jimmy's gonna go off to the army soon, so that'll leave only Donny. He's gentle and doesn't hurt me." Stevie's voice had dropped to a whisper. "He tells Jimmy to stop when he gets too crazy."

Ash put his hand on Stevie's shoulder. "Do you like Donny?"

After a moment, Stevie gave a little shrug. "He's okay."

"Hey, kiddo, don't worry. Maybe I can talk to him—"

"No. You can't. I can't have anyone know I was here. If they ever found out…" Stevie shuddered. "I think Jimmy might kill me."

"And your parents?" Ash's lips curled at those words. How oblivious were these fucking people? "Don't your foster parents have anything to say? Don't they care?"

Stevie nodded his head. "No, you don't get it. They're really nice to me, and Mrs. Harding especially helps me with my homework and everything, but I can't tell her what goes on, 'cause Jimmy will beat me up." He tucked his hair behind his ears. "I don't want to get sent away. I've been there since I was a kid." He sniffled. "She's the only mom I've ever known."

Big, sad brown eyes locked with his. "I'm so scared, Mr. Davis. Why is this happening to me? Why can't they leave me alone? I wish I had a brother at home to talk to or help me."

At one time Ash was that kind of brother. There was nothing he wouldn't do for his brothers. Before he'd fucked everything up and ran away. Before he became the selfish prick he grew up to be. "If you let me contact child services, I can help you, Stevie. You should let me call the cops."

"I-I don't know. I gotta think about it. I'm still afraid that if I report it, Jimmy will find out." Stevie checked his cheap plastic watch. "Oh shit, I better go or I'll be late." He jumped up, got to the opened door, and turned. "Thanks, Mr. Davis. I'll think about what you said and see you next week, all right?" He gave a small yet hopeful smile.

Ash stood and drew the boy into a hug. His skinny shoulders poked out like the fragile wings of a baby bird. How soon before they were permanently broken? "I'm always here for you if you need me. Here's my card with my cell phone. Call me anytime. I mean it." He took out his wallet and gave Stevie his card, which he was happy to see went into the boy's wallet. "Bye, kiddo."

Stevie waved and hurried out of the room. Ash, totally drained, returned to sit, all but collapsing from the emotional struggle within him. No matter what Stevie said, he was going to talk to Drew. Maybe Jordan's partner, the detective, could help. They had an obligation to report it, but they had to keep Stevie's name out of it. That poor, poor kid.

Without warning, it hit him, staggering him with its intensity. Himself at fourteen, helpless in his bed late at night, as his "father" cuffed him to the bedpost, blindfolded him, then touched him all over, kissing him, thrusting first his thick tongue in his mouth, then his thick cock everywhere else. His first kiss, a brutal memory. Any thought of hope or love, destroyed forever by the acts of violence against him. Since then, no man had ever kissed or fucked him. Sex was never about love; it was power and control.

"No, no." He groaned out loud as he rocked back and forth, helpless to stop the tidal wave of emotion crashing over him. Memories flooded through him of his own degradation and exploitation by adults who should have been protecting him, nurturing and caring for him. He couldn't shake off the fact that he'd left the other boys behind. He'd tried to report what was happening in his house when he ran away, but he knew they wouldn't take him, a gay kid from the street, seriously. Not against a respected police officer. He was as bad or worse than his foster father, leaving them there, but he couldn't stay or he'd have ended up killing himself. "Stop, stop it." The tears fell unchecked as he hunched within himself, shaking and moaning. "I'm sorry. I tried. I'm so, so sorry."

Warm, strong arms encircled him. Without thinking, he grabbed on to the person and held him tight, burying his face into a hard chest. Confused, he lifted his head and met the equally bewildered gaze of Drew.

Chapter Ten

TODAY HAD BEEN one hard, long-ass day. Mike had performed magic on the teeth and jaw of a sixteen-year-old who'd been beaten in a schoolyard brawl, simply because she came out as gay. Just because they lived in New York City didn't mean the people weren't as prejudiced and homophobic as any other place. Ignorance existed everywhere.

Flexing his fingers, Drew stretched his arms over his head, feeling the kinks unwind from his back. He removed his glasses and rubbed his eyes. The day had been spent patching up scrapes, stitching up gashes, and getting at least two teens to talk to Keith about pressing charges. Drew managed to coax out of one young man that his injuries were caused by a stepfather who thought he could beat the gay out of him. That reminded Drew. He wanted to speak with Ash about the legal process they might have to face if they did decide to go forward with prosecution. A noise from the hallway caught his attention, and glancing at the clock, he frowned. Six o'clock. Everyone should've been gone already.

He got up from his seat and peered out into the hallway. Spying the receding back of young Stevie North, he shook his head. There was a young man with troubles, and he'd latched on to Ash for some reason. Drew heard a moan further down the hallway then a rhythmic squeaking noise. Fearful of what he might find, Drew sprinted toward Ash's office. He stopped short outside the open door, staring in amazement and consternation.

Clutching himself, tears pouring down his face, Ash sat on the loveseat, in the middle of a full-fledged meltdown of some sort. This wasn't something Drew had expected to see.

"Ash, what's wrong?"

No answer. Ash continued to rock, oblivious to Drew's presence.

His natural instinct to help taking over, Drew entered and sat down next to Ash, taking him into his arms, as if he were a child in need of comfort.

"No, I can't..."

"Shhh, it's going to be fine." Without thinking, Drew pulled Ash in tightly, murmuring soothing, crooning nonsense words. Ash stiffened only a second before burying his face in Drew's chest, the tears soaking through his shirt.

Stunned by the overwhelming emotional connection that flowed between the two of them, Drew froze. Holding Ash felt as natural as breathing. Their eyes met and the veneer of arrogant confidence Ash walled himself up behind peeled away, revealing a broken, frightened man. Drew pressed his lips to Ash's damp, head.

"Let it go. I'm here. I'm not going anywhere. Nothing can hurt you anymore."

Drew rubbed his broad back, feeling the muscles shift beneath his hands. With the tips of his fingers, he pressed and circled Ash's tense shoulders, and Drew closed his eyes, hopeful his touch brought some comfort.

Without realizing it, however, his lips had moved from Ash's hair to his forehead, resting on the warm skin. He trailed his fingers down Ash's cheek, the roughened stubble strange yet fascinating under his fingertips. A slow ache built inside Drew, along with a shocking need to protect this man and keep him safe. Drew could feel his pain; it was a visceral thing, alive and breathing within Ash. He explored Ash's face, tracing the slant of his cheekbones and the hollows of his eyes. Ash's mouth remained pressed against his chest, his breath fanning out in short, hurting gasps.

Why this man? These strange emotions swirling inside him forced Drew to question himself and be more cautious around Ash than he might have been with someone else. These past few weeks he and Ash had grown close, spending long hours setting up the clinic and working together, often having dinner if they both stayed late. He believed they'd become friends; Drew genuinely cared about Ash. To his great shock, after their first visit together, Ash had visited his grandmother on his own, a piece of information Esther had been only too happy to tell him.

Not once in their talks, though, had Ash revealed anything about himself, even though Drew knew without being told something terrible had happened to him as a child. When he'd spoken to Peter about it, his friend shook his head.

"Ash is my friend, Drew. What's even more important is that he considers me to be his friend, and God knows he has no one in his life he can count on. I'd never betray a confidence of his." Peter had raked his hand through his hair, looking exasperated. *"Hell, I don't even know half of what he's lived through, but I assure you, it wasn't pretty. If he wants to talk to you about it, he will."*

Shudders still rippled through Ash's body. What horrors had he seen forcing him to live such a withdrawn and lonely life? The memory of that night in the restaurant hit Drew as he recalled Ash running from the table, returning pale and shaken a while later. Was this the same thing? Did he have some kind of post-traumatic stress disorder that triggered at certain events or times? He'd talk to Rachel about it. Maybe she would know.

"Hey. How're you doing?" He smoothed Ash's hair back from his face, keeping his touch light and gentle. "Feeling better?"

Ash shook his head, still pressed against Drew's chest. "This has never happened to me before and I'm mortified. I never meant for you or anyone to see me like this." His words came out somewhat muffled, but he made no move to pull away from Drew's embrace.

"Don't be ridiculous. Everyone has a breaking point. I was a basket case when my parents died. I cried for weeks."

"Different," Ash mumbled. "You couldn't help yourself. This was my fault. By now I should be strong, able to handle myself."

Without thinking, Drew took Ash's face between his hands, staring deep into his fathomless eyes. "Not everything that happens to us is within our control, my friend. Sometimes life gives us a swift kick in the ass, and we have to do the best we can with what we're given." He bent down but caught himself right before his lips made contact with Ash's bristly cheek. Drew remained suspended there for a moment, feeling the sharp inhalation of Ash's breath, sensing his anxiety, his body tense and coiled tight. Ash had closed his eyes, his long black lashes resting like fans on his skin. With the lightest touch, Drew caressed Ash's face.

"Drew, what are you doing?" But Ash made no move to draw away.

"Damned if I know." But Drew didn't stop trailing his fingertips over Ash's jaw, feeling the tiny ripples flow over his skin.

Ironically Ash pulled away from him. "What's happening here?"

"Why don't you tell me? I walked in, and you were suffering. I've never seen anyone so broken and hurt." Drew put his hands on Ash's shoulders. "Don't turn away from me. We're friends now. Talk to me."

"I-I can't." His gaze remained pinned to the floor.

With a resigned sigh, Drew moved back. "What are you doing tonight?"

That clear, glittering gaze lifted to meet his. A small grin quirked Ash's lips. "I have no plans, Doc. What were you thinking?"

"Get your mind out of the gutter. Want to visit my grandmother with me?"

To his utter surprise, Ash's eyes lit up with a pleased glint. "I'd love to see Esther. I promised her some cookies the next time I came, so we'll need to stop at a bakery."

What an amazing transformation. In what Drew knew must be some kind of survival technique Ash employed to get him through the embarrassment of breaking down in front of someone, the man effortlessly shifted gears, slipping back into his charming, careless personality. Drew decided not to press the issue, thinking when and if Ash wanted him to know, he would tell him.

"Great. Everyone else is gone. I'll lock up the offices and meet you in front."

"Sure. And Doc?" Ash's eyes glimmered for a moment with emotion, then reverted back to their normal, blank façade. "Thanks for everything."

Desperate to keep it light, still unsure of his own strange feelings, Drew cracked a smile and shrugged. "Sure. No big deal."

Within ten minutes, the two were on their way to his grandmother's house. They first stopped in Carroll

Gardens, and while Ash picked up some cookies, Drew ran into the cheese store to pick up some of his grandmother's favorites, as well as his own. He spent a little time tasting both the cheeses and the crackers that accompanied them, and decided to buy several different kinds. That, along with the wine and cookies would make for a nice visit.

After storing their purchases in the trunk of Ash's sporty car, they were on their way again, to his grandmother's house in the heart of Flatbush. After World War II and her escape from Poland, she'd found the few remaining members of her family here in Brooklyn and never left. It was the only place, she once confided to him, she felt safe. He and Rachel loved the small house she and Papa Sy had shared. Their little bit of heaven of the American dream, she always joked. All his fondest childhood memories revolved around Rachel and him visiting their grandparents, spending many weekends helping Papa in the garden growing vegetables and Nana cooking in the kitchen.

They pulled up to the house and parked in the driveway. Her impatiens bloomed in the front yard, the interspersed pink, white, and red colors reminding him of peppermints, while the ceramic pots of crimson geraniums lined the steps up to her redbrick porch. A faint scent of barbecue from a nearby house tickled his nose, causing his stomach to rumble with an ungracious noise. He loved the summertime, when it didn't turn dark until later in the evening.

Ash chuckled. "Hungry?"

His face heated. "I missed lunch, so yeah." Hoisting the bag, he spoke over his shoulder. "The cheeses and rest of the stuff will tide me over, though."

Ash grinned and not for the first time, Drew wondered what went on inside his head. It took an incredibly strong personality to thrust aside the emotional disintegration of a mere hour before. He wished he could learn how to do it.

But, Drew realized, in a way he did—burying his fear, the loneliness so thick and black sometimes he stayed up all night rather than succumb to sleep and his nightmares. Adopting the cat had solved only a small part of his problem. His heart remained lonely.

"Nana? Where are you?" He stepped into the small entranceway, decorated with framed pictures of his family, all the way back to when Nana came to this country from Poland. There were no pictures of her as a young child, or any of her relatives, as she'd come with merely the clothes on her back. All her immediate family, her parents and three siblings, had been lost in World War II. Turning to Ash, he beckoned. "She must be in the kitchen, listening to the radio. Follow me."

"I have been here before, you know. I know where to go." Ash's grumble brought Drew up short, mystifying the hell out of him.

Not for the first time, Drew wondered, *Why would someone like Ash want to spend time with an elderly grandmother?* Another intriguing puzzle piece of the enigma that made up Asher Davis. He shot Ash a strange look. "I don't understand you at all."

Now it was Ash's turn to flush red. "Esther invited me to come whenever I wanted." A defensive note crept into his voice. "I bring her cookies."

By this time, they'd reached the kitchen and Drew saw he was right. The back door was open, as was the window overlooking the garden blooming with roses, azaleas and rhododendrons. One of her favorite radio talk shows played in the background, and a comforting smell of fried onions, garlic, and potatoes perfumed the air.

"Nana." At the sound of his voice, she turned, a smile breaking out across her lined face. He took her in his arms and hugged her. *Please God*, he thought to himself, *don't let anything happen to her for a long, long time.*

"Hello, sweetheart." She gave him a kiss on his cheek, and the old-fashioned scent of rose water she always wore reassured him for some reason. All was right in the world as long as his grandmother was around.

"And you brought one of my other favorite boys. Come give me a kiss too, Asher."

"Hello, Esther. You still won't call me Ash, will you?" Ash dipped his head to kiss her cheek, then picked up her hand and kissed it as well.

"I like the name Asher. It's a fine, strong name you should be proud of. Did you know it is a Hebrew name, meaning *happy* or *blessing*? I think you should remember that, dear." She patted him on his arm, and

Drew studied the incongruous couple as he unpacked the bags.

Never in this lifetime would he have predicted a man like Ash Davis would willingly spend time with his elderly grandmother. Then again, he couldn't imagine why the sight of Ash with his grandmother sent his heart thumping in a peculiar rhythm. "Is anyone else coming, Nana?" He noticed quite a bit of food in the refrigerator when he put his purchases inside.

"Well, the other boys said they might stop by, and Rachel always comes to check on me, even though she says it's to say hello. You can pick up some Chinese food for dinner; those are merely snacks to tide you all over." Hands planted on her hips, she fixed him with a pretend glare, her blue eyes kindled like a gas flame. "You two don't fool me, you know. I see right through everything."

"We love you and want to make sure you're okay." Drew popped a mozzarella ball into his mouth. "I don't see anything wrong with that." He opened the box of crackers and sat at the table. "Do you, Ash?"

Sitting at the table, his chin propped in his hands, Ash stared out of the window to the backyard garden. "I think it would be nice to have people who care enough about you to want to make sure you're safe, but I'm not the person to ask."

Nana threw Drew a sharp look to which he could only shrug his shoulders. With a determined look on her face, she walked over to Ash, and hesitated only a moment before putting her hand on his arm and speaking so softly Drew had to strain his ears to hear.

"Asher, darling. What's the matter? You look so sad today. Do you want to talk to me about it?" Her hand remained on his arm.

Drew could've told her not to waste her time or breath, that a man like Ash would never reveal himself to her. He turned his attention back to the cheese and reached for a bottle of Malbec.

"You know, Esther. I think I might like that very much."

So of all the people in Ash's life, his best friend Peter, Peter's wife, Drew, *anyone*, Asher Davis chose to unburden himself to his grandmother. *Fucking unbelievable.*

Chapter Eleven

THE COZY LIVING room where Esther brought him to sit and talk had that warm, lived-in feeling. Ash imagined her husband coming home after a long day of work to put his feet up on the overstuffed ottoman and settle into his club chair with a drink and the newspaper.

That actually sounded like a perfect ending to anyone's day, now that Ash thought about it. He waited until Esther sat in her favorite chair; then he brought her a white wine before settling into a club chair next to her with an iced vodka. He chose not to put his feet up on the ottoman.

Esther surprised him by talking first. "The Chinese place I sent Drew to pick up dinner from takes a while, so we can have a nice long chat."

It was impossible to be in this woman's company and not smile. "I see. And why do you think I couldn't speak freely with Drew around?"

"Because you've developed feelings for him."

He choked on his drink, then wiped his mouth and

set the glass on a small table nearby. "Esther, I can't imagine why you'd say something so ridiculous but—"

"Deny it to my face." Her bright blue eyes challenged him.

He opened his mouth, then shut it. Then opened it again. "I'm not in love with Drew." Even to his ears, his muttered denial sounded weak at best.

"I didn't say you were in love with him." Her eyes dimmed. "Asher, dear, I know life has not been easy for you, am I right?"

He jerked a small nod, his gaze darting between the floor and her gentle face.

"The first thing you have to learn is to love yourself and believe you're worthy to receive love. Only then can you have a healthy relationship with another person."

At that he barked out a harsh laugh. "Love, love, love. All this talk of love. You say I'm in love with Drew, that I have to love myself. I'm sorry, Esther, but I gave up on love, Santa, and the Easter Bunny when I was a young boy." He rubbed his arms to quell his inner turmoil. "None of them ever appeared in my house when I was growing up."

"Someone hurt you, didn't they?" Those gentle knowing eyes held his and he couldn't look away. "I'll never repeat what you've told me, but after all these years it might feel good to get it off your chest."

Never had he been this vulnerable, not since Mr. Frank had taken him in. But Esther had those same wise eyes. Eyes that looked as though they'd seen things too. Things she could never forget.

Ash needed several deep breaths of restorative air, before he answered her. "I was only a child, but I was made to do and see things that no one should have to endure." Without him realizing it, she took his hand. "I can't speak about it. I want to, but seeing these kids now, helping them brings it all back into full focus." He held onto her surprisingly warm, firm grip like a lifeline.

"I haven't been sleeping well, and today one of the kids got to me in a way that hasn't happened in a long time. Drew found me, and it...well, let's say it wasn't my finest moment."

Esther said nothing, merely giving his hand a squeeze of support every now and then.

"I shouldn't be telling you this, should I? That when Drew found me it..." He gulped nervously, embarrassed to continue, but what the hell? He'd come this far already; he might as well complete his humiliation. "...it felt so good to let go. For the first time in my life I wanted—" He dropped Esther's hand, turning his face away from hers. "I'm so sick of life. It's too much sometimes."

"I know, dear boy—"

"I'm sorry, Esther, but you don't know. You don't know the deep dark hell some people go through every day of their lives. Their despair over a life so hopeless they wonder why they bother to get up in the morning." He faced her, his eyes streaming. "You can't understand."

She sat silent for a while, her face turned toward the window. "How little you young people know about what my generation has seen. Or maybe you do know but choose to forget." Ash stared in silence as she pushed up the sleeve of her sweater to reveal the numbers tattooed on her arm.

His throat seized, and he lost the ability to speak. Not Esther, not this sweet, loving woman. How had she managed to make it out alive?

"Man's inhumanity to man, they said." Her voice quivered slightly. "I saw it all. I won't burden you with my own tales of horror." Esther faced him, her eyes bright with tears. "But I know about despair. I know about fear." Once again she grasped his hand. "But one thing I never gave up was hope. When you give up hope, then you are truly lost. Never give up hope, darling Asher. Never."

"What I hope for, Esther, is either long gone or will never come to pass. I have one hope now and that's to find my foster brothers." A brush of his forearm over the wetness of his eyes cleared his vision in more ways than one. "And I'm sure you want Drew to marry a nice woman, settle down, and have babies."

Simply saying those words hurt his heart. Never in his life had he been more confused. This wasn't him. His only goal was to seek out pleasure, whenever and wherever he could find it. To fuck and be fucked. Emotions and personal involvement—none of it ever entered his plans, but somewhere along the way, he'd gone off course, now with disastrous results.

Through the open window he heard a car door slam and Drew's voice, along with his sister's and his other friends', drifted into the house. He jumped to his feet, afraid of being caught and drew in a shuddering breath.

"Drew's back. I don't want him to see me like this, and I appreciate your willingness to keep our conversation private."

"You have my word. But know one thing." She stopped his departure from the room by the tone of her voice. "The only thing I want for my grandchildren is for them to be happy. They've had enough tragedy in their lives. However and whomever they choose to love and spend the rest of their lives with is up to them." She walked out and left him standing in shock.

DREW THRUST ONE of the bags of Chinese takeout into Jordan's hands. "Here, make yourself useful and take this."

"Chill out, man. What's crawled up your ass?" Jordan hefted the bag and passed it to Mike. He reached for one of the others in Drew's hand. "Here. Give me another one."

Rachel pulled up in her car and beeped her horn. "Hey, guys." She slammed the car door shut and ran over to give Drew a kiss. "How's it going, D, Jordy?" She turned with a wide smile to Mike, who scowled at her. "What's the matter with you?"

"You didn't lock the car, did you? Didn't I warn you last night—"

"Last night?" The bottom dropped out of Drew's stomach. "How did you…wait. You mean you two…" His gaze ricocheted between his best friend and his sister, who wouldn't meet his eye but blushed bright red. Furious, he dropped the bag of food and grabbed Mike's arm. "You're sneaking around behind my back with my sister? What the fuck, Levin? You couldn't come and tell me?"

Rachel pulled at his arm. "Stop it, Drew and listen to me. Mike wanted to tell you, but I said no. Not yet. We weren't sneaking around; it sort of happened. Can't you understand that?" She pressed against Mike's chest, and Drew's jaw tightened watching his friend draw her close in a possessive hold. "Haven't you ever been unexpectedly attracted to someone before and needed some time to figure it out?"

"What's going on out here?"

At his grandmother's voice, his gaze jerked to the front door of the house. She stood on the steps, peering over at them, Ash by her side, a frown twisting his lips.

"Everyone come inside, now."

Obeying Esther's command, they traipsed into the house and stood in the kitchen as Esther, with Ash standing next to her, grim and resolute as a granite-faced sphinx, flayed them with her tongue as if they were children, not grown men over thirty.

"What is the meaning of arguing in the street like common hoodlums? If you have a disagreement, you come inside and discuss it like civilized people." Her gaze shifted to Drew, and he swallowed hard, uncomfortable at being the first under her sharp regard.

"I gather she told you about her and Michael."

Stunned, he lost the power of speech momentarily. "She…she told you?" He raked his sister with an accusing glare, watching her wilt against Mike, who slid his arm around her waist. "I thought we were closer than that."

"Oh no, don't try and make her feel guilty." Her voice cut through him like a whip. "There are some things women talk about with each other first, before we discuss them with men. Do you know Rachel's main concern was how you would react? It wasn't the happiness of being in love. It was about you."

He shoved his hands into his jeans pockets and kicked the toe of his sneaker back and forth across the kitchen floor. This was the last thing he'd ever expected. Mike? Fun-loving, hard-partying Mike? With his little sister? From the corner of his eye he could see the tenderness with which his friend held Rachel, soothing her as she buried her face in his shoulder. His gaze then rested on Ash, who also concentrated on Mike and Rachel, an uncertain expression in his eye.

But his grandmother wasn't finished. "You're angry at your sister for falling in love? This isn't a stranger; it's your friend. A man who's like a brother to you. Rachel was so worried about your reaction she told me not to say anything and of course I wouldn't. Because it's for her to tell you, when the time was right. I didn't like you being kept in the dark, but couldn't imagine you not being happy for her."

The full force of her blazing blue eyes turned back on him. It didn't matter that he was her only grandson; she would never let him get away with what she perceived as a wrong.

"No one has the right to tell anyone who they should or shouldn't love. Maybe one day you'll fall in love again, and the person won't be someone we would've expected." When she slipped her arm inside the crook of his elbow, only then could he tell by the shaking of her slight frame how emotionally overwrought his grandmother was. "Think about this. Are you angry with her because it's Michael, or because she didn't tell you?"

"I'm sorry. Don't get so upset."

"Don't treat me like a china doll. I'm more aware of what goes on in this world than you think." With her free hand she beckoned Rachel to come stand by her. Mike rubbed her shoulders and whispered in her ear. Rachel nodded and came over to them. "Sweetheart, tell your brother how you feel." His grandmother withdrew her arm from his and shooed out Jordan and Ash. "Come, boys. Let's leave them alone now."

Ash leaned over and kissed Nana's cheek. "Actually, Esther, I'm going to head out. I have a case I need to prepare for." Without waiting for a reply he walked out; Drew heard the front door open then bang shut.

Shocked over Ash's precipitous leave-taking, Drew nevertheless concentrated his full attention where it belonged. On Rachel and Mike. "So. How long have you two, you know...?" Shrugging, he couldn't go on. What was he supposed to ask—how long his sister and best friend had been sleeping together? Um. No, thank you.

"Look, Rach, forget it. Nana's right. It's none of my business. I wish you could've told me sooner. But I understand why you thought I might freak out." Their gazes caught, and they both burst into laughter at the same time. "I love you. If you want to be with Mike, it's fine, but God only knows why when there are so many better men in the city."

Mike snorted.

"Hey." Rachel hugged him tight. "Thank you."

"Love you."

"Love you too."

Now to deal with his friend. "Levin, come here." He folded his arms across his chest, glowering at Mike, who gave back as good as he got. For the first time, Drew looked at Mike as someone who might be his brother one day. Tall, brawny and blond, Mike Levin had never lacked for female companionship, despite the loss of almost all the hearing in his left ear. Now that Drew thought about it, recently Mike had been quieter, more settled than he'd ever been in the past.

When they were face-to-face, Drew poked him in the chest. "If you ever hurt her, I'll kill you."

"If I ever hurt her, I'll let you do it. But I won't, D." He threw a loving glance at Rachel. "I never saw it coming, but she's the best thing that ever happened to me."

And that was that. Nothing else mattered, did it? Anyone with half a brain could see the chemistry between Mike and Rachel now that he was aware of it. The man couldn't take his eyes off her. That's the way it should be, and it once again reminded Drew of his own failure of a marriage and lack of a love life.

"Well, all right, man. Be good to her."

"Promise."

The three of them hugged, but it was Mike she stayed with now, her face glowing and Mike's arm remaining in a possessive hold over her. Drew heard a sniffle and glanced over his shoulder. Nana stood in the doorway, wiped her eyes and smiled.

"I'm glad that's settled. Drew, will you help me heat up the food, please?" With neat, precise movements she put on her apron and pulled out the plates they would eat the Chinese food on. "Why don't the rest of you go outside and enjoy the nice weather?" After shooting each other quizzical looks, Jordan, Mike, and Rachel headed out to the backyard.

Obviously, his grandmother had something on her mind she wanted to speak to him about. He took out multiple boxes of food and set them on the counter. "Can I ask you something, Nana?"

Her hands stilled on the door of the microwave. "You aren't still angry about Rachel and Michael, are you?"

"What? No of course not." He shook his head. "I get it, and I'm fine with it." Jordan and Mike tossed a football around in the backyard with Rachel in the middle, laughing and screeching at them to let her catch it once. A smile crossed his lips. Maybe it had been inevitable that Mike and Rachel would fall in love.

And as usual, he was the odd man out. Jordan had Keith, and now Mike had Rachel. Not that Drew missed Jackie at all. What he missed was someone to wake up with, to hold and hold him.

He hated being alone. Even as a child, he'd beg to go wherever his parents went, even if it was only to the supermarket. It was part of the reason he'd gotten the cat after his marriage broke up. As he saw it, his fear of being alone caused all the problems in his life. But as much as he loved Domino, it wasn't the same as having someone to share his bed and his body with.

"What happened with Ash when I went to get the food? Everything was fine until you said you wanted to talk. The next thing I know, he hightailed it out of here as fast as he could."

For the first time his grandmother looked disconcerted. "We spoke, and I told him of my past, in the camps." A tear rolled down her face, and in an instant, he went to her, holding her close. "That poor boy has seen so much pain in his life. I never knew his troubles ran so deep."

A current of unease ran through him. "What are you talking about?"

She tipped her head back to look into his eyes. "You mean you and he have never talked?" Her voice rang with surprise. "I thought you were very close."

He spoke sharper than usual. "What does that mean? Very close?" Jesus, he'd never acted this rudely to his grandmother before. Biting back another harsh retort, he managed to control his temper. "I'm sorry. I didn't mean to snap at you. Why would I be close with him? You don't know him very well, Nana, but he isn't a nice person. He sleeps around, he has few friends, and he doesn't really care about anybody except himself. There's a reason he's alone. He likes it that way."

But even as he spoke, Drew recalled those unguarded moments when he'd seen Ash in a different light. The time he'd bolted from the table at the restaurant, wild-eyed and sweating. And today, when Drew had held a trembling Ash in his arms. The ugly past Ash tried so hard to silence and bury beneath an arrogant, uncaring façade lay too close to the surface for him to hide forever. Drew's conscience pricked at him, as if to chide him for his own mean-spiritedness.

He wished this conversation had never happened and hoped it had come to an end, but he should've known better. Only once before had he seen his grandmother this angry. At the trial for his parents' case against the trucking company, the defense attorney had alluded that maybe Drew's father had been drinking himself. It was a sight to remember, but his grandmother had gathered her shattered emotions and instead, at trial, made an impassioned victims' speech to the judge and jury that left everyone in the court in tears.

Now, here in her kitchen, was the second time. "You should be ashamed of yourself. I'm ashamed for you and surprised. You're basing your beliefs on what others have told you."

Knowing it wasn't possible for him to tell his grandmother of Ash's sexual escapades, he remained resolute in his opinion. "Look, I know you have a soft spot for him, and I like him well enough, but he's a loner, Nana. Yes, he's charming and handsome, but he isn't someone you can get through to." Even as he spoke the words, regret filled his heart. He'd thought Ash could, somehow, meld into his family dynamic as another friend. Sure, their strange sexual attraction unsettled him, but Drew could've dealt with it until he started dating again.

"Believe me, no one likes to be alone. That boy needs people around him. Trust me, I know. He's crying out for help, and I'm afraid if one of us doesn't take him in hand, something terrible might happen to him." The worry in her eyes unnerved him, as she was never one for histrionics. Rachel must have at long last caught the ball as her shrieking and Mike and Jordan's teasing from outside had stopped.

"Did he talk to you?" For Ash to confide in his grandmother would be nothing less than shocking.

"No, not much. He locked himself up tight as a clam and refused to say a word. But I see beneath the smile that never reaches his eyes." With a fierceness he didn't know she possessed, Nana grabbed his arm. "I'm worried after our talk he might do something bad to himself. You think I'm too old that I don't understand the ways of the world. I know he's a homosexual, gay. Why should that matter to me? But something's not right with him. He's a very depressed man. Promise me after dinner you'll go check on him. For me?"

Although there was nothing less he'd rather do than play babysitter to Asher Davis, he agreed, because he'd do anything for his grandmother. All throughout dinner, he allowed everyone to think his silence was still the result of his surprise over Rachel and Mike's relationship. The pleasant dinnertime chatter washed over him, and he made sure to nod at all the right times to keep them from thinking he wasn't paying attention to what they were saying.

In truth, he could only think about Ash.

Chapter Twelve

IT WAS THE usual bitch of traffic on the F.D.R. Drive to Ash's apartment on the Upper East Side. Going home after leaving his grandmother's house and getting his car to drive into the city gave Drew time to think. He'd already made peace with his sister and Mike and let them know he was happy for them. Someone ought to be happy in his family, and since his life was nothing more than work and coming home to collapse in front of a ball game on TV, he wished Rachel the happiness she deserved.

With the radio playing classic rock, and no end to the headlights in front of him in the foreseeable future, he allowed his mind to drift to Ash. Whatever Ash and his grandmother had spoken about affected him, which both surprised and confused Drew. In the brief time they'd spent together, Drew had learned that sharing emotions and personal entanglements wasn't part of Ash's makeup. Drew remembered that Peter, supposedly Ash's best friend, knew only slightly more about the man than Drew did.

Drew got off at the exit nearest to 72nd St. and made his way to Park Avenue. Ash's apartment was located on 86th St. and Park Avenue, and thankfully there was a parking garage down the block. He told the valet he'd be several hours and handed him the keys in exchange for his ticket. It came as a shock that Ash lived in one of the premier addresses in the city. *How the hell did he afford a place like this?* These old, prewar apartments ran in the millions of dollars.

An elaborately uniformed doorman greeted him at the front of the apartment building, and Drew entered the beautiful formal lobby decorated with inlaid marble floors and soaring columns. Various sofas and delicate gilt chairs grouped around an indoor arrangement of plants and flowers. A magnificent crystal chandelier hung over the concierge desk, with smaller, yet still-elegant lighting fixtures leading down the hallway to where Drew presumed the elevators were located. His entire apartment could fit into this lobby.

Both he and Rachel had received payment from his parents' life insurance policies as well as a large, multimillion-dollar settlement from the trucking company, but Drew had invested most of his capital and lived frugally. He didn't need a lot and preferred to spend his money on supporting his favorite charities. This type of luxury was beyond his comprehension, yet somehow, it didn't surprise him to find Ash living here. The man was an enigma and had been since the day they'd met. The fact that he'd been a scholarship student and now lived in a multimillion-dollar neighborhood only added to his mystique.

Drew approached the concierge desk—a beautiful slab of granite surrounded by gleaming mahogany. The young man wearing a dark uniform with more discreet gold braiding than the doorman, looked up with a practiced smile. "Good evening, sir. How may I help you?"

Funny, though he might be a successful doctor, Drew felt underdressed and woefully out of place. "Uh, I'm here to see Mr. Davis?" Somehow he hoped he had the wrong address, and he'd find out Ash really lived in a small, cramped apartment like himself.

"Yes, sir. Who may I say is calling?" The young man had the house phone in his hand, an expectant look on his face.

"Um. Tell him it's Drew."

Although it was late, after eleven o'clock, people still came and went with regularity through the gilded front doors. The men and women passing by him dressed for the evening in clothing that screamed luxury. Their jewelry winked glints of diamonds and who knew what other treasures. Drew didn't know much about high fashion, but living with Jackie for the short time they were married had opened his eyes to how expensive a woman's wardrobe was to put together. With a rueful look, he glanced down at his sneakers, faded jeans, and T-shirt. Perhaps he went too far on the other extreme, but he valued comfort over trend. Maybe Ash dressed so formally to keep up the image he felt he needed to project living here. He'd never seen the man in anything other than a long-sleeved button-down shirt and dress pants, never jeans.

His fashion contemplation was cut short by the young man at the desk. "You can go up, sir. The elevators are down the hallway to your left. Mr. Davis is in apartment 19C."

After thanking the man, Drew followed his reflection along the mirrored walls of the hallway. He laughed to himself as two women sidled away from him when he stepped inside the elevator, choosing instead to stand by the elevator operator. He wanted to take out his business card and say, *See, look. I'm really a doctor. Don't worry.*

They reached the nineteenth floor without incident, and after thanking the young man operating the elevator, he exited into a hushed hallway. Ivory wallpaper inlaid with gold thread covered the walls and the highly polished dark wood floors made no sound beneath his rubber-soled sneakers. Each apartment had a lighted button next to it, with gold apartment letters on the doors.

Nerves buzzing, he pushed the button and heard a soft chime ring within the apartment. After a moment, the door swung open, Ash's unsmiling face greeting him. The apartment loomed as a void behind him.

"Uh, hey, Ash. Sorry if I woke you—"

"You didn't."

The heated intensity in Ash's crystal-clear eyes unnerved Drew. He *so* did not want to do this, but he'd promised his grandmother, and he'd never broken a promise to her, so…

"Can I come in? It won't take long. I promise."

Without speaking, Ash stepped back and opened the door wide. Drew entered the darkened apartment and gaped. Ash had lit candles, placing them on various tables throughout the apartment, but that didn't hide the grandeur of the overall space. The expansive entranceway disclosed hallways branching off to other unknown parts of the apartment. Directly in front of him, a large picture window showcased the glittering lights of the city at night. The airy living room, from what he could make out in the dim candlelight, boasted a baby grand piano and an ornate mantel over a fireplace.

"Christ, Ash, this place is amazing." He glanced over at Ash, who hadn't said a single word.

"It was Mr. Frank's. He left it to me in his will."

That made sense. Jacob Frank had been an extremely wealthy man. He must've lived here until his death. For reasons no one had figured out, Frank had taken Ash in and groomed him as his successor. Somewhere along the way, the two of them had grown close, close enough for Jacob Frank, childless and with no other family, to leave Ash everything when he died.

"That was very kind of him. I heard from Peter he was an amazing man."

Moving across the entranceway, Ash led him into the living room and waved a careless hand at the sofa. Drew spotted a half-empty bottle of vodka and an ice bucket on the table, a full tumbler next to it. After picking up his drink, Ash sat at the far end of the sofa and spoke. "He was the finest human being I've ever met."

There was nothing Drew could say to take away Ash's pain. The dripping wax hit flame as the candles spit and the firelight danced, casting flickering shadows across Ash's bleak face.

"Have a drink, Drew, and tell me why you're here." Ash sipped his vodka and stared at Drew over the rim of his glass.

"No, thanks, I'm driving. But I do want to talk to you." The man was a study in contrasts. Drew couldn't think of a time he hadn't seen Ash perfectly dressed, every hair in place, looking like he'd stepped out of a men's fashion magazine.

Tonight, however...well, he looked off-kilter. Though he still had on his clothes from earlier, his white shirt was uncharacteristically wrinkled and unbuttoned lower than he'd ever seen. Dark stubble shadowed along his jaw, and his hair lay unkempt and disheveled. Drew shifted on the sofa. "Look, I know this may sound stupid, but my grandmother was concerned about you, so she asked me to stop by and check up on you."

"And of course you do everything your nana says."

Drew's face flamed. "Fuck you, Davis."

A tiny smirk hit the corner of Ash's lips and he set his drink down. "What's the matter, Doc? The truth hurts?"

The bastard. After all the nice things his grandmother had said about him, how she'd worried about him, this was his response? To act like the snide sarcastic son of a bitch he'd been at their first meeting? How dare he treat her concern as if it were nothing. And to think he'd actually thought they were friends. "What the hell do you know about the truth, huh? No one knows anything about you; you have no friends, no lover." He stood, ready to leave. "No wonder you're all alone. No one cares about you. You aren't worth it." Even as he spoke, Drew regretted his harsh words—he'd never spoken so cruelly to anyone. But no one had ever gotten under his skin like Ash Davis.

Like a snake uncoiled, Ash jumped off the sofa and grabbed him by the shoulder. "Take that back."

"What's the matter, Davis? The truth hurts?" He mimicked Ash's earlier words and watched the anger flare in those colorless, glittering eyes.

"You fucking bastard. Who are you to say I'm not worth it, that no one cares about me? I have friends. People like me. Don't you ever say I'm not worth it. I matter, goddamn you. I fucking matter."

Ash tried to grab on to him, but Drew wrenched away and took off for the door, speaking over his shoulder.

"People don't like you, Ash; they want to fuck you because you're beautiful. That's not liking. That's not a friendship. How many relationships have you ever had with another man? You've never even had a boyfriend or a permanent relationship, have you? Because you have to have a heart. You have to care about someone.

How can you value someone else in your life when you don't even value yourself?"

Ash grabbed him. "Don't think you can say that and then fucking walk away from me." He shoved Drew against the wall. "Who the hell do you think you are?"

Ash's hand tightened on his bicep. It hurt, and Drew pulled away. He didn't get into physical fights with people; violence never solved any problem. "I thought I was your friend. But now I see I'm not. You don't know how to be a true friend. You run at the first sign of closeness and make fun of relationships. Relationships require effort, a give-and-take. You don't know how to give because you're always the taker." His breath came out heavy and uneven.

Ash slammed him back into the wall. For the first time, unease rippled through Drew as Ash's hard body pressed against his. Unease and something dark and sinuous uncoiled in his stomach, but he ignored it and tried to wriggle out of Ash's unrelenting grip.

"Let go of me. I want to leave."

Instead of moving away, Ash pushed harder against him. There was no mistaking that thick ridge between the two of them. Drew's heart raced until he could barely hear Ash through the pounding in his head.

"You said people don't like me; they only want to fuck me. Then you said I'm a taker." Before Drew could breathe, Ash grabbed his hands and pinned them above his head, forcing their bodies to press against one another. "But you need to know, Doc, that nobody fucks me. So tell me. You want me to take you?"

Drew thought he might faint when Ash's lips touched his temple, his warm breath drifting past Drew's ear. A surge of lust lurched through him as his nighttime fantasy unfolded into reality, there for him to experience if he wanted.

Ash's voice whispered in his ear. "I want you so fucking much. I'm ready to explode. I don't know why, and I don't care. I've wanted you for what seems like forever, and tonight I'm not letting you go until I make you mine. And, baby, you will be mine, make no mistake about it."

With that, Ash buried his face in the curve between Drew's neck and shoulder, his lips and hot, wet tongue finding Drew's skin and nipping, licking, and sucking at the flesh. If Ash hadn't been holding him, for certain Drew would have fallen from the powerful hunger exploding inside him. In all his years of dating women his body had never responded like this. Helpless to move, as Ash had pinned his hands to the wall, Drew wanted to speak, but the electric rush through his blood and the tingling at the base of his cock told him that all too soon he would be ending before he began.

"Uhh." Drew's head banged back against the wall, but he hardly registered the pain. "Ash, stop."

Ash pulled away, his hair in wild disarray, his breath panting, unsteady and heavy. The man looked totally debauched and disreputable, not like the usual in-control, polished executive. Ash swallowed and pulled himself together, raking his hands through his hair, then tugged at the cuffs of his shirt. "What-what's the matter? You don't want this?"

Before Drew could answer, Ash's fingers slid into the palms of Drew's hands, then up farther to entwine with Drew's, flat on the wall. They stood, cheek to cheek, hip to hip, their erections resting against one another. Unlike the harshness of only moments before, Ash's touch now was gentle and soft. Almost caring. Drew's head spun from the sudden shifts of emotion.

"No. Yes. I don't know." Drew leaned his head against the wall to gaze up at the ceiling and licked his lips. "All I know is that if you didn't stop, I was gonna come in my pants."

"How about you come in my mouth, instead?" Ash cupped Drew's jaw and rubbed the pad of his thumb over Drew's lips. "I want you. I want to undress you and touch you, lick you all over. I want you hot, naked, and sweating in my bed so I can know what you'll smell like on my sheets."

The words barely registered in the muddled soup of Drew's brain. His gaze slid over Ash's face, but instead of Ash's usual arrogant smirk, the man before Drew could have been a stranger. His silver eyes shone with hope but also uncertainty, an emotion Drew had never seen before on Ash's usually confident face.

"I don't know what to think anymore," Drew admitted, then sucked in his breath when Ash's lips touched the pulsing vein in his neck The room spun, and then the last candle sputtered out, sending them into a veiled, shadowy darkness pierced only by thin streams of pale moonlight from the windows.

"You think too much." Ash let go of Drew's other hand and with sure, strong fingers popped open the button tab of Drew's jeans. "That can get you into trouble, you know."

Drew didn't know anything except that he wanted Ash's hands on him. "I think I'm already in trouble."

"Tell me to stop, then. I will if you say so, but I don't think you can. You want this, don't you, baby? You want me."

Ash's voice, with that tantalizing slight, Southern drawl, came as if from a distance. All Drew's senses concentrated right there at the juncture between his legs where Ash's fingers pressed, first hard with a firm, sure grasp, then so light his body ached for another touch. Is this what he wanted? Ever since the time he'd caught Ash in the restaurant having sex with the waiter, no woman had piqued his interest or been the subject of his nighttime fantasies.

It had only been Asher Davis.

If Drew allowed himself this night with Ash to experience everything he'd secretly imagined, he'd hopefully get it all out of his system and be ready to return to dating and his regular life. It would be a one-time thing, a curiosity they'd both been dancing around for months. He'd go into it with his eyes wide open, with no expectations, knowing it wasn't meant to be permanent. Drew was too plain and innocent, his tastes not flashy or sophisticated like Ash's. He was beer and pizza; Ash—champagne and caviar.

Drew's mind began to wander until the reality of Ash returned with the touch of his heated breath and wet tongue slipping over Drew's stomach, poking into his belly button, then lapping at the trail of hair leading into Drew's yet unzipped jeans. Drew dug his hands into Ash's hair and wound his fingers around the silky strands to tug him even closer to his body.

"I want it all." He shocked himself, hardly recognizing his own strangled voice, distorted by desire, need and fear.

Ash stared up at Drew, eyes wide and diamond bright.

"Let's go to bed, baby."

And when Ash smiled, Drew knew right then his heart would be broken if this man left him in the end.

Chapter Thirteen

HIS MIND CLEARED; the fog of alcohol swept away, as if a sudden cool rain shower drenched him. Ash waited only a moment, stood, and grabbed Drew's hand, feeling it tremble, then grasp Ash's fingers tight. That small, subtle indication of Drew's trust touched Ash in a way he'd never experienced with a man when they were about to have sex. He didn't understand it, but before Ash knew what he was doing, he stopped and pulled Drew close to hug him tight.

It would be a night of firsts. First time for Drew to have sex with a man. First time for Ash to have anyone in his bed. That it was a man he knew and cared about scared him, but Ash pushed his fears aside to concentrate on Drew. He rubbed Drew's back, soothing not only Drew but himself. "Shh. It'll be all right. I promise." No use alarming the man by telling him how Ash ached for him night after night, not even understanding himself the yearning that brought him to make this move. "You're not afraid of me, are you, baby?" His palm cradled Drew's jaw, the pulse jumping beneath his fingertips.

A shudder rippled through Drew and he spoke against Ash's throat. "Maybe, a little, I don't know." Drew's familiar scent enveloped Ash, mingled with an underlying scent of sweat and fear.

"Let's go inside and lie down." Ash broke their hug and took Drew's hand again, entwining their fingers. They walked down the darkened hallway in silence, but Ash could feel Drew's nerves in the lag of his body and the dampness of his hand.

The sheets lay crisp and freshly laundered a clean unbroken swath of white. The linens, his comforter, everything in his bedroom gleamed of the purest white. Ash needed the cleanliness, that purity around him. He left instructions that the window, no matter the time of year, should be left cracked open. Perhaps for the reassurance that the outside world existed. Or perhaps, he thought, it could be one more escape route should he ever need to run again, no matter it was nineteen stories above Park Avenue. Old habits, especially ones born of fear and pain, die hard, or never at all. Arms around one another, they stood in silence; the room hushed as a tomb.

"Come in and sit. Slip off your sneakers." With a little tug, he pulled Drew nearer to his bed. "Don't be afraid of me. I don't bite." He wrapped his arms around Drew to whisper in his ear. "Not unless you want me to, and in that case the pain is all part of the pleasure."

A shudder ran through Drew, and Ash massaged his

back while his lips found Drew's ear. "What's your pleasure, baby?" He blew a gentle stream of air into Drew's ear, following it with his tongue. Drew's body surged forward as he moaned against Ash's shoulder. Ash nibbled and nipped his way down Drew's neck, the pulse of Drew's vein a thumping rhythm under Ash's mouth. "Don't be afraid. I'll never hurt you."

With one sure movement, he slipped his hands under Drew's T-shirt and pulled it up and over his head. Finally, after months of teasing glimpses and his erotic dreams, Ash's hands roamed over Drew's smooth, soft skin. He slid his fingertips down the waistband of Drew's jeans, and with a gentle, yet deliberate touch, brushed the dip of Drew's ass. "Lie down with me, baby." A whimper broke free from Drew's throat as Ash unzipped him, slid his jeans off, and pushed him onto his bed.

Silky black curls spilling over Ash's pillow stood out as the only smudge of color in their white cocoon. The sight of Drew curled up in his bed spurred Ash to join him. His usually sure fingers fumbled as he tore off his pants and boxers, leaving on his shirt, as he joined Drew. Normally he was neat and fanatical about his clothes being put away properly, but right now, with Drew lying warm and mouthwateringly half-naked in his bed, Ash couldn't care less, and left them in a rumpled pile on the floor.

Strips of moonlight gilded the pale skin of Drew's chest. Ash couldn't help but reach out and run his hands up that tight stomach, loving the silken feel of the curls as they passed through his fingers. From beneath lowered lids, Drew's eyes glinted, watching his every move even as his body trembled.

The men Ash slept with followed a pattern; gleaming, waxed, and tanned within an inch of their life. That had always been his preference. Until now. All the silky curling hair and creamy skin dotted with freckles beneath his hands caused an unfamiliar tenderness to swell within Ash's chest. He touched Drew's boxers and rested there, his hands unmoving on Drew's cock. Ash smiled at the dampness of the fabric. Drew might not understand what his body wanted, but Ash did, and the heat and musky smell emanating from Drew's body signaled to Ash all he needed to know.

Drew's gaze rested on him, his eyes black hollows in the near darkness. "I know I'm stupid for telling you how I feel, because you'll think I'm weak. I'm the desperate one here, the one who's out of control. You're in command, and I don't know what I'm doing."

Ash stretched out on the bed and pulled Drew into his arms. His chin rested on top of Drew's curls as they lay side by side. "Is that what you think, that I'm the one in control and strong? Nothing could be further from the truth. It's you. You alone have the power to bring me to my knees with your body, your skin." Almost choking on his emotion and passion, Ash swallowed and breathed deep to stop his voice from shaking. Where did all this come from? He barely spoke to the men he slept with, yet he couldn't stop the words pouring out from his heart.

He smiled, his lips still buried in Drew's hair. The smell of Drew's citrusy shampoo filled his senses. "Baby, I haven't even been inside you, yet there isn't anything I wouldn't fucking do for you. And you say I have the power?"

The truth he spoke lay between them. The truth, and Drew's obvious desire. The tightness in Ash's chest loosened somewhat, and the smile fled from his lips. His hips moved as if they had a will of their own in a slow and steady rub against Drew's. "Hold on to me, now."

Drew placed his hands on Ash's shoulders, and Ash rocked, their shafts bumping and rubbing. The friction tantalized but proved not nearly enough for Ash. He needed to see Drew naked, touch his cock and taste him. God help him, he wanted to give this man pleasure.

He pulled down Drew's boxers, freeing his cock. Throwing one leg over Drew's hip, Ash drove his hips forward, thrusting his cock alongside Drew's until they found a rhythm. He grasped their two cocks, stroking, sliding, rubbing, as their bodies, slick and heated, heaved against one another. Drew stiffened, his chest, abs, and cock pitching up against Ash, frantic and out of control. With a hoarse, strangled cry, Drew came, pulsing spurts across Ash's stomach and chest. Only a few strokes behind, Ash's body tightened, his cock rigid and hot as he jerked and came. Stars sparkled behind his eyes, and he lost his breath for a moment, then fell back against the pillows.

They lay side by side, panting in tandem. Ash glanced over at Drew, and though his eyes remained closed, Ash knew Drew wasn't asleep. As his own breathing slowed and his erratic heartbeat returned to its normal tempo, Ash reached over to take Drew's hand, but froze before their fingers touched.

What the hell was he doing? Nervous and confused, he pulled his hand back and rolled over on his side, away from Drew.

"You know, I'm not waiting for you to tell me that you love me. I told you I wanted this. Nothing's changed, and I'm not sorry."

Somehow, Drew's quiet voice made him feel even worse. "It's not that."

"Oh no?" The hint of a smile in Drew's question relaxed him somewhat. "What is it then?"

Ash rolled back to his other side, still marveling that he had this man in his bed. Naked. Drew lay facing him, propped up on one arm, chin resting in his palm. The moonlight brightened the room with a pale glow, picking up the green glints in Drew's eyes.

Funny, he could talk circles around his opponents in court and had no qualms about fucking men he barely knew, but now, the simplest of pillow talk with this gentle man, someone he thought of as a friend, made him nervous as hell. Probably because he'd never done it before.

"Uh, I'm not used to this." He bit his lip. "I, um, usually don't talk or entertain. Afterward."

Even in the dimness of the moonlight, Ash could see the hurt enter Drew's eyes.

"Oh."

To his shock, Drew rose from the bed, fumbled around on the floor, and slipped on his jeans. "I'll be going then."

Fucking hell. "No. You misunderstood me." He'd never forgive himself if Drew walked out now, feeling as though he'd been screwed and dismissed. With long strides, Ash reached the bedroom door before Drew and grabbed his arm. "Stop. Where are you going?"

Drew yanked his arm away, then pulled his T-shirt over his head and kept walking. "I'm leaving. You made it clear you were done."

Christ, were they ever going to be on the same wavelength? "Drew, wait." Naked except for his shirt, he nevertheless sped after Drew, sensing that if he didn't stop him now, something vital and precious would be lost forever. "Please."

To his immense relief, Drew's footsteps faltered, then stopped, but he didn't turn around. His back remained stiff and unyielding as a drill sergeant. Ash knew he owed Drew an explanation. Above anything else, they were friends first.

"I wasn't talking about you and me." He licked his suddenly dry lips, wishing like hell he had a drink. Something, anything to calm the firing of his nerve endings. Shit, even his hands shook. "I meant that I'd never done it before because I never wanted to. And now I do, but I don't know how."

When Drew turned around to speak, the hurt had been replaced by a wary, yet puzzled expression. He raked his hand through his hair.

"I don't get it. What don't you know how to do?"

"Forgive me, but I tend to argue a point better when I have clothes on." The sense of relief that the night hadn't all gone to shit hit him with a force so overwhelming, he braced himself against the wall. He held a hand out to Drew. "Will you please come back to bed?"

Although Drew did nothing more than nod, those gorgeous green eyes of his flared for a moment, giving Ash hope that the night had not yet ended for them. And as Drew's hand slipped into his, Ash gave it a gentle squeeze, then laced their fingers together. He could almost hear Mr. Frank's voice in the hallway, speaking to him.

"Take a chance, Asher. Open your heart."

And though that wasn't about to happen, he wasn't ready to let Drew go. Not yet. He sat at the edge of the bed, placing his hand on Drew's chest, holding him in place. By now, the moon had shifted, taking its luminescence with it, leaving the room in near total darkness. The way he liked it. The way he needed it.

Without any words, Drew once again removed his shirt, and Ash slid the jeans and boxers down to his ankles. The outline of Drew's smooth, pale cock was visible in the darkness, and without any hesitation, Ash took it in his mouth, hearing Drew's swift intake of breath, then a long-drawn-out moan of pleasure.

And for him? No fear. Only desire.

This wasn't him lying helpless and alone, unable to fight back. He was in charge. He was in control, and that thought spiked Ash's own pleasure, causing his cock to swell with need. Ignoring his arousal and focusing for once on giving his partner the most pleasure possible, Ash ran his tongue on the underside of Drew's cock, then, sucking the head and tonguing the slit, drew the shaft deep into his mouth. He held on to Drew, rubbing his fingers over the swell of Drew's ass, all the while keeping up the sliding friction of his mouth on his cock.

Deeper and deeper Drew thrust into Ash's mouth, and instead of fighting it like he thought he would, Ash welcomed it, wanted it in fact with an intensity that shocked and scared him to his core. For his entire life he'd denied himself the taste of a man in his mouth, thinking only of his degradation and debasement by his foster father. But with Drew pumping faster and harder, whimpering his pleasure, thrusting deeper into his mouth, Ash suddenly couldn't get enough.

He released Drew for a moment and lapped at the smooth head of Drew's erection, then muttered against the glistening tip, "Go ahead, baby, fuck my mouth. Do it." Once again, he, took him down his throat.

Drew held on to Ash's shoulders, his fingers biting into the skin as he threw his head back, groaning his pleasure. "Oh my God."

Ash slid his index finger into his mouth, wetting it with his saliva and Drew's precome. With a gentle swipe, he inserted it in the crease of Drew's ass.

And like Ash knew would happen, Drew came, harder and noisier than he had before, his salty-sweet essence pumping into Ash's mouth and down his throat, his cry of pleasure echoing throughout the room. Ash swallowed it all, then pulled away. For the briefest of moments the old fear grabbed at him, only to be knocked aside as Drew knelt down next to him, laying his head in Ash's lap.

No pain, no hate. No fear.

"I want to do the same for you." Drew's breath puffed by Ash's erect cock, and he touched Ash with hesitant, gentle fingers, but Ash brushed him off.

"You don't have to, baby." He took Drew's hand in his and kissed his palm. "This night is for you. My pleasure is to give you pleasure. Now come." He lifted the soft white comforter. "Climb in and rest some. I'm gonna go take a shower. You look beat and need your rest."

With a sweet sleepy smile, Drew stretched out and snuggled into the fluffy pillows. "I like that Southern accent." He yawned and patted the bed. "Come on and join me. You need to rest too, considering you did all the work."

Tempted as he was, Ash knew he needed to shower. He was sticky, sweaty, and needed to be clean. And clear his head about what had happened.

"I'll be a few minutes." Resisting the urge to kiss him, Ash turned on his heel and left for the bathroom. Once inside he stripped off his shirt, turned the shower on steamy hot and stepped in. With his eyes closed, he stood under the heated spill of water, letting it pummel his face and roll off his chest. He lathered himself up to wash away the sticky remnants of his and Drew's come.

Without any warning, Drew opened the fogged shower door. "I thought I'd come and join you."

He jumped, narrowly missing hitting his head on the shower fixture. "Fuck, Drew. Why couldn't you wait in the goddamn bedroom?" The pounding water beat down over his head and he held his arms behind his back. His gaze remained rooted to the shower floor, and he watched the rivulets of water swirl down into the drain.

He had no idea how long he stood there, until he noticed the water had stopped and Drew stood next to him, his dry warmth pressed up against his wet, shaking flesh.

"Ash," Drew whispered, kissing his cheek. "Come out now. You're clean. Let's dry you off."

Like a child, he allowed himself to be walked out of the shower, wrapped up in a towel, and patted dry. After leading Ash back to the bedroom, Drew tugged him into bed and together they lay down on the rumpled sheets, holding one another. Ash knew Drew expected an explanation, but he couldn't fathom exposing his tarnished insides to another person, not even Drew, the one person he'd been more intimate with than anyone. He'd die before admitting it, but Ash feared if he told Drew, he'd lose him.

Several moments passed and Ash sensed Drew's

unease; he shifted on the bed and cleared his throat several times, obviously waiting for Ash to ask what was wrong. When it became apparent he had no intention of speaking, Drew spoke against his shoulder. "Whenever you want to talk to me, I'm here for you. But like you said earlier, make no mistake. You *will* talk to me, Asher Davis."

Fucking hell. Tired of it all, of everything in his whole fucked-up miserable life, he turned from Drew's arms, sat up and snarled back at him. "You wanna talk? Well, all right, let's talk. What do you wanna know?" He pointed to the white ridged scar on his wrist, a smile twisting his lips. "You want to know about the first time I tried to kill myself, or the last time I cut myself for fun?" he asked, pointing to a fresh new gash.

"Where do you wanna start?"

Chapter Fourteen

DREW COULDN'T TAKE his eyes off Ash's arms. Up and down, from wrist to elbow, scars riddled his skin. Many were older, thin white lines, but several thick ugly twists of healed, ridged flesh told a story of Ash's deeply-rooted pain. With a practiced eye, Drew knew from their severity some nerve damage existed that could never be repaired.

What troubled him more were the new ones, reddened and fresh, which told him this behavior remained an ongoing problem for Ash. What demons did this beautiful, tortured man battle, even now, that caused him to maim himself like that? His grandmother's sixth sense proved correct once again; she had been right to be afraid.

Whatever drove Ash to cut himself, it somehow had to relate to Ash's past, the past he refused to talk about no matter how hard people pushed him. Drew, Peter, even Drew's grandmother couldn't force Ash to reveal the horrors that gnawed at his soul. With a sinking realization in his heart, Drew recognized this night should never have happened. It wasn't that he regretted it. On the contrary, he'd been willing to go much further, if all had gone well.

Forcing Ash into a corner, pushing him to reveal long-kept secrets wouldn't help either one of them. But neither was pretending all was well and they could continue on as if nothing had happened. While Drew's heart broke for Ash, the man needed professional help.

"I'm not asking you why or to tell me anything you don't want to." Drew kept his tone non-confrontational. "I'd hope that as a friend, you'd feel comfortable enough with me to maybe talk things out. Sometimes that helps."

Shooting him a strange look, Ash scrambled out of the bed and, after rummaging around in his dresser, pulled out a thin sweatshirt and slipped it on. Once covered, Ash visibly relaxed. "Nothing will help. But thanks for the offer."

Drew wanted to deck him. "Thanks for the offer? What am I, a salesman? For Christ's sake, Ash, I'm sitting here naked in your bed, and you're treating me as if I'm a fucking stranger." Considering how this night had degenerated, he climbed out of bed as well and got dressed again. This time he didn't anticipate Ash stopping him.

Ash shrugged. "There's nothing to discuss. You got what you wanted and so did I, so let's say good night."

It was as if he sat at a board meeting. Hello, goodbye, thanks for coming. Literally.

"How do you know what I wanted? You never gave

it a chance. For God's sake I was willing to..." He hesitated, unsure if he could say it. But when Ash sucked his cock, the balance of Drew's whole world shifted and he didn't know if he could ever go back to the way he was before.

"To what, Drew? Let me fuck you to see what it's like? We still could, you know."

Stung, Drew hoped this was a defense mechanism Ash used to push people away and not Ash's actual feelings.

"Why are you acting like such a bastard? I understand you've been hurt."

Like a lion, Ash pounced on him, pushing him back onto the bed. "You understand? You think you *understand*? Why, because you're lonely and took a walk on the wild side tonight with me? You know nothing about me or my life, and that's the way it's going to stay."

Caught by surprise, Drew lost all power to move once those glittering icy eyes held him. "I'm your friend, if nothing else, and that's what friends do, they help one another."

"I don't need friends, or a lover, or anyone trying to make me part of a family. I was fine before I met you, and I'll be fine when you're gone."

Drew shook his head in disbelief. "You think you're fine? Look at yourself. You're a goddamn mess. One moment you're decent, kind, and caring—the next you're a cruel, hurtful bastard. You run from everything and everyone you think might get close to you."

"Isn't this where we started tonight?" Ash's strained drawl didn't fool Drew now. As if he were a balloon, Ash deflated, his shoulders slumping, and his head hung down.

"Yes, I remember now. You told me I wasn't worth it. And you know something; you're right. I'm not worth it. So go home, Doc, find a nice girl to fuck, marry and have babies with. Leave me alone." This time he walked out of the room, and Drew followed.

Ash returned to where he must have been seated before Drew showed up tonight. The club chair stood by the dark, cold fireplace, the bottle of vodka and ice bucket resting like sentinels on the small table, awaiting his inevitable return. In his heart, Drew knew this was where Ash spent most of his time when he was at home. In that chair, with a bottle, staring off into nothingness. What ghosts did he see as he sat all alone, deep into the night? Was it shadows of his past come to haunt him in the present? The vision of those twisting, ugly scars remained imprinted in his mind's eye, and Drew winced in sympathetic pain.

"Ash, I said I was wrong, and I'm sorry. I spoke out of anger."

The ice must've melted, as Ash peered into the bucket, shook his head, then sloshed some vodka in his glass and, with a practiced flip of his wrist, drank it off in two gulps. He poured another and repeated the action. Only then did he answer. "No, you merely spoke the truth, what I was always told." He poured another glass and Drew watched in amazement as he drank that down as well. In the span of minutes, he'd gone through three full tumblers of straight vodka like they were water.

"I'm not worth it. Jus' a poor kid with no family." He stood and began wandering around the spacious room, then tipped his head back to stare at the ceiling. Flinging his arm out, he spun around. "But I showed them all, didn't I, Mr. Frank? You said I was smart and I could make it."

His heart breaking for this tortured man, Drew approached him with care. No way could he'd leave him alone tonight in his fragile condition. He'd never forgive himself if something happened to Ash.

"Why don't you lie down?" Drew placed his hand on Ash's shoulder. "I'll help you back into the bedroom."

Having stopped spinning, Ash stood swaying in the middle of the room, looking decidedly pale and ill. "I don' feel so good." He squinted into his empty glass. "Wha' happened to my drink?"

He plucked the glass out of Ash's hand. "No more drinks for you, my man. You need to lie down and go to bed."

"With you?"

The hopeful note in Ash's voice struck a chord deep within Drew's heart. How could he walk away? After his revelations tonight, Drew knew he couldn't leave. It had nothing to do with the sex, although his face warmed remembering the feel of Ash's mouth on his cock. Knowing how hard Ash worked at the center, how dedicated he was to those kids, a beautiful shell existed under the glossy exterior Ash had built up to shield and deflect anything that might hurt him.

Now wasn't the time to think about that. He slid his arm around Ash's shoulders and pulled him close. It was a little difficult, as Ash had several inches and well over twenty pounds on him, but after a few stumbles, he managed to push Ash back down the hallway and rather indelicately dump him into his bed. Drew turned on a night table lamp, casting a low glow over the room.

"Ow." Ash rolled onto his back, his bleary face turned sideways as he mumbled into the pillows. "My head's spinning." Quicker than Drew thought possible considering the man's drunken state, Ash grabbed Drew's T-shirt and pulled him down on top of his hard body.

"Oof." He landed with his pelvis nestling in perfectly with Ash's. As expected, Ash was most definitely aroused, but Drew had already made up his mind not to engage in any more sexual games with Ash until they had a chance to clear the air.

"Hey, none of that. You're drunk, and I don't think it's a good idea."

A heavy hand clamped around his waist, and Ash's lips found his neck. "I'm usually drunk when I fuck somebody, so I think it's a great idea."

Dismay, like an icy bucket of water cleared Drew's mind. His erection wilted and with surprising strength, he wrenched away from Ash's drunken nuzzling and stood up, spitting in anger.

"I'm not 'somebody.' I'm not some piece of ass you picked up at a bar to screw and forget. I'm your friend, goddamn you. Friends are different." Christ, he almost let this guy…it was too much to imagine. Almost without thinking, he stuck his face in Ash's. "I'm different, or at least I thought I was."

Ash merely stared back, those silvery eyes unblinking.

"Are you telling me I'm no different than that waiter who blew you in the hallway, the same as all those anonymous men you've fucked?"

Ash opened his mouth, then closed it, bowing his head. "The fact you're even here, in my home and in my bed, and we're having this conversation shows how different you are." He fell back onto the pillows. "Drew, what the hell do you want from me?"

Good question. He hadn't a clue. As a friend, he would help any of the people dearest to him, no questions asked. But Ash had become more than a friend. What had happened between them tonight carved a special place in Drew's heart, even if they never took it further. Drew hurt for Ash, felt his pain. The pit of ugliness Ash had lived in prior to his arrival in New York must have been so deep and black it was a miracle he'd been able to climb up out of it.

"I want you to talk to me." With a gentle hand, he stroked Ash's sweating face. "Please tell me about it. Maybe I could help you."

Ash's laugh rang bitter. "Help me? You're nice,

Drew. Good and pure at heart. You see the best in people and always think of how to help them." He rolled onto his side, presenting Drew with his broad back. "It's impossible for someone like you, who grew up normal, loved and sheltered by a family, to understand what can happen to the throwaway children left behind. The ones no one wanted."

Drew sat on the bed, his weight tipping the mattress, forcing Ash to slide closer to him. The warmth of his large body tempted Drew to reach out to hold and comfort him, but he didn't want to break the spell of Ash revealing even the smallest piece of himself. Something, anything, though, would be helpful in unraveling the mystery of this man. "Talk to me."

Ash's dark head burrowed farther into the pillows. "I can't drag you into the mess of my life. As it is right now, you know more about me than anyone else. You don't understand how hard I've worked to put it behind me, but I can't. It's like a horrendous jack-in-the-box that keeps springing up when I least expect it, to scare the shit out of me and drag me back down."

"That's why you relate so well to those kids at the clinic, right?" He took a deep breath. "To Stevie? You know what he's going through, don't you, because something similar happened to you. Am I right?"

At Ash's quick nod, Drew instinctively touched his shoulder in sympathy, but Ash flinched away. "We were all thrown in together. The kids no one wanted. No family who cared whether we lived or died, but we had each other, you know? Years we spent waiting for someone to help us. And they looked up to me 'cause I was older, but I couldn't help myself; how could I help them?"

Drew held his breath, knowing Ash had withdrawn inside himself once again, reliving his youth.

Ash flipped over to lie on his back, eyes flat and blank, his handsome face ravaged by inner torment. "We thought he cared at first, our foster father. He'd buy us candy and take us to ball games and the circus. Our foster mom was timid, churchgoing, and clueless." He hugged the pillow to his chest. "Later on we found out he'd hit her if she didn't do what he said, when he said it. Dinner on the table and beer in his hand when he walked in the door. If not…" Ash punched the pillow. "But never where anyone could see. Or bad enough so she'd hafta go to the doctor. She'd lie for him anyway. He was a cop, a good ol' boy. Who'd they believe, him or us?"

It was worse than Drew had imagined. These were the stories he'd only heard about, the ones he saw on the television that made him start the clinic in the first place.

Ash let go now, the words spilling from him like water freed from a dam. "When he moved on to us boys, I let him do whatever he wanted to me, 'cause they were littler, you know? I tried to protect them from him." A lone tear trickled down his cheek. "I thought when I left they'd come with me, but they were too afraid to leave."

"Who were they, Ash?" Drew covered Ash's hand,

shocked at the cool, clammy feel of his skin.

"The closest thing I've ever had to brothers. But I abandoned them, left them with him." Ash's eyes, huge, wounded, and now shiny with tears, captured Drew and pulled him into their gray depths.

"I didn't want to leave, but I knew I'd end up dead if I stayed. I never thought they wouldn't come with me, but at the last minute Luke changed his mind and Brandon was too young. I shoulda stayed."

"You don't know. Maybe it worked out for them. Maybe he left them alone." Drew stroked his hand, trying to soothe his agitation.

"No, no, I know something terrible happened." Ash sat up, pale and trembling. "You don' understand." He put a hand to his mouth. "I'm gonna be sick."

Stumbling out of the bed, he rushed to the bathroom. Drew followed him silently, watching as he retched in the toilet. He slid down next to Ash and put his arm around his shoulders, holding him close, letting the man lean against him. He smoothed back the sweat-drenched hair and murmured quiet, nothing words of comfort into Ash's ear until he finished. Without saying a word, he rinsed out a hand towel in cold water and placed it on the back of Ash's neck.

A moan broke free from Ash. "Drew, why are you still here?"

"Because you're my friend. And I don't abandon my friends when they need me." Without giving it a second thought, he brushed the hair off Ash's face and kissed his cheek. Ash grew still, and Drew immediately sensed his withdrawal.

"Uh, I think I need to rinse my mouth and brush my teeth." Although Ash stood without help, Drew noticed he still needed to brace his hands against the sink to steady himself. Their eyes met in the mirror. "I can take care of myself."

Shut down by Ash's aloof and cold behavior, Drew nodded and returned to sit on the bed. After waiting several moments, a horrified thought crossed his mind. Was Ash *hurting* himself in the bathroom? Visions of the man bleeding had him up and off the bed, halfway across the room, when Ash opened the bathroom door, wrapped in a robe.

"Are you all right?" His gaze flickered to Ash's arms. "I, was, uh getting a little worried."

Ash's hands tugged at the sleeves of his robe; a gesture Drew now knew to be defensive, from a long-standing habit. "About what? Thinking I was doing something to myself in the bathroom?"

The cruel tinge to his words hit Drew like a slap, but knowing Ash better now, he understood. It was Ash's way of keeping him at arm's length so he wouldn't dig deeper into the past and get closer. Drew, however, had an infinite level of patience. Ash could take as long as he wanted, but now that he told his story, Drew would find a way to help him.

"Are you back to being that asshole from when we first met? Is that how you think you're going to push me away? Maybe Peter's afraid to step on your toes, but I'm not." Drew tipped his head back a little to stare into Ash's eyes. For a moment he thought he saw a flicker of hope in those clear, silvery depths before the shutters came down, blanking out any expression.

Ash opened his mouth, but the phone rang, cutting off whatever spiteful remark he might have planned. Drew watched alarm flare in Ash's eyes before he hastened over to the night table and picked up.

"Hello?" His breathless voice caught, then became sharp with excitement. "No, no, it's not too late. I told you to call no matter what the time. Are you sure, Martinson? Tell me everything you know." He listened for a moment, and Drew could tell by the expression that lit up his face, something important had happened. "Wait, can you hold for a moment?" Ash put the phone down and gave him a sideways glance.

"Um I have to take this call, and it's private, so…" Ash shrugged, his gaze flickering back to the phone.

Son of a bitch, he's dismissing me as if I worked for him. Hurt, Drew gave a tight nod. "Sure. See you around." Ash had already returned to the phone as if he didn't care what Drew's answer was.

Before he left the room, he heard Ash's voice, raised in excitement. "You found both of them, or one? Tell me everything."

I'm doing this to try and help him. That was the justification Drew played over and over as he listened in the doorway, trying to make sense of the conversation.

Chapter Fifteen

AFTER HE HUNG up the phone with Martinson, instructing him to spare no time or expense to continue his search, Ash glanced at the clock by his bed. Surprised to see it was only one thirty in the morning, and restless enough to know he wasn't ready for sleep, he threw on a pair of pants and a shirt, drank a bottle of water in a few gulps, and left his apartment. His body hummed with excitement as he exited his building, automatically heading toward a bar he frequented when he wanted anonymous, hot sex.

The dim, below-street-level bar was packed, he noted with satisfaction. There would be no problem working off the buzz of pleasure that had built up in his body during Drew's aborted visit.

At the thought of Drew, regret slammed through him, hard and vicious, but he quashed it down, unwilling to face those feelings at the moment. He slid into a vacated seat at the bar, and Danny, his usual bartender, had his vodka poured and ready.

Though still somewhat light-headed from the evening's earlier drinking, he needed the sweet, beautiful oblivion only alcohol could give him to help him forget what a piece of shit he'd been toward Drew.

"Hello Ash, how's it shaking tonight?" Danny winked at him as he shook a martini for another customer.

"Good, my man." The vodka slid down his throat like water. "Another one, Danny. It's been a bitch of a night."

The bartender laughed as he poured his drink. "I know how you feel, bro. Some nights all you need is a stiff one."

He looked at Danny, and they shared a laugh. Ash gulped the second one as quickly as the first, wanting to drown out the voices in his head scolding him for his shitty treatment of his friend. Two drinks in this short a period of time, coupled with his earlier vodkas, had him swaying on his seat, slightly dizzy and unfocused.

As he tossed down half of his third drink, a hand touched his back and caressed his shoulder. The heat of the man's palm seared his skin through his shirt. He jerked away, stood, and faced the man whose hand remained on his body.

Long, buttery-yellow blond hair framed a pale, high-cheekboned face. Deep brown eyes stared at Ash with a hunger that kick-started the blood racing through his veins. Ash raised a brow as he pushed the hand away. "Can I help you?" Yeah, he was drunk but Ash didn't care. His body burned and he needed to quench his hunger.

A slow smile crept over the blond man's face. "I know how I can help you." He took Ash's hand. "Let's go to the back." The press of the crowd pushed Ash's body against the stranger, and he could feel every dip and curve of the man's lithe, muscled torso through his thin T-shirt.

This was what he came for, to drown himself in another hot, willing body. As he walked to the back, Ash couldn't wait to feel the man's lips slide over his cock. He needed to bury himself inside of someone, anyone to forget about Drew.

"Hey, man. This is good, right?" They entered the restroom, and the man locked the door behind him.

Ash didn't answer, having no use for petty small talk. He unzipped his pants, then closed his eyes and stroked himself, picturing the face of a hot, green-eyed angel with silky dark curls staring up at him. His head spun from all the vodka he'd gulped down at the bar.

Wet warmth enveloped him as a twisting, flickering tongue swept over the head of his cock. He widened his stance, bracing his back against the wall, and none too gently began thrusting into the willing mouth.

His mind blanked until all feeling and sensation centered around his groin, and he grabbed the head of the man on his knees before him. "Christ, Drew, fuck me, yeah."

Hazy with desire, he opened his eyes, expecting to see the dark-haired Drew at his feet. At the sight of his hands buried in blond straight hair, not black curls, Ash grew confused. His blurred mind couldn't separate who kneeled between his legs, from who was in his head and he yanked himself away, his erection wilting.

"Wait, what the fuck is going on? Where's Drew?"

The blond let go of his cock with a wet, sucking sound, his hand still wrapped around his own erection. "What the hell, man? Are you on something?" His pale face, flushed with lust, tightened. "I was close and so were you."

Dizzy and slightly nauseated, Ash shoved his now limp cock into his pants and zipped himself up. "Uh, look, I'm sorry, I shouldn't have come in here with you."

By now the other man had finished jerking himself off and stood, brushing his knees with his hands. "You're right. I don't know who this Drew guy is, but you need to figure it out if you're gonna call his name when your dick is in someone else's mouth."

The stranger unlocked the door and opened it. "Better get your fuckin' head together, man."

Ash leaned back against the coolness of the tiled wall. A perfect ending to this night. He relieved himself, washed his hands, and splashed cold water on his face. After leaving the bathroom, he wove his way through the crowd, paid his tab at the bar and returned home.

Now three o'clock in the morning, Ash fell into a restless sleep, where the old nightmares mingled with new. He jolted upright to a sitting position in the bed, eyes wide open and bulging with alarm, a name on his lips.

"Drew…"

With a sinking heart, Ash remembered he'd sent Drew away, and not nicely either, but rather dismissively and brusque, as if they'd finished a business transaction. Rather like the way he usually ended all his sexual encounters, except this time he knew the man's name and had to see him again.

"Shit, I really fucked this up." Wide awake now, he peered over at the glow of the bedside clock. Five thirty-five. Well, wasn't that fucking wonderful. Knowing there was no sleep left for him tonight, Ash tossed back the covers and walked naked into the living room. The bottle of vodka awaited him like a long-lost friend, offering warmth and forgetfulness. Exactly what he needed after the complete shitstorm of a night. He poured a little into the glass and drank it back straight.

Warmth, such as it was, seeped into his chilled body but couldn't erase the cold manner he'd treated Drew. "Fuck." He poured out a little more, the neck of the bottle knocking against the rim of the glass, but he couldn't bear to drink this one warm. With a sigh, he grabbed the bottle, crossed the living room, and entered the kitchen. After filling his glass with ice, he poured it full and waited a moment, letting it chill, as he wrapped his mind around the phone call from Martinson.

The news he'd received tonight was the closest he'd ever come to concrete information about one of his brother's whereabouts. Luke might be in New York City. He trembled, knowing that no matter how many millions of people lived in the city, he and Luke might soon see each other. And once again, he'd allowed alcohol to numb his fear. He was such a goddamn coward. That's why he'd pushed Drew away, or tried to. At the thought of Drew, he drank a little more vodka. How many did that make tonight? Not nearly enough to dull the searing pain, remembering how he'd basically thrown the best man he'd ever met out of his apartment.

Could he finally let someone share his hurt, his life? Could he tell Drew about what really happened to him as a child and young man? He pulled open the drawer. He might be a little drunk but in the twilight of early morning, he knew the ritual and could do it with his eyes closed.

In a macabre sort of way, the smooth edge of the knife handle comforted him. Still holding his drink in his left hand, he slid to the floor, his legs pressed up into his chest so his chin rested on his knees. With deliberate care, he placed his drink on the floor, then rubbed his right arm, searching for a smooth, yet unblemished spot.

The thin blade slipped into his skin, and he welcomed the sting. A thin line of blood appeared, and he smiled.

Absolution.

Each cut on his body reminded him not only of how he'd failed his foster brothers, but in a twisted way gave him strength to push the nightmare of Paul Munson's abuse behind him. Now he could add the cruel and callous way he'd treated Drew to his litany of failures. It didn't matter if it made no sense to anyone. He knew. It was his body and his choice to do with it what he wished.

The knife clattered to the white tiled floor, sending drips of blood splattering across the pristine surface. He watched with almost clinical disinterest as the tiny rivulets of red trickled down his arm to land on his knee. Years of experience now enabled him to judge when to stop to prevent losing too much blood. In the early years he'd had some close calls and the heavier, deeper scars to show for it.

Drew would know how to help him prevent further scarring, but he wanted them, needed those scars to prove he was still alive and capable of feeling pain.

Most of his life, he'd felt nothing at all.

Being the selfish bastard he was, until he'd spoken with Esther and understood the horror she'd not only witnessed but endured and triumphed over, he'd never thought about anyone else's suffering. That tiny woman had wormed her way under his skin like no one else had. After leaving her house yesterday, he'd planned to hurt himself, badly, but then Drew had come by.

Drew. It all came back to him and that damn sweet smile he couldn't get out of his mind. "I really fucked up, didn't I?" he groaned to no one in particular. Maybe not. More tired now than drunk, he lifted himself off the floor and, after rinsing his arm off in the sink, picked up the phone on the counter.

After four rings a husky, sleep-roughened voice answered. Shit, the man sounded so fucking sexy, even half-asleep.

"Ash? What the fuck are you calling me at six in the morning for?"

Half-asleep and angry as well. He suddenly lost his nerve and swallowed hard.

"Are you all right?" Now Drew sounded both awake and anxious. "Do you need—"

"I need you, Drew." He leaned against the counter-top, the hard edge digging into the naked skin of his back. "I fucked up, and I'm sorry."

"Hold on a minute." In the background he could hear rustling, and all Ash could picture was Drew naked in bed. Though his mind ached with vodka and tiredness, his body proved itself wide awake as he looked down to a large, healthy erection bobbing in front of him. He walked to his bedroom and lay down, slowly stroking his cock.

"I wish you were here with me." His lips pressed against the receiver as he breathed the words into the phone.

Drew sighed into the phone. "Come on, Ash. You told me to leave, dismissed me, as a matter of fact. Let's leave it at that."

"No, I can't." He continued to stroke himself and couldn't contain a groan that came from his lips.

"Are…are you jerking off while you're talking to me?" Drew's voice rose with incredulity. "Seriously?"

"I wanted you so bad tonight. I can't stop thinking

of your body and your cock." His hand was slippery with all the wetness leaking from the engorged head of his dick. It was easy to slide his hand up and down, faster and faster.

"Ash, please." Drew's voice came through the receiver, pained yet curiously short of breath.

"Are you hard too, baby? Did you like it when I took you in my mouth, hmm?" Ash's hips thrust upward now, pushing his cock through his fist.

"I can't believe you're doing this over the phone."

"Touch yourself, baby. Go on. Do it where my mouth was and pretend I'm there with you now. Remember how my mouth was on you? All hot and wet and tight?" Ash jerked his cock a few more times, and then his orgasm came upon him, thundering in his chest and lighting up his balls. He spurted hot, creamy jets across his stomach and chest.

"This is crazy."

"Mmm. I was thinkin' of you, baby. Of your hot sweet mouth and your tight ass."

There was no sound, and for a moment he feared Drew had hung up.

"Are you still there?"

A heavy sigh blew in his ear. "Yeah. I don't know, Ash. We have so much to talk about."

"Talk is overrated. Stroke yourself, come on. Harder and faster. Think of how good it felt before. Remember me licking you, sucking you, and touching you all over? Your skin is so soft, baby. Like a juicy ripe peach."

A small sound came through the earpiece and Ash imagined Drew naked in his bed. He wanted to be there with him now, watching he face tighten with desire and see him lost in passion. His own bed, always a sanctuary, now seemed barren and cold.

"I wanted you so bad tonight, Drew. I wanted to sink into that beautiful ass of yours and pound you into my bed. I wanted to make you mine. Can you imagine me inside you, baby?"

Ash could imagine it; he'd spent weeks wondering what Drew looked like naked beneath his clothes and now he knew. Pale soft skin, silky black hair and a lean body he could spend hours examining with his mouth and tongue.

"I've never, ah…"

"Had phone sex?" Ash chuckled. "Obviously. But everything I said was the truth. I know I fucked up earlier."

"Well, I know how you can make it up to me."

"You'll come over tonight, and we can finish what we started?" The pleading tone in his voice at one time would've made his skin crawl if he'd heard it from another man's mouth. How quickly things changed, how he'd changed. But the fact remained that he wasn't yet willing to let Drew slip out of his life.

"That's not what I was thinking."

With a sinking heart, he knew exactly what the good doctor was thinking. "Oh?" If his casual tone didn't fool himself, it certainly wouldn't fool Drew.

"Look, Ash. Like I said earlier, aside from whatever

this physical thing is between us, tonight disturbed me on so many levels."

"There's nothing to discuss."

The frustration in Drew's voice came through the phone receiver loud and clear. "Are you kidding me? I know something terrible happened to you when you were young. Your arms are covered with self-inflicted scars, and you say there's nothing to talk about?"

"It's not for you to get involved in. It's my personal life."

"You are fucking unbelievable." Drew laughed, but there was zero humor in him. "I shouldn't get involved because it's your personal life? Ash. My dick in your mouth is about as personal as two people can get with each other. Shit, if things had gone on..."

He swallowed hard, and Ash closed his eyes.

They were two immovable objects banging against one another, neither willing to give an inch. Like a wave smashing against a rocky cliff, the wave would forever pound against that immovable wall, but the cliff would always stand strong and battle it back.

"It's my life, Drew. There are certain parts of it I don't share, not with you, not with anyone. I can't." He got off the bed and, still naked, pulled the curtain back and stared out the window. Cabs whizzed down the early morning streets of Park Avenue, beginning their early morning pickups.

"What are you afraid of? Can I at least ask that?"

Everything. Letting the curtain fall, he turned his back on the window and returned to the bed. "I don't know. My whole life I've been afraid. When I was younger, I was afraid to be alone, without a family. Then when I was taken in"—his voice caught, and he coughed—"I was afraid for the younger boys in the house. After a while I hated the person I became."

"What type of person? I'm not afraid of you, even though you try and hide behind a mask, like you don't care about anyone or anything." Drew's comforting voice had Ash curling up in his bed, hugging the pillow to his chest. This was nice, talking to Drew, almost normal, but he knew it was all a façade.

"Someone without a soul. Someone who wouldn't think twice about hurting another person."

"I'm sure you had a reason." No hesitation or doubt in Drew's tone. Like he actually believed in Ash as a decent human being.

"My fear and selfish actions left my friends...*my brothers*...alone with him and defenseless. I should've been stronger and fought back, or found another way to deal with it." Funny how talking it out now released a bit of the tightness in his chest. For the first time in forever, he could breathe a little deeper.

"How old were you when all this happened?"

"I was eighteen when I left there." Eighteen, scrawny, and scared to death. He'd never even been out of the small town in Georgia until he ran away that night.

"You were a kid, for Christ's sake. Stop beating yourself up over it."

"You don't understand, Drew. I left because I

couldn't take it, and I knew if he kept coming to me, one night I was gonna kill him. So I left when I shoulda stayed and had it out with him."

Drew scoffed. "You said the guy was a cop. He would've put you in jail or killed you himself and made it look like an accident."

Visions of Luke's tearstained face flooded his mind. No matter how many years passed, Ash could never forget how Luke pleaded with him not to go. "Maybe it would've been the best thing." No more pain.

In the yawning silence from the other end of the phone, Ash's heart throbbed in a gruesome concert with the throbbing in his cut arm.

"Is that why you do it? Hurt yourself."

The man should've been a psychiatrist, not a plastic surgeon. Ash blew out a harried breath. "Drew, like I said before. You're good, and I'm not. I'm bad, and if you get too close, bad things will happen to you. I should've stayed away from you, and from now on I will." He looked at the clock. It was now almost six thirty in the morning. The room had lightened around him, and the angry honking of the cars on Park Avenue filtered even up to his floor. "I have to get ready for work. I'll see you at the clinic."

"But, Ash—"

"Bye, Drew." He set the handset down on the bed and rolled over, still hugging the pillow, staring at nothing for a very long time.

Chapter Sixteen

WEEKS PASSED SINCE that night they'd talked, and Ash continued to avoid him. No matter when he showed up at the clinic, if Ash was there, he was either meeting with kids or managed to slip away before Drew could catch him to sit and talk. The one time Drew had swallowed his nerve and gone back to Ash's high-end apartment building, he was informed by the concierge that *"Mr. Davis isn't home for visitors."*

There was no denying how good Ash was with the kids, especially the ones who came in leery of the clinic's good intentions, and disbelieving that anyone could help them. They'd meet with Ash, and something inexplicable resonated between them, validating all their hard work. Speaking with Ash allowed them to see someone who'd made it and gave them hope they too could escape and become a success.

Everything he'd ever dreamed could be accomplished in his life was happening.

Rachel submitted her doctoral thesis, and she and Mike were stronger than ever. Jordan and Keith were in the midst of planning a wedding in the not too distant future, as Keith had proposed to him over the summer. As usual, Drew was the one left alone.

He finished his chart on the last girl, who'd shown up with a facial laceration she said she received from banging into the door when she woke up in the middle of the night. To Drew, the mark looked like the cut from the sharp edge of a ring, as if she'd been slapped and it cut her face. Though she vehemently denied it, she wouldn't let them call her mother, coming instead with her older brother who stood to the side, his jaw clenched and hands fisted.

Drew recognized that pugnacious look. The young man was spoiling for a fight, and Drew had no doubt he would go home and want to beat the crap out of whomever he thought had done this to his sixteen-year-old sister. He'd had Rachel talk to the two of them, she later told him she'd given them the number of someone who would talk to them free of charge about family abuse.

He threw down his pen and took off his glasses to rub his tired eyes. As it so often did when his mind wandered, he found himself thinking back all those weeks ago to that one amazing, intense night with Ash. Nothing could have prepared him for the feel of Ash's mouth on his cock. No blowjob he'd ever gotten from a woman had even come close to the blinding, white-hot desire that had flamed through him. The mere thought of it set his cock twitching, swelling with an insistent need he'd neglected for far too long.

He should start dating again. Once he found a woman and started having sex on a regular basis, the strange fascination with Ash would fade. As a matter of fact...Drew opened the laptop on his desk, put on his glasses, and logged on to that dating website he'd registered with several months ago but had never used. Again, as he remembered, page after page of young women appeared, but this time he looked carefully at their profiles, making a list of the women he thought might be compatible with his lifestyle.

After about forty-five minutes, he had seven names. He e-mailed each one to see if they wanted to meet for coffee. First, he needed a cup for himself right now and a little snack. Mug in hand, he wandered over to the kitchen, brewed a cup of hazelnut, and stuck his head in the refrigerator to see what was there for the taking.

He'd grabbed a meatball sandwich when he heard Ash's voice. His heartbeat quickened, as this was the first time since they'd parted on such bad terms that the two of them had been together, alone, in the office. Then another younger voice spoke, and Drew recognized it as Stevie, the boy Ash so desperately tried to help. The sandwich forgotten, he walked over to Ash's office.

When he approached the open door, he saw Ash, elbows on his desk, sleeves unbuttoned and shirt collar undone at the throat, looking tired, rumpled, and upset. Stevie sat hunched forward in his chair, his hands over his face.

"Anything wrong? Can I help?" Drew's main concern was Stevie. Ash had filled him in from the beginning on the boy's miserable bullying. "Are you hurt, Stevie?" Drew strode into the room and dropped to his knees by the boy's chair. He put his hand on Stevie's arm, and his heart skipped seeing how even that slight, nonthreatening action caused the boy to flinch.

"Stevie?" Ash spoke in a quiet, affectionate tone Drew hadn't heard before. "You can talk to Dr. Drew."

When Drew glanced up, he caught a glimpse of the pain in Ash's eyes before they shuttered, turning flat and blank. When the boy didn't answer, Ash continued to press him. "Would you want me to talk to him for you?"

At Stevie's tentative nod, a breath Drew wasn't even aware of holding escaped him. He stood, as did Ash, and they left the room to stand in the hallway together.

It was the closest he'd been to Ash in almost a month. Dark smudges beneath his tired eyes coupled with an overall exhausted appearance evidenced Ash's internal suffering, yet those glittering eyes still had the capacity to render Drew breathless.

This admiration of Ash didn't help Stevie, though, which was why they were here in the first place. "Uh, so what's going on? You two seemed very intense in there."

Ash raked his hand through the tangles in his hair, and his shirtsleeve fell to his elbow, revealing a fresh new bandage. Drew's breath caught in his throat; it sickened him to think of Ash continuing to abuse his body.

"Damn it, why?"

"We're here to talk about Stevie, not me, correct?" Ash's clipped tone screamed, *Hands off, stay away, don't ask questions.*

Drew was never one for following directions.

"You're still doing it, aren't you? I'm begging you to get some help, before it's too late." In an instinctive, comforting gesture, Drew reached out, but Ash pulled away from his touch.

"So you don't want to help Stevie; is that what you're saying?" Good deflection by Ash. First point to him.

"Of course I do. What's going on?" Drew tried to smile but failed. For weeks now, he'd been frozen with unhappiness.

"Jordan saw him today. Severe bruising around his ribs, as well as a sprained wrist. Nothing permanent, but I'm trying to talk him into allowing Jordan to have Keith arrest the two other young men."

"He won't cooperate, will he?" Drew already knew the answer.

"Nope." Ash shook his head in disgust. "He's still too afraid. I've had child services over to the house, but they find nothing wrong and no one's reported any problems. The parents aren't the problem. It's those two kids in the neighborhood who torment him on an almost daily basis. And Stevie's scared to death of them. Maybe Keith could pay an unofficial visit and scare the shit out of them."

Drew thought for a moment. "It might work. Bullies tend to back off if they feel their secret is out. Want me to try to talk to him?"

Ash blew out a breath of exasperation. "You can try, but he's so fucking afraid, he's a heartbeat from running away." He rested against the wall with a sigh, his eyes closed.

"Hey." Drew took a step forward, close enough to see the trembling of Ash's eyelashes against his cheeks. At his voice, the long black lashes fluttered open, revealing those odd, translucent eyes that picked up every color, like the reflection of diamonds. "Please talk to me. I know you've been avoiding me."

Drew caught a scent of Ash's light cologne and body heat. Without thinking, he took another step closer, never taking his eyes from Ash. Drew's gaze fell to the other man's lips. Soft breaths fanned his face; he could feel the imprint of Ash's mouth on his.

Hot, firm, and wanting.

I must be insane.

"I come here to help. That's the only reason I'm here." Ash licked his lips. "I do it for Stevie and the others."

They stood close enough to share the same air, yet the yawning emotional distance between them was as great as the first day they'd met. Impenetrable, for Ash had gone cold and still. Drew thought back to his grandmother and how she sensed the truth of what lay inside Ash. Not the chilly, confident lawyer, quick on his feet with a smirk or a snide remark. Instead, as always, she saw straight to the heart. To the inner truth of what lay deep within the person. From the start, she'd sensed Ash's innate decency, no matter how he walled it off from the rest of the world.

And because of that, Drew held on to Ash as both a friend and a man he believed in. He couldn't, wouldn't press Ash now. There would be time enough for that, when they were truly alone and able to lay their feelings bare to the blood and bone. Whether it led to something more intimate wasn't the point. The terrible loneliness Ash endured each day was no stranger to Drew. As his own family and friends paired off to begin new lives and build their own worlds, Drew remained cocooned like a caterpillar in his chrysalis.

His tentative flutters to break free resulted from a need to connect with another human being. To give and receive a touch against warm flesh. Drew thought back to the women he'd arranged coffee dates with not even an hour ago, and forced himself to feel excited at the prospect of meeting new people and a possible fresh start to his life. It didn't help that the person he most wanted to spend his time with stood in front of him with a heart as impermeable as a granite-faced mountainside.

He stepped back now, relinquishing the space to Ash. The tension broke between them. "I'd like to still talk to Stevie. Maybe if he could meet Keith with Jordan and me there, he'd feel less scared."

Ash shrugged. "I guess it's worth a shot."

Drew nodded; his gaze now instinctively drawn to

Ash's arms. When he looked up again, the cool indifference on Ash's face hit him like a physical slap. Would he ever figure out this man? As he moved past Ash into the office, he couldn't help but murmur, "What you started that night isn't over between us."

A harsh hand came down on his shoulder. When Drew turned his head, he scarcely recognized Ash and the bitter smile distorting his face. "It is, because I said it is."

Drew pulled away and put aside his anger at Ash's stubbornness. He chose instead to focus on the immediate problem at hand, Stevie. The boy sat back in his chair, his long hair tucked behind his ears, exposing the pale white curve of his throat, a faded bruise running down its length.

"Hey, Stevie, how's it going?" Drew kept his voice light and easygoing, hoping not to startle the youth.

Stevie opened his eyes and gave a tentative smile. "Hi, Dr. Drew. I'm okay. Really. Ash is making a big deal out of nothin'. Honest."

Ash made a move as if he was going to speak, but Drew put up a hand, forestalling him. "I'm glad to hear you're feeling better, but I want to talk to you for a few minutes, okay?"

Stevie's brown eyes turned dark and wary. "Um, well, I guess, but—"

"I know the whole story, so you don't have to worry about hiding stuff from me. You know Dr. Jordan's partner, Keith, is a police detective, right?"

Stevie swallowed and nodded, eyes huge in his pale

face.

"Well, what would you say if we all had a talk, you, me, Dr. Jordan, and Keith? You could maybe let Keith know, and he could help somehow."

Stevie bolted upright in the chair. "No. I can't. They'd kill me if I ever went to the cops. They told me."

"Calm down, kiddo. You know bullies say that to frighten people they think are weaker than them." Drew knelt next to Stevie's chair. "You're stronger because you came here to try and find a way out, and we are going to help you. I think once they see you're serious, they'll back off and stop hurting you."

Stevie's wide-eyed gaze searched his face. "Do you really think so?" He turned his head to the doorway, where Ash still stood. "Do you think so too, Ash?"

The reply was immediate. "Yes, I do."

Drew exhaled. At least Ash didn't allow his personal feelings to overrule what he knew was best for Stevie. After hearing of the beatings the boy endured, Drew knew it might only be a matter of time before those bastards would take it a step too far.

Stevie's face screwed up as if he was in physical pain. Drew noticed him rubbing his side, obviously in discomfort from his bruised ribs. "Hey, buddy, how about right now? You call your foster mom and tell her you're at a school thing, and we can all go to my house and you can talk to Keith. Right, Ash?" He knew enlisting Ash's help was the key to Stevie's participation.

"Yes. I'll be right here with you when you make the call. Will that help?" Ash walked over to Stevie and laid his hand on the boy's shoulder. Drew watched as a look passed between the two of them. This case went well beyond work for Ash.

It came to Drew then that Stevie was Ash's gateway to self-forgiveness. In Stevie, he could right the wrong he thought he'd made by leaving his foster brothers behind.

Oh, Ash. Forgive yourself already. What happened years ago wasn't your fault.

To his great surprise, Stevie picked up the phone and, with Ash's hand still on his shoulder still, made the call home. White-knuckled, his hands shook as he spoke to his foster mother, who allowed him to stay. The boy hung up the phone and wiped the sweat off his forehead. "She was so happy I was getting involved in school. I feel really bad lying to her." He clutched at Drew's knee. "They aren't gonna get in trouble, right? They don't know anything. I never told them about what Jimmy and Donny do to me."

Drew stood, deliberately not answering him. "Why don't we grab some food and head on over to my place. I'll call Jordan and have him and Keith come over. Sound good?"

"You aren't answering me." Stevie's spurt of defiance surprised Drew. "If you tell the cops and they get in trouble, I swear I'll lie and say nothing happened and you made the story up. Mr. and Mrs. Harding are really nice to me. Promise you won't say nothing."

"Stevie—"

"Promise me or I'll run away, and you'll never see me again."

Ash's hand fell on Drew's shoulder and squeezed it. Hard. "We promise, Stevie. But that doesn't mean we won't watch out for you and keep our eyes out for any trouble. Right?"

"It'll be okay, right, Dr. Drew?" Stevie's worried eyes held his.

Like quicksilver, a smile came and went on Drew's lips. "Of course."

Ash dipped his head in acknowledgment as if to concede that Drew won this round.

They left the office and decided on Chinese take-out, then headed to Drew's apartment. Not five minutes after they'd arrived, Jordan and Keith showed up. Stevie lay stretched out on the sofa, Domino curled up in his lap.

Drew dished up Keith's chicken with broccoli, and Domino jumped off Stevie's lap to stalk over to Keith, tail held high, yellow eyes wide and bright.

"Not on your life, big boy. You're too fat." Keith stared the cat down.

The cat's tail swished back and forth on the floor.

"Don't be rude, Keith. He's a growing boy." Drew held out a piece of steamed chicken to the cat, who took it in his mouth and left the room, tail once again held high like a triumphant banner.

The blond, blue-eyed police officer snorted, and Jordan poked him in the ribs. "You're insulting Drew's baby."

Keith finished chewing, then put his plate on the coffee table and turned his attention to Stevie. "So from what I've been told, there're these kids in the neighborhood bullying you and they have been for a while, right?"

Stevie nodded. "Um, kind of." His voice, little more than a whisper, crackled in the silent room.

Keith gritted his teeth, the muscle in his jaw flexing beneath his skin. "These boys are assaulting you, Stevie. You can't let them get away with it." He left his seat and sat on the floor next to Stevie. "I have to report this to child services, son. But I give you my word, you'll be safe."

Stevie winced as he sat up on the sofa, a cushion propped behind his back. "Dr. Drew promised to leave my parents out of it. 'Cause if you do, I won't stay around."

Before Keith had a chance to answer, Ash spoke. "You can come live with me. I'll make sure you're safe."

Drew held his breath. Was Ash getting in too deep? It was never a good thing to become so personally involved with your cases, but by the determined set of his jaw, Drew knew no one would be able to talk Ash out of it. Besides, weren't they all in a little deeper than they should be?

Keith shook his head. "That won't work, Ash, but thanks for offering. I have some friends at child services. I'll talk to the social workers first." He patted Stevie on his knee. "Don't worry, buddy. We're going to do this right so you'll end up safe, and your parents won't get in trouble."

He returned to sit next to Jordan, who put an arm around him and gave him a kiss on the cheek. "Thanks, babe."

Drew watched their interaction, not without a twinge of envy. They were so perfect together. As corny as it might sound, Drew had known from the moment he introduced Jordan to Keith that they would fall in love. They complemented each other, no matter that their personalities were so different. Keith tempered Jordan's type A, perfectionist behavior. Keith never raised his voice, never got mad when Jordan occasionally lapsed into rudeness or made snide comments. A simple raised brow and a, "Really, babe that was uncalled for," quickly had Jordan issuing an apology for his behavior.

They all gathered up their plates and dumped them in the garbage, signaling they'd finished what they could, at least for tonight.

Keith, car keys in hand, knelt next to Stevie on the sofa.

"Think about what we talked about and I'll be in touch with you either way in the next few days."

"Okay, I promise."

Drew let them out, then returned to Stevie.

"Keith will make sure it'll work out, and Ash will keep you safe." Drew ruffled the Stevie's hair. "He's a great guy, huh?"

With a face full of hero worship, Stevie sat up and

turned to Ash. "You're the best. I only wish it would all happen like Keith says."

Drew held Ash's gaze. "When Keith makes a promise, he keeps it. Don't worry, Stevie; it'll all be over soon." They left, Ash not saying another word, his hand remaining on Stevie's shoulder in a protective clasp.

Drew cleaned up and remembered he had sent out invitations to the women from the dating website and when he checked his e-mail, he found that three of the seven had already accepted. That thought brought him no joy or excitement as it once might have.

Somehow the clinic had become his reality; but without any human comfort he'd go mad from loneliness and heartache. So whether or not he was excited about meeting these women, he'd do what he must to start to feel alive again.

Chapter Seventeen

"WHERE THE HECK do you put it, kiddo?" Ash couldn't help but laugh as Stevie came back with a second burrito, a bag of chips, and guacamole.

Instead of apologizing as he might have when they first met, Stevie grinned and peeled back the foil wrapping. "Hey, I'm a growing boy, like Dr. Drew's cat." He took a big messy bite and chewed away as he rummaged around in the bag for a handful of chips.

Regret burned through Ash at the mention of Drew's name, leaving a scorched, bitter path in its wake. That night they had together all those weeks ago seemed almost dreamlike, and as the brightness of the memory turned hazy with the passage of time, he wondered if the intense emotions of the night were as real as he recalled.

Better that they moved on with their separate lives. He leaned back in the chair, enjoying the sight of Stevie demolishing his Mexican food. After that talk with Keith, Stevie started working at the clinic, helping Javier at the front desk. He'd gained confidence and even admitted to Ash he had a little bit of a crush on the older boy. Ash knew Keith had tried to find the kids who bullied Stevie to scare some sense into them, but he no longer felt comfortable enough with Drew to ask if there'd been any progress made.

Luckily, Stevie seemed more at ease. He'd begun to gain weight and grow, although Ash suspected it was meals like these and the ones Drew's grandmother provided him at the clinic that contributed to his healthier look. "So, you're going into junior year of high school. Have you thought about what you want to do after you graduate, like college?"

Stevie chewed and swallowed. "I talked to Dr. Drew, and he said he'd help me with tests and my applications and stuff. I know I'm not smart enough to be a doctor, but I thought I could maybe be a technician or something."

"You can be anything you want to be. Remember that." Ash leaned forward, elbows on the table.

"Well, yeah, but my grades aren't so good. But I wanna help the doctors, you know?"

The excitement in Stevie's eyes warmed Ash's heart. To think that only two months ago he'd been a scared, shy child, afraid to look people in the eye or express an opinion. Now his confidence, while not at its peak, had certainly soared to heights never before imagined.

"Take your time, and when you get ready to apply, we'll all be here to help." Ash checked his watch and asked in what he hoped sounded like a casual voice, "You've gotten to be very friendly with Dr. Drew, haven't you?"

Stevie's eyes lit up. "Yeah, he's really nice and friendly. Did you know he has a girlfriend? I met her when he invited me to his apartment. She came over, and we played with his cat."

The taco chip he'd been holding crumbled to bits between Ash's fingers. "No, I didn't know. What's her name?"

"Um, Shelly. She seemed nice. And she's pretty." He grinned. "I think she really likes him. She kept standing close to him and touching his shoulder." He made a face. "I even caught them kissing once."

Another good thing in his life he'd fucked up. What did he expect? Drew wasn't going to remain celibate forever, and his divorce would be final soon. Obviously he'd decided to move on and found a perfectly nice woman, like he should. The pain lancing through him made it impossible to breathe. "What time do you have to be home? It's almost five o'clock." He barely managed to choke out the words.

Stevie gulped down his soda, then wiped his mouth. "Yeah, I'd better get back now, or I'll be late for dinner." He stopped and stared. "You okay? You look kinda funny."

"I'm fine. Come on." Ash stood and took Stevie's tray to the front of the restaurant as they walked outside. "I'll drive you home." He draped his arm around the boy's shoulders.

"Do you think you should?" For the first time, Stevie sounded uncertain. "I don't want those guys to see me drive up in your car."

"Don't worry; I won't drop you off right in front of the house." He took the keys from his pants pocket and disabled the alarm. "Hop in."

With a grin, Stevie slid into the front seat. "This is such a cool car." His hands smoothed over the leather seat. "It must cost a ton."

"You know, Stevie, remember I started off like you, no family, gay, and abused. But I knew if I wanted to get out, I had to get an education and make something out of myself." Ash drove toward Red Hook, where Stevie lived.

"But I'm not smart like you or Dr. Drew." Stevie stared out of the window. "I can't be a lawyer or doctor."

"You do your best and be whatever you can be, only be the best at it, and help people along the way. Paying it forward is the best thing you can do." Ash turned down Van Brunt St. and pulled into a space about a block away from Stevie's house. "They've been leaving you alone lately, haven't they? You haven't complained or shown up hurt."

Stevie didn't answer for a few moments, fidgeting instead with the seat belt. "They have, but I don't know." He shrugged his thin shoulders with the bravado of the very young and spoke with surprising strength. "Something's off with them, but as long as they leave me alone, I don't care." After unbuckling his seat belt, he gave Ash a shy smile. "Thanks for the ride."

"No problem." After Stevie got out of the car and came on to the sidewalk by the driver's side window, Ash continued to speak. "I'll see you tomorrow, right?"

Before Stevie could answer, a yell echoed from down the block. "Yo, shrimp."

Stevie paled. "Oh shit, no."

From the description Stevie had given him, Ash knew right away these were the boys Stevie told him about, Jimmy and Donny. He got out of the car and leaned against the hood, arms folded across his chest. The two young men swaggered over wearing tight muscle T-shirts and baggy cargo shorts. Ash pegged the one with the cruel face, hair buzzed short over a bullet-shaped head, and sneering expression as Jimmy. The other one, Donny, he presumed, danced on the balls of his feet, his face covered in stubble and a mistrustful look in his eyes.

"Shrimpy, who's the dude?" Jimmy's eyes brightened with an evil light. "He must be a rich man with that car. Is he your sugar daddy? You fucking him?"

A sickening feeling crept through Ash. This could go very wrong, very fast if it wasn't handled carefully. "Hey, guys, I'm a friend of Steve's. I gave him a ride home from work."

Jimmy eyed him with undisguised hostility. "Yeah? What's he do for you? Ride your dick?" He laughed at his own joke and high-fived Donny.

Ash's lips tightened. "Steve helps out the doctors in the clinic. I know he's told you. He's a very valuable member of our staff." Shit, he'd love to punch these two punks in their leering faces.

"Yeah, he's told us. We're sick of hearin' about Dr. Drew this and Dr. Jordan that. Bunch o' fuckin' pussies, all of you." Jimmy cracked his knuckles. "Comin' around here in your rich-ass car showin' off to everyone, thinkin' you're better than us." He walked away, Donny following him, then called over his shoulder. "Better kiss him good-bye and go home, Stevie boy. Don't wanna make everyone mad." Then he kept walking. Donny hurried to keep up with Jimmy's long strides, shooting uncertain looks over his shoulder.

"Shit, are you going to be all right tonight?" Ash raked his hand through his hair, frustration tightening his voice. "Text me later and let me know if everything's fine."

"I will." Stevie hefted the backpack he always carried with him onto his back. "Thanks for the snack and everything. I gotta go."

"Bye, kiddo." Ash watched him hurry up the block to his house. After he disappeared around the corner, Ash shook his head, returned to his car and drove off, back home to his Park Avenue apartment, a million miles away.

The phone rang, and he pressed the button. "Davis here."

"Mr. Davis, this is Martinson. I have some more news."

Good thing he was at a light; otherwise he might've rear-ended the car in front of him. "Go on, tell me."

Martinson cleared his throat. "I found him, sir. Mr. Luke Conover lives in an apartment in Chelsea. He changed his name legally from Carini five years ago. For the past two years he's worked for the investment firm of Lambert and North as a financial consultant. He's single and has no children. The people at his firm speak very highly of him, but they all say he's quiet and doesn't socialize much. He doesn't drink, smoke, or do drugs and has never been arrested."

Ash let out a long stream of breath. *I didn't think you existed, but thank you, God.* Un-fucking-real. All these years Luke had lived here, in the same city, and he didn't know it. "Do you have an address for him?"

Through the phone, the pages of a notebook crack-led. "It's 1655 West 19th St., Apartment 4C."

Glancing at the dashboard clock, Ash saw it was after six o'clock. Still early to be home, but he'd take a chance. If he had to camp outside all night, he was going to see Luke. "Thank you, Martinson. Excellent work. Any news of Brandon?"

"No, sir. But now that I've located Mr. Conover, I can concentrate my attention on his case. I presume that is what you want."

"Absolutely. Keep me posted. And thank you, again." Ash clicked off and headed over the Brooklyn Bridge. Traffic was heavy, but he made it down Chambers St. to the West Side Highway. By the time he reached the exit by Chelsea Piers, it was almost six forty. Nothing like rush hour in the city to eat away valuable time. Ash maneuvered through the maze of downtown streets and soon found himself on West 19th St.

He pulled into a parking lot and walked toward Ninth Avenue. There were some new high-rises and lovely brownstones in this neighborhood. Obviously, Luke had done well to be able to afford to live here. His heartbeat quickened as he spotted the glass-and-steel high-rise where Luke lived.

Pulse racing, he could hardly contain his excitement as he approached the concierge desk. "I'm here to see Mr. Conover. Is he home?"

The concierge, an older gray-haired man, barely looked up from the desk. "I'm sorry, sir. Mr. Conover is away on business. He isn't expected back for several weeks."

Joy faded, replaced by the pain of disappointment. "I see. Thank you very much."

"You're welcome, sir. Have a good evening."

His steps dragging, Ash returned to his car. Now that he knew where Luke was, he wanted to swing from the trees and yell from the rooftops. A sobering thought hit him as he started the car. *What if Luke doesn't want to see me?*

TWO WEEKS PASSED and Ash returned once again to Luke's building, only to be met with the same response. Mr. Conover was still out of town, and they had no firm date for his return. His phone vibrated in his suit pocket, and when he saw several missed calls from Drew, he grew alarmed.

"What's the matter?" Aside from hurried hellos and good-byes in the clinic, he and Drew had barely spoken to one another in the past month. Ash had caught a glimpse of Drew's girlfriend when she stopped by the clinic one evening to meet him for a date. Small, with long dark hair and big brown eyes, she gazed at Drew as if the sun rose and set on his every word. Everyone in the clinic except him had met her earlier, but he had no desire to sit and watch her put her hands and lips all over the man he couldn't stop thinking about.

He remembered all too well what Drew felt and tasted like.

"It's Stevie. I've called Keith and Jordan. Can you come over to my apartment?" Drew's tense voice sent a chord of anxiety thrumming through him.

"I'm in the city. It'll take me a while to get back to Brooklyn."

"Get here as fast as you can."

Drew's terse voice had him speeding through yellow lights. He took the Battery Tunnel back into Brooklyn since it was less crowded, and within twenty minutes, he pulled up in front of Drew's apartment building. He recognized Jordan's car as he ran across the street and up the front steps. Someone buzzed him in right away, and he pounded up the stairs. Jordan held the door open for him.

"It's bad." Jordan's tone was grim. "Luckily nothing was broken, but he's scared to death." He pointed to the living room. "Drew has him lying down on the sofa."

Ash barely heard him as he hurried past. His gaze fell on Stevie's huddled body on the couch, his face hidden from sight. Drew's cat lay curled up next to him, his large furry body pressed against the boy as if to give him strength.

"Hey, kiddo. What's going on?" He knelt beside him and touched Stevie's hand. The boy shuddered, then spoke, his voice muffled as his lips were buried in the crook of his arm.

"Ash? Is that you?"

Tears stung his eyes. "Yeah, it's me. Come on, talk to me. I'm not going anywhere." He laid his hand firmly on Stevie's back and rubbed it in a soothing circular motion. "It'll be all right." Behind him he heard Rachel and Mike speaking quietly. The whole protection squad was here to rally around this broken child.

When Stevie picked up his head, Ash's breath caught in his throat. Dark bruises mottled his throat and the top of his chest where his collarbone stuck out. Both eyes had been blackened and his knuckles were scraped raw, as if he'd tried to defend himself.

For a moment everything went black before his eyes. Bile rose in his mouth, and a faint buzzing sounded in his ears. If he didn't get control of himself, he'd pass out. Several deep breaths later, he had it under control. "Who did this to you? Was it Jimmy and Donny?"

Stevie shook his head. "No. I was jumped by some random kids. I swear."

But Ash had seen the flicker in Stevie's eyes and suspected he wasn't telling the truth.

"Did they hurt you any other place, Stevie?" Ash held the boy's gaze, searching his eyes for the truth. But Stevie wouldn't look him in the eye when he answered.

"No, I'm really fine. I don't know why I came here." He shifted on the couch and sat up, wincing a little at the movement.

Ash spoke over his shoulder. "Jordan, you checked him out already?"

"Yeah. No broken bones. The nose will be swollen for a while and turn all sorts of amazing colors."

Mike stepped up next to Ash. "Hey, buddy boy. Can I check your mouth?" At Stevie's nod, he manipulated his jaw and checked his teeth. After he was finished, he stood back, hands on his hips.

"Hmm. I'd like you to come in for some X-rays tomorrow. I need to check to make sure your teeth are secure. Okay?"

Stevie nodded. He pulled on Ash's shirtsleeve. "Can I talk to you and Dr. Drew?"

"Sure, kiddo." He got to his feet and approached Drew, who was in the center of the group. And there stood his girlfriend, in the middle of telling Rachel how Stevie had shown up at the apartment while they were eating dinner. Never one to care about what people thought of him, Ash interrupted her.

"Drew, Stevie wants to talk to us."

The conversation halted in midsentence. Drew left the circle and came over to him. "Did he talk to you? He said he tried calling your cell phone but couldn't get in touch with you."

Guilt squeezed in his chest. Right, he'd been busy stalking Luke's apartment building. Helping no one and failing everyone again.

"Hi, I'm Shelly, Drew's girlfriend." Her smile faded when he failed to return it with one of his own.

"I'm not here to make friends, sweetheart. This isn't a dinner party." It didn't bother him in the least to see her face flame with embarrassment and her big brown eyes fill with tears.

"Don't be such a prick, Ash." Drew kissed Shelly's cheek and murmured something in her ear. She shot Ash an unreadable look, then returned to the others.

"Was that really necessary? She didn't mean any harm." Drew's exasperated tone bugged the shit out of him.

"Yes, it was. I'm not going to be her friend. I'm here for Stevie." Ash glared at him. "I never would've come back here if it wasn't for him. Christ, Drew, I'm barely your friend anymore."

"Whose fault is that, you bastard? You walked out on me," Drew shot back, obviously a little louder than intended as the room quieted around them.

Ash cocked his brow. "Are we done? I want to talk to Stevie and go home."

Drew, pale and scowling, brushed by him to sit with Stevie on the couch. "What's up, buddy? Are you gonna let Keith arrest those two now?"

Alarm flared in Stevie's eyes. "No. It wasn't them. I swear. Don't do anything, please, Dr. Drew."

Ash knew child services had again been to the house at Keith's urging. Nothing untoward had been found. The home was neat, there was food in the refrigerator, and the fact that Stevie was doing much better in school as well as holding down an after-school job lent credence to his foster mother's claim that everything was going well. There had never been any reports of abuse from either the school or the neighbors. In other words, as of now, there was no reason to remove Stevie from the home. Drew held the young boy close. "Please tell us the truth, Stevie."

"I am. I swear. I was jumped coming home from the bus stop."

Putting on a smile for Stevie, Ash replied, "How about you spend the night at my house tonight? Call home and tell them you're with a friend from school." He put his arm around Stevie. "You'll have to tell them the truth tomorrow when you get home with all those bruises on your face."

"Okay. I'll tell them the truth. That I was beaten up coming home from school and I spoke to the police."

Maybe his story was true. Ash knew the neighborhood was a dangerous one, and for a slight boy like Stevie, it made him an all too easy target.

He made the call to his foster parents and after saying his good-byes, they left together.

Ash didn't say good-bye to Drew, as his little girlfriend had plastered herself to his side. But when he glanced up at the window of the apartment after he shut the car door on Stevie's side, he saw a figure, silhouetted in the lamplight. Though shrouded in shadows, Ash knew it was Drew. Like a sixth sense, he always knew where Drew was when they were together.

He got in the car and drove away.

Chapter Eighteen

HE'D MISSED HIS usual Sunday dinner with his grandmother, as Shelly had gotten tickets to a ball game, so Drew's visit had to wait for Monday night. It had been the source of his and Shelly's first argument last week when she surprised him with the tickets.

"I told you not to make plans for me, Shel, especially on a Sunday." He'd never raised his voice to her before, but she had to understand his priorities. "Sundays I visit my grandmother. She always comes first."

First all he heard was sniffling, then, when he glanced over at her, tears were rolling down her face. "I'm sorry, Drew. I know how much you wanted to see the game." She hung her head. "I wanted to do something nice for you."

Guilt sliced through him like a hot knife through butter. Shit. Once again, he was the bad one. "C'mere." He held out his arms, and she threw herself into his chest. "It's okay this time but please don't do it again."

All this ran through his mind as he parked his car in front of his grandmother's house, noting that her grass had been freshly cut. That was nice of Mike. He knew his friend and Rachel had been over yesterday.

After he rang the bell, he heard her steps tapping on the hardwood floor and the rattle of the inner door being unlocked. A wonderful smell of baked cookies greeted him as she opened the front door.

"Come in, sweetheart." She gave him a kiss, and he hugged her. "I made your favorite. Chocolate chip." She looked behind him. "The girlfriend isn't with you?"

"She had to work late. I'm happy it's the two of us." He reached the kitchen and lowered himself with a contented sigh onto one of the wooden chairs, covered in a flowered cushion. A platter of cookies sat on the table, as well as coffee mugs, milk, and sugar. The cookies were the way he liked them, soft in the center and a little crisp on the edge with lots of big chunks of chocolate.

Biting into one, he moaned his pleasure. "Nana, no one makes these better than you."

She didn't answer him, and he opened his eyes. "What's wrong? You're looking at me strangely."

"What's really the story with you and this girl?" She stirred her coffee and took a sip, then put the cup down as if she wasn't really interested in it. "Tell me the truth."

He took a mouthful of the strong and bracing coffee. Leave it to his grandmother to cut straight to the chase. "There's no story. We're dating. We have fun together."

After studying his face for a moment, she shook her head. "You don't love her." Not a question, merely a statement of fact.

Horrified, he choked on his cookie. It took two large swallows of coffee before he could speak again. "Love? Of course not. We've only been dating a month or so."

With a fond smile, his grandmother shook her head. "How long you know the person doesn't matter when you're in love. It could happen the first time you see them. But when you're apart, the time stands still until the person you want to be with is with you again." She took his hand. "You don't feel that way about her, do you?"

With a heavy sigh, he shook his head. "I'm not going to either. I shouldn't lead her on like this."

Nana patted his hand. "She was in love with you from the first. I could tell the moment I laid eyes on her. She didn't know you, but she loved you."

Reflecting on what she said, Drew knew it was true. Shelly was so much more into the relationship than him. She was the one forever planning and setting up their dates. He didn't miss her when she wasn't there. In fact, he could go a whole day without hearing from her, and he wouldn't think twice about it. He sipped his coffee more slowly now, savoring its heat.

"What does Asher think of her? I couldn't get a straight answer from him yesterday."

He choked again, this time sputtering coffee on the table. "Sorry, Nana." He wiped up the drops with his napkin. "Ash? Here yesterday?" The thought made him dizzy, as did all his thoughts about that infuriating man.

"Yes. He comes by at least once a week. We have lovely visits." Her eyes glimmered. "That boy is very special to me."

"Was he the one who mowed your lawn?"

"No. Some young boys came by and offered to mow the lawn and trim the hedges. Why not? Usually one of you boys do it, but you shouldn't waste your visits doing yard work."

His mind still couldn't wrap around the fact that Ash came by to see his grandmother even though they weren't really friends anymore.

Still, curiosity gnawed at him. "What did he say about Shelly?"

"Who?" She gave him a questioning look. "Asher?"

At his nod, she gazed out of the window for a moment. "What really happened between you and him that you don't talk anymore?"

Drew swallowed. Leave it to his grandmother to answer a question with one of her own. How could he tell her the truth? Her bright blue eyes stared back at him, unwavering and full of love.

"We became too close too fast, and it got a little overwhelming. Ash won't trust anyone, and I can't have a friend who doesn't believe in me."

"Sometimes you need to give people a little time to learn how to trust. Especially when they have been hurt so badly." Nana took his cup to the sink to rinse out the cold dregs, then brought him a fresh hot cup. "Asher does care about you; he's not sure how to show it."

The bittersweet memory of Ash's mouth on his cock, that wicked flickering tongue sliding down his hard length, confused him as always. The sharp pain of hurt, of a friendship gone as quickly as it arose, mixed together with his never before dreamed of desire for a man. "Nana. Trust me when I say he knows how to show it. He cares for Stevie, the young man in the clinic we're all trying to help. I didn't give up on Ash; he gave up on me, on our friendship."

He stood and took both their now empty coffee cups to the sink. "Why don't you let me take you out for dinner?" At her hesitation, Drew sat next to her and hugged her.

"Come on. I'll buy you a nice corned beef sandwich and a big pickle."

She sniffed, but her eyes twinkled. "You think you know me so well." As they passed through the front door and he locked it for her, she said, "I may get pastrami this time."

He grinned and took her hand as they walked to his car.

AT 7PM ON Thursday night, he and Shelly sat in the coffee shop around the corner from his apartment in Brooklyn Heights. He'd wanted to meet in his apartment, but she couldn't stay long so they were having a quick date.

Every day this past week he'd planned on calling her, to set up a time to get together and have a talk. The talk that would more than likely end their relationship. Without a doubt he couldn't continue to see her; he didn't feel right leading her on, letting her believe they had a relationship when he knew he'd never fall in love with her. Hell, he thought she'd get the hint when he told her it was too soon for them to have sex.

They'd sat at the table for only a moment when his phone rang. He looked at the screen but, not recognizing the number, didn't bother to answer it. The coolness of the iced latte quenched the dryness in his throat. Ever since his conversation with his grandmother, guilt ate away at him. He knew he should break it off with Shelly, but something always managed to prevent them from having "that talk."

Drew sipped his coffee. "How's your week going? You've been busy, huh?" An incoming text buzzed, but he ignored it as well. Why couldn't people leave him alone? "You're looking tired."

As a menswear buyer for one of the major department stores, Shelly had explained to him how she was responsible for what clothing he saw in the stores. It was all Greek to him, since he cared very little about fashion.

She nodded. "They're running us ragged planning the Christmas season sales already. I have to work late all this weekend, so we won't really get a chance to see each other."

"That's okay. You have to do what's best for work."

She shot him a strange look but didn't say anything and drank her coffee.

His phone rang again, this time with Rachel's familiar tune. "I'm sorry, Shelly. I have to take this. It's Rachel.

"Hey, wh—"

"Drew, where are you? Why aren't you answering your phone?" Her voice, normally so cheerful, sounded strained and on the verge of tears.

"What's wrong?" His heart bottomed down to his stomach.

"It's Nana. She's in the hospital." In the background he heard Mike's voice; then his friend came on the phone.

"Drew. Get over to Methodist Hospital right now. We're in emergency."

He shoved the phone in his pocket and stood so abruptly his chair overturned. Shelly's alarmed voice seemed to come from a great distance.

"What's wrong?"

"It's my grandmother." *Please, please don't let anything happen to her.* "She's in the hospital. I have to go." He took off, not paying attention if she followed him or not. But she was there as he raced to his car and flung the door open. Without a word, she jumped in the front seat next to him and they took off.

Fortunately the hospital was less than ten minutes

away. He parked in the doctors' parking lot, threw his parking permit on the windshield, and jumped out of the car. Drew found the emergency room its usual chaotic morass of patients waiting to be seen, plus EMS personnel, doctors, nurses, and technicians. Within moments he spotted Rachel and Mike.

"What happened?"

Rachel flung herself into his arms, sobbing. "I don't know. It's her heart, they said. I called and called her house, but no one answered, so I called Mrs. Delaney. She went over, and the front door was wide open. She called the police, then me."

Mike picked up the story as Drew continued to hold Rachel. "Keith was in Brooklyn investigating a case and said he tried to get you when he heard the call come in. He recognized your grandmother's address."

"I wasn't picking up my phone. Shit." He swore so loud, several people across the room stopped talking and stared. He didn't give a damn. "Let me see what I can find out."

He left Shelly with them and entered the emergency room triage area. They recognized him, as he had admitting privileges in the hospital, and one of the nurses pointed him to the curtained-off area where they said his grandmother was. There were several doctors there already, and he approached the one he recognized.

"Rob, what can you tell me?" Dr. Robert Porter was a cardiologist and one of the best. Drew's heart rate steadied, knowing his grandmother was getting the finest care she possibly could. "She's my grandmother."

Rob's eyes widened, then softened with concern. "Her heartbeat is irregular. We need to keep watch on her. I'm moving her to ICU now." He gave orders to the two doctors standing next to him, handing the chart to the closest one. Taking Drew's arm, he led them away, back toward Rachel. "They came in with her, so I'm presuming one or both are relatives?"

"It's my sister and her boyfriend." Shelly stood there as well, but he couldn't be bothered to introduce her right now.

As Rob explained to them about the problem with her heart, Jordan and Keith showed up, concern etched on their faces. Keith came straight to him and hugged him hard. "I tried to call you, man, but you didn't pick up."

"It doesn't matter. Let's go. They're transferring her to ICU. It's on the fifth floor." Like the Pied Piper, he led the line of family and friends to the elevators. They crowded in together, and he was surprised to see Shelly still there.

"I thought you had to go back to work, Shel."

Her big brown eyes stared back at him, incredulous. "Drew, I called and said I couldn't come in because of your grandmother. Did you expect me to leave you?"

Mercifully, the doors opened so he didn't have to answer as Rachel took his hand. They approached the ICU and saw their grandmother's suddenly frail-looking body in the bed, surrounded by tubes and beeping machines.

"Oh, Drew." Rachel buried her head in his shoulder. "Please tell me she'll be all right."

He didn't answer as Rob opened the door and beckoned him inside. Mike took Rachel from his arms and held her close. The door closed behind him.

"How is she really? Tell me the truth." Drew stood by her bedside, watching the faint rise and fall of her chest. "I feel so fucking helpless."

"We're monitoring her carefully. Her heartbeat seems to have stabilized for now." Rob's lips quirked in a faint smile. "She's tough and a fighter. That's in her favor."

"So she'll be all right?" As a doctor he knew it wasn't a question he should ask, but now he was merely a family member of a patient, grasping for answers.

"Let's say I'm cautiously optimistic." Rob patted his shoulder as he walked by him. "Only one visitor at a time, even for a doctor's family."

Drew barely heard him as he stood next to his grandmother. "Nana. It's me, Drew. You're going to be fine."

But she didn't waken. He kissed her on her cheek, and he smelled her familiar scent of rose water. For some reason that comforted him. "Rachel's outside with Mike. Jordy and Keith too. All your boys. You didn't have to go to this extreme to get us all together, Nana." The tightness in his throat made it almost impossible to speak. Or breathe.

"I'll let Rachel come in to say hi to you." He kissed

her again and left the room. Rachel ran over to him.

"How is she? Did she wake up yet?" The rest of his friends crowded around him.

"No, but she's stabilized. You can go in, Rachel." The stress of the night caught up with him, and he leaned against the wall and closed his eyes. How could this have happened? His grandmother's blood pressure was normal. He knew because he checked it regularly.

"Drew."

His eyes remained closed. Why now, of all times, did he hear Ash's voice? He'd hardly spoken more than a dozen words to him lately.

"Drew." The voice became more insistent. He opened his eyes to Ash standing behind everyone.

"Ash."

Without a second thought he rushed into his arms and held on for dear life. Without shame the tears flowed, wetting the fine linen of the shirt beneath his cheek. Ash's strong, broad arms held him tight; his quiet voice murmured soft words in his ear.

"It'll be okay, baby. Don't worry. She's a strong lady." Ash's fingers slipped through Drew's hair. All Drew needed was Ash holding him tight against the hard planes of his chest. A deep sigh shuddered through Drew as his body and Ash's settled and fit together, like two long-lost puzzle pieces, finally found.

The heated scent of Ash's skin, almost forgotten, yet instinctively familiar to Drew assailed his senses, returning him to that long-ago night of dreamy desire. He needed no one else; only Ash.

"Drew?" From somewhere in the background of his mind, a voice pricked his conscience. "What's going on?"

Ash's hands dropped from his body. Almost immediately he missed the all-encompassing warmth and security. His lips moved against Ash's shoulder. "Make them go away."

"Drew." The voice grew more insistent.

"I think you should talk to her."

"Don't leave, though." He clutched at Ash's shirt, wrinkling the fabric beneath his desperate fingers. "Promise you won't leave?"

Ash's mouth whispered against his ear, speaking words only meant for him to hear. "Shhh. I won't, baby. I'll stay as long as you need me to."

Drew closed his eyes, swiping his fingers over his wet cheeks and damp lashes. When he turned around, Shelly stood there, her eyes wide with shock. Damn, he'd forgotten all about her.

"Shelly, we need to talk."

Chapter Nineteen

ASH WATCHED AS Drew walked his girlfriend around the corner to the lounge area. He hated hospitals and hadn't been in one since Mr. Frank died. That sickly sweet smell of chemicals, mixed with the pungent odor of antiseptic made his skin crawl.

But when he heard what had happened to Esther, he'd almost lost control right in his office. My God, that woman was as dear to him as actual family. And, right now, when Drew said he needed him, that settled the matter. At a touch to his shoulder he started. Jordan stood next to him, a curious look on his face.

"What are you doing here? I didn't think you and Drew were even friends anymore."

Neither did he, yet when Rachel called to tell him about Esther there wasn't a moment's hesitation as to where he had to be. And for whom. The time had come to put aside all the petty bullshit of the past few months. Life crises usually brought people together, and this time Ash might stay and fight for the man he couldn't get out of his head and his heart.

"Things have a way of coming into perspective when you're faced with an emergency. Rachel called me, and here I am." What he really wanted to do was tell Jordan to fuck off, but out of respect for Esther, he'd hold his temper.

"Don't mess with him, not when he's so vulnerable."

Ash's lip curled in a sneer; the thought of Jordan scaring him away from here was almost ludicrous.

"Listen to me carefully, Jordan, since I'm only going to say this once to you. I am not your friend. I don't give a shit what you think. I'm here for Drew. If you can't deal with it, not my problem, buddy boy. Now go back to your boyfriend and leave me the hell alone." Without waiting for an answer, he stormed off in the direction he'd seen Drew and his girlfriend walk. Angry voices slowed his footsteps and he stopped dead in his tracks, not wanting to intrude, but when he heard his name mentioned, Ash felt no shame in eavesdropping on their conversation.

"What the hell was that about with Ash? You've barely spoken to that man in months, yet he shows up and you're hugging him like a long-lost brother."

Ash crept up quietly and peeked around the wall. Shelly and Drew stood facing each other, but neither one could see him.

"I don't owe you any explanation. Plus, this isn't the time or place to have this conversation." Ash could tell by Drew's body language that he was holding something back.

"We're a couple. We love each other. How can you say you don't owe me any explanation?" Ash winced at Shelly's strident, desperate tone.

Drew took her hand, a pained expression on his face. "I didn't want to talk here, but you're forcing me to."

For the first time, Ash felt sorry for Shelly. He could tell by the dawning expression of shock on her face that she knew what was coming before Drew even spoke.

"Oh my God, you're breaking up with me, aren't you?" She pulled her hand from Drew's as if it were singed by fire. "But I love you." Tears coursed down her cheeks.

"This all happened too fast. You don't really love me. We barely know each other." He took her hands in his. "It has nothing to do with you, please believe me. You're a great person."

She gave a shaky laugh. "The 'it's not you, it's me' speech, huh?" A shudder rolled through her slight frame. "I think it's more than that."

"What do you mean? I'm not ready for a serious relationship right now." Drew turned away from her to walk over to the window. Ash could see the tension in his back and, strangely enough, itched to hold him.

"You're fooling yourself, and I should've seen it. It's Ash, isn't it?" She joined him at the window, putting her hand on his arm. "I saw it for a moment the first time I met him at your apartment, but tonight it was blatantly obvious."

Drew stared at her, his face pale. "What are you saying?"

"When you saw him tonight, you needed him. It showed on your face. You never looked at me the way you looked at him." Her voice caught on the hiccup of a sob. She passed her hand over her eyes, then shook her head. "You've never needed me."

She picked up her purse from the chair and turned to leave. Ash stepped in front of her. "I owe you an apology. I was wrong about you."

For a moment she studied his face. "No, you weren't. If I thought there was a chance, I would fight for him. But I'm not who he wants." She walked away, back straight, head high.

A classy woman.

"Ash." Drew's voice drove all thoughts of Shelly from his mind.

"I'm sorry; I didn't mean to eavesdrop, but I wanted to make sure you were all right." His gaze raked down Drew's body with a hungry intensity. "Was she right? Do you need me?" He advanced on Drew until they stood so close their breaths mingled. The green of Drew's eyes darkened until they turned almost black.

"I think so." Drew tipped his head back to stare at the ceiling, but all Ash could think of was licking his Adam's apple and biting that beautifully pale skin down his neck.

"That's good, because I think I need you too." The words slipped out before he could stop them. Need. He'd never needed anyone. Wanted, yes. Desired, certainly. But need? Staring into Drew's eyes, the decades-old wall Ash had built around himself begin to crumble. Maybe he wasn't such a bad person after all, if someone like Drew could care about him. Maybe Mr. Frank was right.

He took Drew's hand and pressed a quick kiss to his palm. "Let's go back now and see how your grandmother is doing."

Drew held on to his hand for a moment, then squeezed it. "Yes. Then I think we should talk." Their eyes locked, and Ash nodded.

"Agreed."

They returned to the ICU waiting area. Mike had Rachel wrapped in his arms, while Jordan sat talking quietly with Keith. Rachel broke away from Mike's embrace.

"They told us to go home now and come back in the morning. If anything happens, they'll call us immediately." Her gaze returned to the windowed room where Ash saw Esther being attended to by several nurses. "I hate leaving her here all alone, though." Her eyes welled with tears, and her lip quivered.

Drew hugged her. "She's getting the best care possible, and I'm only ten minutes away. We won't be any good to her tomorrow if we can't stay awake because we were up all night watching her sleep."

Rachel nodded. "You're right. Then we should go."

They traipsed to the elevator, and it whisked them down to the main level. The hospital doors opened to the sultry night air, where surprisingly, the avenue still buzzed with activity. Strains of jazz music drifted out of the doorway of the bar across the street, its winking neon lights announcing that twenty different kinds of beer were to be found within. A crowd of rowdy teens spilled onto the sidewalk outside the diner on the corner.

Rachel and Mike hurried away to their car. Jordan looked as though he had something to say, but Keith pulled him away, leaving him and Drew standing on the sidewalk.

"Come on. My car is this way." Drew started walking up the block.

Ash hurried after him, thoughts bumping furiously around in his mind. What next? He'd never had this happen before; sex was always easy to find. This had nothing to do with sex and everything to do with his mind and his heart. *Shit.* He was in way over his head.

They climbed into the car, and Drew began to drive. Ash studied Drew's long-fingered hands on the steering wheel and thought how they would feel wrapped around his cock. He shifted in his seat. "Will you come home with me?" His voice croaked, rusty and dry.

Drew didn't answer. He continued to drive until they pulled up to a familiar street. He parked, then shut off the engine. Ash's breath caught in his throat as they faced each other.

"No, I won't. You're coming home with me." Drew reached across the seat, his hand extended. Without any hesitation, Ash took it and gave a gentle squeeze, then opened his door and got out. Together they walked to Drew's building, neither speaking.

The leafy oak trees on both sides of the street created an arched canopy nearly blocking out the night sky, allowing only mere glimmers of luminous moonlight to filter in between their branches. Ash held back, looking upward toward the darkness.

"It's so peaceful here, so safe. One could almost believe nothing bad happens in the world when you stand here."

Drew touched his shoulder. "Come. Let's go upstairs."

He followed Drew, desire building with every step. By the time they'd reached Drew's door, Ash trembled with restraint. Damn, he couldn't ever remember being this desperate to be with a man. The door opened, and he pushed Drew inside. With a rough intensity that surprised him, he grasped Drew by the shoulders yanking him close, eager to feel his hardness against his own arousal.

"I want you," Ash gasped as he licked and nuzzled Drew's throat. "But you need to tell me."

Drew bucked against Ash, his own hardness evident through his jeans. "Tell you what?"

"That you want me. Tell me you want this, want me in your bed, in your body." Ash bit down on Drew's shoulder while rolling his hips into Drew's groin, and was rewarded with a deep moan.

"God, yes. Fuck it, Ash. I want you so badly it's

killing me. I was dying inside being without you." Drew brushed his lips against Ash's cheek, soft and warm, his breath gusting sweet. "I'm tired of worrying about what everyone thinks I should be. I only know even when I was with Shelly I was still lonely. And all I could think of was you."

Ash could barely recognize his own voice, hoarse from desire and need. "I haven't been with anyone since I met you. No one. I want you so fucking bad, baby, my head is goin' to explode." He pulled Drew against him. "Let's go to the bedroom."

Drew kissed his cheek. "I haven't been with anyone either. I never had sex with Shelly; I couldn't when all I wanted was you."

Arms entwined, they stumbled into the bedroom. Ash pushed Drew onto the bed and caging his legs, pulled off his shirt. Drew's pale skin glowed in the moonlit room. Ash made short work of his own shirt, pants, and boxers, until he stood naked and fully aroused in front of Drew, who stopped undressing to stare.

"I remember in your apartment how you took me in your mouth." Drew's fingers clasped his erection, his eyes bright with desire. "I want to do that for you. Let me feel you, taste you."

Sex had always calmed the empty space inside him, but never for long. Desperation lingered there, a hope and longing that maybe this time he'd be freed from the prison inside his mind. He'd been so alone for so long he'd forgotten what happiness felt like.

Seeing Drew's shining eyes, the longing etched in his face, and knowing he was the reason for it, broke down the final barrier isolating his heart. He joined Drew on the bed, stretching out next to him.

"I don't want to force you; it's your first time."

Drew wrapped his fingers around Ash's cock and rubbed his cheek along the rigid length. "That's why I want to do it. I want it with you." He kissed the tip and Ash bit back a groan. That simple soft touch rendered him weak.

"It could only be you."

When the sweet, wet warmth of Drew's mouth closed over the head of his cock, sliding down, grazing the sensitive underside with his teeth, Ash groaned.

"Fuck, Drew. I'm gonna come in your mouth if you don't stop."

Drew hummed and swirled his tongue all around his shaft, running the tip of his tongue hard along the sensitive underside. While one hand gently pumped him, the other tickled his balls, teasing the sensitive skin.

"I hope you do. I want to taste you."

Mindful that it was Drew's first time, Ash couldn't help but get swept away by the overwhelming sucking sensation of Drew's talented mouth. He tried to show restraint, but his hips began to thrust, forcing his cock farther into Drew's mouth. Without stopping, Drew's tongue traced a teasing, tickling path.

"Baby, be careful; don't wanna hurt you." Ash gritted his teeth. "Fuck me, it feels too good." Drew took him in all the way, and after a few more pumps, Ash's body seized and shuddered as he came hard, crying out in the night.

"Oh God."

Drew swallowed everything Ash gave him and sat back on his heels, lips glistening, eyes wide and dark.

"Was it okay? I didn't really know what to do. I listened to your body. Your skin is very responsive to touch."

Breathing heavily, Ash watched Drew's fingers trail up his body and caught his hand, holding him tight.

"Only your touch. But you didn't need to do that. Tonight I was supposed to take care of you." He kissed the top of Drew's silky head.

Drew burrowed in next to him, burying his face where Ash's neck met his shoulder. The movement of Drew's lips against his skin sent shivers of delight rippling through him. "Who takes care of you? It's time you let someone know you and be there for you."

Emotion threatened to overcome common sense as Ash wanted to say words he'd never before imagined possible. Instead, he rolled on top of Drew, their bare chests rubbing together, creating a delicious friction. The walls came crashing down as he held Drew's face in his hands. "I want to kiss you."

Drew's eyes glimmered and Ash dipped his head. Warm lips met his, their touch soft and gentle, not rough and punishing and Ash's breath caught. The taste of Drew intoxicated and Ash shifted, licking at Drew's mouth, sucking at his lips, all the while holding

Drew's face in his hands as if to prove he wasn't a figment of his imagination. He ached for more, not less of Drew and Ash slanted his mouth across Drew's, hungry, needy desperate. Their tongues met in a slick, heated slide and Ash could have sobbed with the rush of pleasure that drenched him with its sweetness. Denied for so long, Ash's lips throbbed as Drew nipped and nibbled at them.

This exorcism of his sordid past could only be with Drew. He made everything possible. As they learned each other's bodies, tasted one another's lips and breaths, Ash knew no matter how much time would pass, he'd never be able to remove the mark that Drew left on his heart.

Their deep kisses turned to sweet, light brushes of lips. Ash rested his forehead against Drew's. "You're still wearing your clothes. That's not acceptable. Take them off."

Drew's fingers trembled against his stomach as he popped the tab on his pants, pulled down his zipper and kicked them off so he lay only in his boxers. Still straddling him, Ash flexed his hips so their cocks brushed each other. And though he'd enjoyed an eye-popping orgasm only minutes before, his cock twitched at the contact. He braced his arms on either side of Drew's head and bent down to once again kiss his lips. Hearing Drew sigh his pleasure, Ash's lips curved in a smile.

"Happy, baby?" He couldn't help but nibble on Drew's neck. The man tasted so damn sweet. Like a cat, Ash rubbed his cheek against Drew's neck, nuzzling into his warmth as he reached down to pull Drew's boxers down then grip Drew's hard cock. He caressed Drew's length and rubbed the thick head to pick up wetness.

"Oh yeah, I'm so happy I could die right now." Drew sighed as he thrust his cock into Ash's hand, pushing hard.

"We have all night. Don't die on me now." Ash chuckled, the laughter catching in his throat as Drew continued to drive hard, his cock sliding and rubbing against his palm. Within minutes Drew's body arched off the bed, and with a grunt, he came all over Ash's stomach and hand.

Drew sank back on the bed, and Ash collapsed on top of him. They lay belly to belly, chest to chest, their cocks spent for now. After a few minutes, Ash got up to go to the bathroom to clean himself. He brought back a warm, damp washcloth and rubbed down Drew's stomach, kissing it after wiping him dry. Tossing the cloth off the side of the bed, Ash put his arm around Drew and pulled him close, smiling as the sleepy man curled around him. As he drifted off to sleep, it occurred to Ash that this was the first time he'd ever slept next to another person or shared a lover's bed.

Chapter Twenty

"NO, PLEASE. IT wasn't my fault; it wasn't my fault." Drew bolted upright in bed, sweat pouring off his face. Strong arms came around to hold him, and he stared into the steady, compassionate eyes of Ash.

"What's the matter, baby? You had a bad dream?" Ash kissed the top of Drew's head and hugged him close. The beat of Ash's heart thumping, so real and strong, calmed Drew, but the violent images of his nightmare remained branded in his mind. He nodded, then rolled away from Ash.

"I'm sorry I woke you. I've had them since my parents' accident." He stiffened, shocked at how easily that confession, never before revealed, slipped out.

"Do you want to talk about it?" Ash lay on his side, his face all but hidden in the shadows of the night, aside from the glint of his eyes and the gleam of his white teeth. "You've never really told me about your parents. Unless of course it would bother you too much."

Drew flopped onto his back, the black emptiness of the bedroom perfectly matching his dark mood. “I had the best of childhoods, yet for some reason, I lived in a constant panic it would all be taken away from me. I never liked being alone, thinking that if people left, they wouldn’t come back.”

From the living room he heard his cat’s plaintive meow. Domino, now used to sleeping in his bed, didn’t appreciate being evicted. Perhaps he didn’t like being alone either. They were alike, he and his cat. Two strays, lonely for companionship. He pressed the heels of his hands into his eyes, determined not to let loose the tears threatening to spill over.

“It was my fault they died.” He gulped air down his swollen throat and curled himself in a ball, facing away from Ash.

“I thought they died in a car accident?” Ash sounded confused.

“They did.” Oh God, why did he have to have that nightmare? Perhaps he could distract Ash, and he’d stop asking questions. He sat up and grasped Ash around his neck.

“Kiss me?” He tried to press his lips to Ash’s, but to his surprise, Ash drew back and sat up in bed.

“You’re deflecting, Drew. If you don’t want to talk about it, fine. All you have to do is say so. But I think you need to get this off your chest.” Ash took his hand and laced their fingers together. “Talk to me, baby. Let me help you through your pain. Share with me; tell me your secrets like I told you mine.”

Drew rubbed their entwined fingers across his lips. Compared to what Ash had been through, he had no right to complain. "It's stupid, but when I started college, I lived away from home for the first time, and I missed my parents and my friends. I was so lonely and spent most of my time in the library. I guess I was the nerdy little premed everyone thought."

Ash gathered Drew in his arms, his body a solid wall of comfort. "I bet you were a hot, nerdy premed, though."

Drew rubbed his head on Ash's shoulder, inhaling his heady scent of coffee, warmth and male. "Actually I had few friends. I missed everyone at home so much, I used to beg them to come visit me all the time."

Ash said nothing, merely stroked his hair, occasionally planting kisses on his head and cheek.

"My mother didn't drive, and my father hated taking long trips, but I guess I made them feel so guilty, they finally agreed. We had a great weekend, but on the way home," he took a deep breath, forcing air into his lungs, "a tractor trailer crossed the divide, hitting them head on." Hot tears coursed down Drew's cheeks. "If I wasn't such a needy, pathetic bastard, they'd still be alive. They'd told me they'd almost brought Rachel. For God's sake, I could've killed her too."

He lost it then and sobbed into Ash's chest. The pain and self-reproach that had clawed at him all throughout Rachel's minor breakdown and his grandmother's grief broke free.

"Let it out; it's okay. Baby, it's been over ten years.

You need to let it go. It wasn't your fault. It was a horrible accident with your parents being in the wrong place at the wrong time."

Drew wiped his eyes and gazed into Ash's face. "All these years I always blamed myself and tried to make myself a better person. I grabbed on to any woman who liked me, whether or not I liked them."

"Like your ex-wife?" Ash murmured, his hands drifting downward to massage Drew's shoulders.

Drew shrugged. "I guess so. Yeah."

Ash's hands roamed over his body, tweaking his nipples, reaching down to grasp his cock. In between biting his ear and kissing his jaw, Ash licked his neck and whispered, "I think you're amazing with what you've done with the clinic. You care so much about people, and you're so good with the kids. I've never known anyone as good as you."

The gentle caresses turned more purposeful. Hands still clasped, Drew kissed Ash's fingers and wondered why it didn't seem odd to lie in his bed with a man instead of a woman. Instead of soft breasts and smooth, perfumed skin, he now craved a strong jaw and hard muscles to touch and kiss.

It didn't feel strange nor did he find it uncomfortable. He'd known Jordan his entire life and loved him as a friend for almost as long. Man or woman, what did it matter who he slept with, and why did people think it was any of their business? As his body warmed to Ash's touch and his cock swelled with need, everything faded away until the only thing that mattered was this man, their hearts, and how they felt about each other.

"I want you. Make love to me. Now."

In one fluid motion Ash trapped him beneath his body. "You're sure? You want me? It will never be the same after this."

Drew shivered. A hard throbbing need uncoiled from within, releasing something wild. "Yeah. Fuck me. It's all I can think of." He writhed underneath Ash, seeking the friction he so desperately craved.

"Oh God, you're gonna kill me." Ash's strained voice broke, then gasped out raw and needy. "Tell me you have condoms. And lube."

"Night table," he rasped. Drew heard the drawer open and Ash rustling around. Cursing, Ash turned on a lamp, casting a glow of light over the room. A strip of condoms hit the bed along with a bottle of lotion; then Ash came crawling back to him on all fours. Drew lay back, admiring his handsome face and muscular shoulders. Dark hair sprinkled down Ash's broad chest leading a trail down to his cock, which rose up against his taut abs, flushed and hard.

The intense look on Ash's face rocked Drew's mind.

I'm about to have sex with a man—with Ash.

He struggled for breath and his sanity.

"You're sure about this, right? Because I know once I taste you this time, I'm not stopping until I make you mine." Ash swiped his tongue along the head of Drew's cock, licking up the wetness, but never breaking eye contact in a move so erotic, so intimate, Drew almost came right then.

"You know if you keep this up, you're going to ruin your rep as a ruthless bastard." Drew watched Ash's lips, wet and gleaming, curve in a wicked smile.

"Then we'll have to keep it our secret, won't we?" Ash slid his bulk over Drew until their lips almost touched. The smell of sex and man created a heady perfume. Without thinking, Drew wound his arms around Ash's neck and kissed him, the salty-sweet taste of his come bursting over his tongue as Ash groaned into his mouth.

Their cocks bumped and slid even as their mouths devoured each other. A heavy, muscular thigh pushed between Drew's legs. "Want you so bad, baby." Ash's heavy pants matched the throbbing of Drew's cock.

Drew opened his legs wide. "You have to know how much I want this, want you."

Ash dropped his head back down for a quick kiss, then reached for the lotion. Drew couldn't help but tense as Ash's cool, slicked fingers touched his ass, then breached his hole. Everything faded away, all fear and hesitation, at the touch of Ash's finger sliding inside Drew for the first time. He gasped as it sank in slowly past the first ring of muscle, then reached farther until it was settled to the hilt.

"Okay, baby?" Ash's eyes glimmered with concern.

"It feels strange, but yeah, I'm fine." Drew smiled, then groaned when Ash inserted another finger to join the one already inside and curled them upward. "Oh damn, that's strange." It burned a bit and stretched, but no pain.

Ash continued to twist his wicked fingers inside him when he hit something. His prostate, Drew thought almost clinically, then his nerve endings burst into flames and he almost forgot how to breathe. He cried out, sliding down on the bed, greedily pushing against those fingers as they continued to thrust in and out of his trembling body. Pleasure rolled through Drew, so intense and raw he wondered how he'd lived without it all these years.

"Oh God. Please. Now."

He heard the foil tear on the condom wrapper and the slick sliding as Ash rolled it on and lubricated himself.

"Pick up your legs, baby, and put them on my shoulders." The thick, wide head of Ash's cock nudged his entrance, and Drew tensed for a moment. "Ssh. I'll be gentle with you. It's my first time too. I've never been with a virgin, so we'll learn together."

Drew bit his lip hard as Ash reached down to guide himself inside. The pain proved to be much greater than with Ash's fingers, but he knew to relax and keep breathing. Once the head passed through that tight ring of muscle, it was done, and Drew struggled to breathe from the overpowering sensation of having a part of Ash inside him.

"You okay, baby?" The strain and need in Ash's hoarse voice caused a pang in Drew's heart. No one had ever shown him such tenderness and care.

"I'm good. I need you to move."

"Giving orders, Doctor? I'll see what I can do." Starting with short, careful thrusts, Ash pushed deeper and deeper into his body until Drew knew by the feel of Ash's balls against his ass that he sat firmly slotted inside.

Ash began the slide in and out, the push-pull of their bodies moving in pace with the frenzied beating of Drew's heart. Drew shifted, picking up his legs a bit higher, and once again, that blinding streak of pleasure-pain overtook his body.

This time Ash thrust deeper and deeper until Drew thought he touched his very soul. He stroked his cock in time with Ash's movement, his need building, twisting, burning through his blood to pool at the base of his cock.

"Ash, my God, what the hell—" His moans echoed off the bedroom walls as Ash continued to thrust inside him.

Ash gave two hard, almost brutal thrusts, and fire sizzled within Drew, melting him from within. Drew thrust his cock into his fist and came in spurts across his stomach, gasping for air. His ass clenched, and Ash stiffened and groaned as he climaxed inside him. After a moment he carefully pulled out and took care of disposing of the condom, then crawled back into bed.

What would happen now? Drew wasn't stupid enough to think a man like Ash would go for postcoital pillow talk and cuddling, yet still he hoped for some of the kindness and affection Ash had shown before they'd made love.

Because for him at least, it was making love, not fucking. He could hear Ash's harsh breathing as they relaxed side by side. Strange that the man had been so intimate with him, more than anyone ever had been before, yet now, lying here next to him, with every passing minute Drew anticipated not only a physical chasm but an emotional one as well, moving them further and further apart.

"Drew?"

He rolled over at Ash's question but kept his eyes averted. "Yeah?" He braced himself for a brush off. Even remembering Ash's gentleness, he couldn't be sure that wasn't a ploy by the silver-tongued attorney to get what he wanted, and now that he'd screwed him senseless, he planned to make his exit.

"Are you all right? I...I didn't hurt you, did I?"

Drew flashed an incredulous look upward at Ash's concerned face. "You're worried about me?" A kernel of hope built in Drew's heart that Ash might want to stay.

Ash's brow furrowed. "How could you think otherwise?"

"After our last time, I'm not quite sure how you feel or what to expect now." He broke eye contact and looked toward the foot of the bed. Anywhere but at Ash.

To his surprise, Ash slid closer to him, hauling him in tight, pressing his face into Drew's hair. "I feel like the luckiest man alive, 'cause you're so fucking perfect and for some reason you want me. That's all I know." Ash's arms tightened around Drew. "You do, right?"

Once again, that vulnerable, uncertain tone of Ash's did funny things to Drew's breathing and his heart squeezed painfully tight. The magnitude of his feelings for this beautiful, damaged man surpassed anything he'd ever imagined possible. Words trembled on his lips but he refrained, knowing it was too fast, too soon.

"I wouldn't want to be any other place in the world."

Drew turned in Ash's arms to see his handsome face break out in a smile. On impulse he initiated a kiss, slipping his tongue in to tease with Ash's. After an initial hesitation, Ash eagerly responded, and they spent several moments kissing until Drew realized how sticky and sweaty he was. "I'm gonna take a shower." With a sleepy nod, Ash closed his eyes, and Drew climbed out of bed.

Upon entering the bathroom, he looked at his reflection in the mirror. With his jaw scraped almost raw by Ash's beard, his chest all sticky and faint reddened marks on his neck and chest, Drew had to admit he looked thoroughly fucked. He grinned and turned on the shower.

Steam rose in the bathroom, and he entered the stall with a satisfied groan and closed his eyes. Almost too tired to move, he stretched out his hand, reaching for the soap.

"Looking for this?" Soap-slicked hands caressed his chest. "Let me wash you, baby. Take care of you. You had a rough night."

For a brief moment, Drew considered opening his

eyes, but the effort seemed almost too much to bear and he smiled his assent. "I'd love that." Between the heat of the water, the sensuous stroking of his skin, and his overall fatigue from the scare with his grandmother, his legs nearly gave out. He could feel himself sliding down the tiled wall, only to be caught and pulled against Ash's hot, wet body.

"Come on now. Let's get you dried off and ready for bed." Ash reached up and turned off the water.

He allowed himself to be led out of the shower stall, where Ash enveloped him in a large towel and dried him off. Ash wrapped a strong arm around him and helped him into bed, tucking him under the thin comforter.

"You need a good night's rest."

"Wait." He reached out and grasped Ash's hand, lacing their fingers together. "You aren't leaving, are you?" The silence stretched out until it became impossible not to speak. "Why? Why do you want to leave?"

"I haven't been asked to stay. I didn't know how you'd feel about me…us. I've never wanted to stay." The bed sagged under his weight as he perched on the edge. "Until now."

Still holding on to Ash's hand, Drew tugged him closer until he could rest his head on Ash's shoulder. "I want you to. Please? Stay with me."

Ash smiled and joined him underneath the comforter, holding him close. His very presence gave him the strength to face the worry from his grandmother's illness and confront his guilt over his parents' deaths. Drew closed his eyes and drifted off to sleep.

Chapter Twenty-One

ASH AWOKE SLOWLY, cracking one eye open, an unfamiliar warmth snuggled into his chest. Soft puffs of breath wafted across his cheek, and one of Drew's legs rested over his thigh. His cock swelled full and heavy, pressing into Drew's belly, but he made no move to initiate early morning sex. Drew had been so bone weary last night when they'd gone to bed, Ash wanted to give him a few more minutes before he'd have to wake up and jump into what promised to be another overwhelming and exhausting day.

Instead, he took the opportunity to hold Drew close. With the pads of his fingertips, he traced the smattering of freckles dotting the fine, pale skin of Drew's shoulder. Like a game of connect the dots, Ash followed his fingers with his tongue, as little dips and tastes of all that sweetness would have to be enough to hold him for another day. Drew shifted, mumbling in his sleep, and turned on his other side, so now Ash's cock nestled in the hot crease of his firm ass.

It would be so easy to slide between those tight

cheeks and rock himself to oblivion. Take his pleasure without thinking of Drew's. But it wasn't what Ash wanted anymore. Like he did last night, Ash wanted to see Drew's face when he entered him and watch Drew's eyes grow blind with lust when he came.

Shit, he sounded like a fucking cheesy Hallmark card. Easing out from underneath Drew's body, he stood and gave a lingering look at the sleep-warmed man lying in the bed. For the first time Ash shared a bed with someone other than when he, Luke and Brandon had huddled together in his bed back at their foster home. But that didn't count. They'd come together then because they were scared of storms or when Munson was beating up his wife. Not the fondest of memories.

This was different. And when Drew sighed and cuddled the pillow, an unfamiliar twist curled through Ash's heart and he wanted nothing more than to climb back into that bed. Instead, he forced himself to turn on his heel and, after finding a toothbrush and disposable razor in the bathroom, cleaned himself up. He picked up his wrinkled clothes from the floor with distaste. He couldn't go to the office like this, but nothing Drew owned would fit him.

He wandered into the kitchen, determined to wake up and make himself some coffee. The sight of the large black-and-white cat sitting in the center of the kitchen floor, staring at him with those wide, unblinking eyes, unnerved him for a second. "Hey, cat. Are you hungry too?"

No answer, merely a swish of the tail.

Hmm. He saw the cat bowl on the floor, but finding the food would require a search of the cabinets, which was kind of personal, but what the hell. After opening and closing several doors, he found a bag of dry food. Success. When he picked up the bag, the cat came to life, meowing and winding himself around Ash's legs. After he filled the bowl with food, Ash replaced the water. The animal now taken care of, Ash discovered the coffee and set out to brew himself a cup.

Minutes later the sweet aroma of vanilla-bean coffee filled the air and he poured himself a cup. He glanced at the kitchen clock, registering it was barely eight o'clock. Remembering he had a business to take care of, he picked up the phone and called the office.

"Davis and Frank. How may I help you?" Laura's early morning, perky voice greeted him.

"Hello, Laura. Is Walker in yet?"

"Good morning, Mr. Davis. Yes, Mr. Walker is here, preparing for your ten o'clock."

He sipped his coffee. *Good.* "Put him on, please."

"Of course, sir. One moment."

A click and then a nervous-sounding Walker came on. "Mr. Davis? Is everything okay?"

Walker had been with him for eight months now, but Ash still thought the man believed he'd be fired anytime they spoke.

"Everything's fine. I've had a bit of a family emergency, so I won't make the meeting."

"I see." A cautious tone crept into Walker's voice.

"I can reschedule them."

"No, no." Ash heard movement from the other room, and suddenly anxious to see Drew again, hastened to end the call. "I trust you to handle it."

Silence for a moment. "You do?" Walker sounded so incredulous Ash had to laugh.

"Yes, I do, unless you think there's a reason I shouldn't?" Ash chuckled to himself as Walker stuttered in his ear.

"N-no. Of course not. Thank you, sir. I'll make sure everything turns out the way you intended it to. You can count on me."

"I know, Walker. I'll talk to you later." He clicked off and made another cup of coffee. He found bagels in a bag on the counter and had taken out a knife to slice them for toasting when a noise behind him caught his attention. He whirled around.

"Oh my God, Ash. No." Drew stood at the doorway to the kitchen, naked except for a pair of boxers, a frightened expression on his pale face. "Put the knife down, please."

What the fuck? Then he looked down and saw his hand still gripping the large serrated bread knife and knew immediately what Drew had thought. Embarrassed, he instinctively struck out. "What? Afraid I'm going to bleed all over your kitchen?" After that cruel jab, he couldn't look at Drew, so he turned around, his entire body tight with shame, anger, and regret. He tossed the knife onto the counter and bowed his head, struggling to keep from lashing out further.

How stupid to give in to his desire to sleep with Drew. The man knew too much about him. Drew had stripped back his layers, almost to his center core. The part of him he'd always kept hidden, for fear if anyone ever got to that point, they'd see what and who he truly was.

Nothing. A nobody.

A warm palm flattened against his back. Ash flinched and tried to pull away, but the other hand slipped around his waist. Drew leaned against Ash's back and held him close, his cheek pressed into the muscles of his shoulders.

"I'm sorry I jumped to conclusions. I got so scared when I saw you holding the knife everything else flew out of my head." Drew's soft, warm lips kissed his neck. "Forgive me."

Ash turned and faced Drew, his green eyes so open and honest Ash couldn't help but pull him close. "No, I'm sorry I yelled at you. You had every right to think something might happen, especially now that you know."

Drew stepped back but held on to his wrist, his fingertips trailing over the old scars. Though long healed, the nerve endings had never fully recovered and numbness remained at the surface. "Will you tell me what happened?" Drew's voice struggled to remain neutral. "Only if you want to, of course."

Thoughts scurried through Ash's mind like mice. What to say, what to hide? Then he remembered last night, watching Drew's open face under him as they made love. The trust he'd been given was a gift. He couldn't lie to this man if his life depended on it.

"I made you coffee." He handed Drew his cup. "Let's go back to bed, and I'll try to explain." Glancing at the clock, he saw it was eight thirty. "We have time before we go to the hospital."

Drew accepted his cup and they walked back to the bedroom. "Thank you." A small smile curved his lips. "You're coming with me?"

Ash got into bed. "Of course. If you want me to, that is."

"Of course I want you with me."

Warmth suffused him. No one had wanted or needed him since his foster care days.

After Drew set his cup down and joined him in the bed, Ash put his arms around him and gulped a deep breath. "It all started when I was fourteen. The first time Munson raped me. He tried to be nice at first, but when I wouldn't give in to him, he beat me with the butt of his gun and cuffed me to the bed. He told me I was a bad boy because if I fought him, that meant he would go to Luke and do what I wouldn't let him do to me. I had no choice but to give him what he wanted."

Ash could see it all again, the images rising in his mind, imprinted in stark relief. Oddly it was things like the lumpy mattress cutting into his back that came to mind first, along with the scratchy, bright blue blanket that provided little warmth. Then the memories of the pain. The gun hitting him, the cuffs on his wrists, and the ropes on his ankles as he struggled, and ultimately, the hated touch of his foster father invading his body.

"Oh Ash." Drew took his hand and he held on.

"I let him do whatever he wanted to me, as long as he left the other kids alone. But one night when it got too much, I took a knife here"—he pointed to the thickest scars on his wrists—"and here, and I tried to kill myself."

There'd been so much blood and pain, but his foster mother found him and took him to a lady who lived two houses down from them. No questions asked. The neighbor, Mrs. Cartwright, simply stitched and bandaged him up and he went home.

Drew looked horrified. "No one reported it? My God, you could've died."

Ash chuckled at his naïveté. "Baby, we lived in a small, one-road town. One way in and out. No one was gonna go against a cop, especially a mean son of a bitch like Munson. After that I got smart. I'd let him do what he wanted, but he hated when I marked myself." It was worth every slap he got, whenever Munson saw a new knife cut on his arms. "It only made me want to do it more. To let him know he couldn't tell me what to do with my body."

He fell back on the pillows, taking Drew back with him to rest on his chest. Ash held Drew close, comforted by his nonjudgmental silence. "When I ran away, I cut myself again and wound up in the hospital, but by then I was eighteen, and they couldn't send me back. I walked out of the hospital during the night and came up to New York, got a job in a fast-food place, and studied every night for my GED."

Now that he'd started, the words rushed out from him, fierce and unstoppable. "I saved every penny, slept in shelters or wherever I could find a place. I never sold myself, though, 'cause I was too scared of gettin' a disease. I went to a community college, then to a four-year one. That's when I knew I wanted to be a lawyer to help kids like me."

Still Drew said nothing, merely letting him talk out his pain.

"During college, my manager at the restaurant felt sorry for me, so he rented me a room in his house. I thought he'd want sex from me in exchange, but he was honest and only took some money from my paycheck. I got to study and graduated top of my class. That's how I got the scholarship from Mr. Frank to go to law school."

Drained, he closed his eyes but kept talking. "Everywhere I went, I looked for Luke and Brandon. I knew I'd failed them. And every time I thought about how much I'd let them down, I'd carve another little piece out of my arm to keep me focused on finding them."

Drew kissed his cheek and placed his warm hand over Ash's heart. "You'll find them one day. I can help you if you want. I'll help you through it all."

Ash slid his palm over Drew's hand to hold him tight. He couldn't stop touching Drew, needing the connection, like a lifeline to his heart. "I found Luke. He's away on an extended business trip, but he lives here, in the city."

"That's wonderful." Drew sat up, and Ash sensed his nervousness. "I hate to stop you here, but I want to get to the hospital early to have a chance to speak to the doctors."

"Of course. Let's get dressed and go." He jumped out of bed, no longer caring that his clothes were all wrinkled. Let people think what they would about him and Drew; it was nobody's fucking business but their own. The weight he'd carried for years no longer suffocated him. He'd talked to Drew about some of what happened to him, and hadn't been turned away. Maybe they could make this work.

He smiled as he buttoned his shirt and tucked it into his slacks, trying to smooth out the wrinkles. Drew came out of the bedroom looking good enough to eat in a pale green shirt, dark blue tie, and black pants. Ash couldn't resist pulling Drew close to grab his ass with one hand. Now that he'd finally kissed Drew on the mouth, he craved more of him. He crushed his lips over Drew's, loving the softness. Drew's mouth opened, accepting the slide of his tongue inside.

Drew whimpered as their tongues tangled together. Showing restraint he didn't know he possessed, Ash pulled away and huffed out a laugh. "If we don't leave now, I'll keep you in bed all day."

Something dark flashed in Drew's eyes; then he seemed to realize where they were headed. "Right, we'd better hurry."

Ash nodded, grabbed the bagels from the counter, and followed Drew out of the apartment and down the stairs.

QUITE A DIFFERENT scene greeted them this morning than when they'd left the night before, with the most important thing being Esther was awake and talking. A circle of doctors and nurses surrounded her. Drew, who'd put on a white doctor's coat, looked incredibly hot and sexy, even when he told him to wait outside while he went into the ICU to consult with the cardiologist.

For a moment, Ash almost forgot himself and went to give him a kiss good-bye. And it seemed as though Drew was of a like mind as he too leaned in as if to accept it. Only the sound of Jordan, Rachel, and Mike's voices stopped him short.

"Drew, how is she? Have you seen her yet?" Rachel came running up and grabbed Drew's arm. Drew put his arm around her and walked her away to speak with her in private.

Ash turned to greet Mike. "Hey, how's it going?" Mike gave him a fist bump, then continued on to join Rachel and Drew. Ash watched as Drew spoke with them for a few minutes more, then left to go inside his grandmother's room. The white coat gave him an air of authority, and those tortoiseshell glasses turned Ash's insides soft with desire. Let people think what they wanted. Ash couldn't take his eyes off him. Who knew he'd go for that sexy, intellectual look? His lips curved in a smile as he watched Drew lean down to kiss Esther.

Someone poked him in the back. "What the fuck is going on?" Surprised, he turned around to find Jordan up in his face, icy blue eyes spitting fire. "You better have a goddamn good explanation, Davis." Jordan poked him again, this time in the chest.

Ash leaned back against the wall, a lazy smile on his lips, but his voice clipped out cold and hard. "You fucking put your hands on me again, I'll make you sorry. I don't care that you're Drew's friend or that your boyfriend's a cop. Got it?"

Jordan rocked on the balls of his feet, his arms crossed in front of his body. "Go to hell, Davis."

"Been there, done that already." Ash smirked, mimicking Jordan's body language. He didn't think they'd end up in a brawl inside the hospital, but he wasn't about to get caught short. Not by Jordan. "What's your problem?"

"What are you doing here? You're not family or close with us. And why are you wearing the same clothes you had on yesterday?" Jordan's disdainful gaze raked him up and down, but there was nothing sexual in his appraisal. If anything he looked angry and disgusted.

Since when did Jordan think he owed him any explanations? Ash raised a brow and smiled. "Fuck off. I don't answer to you, and neither does Drew." Then, knowing how it would infuriate Jordan, Ash turned his back on him and walked away, toward Mike and Rachel.

Ash didn't count on Jordan's tenacity, however. Before he reached the seating area, where Mike and Rachel waited for Drew to come back and tell them about Esther, Jordan grabbed his arm.

Ash stopped dead in his tracks. "If you want to have your hand remain intact to perform surgery, I suggest you get it off me. Now." No one touched him unless he wanted them to. Years of getting tied down and brutalized would do that to a person. Jordan, however, didn't know that and continued to hold on to him. Beads of perspiration popped out on his forehead and Ash shook from the combination of rage and fear spiraling though him. Spots whirled before his eyes, and his breath caught in his throat. If he didn't get Jordan off him, he'd end up in the midst of a full-fledged panic attack in the middle of the hospital.

With one gigantic effort, Ash pulled away from Jordan's grasp, though the nausea and dizziness remained. The coolness of the tile wall he braced himself against seeped through his sweat-soaked body. Jordan took a step closer, and Ash stiffened, then snarled at him. "Get off me. Leave me alone."

Jordan got the message at last and allowed Mike to lead him away, though both men kept shooting confused looks over their shoulders as they found seats in the waiting area. Rachel came over to him and, speaking very gently, touched his hand. "Ash, are you all right? You look like you're about to pass out."

He gazed down at her concerned face. Unlike Jordan, Rachel radiated only warmth and compassion. He gave a weak smile. "Yes. Thanks. I, um, don't like people grabbing me, that's all."

She shot him an unreadable look, but then Drew came out of his grandmother's room, and she left his side to run to her brother.

"How is she, Drew? Is she going to be all right?" Rachel held his arm, and Drew hugged her to him. Ash remembered last night and the feel of Drew's arms around him. Heat rose in his face.

Drew smiled at Rachel and at all of them as Mike and Jordan, who wisely skirted a wide berth around Ash, joined their small group. "Yes, she's much better. Her heart remained stable all night, and she's breathing on her own and is awake and demanding to go home."

Recovered from his earlier anxiety, Ash chuckled, knowing that sounded exactly like Esther. Drew caught his eye and grinned, then took Rachel by the hand. "Come, Rach, we can see her together now. She says she remembers what happened." He took a few steps, then stopped and turned around. "Jordan, could you call Keith? I'd like for him to hear what she has to say."

Jordan nodded and immediately pulled out his cell phone to call his detective boyfriend. Begrudgingly Ash admitted Jordan was a good friend to Drew, no matter that he was an arrogant dick. Did it matter if he and Jordan got along? Not really. He knew the man would always be suspicious of him because of his past behavior. Watching Drew through the glass window of the ICU room interacting with his grandmother and sister, Ash wondered how long it would take before he'd screw up or hurt Drew. He didn't know what it was to care about someone. He'd spent his whole life with a barrier around him—don't touch, keep away. The only one who'd ever penetrated it was Jacob Frank. Except for last night. Being with Drew had cracked open his shell, and he didn't like it. The feelings of helplessness and pain rushed in like floodwaters after a rainstorm. He'd spent years making sure he'd locked himself up tight, only to have it all come crashing down with the press of Drew's mouth on his and the feel of his body underneath him.

It wasn't part of the plan.

Maybe Jordan was right and it would be better if he disappeared like they all probably wanted, and let the people closest to Drew help him. After all, he was a stranger, like Jordan said, not part of their family. They didn't need him. With one final look through the glass, he hastened to the elevator, managing to make it inside before the doors slid closed.

As the elevator whooshed downward, he wondered at the emptiness inside him now that he'd left Drew, and the yawning sense of loss, like he'd left something behind he might never be able to find again.

Chapter Twenty-Two

"NANA, YOU HAVE to lay back and relax. It won't do you any good to fight us." Drew gazed down at his grandmother with affectionate exasperation. Now that she was no longer in any danger, he had no problem exerting his authority as a doctor rather than a worried grandson. "You aren't going to leave here a moment before Dr. Porter says so." He allowed himself a brief glance out of the window to catch a glimpse of Ash but didn't see him. Dr. Porter came in with a bevy of young interns and residents following him.

"Well, Mrs. Klein, you gave your family quite a scare." He flashed a broad smile at her.

One thing his grandmother loved was a nice-looking man, no matter the age. Tall, with dark hair and piercing light-blue eyes, Rob Porter was one of the hospital heartthrobs, and Drew noticed with amusement how she turned her charm on the doctor. Esther might be close to ninety, but she was still a flirt.

"Why, I didn't mean to, of course." Her brow

furrowed as the smile dimmed from her face. "These two young men came to my door and said such awful things." The pink color drained from her face, leaving her pale. Alarmed, Drew grabbed her hand while Rachel brushed back the hair from her face.

"Mrs. Klein, try not to get upset. I'm sure your family will see to it that you are given the best of care and that something like this never happens again." Rob beckoned Drew over to the door.

Anxious to hear what Rob had to say, Drew jumped up from the chair, first stopping by his grandmother's bed to give her a kiss. "I'll be back in a few minutes." When he joined Rob, the doctor was frowning.

"Drew, she's fine. I'm going to keep her here one more day for observation but I recommend you have someone stay with her once she returns home. She shouldn't live on her own."

That's what Drew was afraid of. His grandmother never wanted to be one of those people who had to rely on external help. He and Rachel would have to tread carefully to preserve her independence. "Don't you worry, Rob. She's going to have to listen to us now."

"Good."

After making some notations on the chart, Rob said good-bye and left, the group of doctors trailing in his wake. Drew returned to Rachel and his grandmother. "Nana. You're going to have to have someone with you from now on. No argument."

Rachel got up from the bedside. "I spoke with Mrs.

Delaney. Now that her husband is gone, she told me she was thinking of selling the house, since she can't afford the taxes and the upkeep. She'd love to move into your spare bedroom, Nana. It would be the perfect solution. You like and trust her, and she could keep you company, as well as help out."

"That's a wonderful idea, Rach. A win-win in my book, right, Nana?" Drew said.

He had to give her credit. She didn't fight back, merely glared at them and said nothing. Knowing her, she was coming up with some convoluted plan in her mind to counteract their plans.

Before he could say anything else, someone knocked on the door. Spotting Keith's blond head in the window, Drew motioned for his friend to come inside. Keith was in his official capacity as an NYPD detective, as he wore a shirt and tie and Drew spotted his detective's shield clipped to his belt.

"Hey, thanks for coming so fast." They hugged briefly before Keith went over to his grandmother.

"Well, Esther, what do you have to say for yourself?" Keith's bright blue eyes twinkled.

"My, you boys all look so handsome in your suits and ties. It was almost worth getting sick to get to be surrounded by you all." She laughed.

"Nana, really." Rachel's exasperated groan sent him and Keith laughing and shaking their heads.

"Okay, Esther. Drew said you had some visitors. Can you remember and tell me what happened?" Keith pulled out a little notebook and pen, then sat in a chair next to her bed.

Drew glanced at the heart monitor attached to his grandmother and setting off steady beeps. At the first sign of any change, he'd make sure to cut off the questions. Rachel stood by her bedside, like a protective sentry, holding her hand.

"Well, it was funny. Remember I said two young men had come by and cut my grass and trimmed the bushes for me the other day?" They all nodded, and she continued. "They came back, which I thought was strange, since I obviously didn't have any work left for them to do."

"Did you tell them that, Esther?" Keith had stopped writing in his notebook.

She nodded. "I did, and they laughed at me and said some strange things."

"Like what, Nana?" Rachel dropped her hand and sat on the edge of the bed.

His grandmother looked at him. "They mentioned you, Drew. Not by name, but said, 'Tell your grandson and his friends to keep out of our business.' " She dropped her voice and fingered the edge of the sheet. "They started cursing and saying horrible things about you, darling, and Asher and Jordan."

Keith's eyes turned into chips of blue ice. "Did they threaten you, Esther, or touch you?"

After a little hesitation, she nodded. "They pushed me against the wall and said to tell Dr. Drew that things would get worse if he continued helping those kids." She glanced up at Keith. "They used a slur, and

I'm not about to say it, even for you, dear. I don't use that kind of language."

Keith's normally smiling face vanished, replaced by a stone-like mask. He patted Nana's hand. "Don't worry about it. I know what you mean." He wrote for a few minutes in his notebook. "Is that all?"

Nana thought for a moment. "Yes. They left, laughing as if it were a big joke, but not before pushing me around a little." Her voice rose with indignation. "What kind of world are we living in with such a lack of respect for women and someone of my age? Who's raising these hoodlums?"

The machines kept up their steady beeping with no change, Drew noted. He turned his attention back to Keith, who continued to ask questions.

"Esther, what did they look like, and did you hear them call each other by any names?" Keith watched her with an expectant look on his face.

Her face scrunched up in thought for a moment. "They were both young—teenagers, I'd guess. One was tall and nice looking. He had very short hair and brown eyes, but his lips were thin. I tell you I've never trusted a man with thin lips. The other was shorter with that crazy hair all over his face, like they like to wear nowadays." She shrugged. "I don't know why they think it's attractive."

Drew looked over at Keith and caught his lips twitching as if to hold back his laughter. He turned back to her. "Any names, Nana?"

She shrugged. "No. I'm sorry. But I would definitely recognize them again if I saw them." Her eyes brightened. "Maybe you could bring me down to the police station, and I could look through pictures."

Keith laughed. "Esther, I have a feeling you think this is like an episode of *Law and Order*."

"Well, I do love that show," she grumbled. "And that's what their witnesses to crimes always do."

Keith stood and went over to the bed to give her a kiss. "I'll take you myself in a squad car with the lights on the top and let you look through pictures, but only after your doctor clears it." He stuck out his hand. "Deal?"

She took his hand and shook it as everyone in the room laughed. "Deal."

The nurse came in and shooed them out. "Mrs. Klein needs her rest. Everyone out now please, including you, Dr. Klein. No special treatment for you because you're a doctor." Mrs. Albright winked at him. The two of them went way back, to when he was a resident here and she was the toughest nurse, always giving the new doctors the hardest time.

"Yes, ma'am." They filed out of the room into the waiting area. Drew was surprised to see only Jordan and Mike. Where was Ash?

When he posed the question to Jordan, his friend merely shrugged. "He left a long time ago. Got in the elevator and went. Forget about him, Drew. I told you a long time ago he's a player and a bastard. He's no friend to you."

Drew couldn't believe Ash would simply up and

disappear. Not after last night and the truths they'd bared to each other this morning. Without being told, he knew Ash had never revealed to anyone else the brutality and degradation he'd suffered before he reinvented himself. The scars that left, both physical and emotional were not to be taken lightly, nor were they something to slough off and bury away, as he feared Ash did to survive.

Remembering how gentle and caring Ash had been with him the night before, Drew wasn't about to let him withdraw back into that cold, lonely shell. Now that he'd seen the best of the man, he was ready to help him through his worst.

"Jordan, did you say anything to him to make him leave?" Everyone turned to him, Jordan's face a picture of astonishment.

"Are you implying that I drove the man away? I did nothing of the sort. He walked away of his own free will." Keith put a hand on Jordan's shoulder, but he shook him off and advanced upon Drew. "Why do you care if he's here, anyway? What happened to Shelly? Where's your girlfriend?"

Everyone now stared at Drew. Damn, the back and forth was like a tennis match. "We broke up."

Rachel's mouth fell open. "Oh, Drew. I'm sorry."

He shrugged. "It was for the best. She was way too serious about the relationship. Much more into it than I was."

Jordan made a sound of disgust. "I'm sure your buddy Ash was happy about the breakup."

This was getting ridiculous. "What the hell is your problem? You've had a stick up your ass about Ash since we first met him. So what if he made a pass at you years ago? Shit, man, let it go."

Jordan persisted. "But don't you see—"

"What I see is you bad-mouthing someone who's never said a bad word about you. There's no reason for you to hate him so much."

"He's a user, and you're too nice a guy to see it. He screws people and then dumps them. That's his MO."

Worried, pissed off, and tired, Drew had enough. "I'm not that nice, and I can take care of myself. And as for Ash, you've never given him any slack, no matter how hard he's worked at the clinic or tried to protect Stevie. You think you have the right to judge everyone and everything, and we should let you run our lives. Who the hell are you to treat me like some fucking child who doesn't know any better? I decide who I take to my bed, not you, Jordan." He stopped for a moment to catch his breath. "And for the record, Ash didn't have to try too hard to screw me, 'cause I wanted him as much as he wanted me."

Keith had come over to Jordan's side but for the first time it seemed he wouldn't be able to calm his lover down as Jordan continued to bad-mouth and rant about Ash.

For some reason, Jordan thought he had the right to decide who Drew dated, screwed, and fell in love with. Drew always knew the man had an ego a mile wide, but this was ridiculous. "You know what, Jordan?

I'm done. I thought as a friend you'd trust me to make the right decisions and stand by me." They'd known each other since he was four years old, and this was the first test to their friendship. "I always thought I could count on you. Has that changed?"

Jordan couldn't hold his gaze. "I trust you. It's him I don't trust."

Drew came right up into his friend's face. Jordan could be stubborn, arrogant, and high-handed but never deliberately mean.

"If you trust me, then you have to understand I know exactly what I'm doing here."

Jordan's mouth tightened. "It's different. Snakes never let you know when they're coming toward you. They slither around you, and before you know it, they've swallowed you whole. That's what Ash Davis is. A snake. I've seen him in the courtroom. He's got a way with words that'll make you think black is white and up is down. Never mind silver-tongued, the man has a forked tongue."

Remembering where Ash's tongue had been on him last night, heat rose in Drew's face. Irritated with himself for getting distracted, Drew folded his arms across his chest and glared at Jordan. "It's not the same, and you know it. You're bordering on the irrational the way you feel about him."

He turned on his heel to walk away; if he didn't leave now, he'd do or say something he'd regret. Something that might irreparably damage their lifelong friendship, and Drew wasn't ready for that to happen.

He knew everything Jordan said to him was out of love and concern, but for so many years, people had managed his life and he'd acquiesced, out of disinterest and boredom. His one act of rebellion, marrying Jackie, turned out disastrous, and that was all the fodder they needed to show him he wasn't strong or smart enough to pick the right person for himself.

No one understood him. Pathetic as it might be, Drew still felt like that scared and lonely child when his parents left for work and he'd stay home with Nana. He'd constantly needed reassurance that they'd be coming back home and hadn't disappeared forever. Was it so wrong to want someone to hold, someone to love? He'd always been that little boy lost.

After his parents died, he'd gone slightly crazy and thrown himself into the wildness of the college party scene. Anything to not be alone. Many a morning found him in a strange girl's bed, with no idea how he'd gotten there. Nor did he remember the three-somes, occasionally waking up sandwiched in between two girls, or even once or twice tangled up with another girl and guy. He'd always been so drunk he couldn't remember the sex at all. Total oblivion was what he'd been after, to wash the pain away.

That hadn't lasted long, as fear for his health as well as his studies overcame his irrational behavior, and he'd settled down to being the studious bookworm he'd always been. He may have opened his mind to his studies, but he'd walled off his heart to life.

Now Ash had up and left him at a time when he

needed someone to lean on the most he had in years. They might have been lovers—he'd let Ash inside his body—yet Drew still didn't fully understand Ash.

After last night, though, he assumed he'd have a chance to try.

Perhaps Jordan was right, and Ash had used him. It wouldn't surprise him as he'd had to live his whole life by his wits and quick mind. But even as those thoughts tumbled around in his muddled brain, he remembered the quiet strength of Ash's voice as he revealed his childhood to him. The self-loathing and pain etched on his face, the halting way he disclosed his story of debasement and cruelty, scoring a path of not only pity across Drew's heart but something fresh, unexposed to light before, as if he'd come out of the darkness from a long trip. Feelings he'd never experienced and wasn't yet ready to face.

When he glanced around the small room, everyone he cared about was there. They all looked at him with varying degrees of surprise, dismay, and pity to some extent. He knew they loved him, but only as a brother and a friend. Right now he needed more than that. He needed to find out if the man he'd shared his secrets with and let possess his body was merely a figment of his imagination.

"I gotta go find out where Ash went. I'll come back after lunch and check on Nana." Drew kissed Rachel good-bye. "We'll talk later, about everything."

"You better mean everything, you know," she called after him as the elevator doors closed on him, and he traveled downward to the first floor. That promised to be an interesting conversation, for sure.

Chapter Twenty-Three

BY THE TIME he got to the office, Ash's poor mood had deteriorated to anger. Anger at Jordan for getting under his skin, anger at Drew for caring, but most of all Ash was angry with himself for revealing his pathetic life. He'd first gone home to shower before heading to his office. Now that he'd changed into a suit and tie, the outside of him reflected his normal hard veneer, a fresh suit of armor ready to deflect whatever life planned to throw at him. His insides, however, now that was a different story altogether.

His stomach churned with anxiety, and his nerves were shot. Each time his phone rang or Laura knocked on his door with papers to sign or to escort in his next appointment, he foolishly hoped it was Drew.

What would he say to the man anyway? He buried his head in his hands, embarrassed at his emotional outburst so early this morning—it seemed a lifetime ago. How could he have been so foolish to tell Drew everything about himself? Now the man would pity him and see him as nothing more than another one of his projects. Someone who needed saving, when that wasn't what he wanted and needed at all. He stood at the window, gazing down at the busy avenue below.

A knock at the door mercifully ended his self-flagellation. "Come in." He brushed back his hair, hoping it lay properly. The least he could do was look the part of the unruffled executive. He didn't want anyone in the office to know the turmoil he faced inside.

Laura's slightly confused face filled the doorway. "Mr. Davis, there's a Dr. Klein to see you. He doesn't have an appointment, but he said he'd wait as long as it took." She pursed her lips. "Do you want me to send him away?"

Ash had to smile at her protective behavior. Laura had been with Jacob Frank for almost twenty years, right out of high school. She was a tiny woman, always dressed to perfection with sky-high heels and color-coordinating purses to match her outfits. She ran the office with almost military-like precision and accepted Ash as if he were her own son.

"No, give me a moment, then send him in." She turned to go. "Oh, and Laura? Hold all my calls, please. If anything important comes in, direct it to Mr. Walker."

Her heavily made-up eyes widened enough to let him know her surprise, but all she said was, "Yes, Mr. Davis," before she left, closing the door behind her.

Ash gulped the coffee sitting on his desk, wincing at its lukewarm taste. It had been sitting there for quite some time, and its sourness only added to the roiling in his stomach. He knew the best thing he could do would be to send Drew on his way, give him a, *Thanks for the fun night, but let's keep it strictly professional* speech. A kiss-off. After all, they worked together, and as such, they'd have to keep seeing each other at the clinic.

Ash had no illusions about Drew eventually returning to his straight lifestyle. The man wanted to experiment, and Ash was more than willing to be his guinea pig. But Drew had home and family spelled out in bold letters across his heart, and Ash had no clue what that entailed. Caring for himself was all he knew. He had no expectations of permanency.

Still, his pulse ratcheted up when Laura let Drew into the room. Drew's furious face didn't bother him; he could deal with anger.

"How's Esther?"

Drew stared at him. "She's much better, but what the hell happened to you? One minute we were there, together, and the next I looked for you and you'd disappeared. Why did you leave me?"

The confusion and disappointment on his face pricked Ash's conscience, but he steeled himself against the emotions beating in his chest. What he really wanted to do was come around from behind his desk, grab Drew, and hold him tight. After last night he found it impossible to forget the perfect way Drew's slim body curved around his. The thought that it might have been both the first and last time hurt Ash more than he imagined possible.

But like a coward, he remained standing behind the fortress of his desk, where he was safe from his impossible attraction to Drew. "You were busy with your family, and I didn't belong there, so I went home to shower, change, and come to work." Ash laced his fingers together, and could only hope Drew didn't notice how they shook.

"What the hell does that mean, you didn't belong there? I brought you there. I wanted you with me." Drew swallowed, and Ash heard the hurt in his voice. "I thought after last night, you wanted to be there with me too."

Tell him, now. This is the perfect time to tell him how you really feel about him.

Ash could almost hear his inner conscience screaming. And God knows he wanted to. He'd kissed the guy. He'd never done that before. Spent the night holding him as they slept. Another first for him. But Ash bit down hard on his inner cheek to stifle his words. Drew was better off without him. What happened last night was something Ash would relive for years, but Drew could move on, like he had from his girlfriend.

Ash opened his mouth to speak, but before he could say anything, Drew advanced on him, coming behind his desk, crowding up against him. The damp heat of Drew's breath drifted past his neck and the top of Drew's silky head of curls brushed his chin. Ash bit back a frustrated groan. He tried to do the right thing and stay away, but the inexplicable pull of his body toward Drew left Ash curiously weak in the knees. He might be a mass of confusion but with Drew near he could draw an easy breath for the first time since they separated.

"What are you afraid of, Ash? I let go of my fear last night when we made love."

Drew's body heat encompassed him, and his knees shook. *Made love? Shit.* What happened to him? Usually he was the dominant one, the one who made other people give in to his demands. Now his stomach did flip-flops as he responded to Drew.

"Uh, I'm not afraid. I don't think—"

"Yeah, you're right. Don't think." Drew slipped an arm around Ash's waist. "I never thought I'd want to be with a man, but when I stopped thinking with my head and let go with my heart, there wasn't any place I wanted to be more than there with you last night."

Ash whispered, gasping for air. "I took advantage of you. It's what I do. Jordan said—"

"Forget about Jordan. He doesn't know what I want or what I feel." Drew's gaze touched Ash briefly; he strode back to the office door, locked it, and returned to Ash's side. "For years I've been alone, even when I was with my friends or after I got married. I never felt safe, thinking everything I had would one day be taken from me."

"But you deserve someone better. And you want a family, a home. I can't give you that." Ash shuddered as Drew's hand brushed over the thin, tropical wool of his trousers to unbuckle his belt. "I don't know how."

"I disagree." Drew unbuttoned the top of Ash's pants and unzipped them. They fell straight down to his ankles, leaving him only in his boxers, his cock bulging out, already wet and aching. "You showed me last night how caring and gentle you are." Drew pushed down the boxers, exposing Ash's stiff erection to the cool air.

Ash grabbed hold of the chair to steady himself. His legs trembled, and his head spun. Drew was wrong. He wasn't good or caring. Then Drew dropped to his knees, and the sight of the man kneeling at his feet blew his mind. "Drew." He couldn't help moaning as he reached out to touch that head of tousled curls he'd dreamed of too many nights to ever forget.

The warm wetness of Drew's mouth engulfed Ash's cock. He wanted to pull away and tell Drew he should leave, but his body had other ideas as his cock swelled and his hips began to thrust a slow, steady rhythm into Drew's mouth.

The rough-smooth feel of Drew's tongue soothed him, a balm to his tortured soul. Drew's hands rested on Ash's thighs, the tips of his fingers rubbing gentle circles on his hipbones.

"Oh God." In a smooth movement, Drew placed one hand on Ash's hip while the other kept a steady stroking motion on the part of Ash's cock that wasn't inside his mouth. He was far from expert and lacked the finesse of a more practiced technique, but for Ash it was perfect. It came from the heart, and Drew's need for Ash. It was pure Drew.

Heat flooded through him as his heart began to race, his balls tingled, and with a hushed groan, he came, filling Drew's mouth. Ash worried for a moment Drew wouldn't be able to handle swallowing, but when he'd recovered enough to open his eyes and search Drew's face, nothing but a smile resided on those glistening lips.

He pulled Drew up and kissed him, enjoying the soft heat of his mouth. Ash discovered he loved kissing Drew and couldn't stop thinking about his lips. "Baby, you were amazing. But why?" He held Drew close, listening to the pounding of his heart matching its beat with Ash's own. Totally in sync. "Why me?"

"Because I'm tired of watching life happen around me. Everyone thinks they know what's best for me—my sister, my friends. They treat me as if I have no backbone or I'm too emotionally immature to make my own decisions, especially after the disaster with Jackie."

Ash kept silent, holding on to Drew and stroking his back. He'd seen it—the way Drew's friends took over his life and made decisions for him. He'd never thought to say anything before, as he hadn't known it bothered Drew so much. But with a sinking feeling, he understood the meaning behind Drew's words.

"So I'm your rebellion? A way to show everyone that even though they don't like me, you'll do what you want?" Ash held his breath, waiting for the answer.

"Hell no." Drew's emphatic denial comforted him, and when he tipped his head back to gaze into Ash's eyes, Ash saw straight into his heart. "Don't you get it yet? You're so much more than that to me. We need to talk, but I have to get back to my grandmother, and you need to get dressed and go back to work."

Drew's lopsided grin as Ash reached down to pull up his boxers and pants caused a funny thump in Ash's chest. He zipped himself up but didn't let Drew move out of reach.

"It's not my fault I was attacked at my desk. I was trying to do work." Ash grinned as he slipped his hand under Drew's collar, resting it on the nape of his neck. His thumb swept back and forth against the soft skin there. What was it about this man that rendered him helpless? He kissed Drew's cheek, enjoying the barely-there shiver that rippled under Drew's skin as Ash held him tight. "You really want me with you at the hospital?"

Drew sighed and nodded against his chest. "I do. I want you with me. Period. Do you want that?"

"Why? I know I want you. But you've never been with a man before, and from what I've seen, it was never on your horizon." Ash still didn't understand Drew's ease with their sexual relationship.

Drew leaned his hip on the desk. "We had an unconventional upbringing. I've never been hung up on sexual labels. When my parents were alive, they told both Rachel and me that as long as we loved the person, it didn't matter who we slept with, man or woman. After our parents died I went a bit wild, like I told you before, and Rachel did also. It's obvious she's now very much in love with Mike, and I hope it stays that way forever."

"Your parents were very special." Ash wondered if his own parents knew he was gay even at his young age and that was one of the reasons they'd dumped him and ran. "But aren't you concerned about what people might say now, if they found out?"

Drew's voice came out uncharacteristically hard. "It's nothing that I ever needed to discuss with anyone and still don't. My sexuality is my own personal business, and like I said to Jordan, who I choose to sleep with is my decision."

Ash contemplated Drew's profile. Drew might not have an overpowering physical presence, but Ash could take a lesson from his emotional strength. "Baby, you're amazing. I'd be proud to be with you anywhere."

The sweet smile that broke across Drew's face took his breath away.

"So don't disappear on me again. Talk to me and tell me how you feel. Okay?"

Ash nodded. "I promise." He leaned over and kissed Drew's cheek again, his lips lingering on his freshly shaven skin. "Come home with me tonight?" He kissed Drew's lips. "Stay with me?"

Drew's hands crept up to hold on to his shoulders. "I want to, but the cat…" He moaned as Ash planted kisses along his lips, nipping and licking their softness.

"Please, baby. I want you so much. Bring the cat with you. Stay with me." Before Drew, Ash had never needed to touch his lovers beyond the physical necessity to achieve release. He didn't pay much attention to whether or not they received pleasure of their own. Being with Drew changed him from a selfish lover to one who cared about giving pleasure.

"Bring Domino to your apartment?" Drew sounded incredulous. "But what if he ruins something or has an accident?" His eyes danced with laughter. "He can be a little vindictive if he gets annoyed."

Ash thought of his pristine apartment and winced. But he really wanted Drew in his bed tonight. "Maybe we could go over to your apartment and feed him, then go to mine?" His eyebrows waggled. "I'll make it worth your while." Ash bent Drew backward over his desk, prepared to convince him with his lips and his body, when his personal cell phone buzzed with the specific ringtone he'd assigned to Martinson.

"Shit, I have to take this. It's the private investigator I hired to find Luke and Brandon." When he saw Drew stand and make his way to the door, he asked Martinson to hold. "Where are you going?"

Drew stopped and turned around. "I figured you wanted me to leave, like you did the last time he called."

"Don't be an idiot. Please wait? Sit down on the sofa where you'll be more comfortable." He pulled Drew to him for a quick but fierce hug, then turned his attention back to the phone.

Martinson's no-nonsense voice reassured him. "It seems that after Luke Conover left the house, Paul Munson and his wife took the other boy, Brandon, and left the state. They ended up in Pennsylvania, where

Munson got a job with a small sheriff's department, and Grace Munson taught Sunday school in the local church. Brandon went to high school, played baseball, and was well liked by everyone."

So excited he was practically shaking, Ash asked, "And now? Do you know where he is now?"

Drew came to stand next him, and Ash hugged him tight, his anchor against the storm of his life.

"That's the strange thing. He disappeared the week before he was supposed to leave for college. No note and no trace of him."

Ash's heart sank. "But that's almost eight years ago. No one's heard from him?"

"Only a few letters to his mother that showed up with no discernible pattern. They say 'Don't worry, I'm well.' Nothing else."

In a tight voice, Ash asked, "Postmarks?"

"Different states in the Northeast." Ash could sense the man's frustration over the phone. "I'm not giving up, sir."

Ash sighed. It wasn't Martinson's fault that he wanted to throw the phone through the window or punch something or someone hard. "I know you aren't. It isn't your fault. Keep going. Spare no expense."

"Yes, sir. I promise I'll find him."

"Thank you." Ash clicked off and threw the phone onto the couch. "Fuck."

"I'm sorry." Drew squeezed his hand. "I know you've been looking for a long time. You'll find him one day."

Ash stalked around his office. "I'm beginning to wonder. Now that I know he disappeared willingly, it's clear he doesn't want to be found. Those are the hardest kinds of people to find."

Drew stepped in his path, forcing him to halt his steps. "Listen, whatever happens, you don't have to handle it alone anymore. We can work on it together."

Exactly like he'd thought. The man was too fucking good. "So you'll come home with me tonight?" Ash dragged Drew up against him, palming the man's perfect, taut ass. He could feel the muscles flexing underneath his fingers. "Say yes." He kissed Drew's neck, his jaw, and then rested his lips at the corner of Drew's mouth. "Please," he murmured, watching Drew's eyes flutter shut.

"Okay, yes, whatever you want." Drew shifted his head, and their lips met.

Soft, sweet, and the lightest touch. Not hard or brutal, with a thrusting tongue and clashing teeth. Still somewhat uncomfortable with kissing, Ash stiffened at first, but when Drew flickered the tip of his tongue along the seam of Ash's lips, desire overpowered fear and he opened his mouth to fall into the eroticism of the simple kiss. They stood that way, kissing, learning each other's mouths and breaths, until Drew pulled away with a look of regret. "I need to get back to the hospital."

"Then I'm coming with you." The smile on Drew's face let him know he'd made the right decision. Fuck Jordan and whoever else had a problem with him and

Drew. From now on he'd make sure to be by Drew's side to support him as he stood up to his friends and family.

Whatever he needed.

Chapter Twenty-Four

THEY ARRIVED AT the hospital around lunchtime. Drew could tell his grandmother was almost back to normal, as she was giving the nurse her special recipe for apple cake, which as he knew, was the best thing in the world. He bent down and kissed her cheek.

"They're moving you to a regular room in a few minutes." He greeted the nurse, then checked his grandmother's chart, pleased to see all her vital signs were normal. The nurse left the room, leaving him alone with her.

"Why can't I go home? I feel perfectly fine." She scowled at him.

"Because they need to observe you for one more night and I agree. So does Rachel, so you're outvoted." He folded his arms and scowled right back at her.

She relented. "Only one more night, though. I want to go home. I miss my bed and my flowers." She peered behind him, looking over his shoulder, her face brightening. "Oh, Asher is here. I wondered if he was going to come by."

Drew sat in the chair next to her bed so she could wave to Ash through the glass. "He was here last night too, but had to leave early this morning."

"I hope you two put aside your differences." She dragged her gaze away from Ash to glare at him.

Oh, Nana, you have no idea. "Um, yeah. We're good now. He was very worried about you."

"I'm glad you two are friends again." She pursed her lips and studied her hands.

Drew could tell she wanted to say something but held back, which was unusual for his outspoken grandmother.

"Nana, what is it? I know you want to ask me something, so go ahead and spit it out."

Her gaze slid over him; then she turned her attention back to study her fingers. "Where's your girlfriend? Isn't she here?"

Drew took her hand in his, noting how thin and fragile it felt. Her pale skin revealed every blue vein, reflecting all the hard work she'd endured during her life. He kissed her fingertips. "We broke up."

Her eyes opened wide. "You did? Why?"

He shrugged. "You were right. She got too serious, too fast. She told me how much she loved me, and I freaked out." He placed his grandmother's hand back on the bed and, with a quick glance through the window, saw Ash standing there, talking to Mike and Rachel. "I didn't love her, and I'm never going to fall in love with her. So I told her, but in a nice way."

Nana nodded with approval. "Good. I knew she

was crazy about you, and you didn't feel the same way. It wasn't right for you to string her along. She's a sweet girl, but not the right person for you."

Nana held his gaze, and he shifted on his feet, a little embarrassed. For some reason, he thought she wanted to say more, but then the orderlies came in to transfer her to her regular room.

"I'll see you later." He gave her a quick kiss and left, joining his sister and the others waiting outside.

Drew could tell by the side looks Rachel kept giving him that she was dying to get him alone to talk about him and Ash.

Because he loved her and they were so close, he decided it was only right he talk to her first. But not with Mike. "They're transferring her to a room for one more night of observation." He smiled at Rachel. "Everything looks normal."

Rachel hugged him. "Thank God. I don't know what I'd do if…well, let's not think about it anymore." She held on to him.

"Mike." Drew held onto Rachel. "I want to borrow my sister for a while, all right?"

His friend had his bad ear turned toward him and didn't hear him. When he went to tap him, Rachel put a hand on his arm.

"Don't." Her voice was quiet, her eyes sad. "He's still jumpy from the attack, and if you startle him, it makes it worse." She left his side to stand in front of her boyfriend. "Hey, love. I'm gonna go talk to Drew for a few."

Drew watched them closely. The look on Mike's face as they spoke was almost worshipful. His sister deserved nothing less.

She returned to his side. "Okay, I'm ready."

After saying goodbye to Ash and Mike, he and Rachel left the hospital and went to the diner across the street. They settled into a booth and the waitress brought their coffees right away, but she didn't take a sip, instead jumping right into the conversation.

"What's going on with you and Ash?"

Here goes nothing. "We've sort of started a relationship." He took a quick sip of his iced coffee, welcoming the shock of cold as it traveled a path down his throat. A quick glance at her face let Drew know, yep, she was surprised.

Her eyes narrowed. "Jordan said he'd take advantage of you. I like Ash but—"

"Listen." He sensed his anger rising and struggled to keep it under control. "I'm tired of everyone telling me who they think is right for me and who I should or shouldn't date, sleep with or marry.

"But you have to admit I was right about Jackie." Rachel shot him a pointed look.

"Yes, Rach, and I said it, fine. You were right about that. But it's my life to live and make decisions and mistakes, if they happen. You all need to stop thinking you have the right to tell me what to do and not do. Stop treating me like a little kid instead of your older brother."

"But Drew, you and Ash? I like him. I really do,

but Jordan says he's a player. I don't want you to get hurt."

Exasperated, he rolled his eyes. "So what? What if I do get hurt? It's my life and my choice."

"Well, you chose Jackie, and look what a bad choice that was. So maybe you need someone to tell you you're making a mistake." Her voice dropped to a whisper. "And you're really sleeping with him? You're not gay, so what are you doing?"

His stomach dropped. One thing he'd always thought he could count on was support from Rachel. If he didn't have that, he might be lost. "Would you be upset to find out I was bisexual? I thought you of all people didn't care about things like that."

Now it was her turn to roll her eyes and make a disgusted sound to go along with it. "Don't be a jerk. I'll love you no matter what. I don't care if you're gay or bi or straight, but this seems so sudden, that's all."

"It actually isn't," he admitted. "I've been attracted to Ash for a while now but denied it. Things happened the other night, and now this is exactly where I need to be." He took her hand and squeezed it. "He's a good man, Rach. His childhood was unbearable; you have no idea. I'm in awe of what he's made of himself." His lips tightened. "I won't let Jordan bad-mouth him. If he has a problem with Ash, then he either needs to deal with it or not be my friend anymore."

A small sound of dismay slipped out of Rachel's mouth. "You've known Jordan all your life. You can't cut him out like that. He's practically family."

"Family should stand by you and support you. That's what I'm asking. As long as you're there for me, for us, that's all I need." He stood and kissed her cheek. "I have to get to the clinic. Are we good?" He held his breath, waiting for her response.

She jumped up and flung her arms around him. "Of course. I love you no matter what. And I promise to try and back off." Being Rachel, she had to get in her parting shot, like she always did. "But if Ash hurts you, all bets are off."

He laughed, shaking his head as he left the diner.

THAT EVENING, DREW lay spread-eagled on Ash's enormous king-sized bed. Through heavy-lidded eyes he watched Ash kiss a path down his chest to the line of hair that led a trail from his stomach to disappear beneath his boxers. Who would have ever thought he'd be lying here in a man's bed, reveling in kisses so intense he could barely breathe? Then Ash dipped his tongue into Drew's belly button, and all thoughts fled leaving only pleasure and lust remaining. Ash caressed his cock through his thin boxer shorts and tugged them down, allowing his erection to spring free. The coolness of the air conditioner hit his fevered skin, causing him to shiver with delight.

"That feel good, baby?" Ash whispered, his cheek resting on Drew's thigh as he stroked Drew's cock with a strong hand. Drew arched up into his touch.

"Incredible. Don't stop." Drew couldn't help thrusting into Ash's hand, his cock leaking wetness from the head. He never remembered it being so easy to get hard. It seemed now all Ash had to do was look at him, and he had an erection. "Faster."

Ash chuckled. "Not so fast. The pleasure is better if you prolong the wait." He laid off for a moment, then straddled Drew, his large powerful thighs entrapping Drew's lower body. "I love to see you under me, begging for it."

Drew raised a brow. "Begging? I don't think so."

Ash shot him a look then dipped his head down, to Drew's surprise, bypassing his cock to tongue his balls.

Drew shifted nervously, "You have a very evil look in your eyes. What are you planning?"

Ash said nothing, then lifted Drew's hips in the air and held his legs wide open. He ran his tongue down the crack of Drew's ass, stopping at his hole.

"Shh. Close your eyes and feel."

A dark thrill ran up Drew's spine, and he complied, concentrating on the warm wetness of Ash's tongue as it licked around his hole. Trembling, Drew sought to keep his equilibrium at the first slide of Ash's tongue inside him.

"Oh God." His legs shook. He could feel Ash's smile against his skin, but he didn't stop and continued to lick and play at his hole until Drew came in a passionate rush of desire. His vision faded to black as the shattering orgasm left him boneless, sated, and half-dead with pleasure.

After several minutes, he caught his breath. "My God, Ash, what you do to me." He blindly reached out his hand, unable to even open his eyes. A smile tugged at his lips at the feel of Ash's palm sliding up to hold his hand, lacing their fingers. Lovemaking had never been so intensely personal as this. He cracked open one eye to see Ash stretched out next to him, his own cock still hard.

"I want you, Ash." Drew reached out and traced the tip of Ash's cock, tickling the slit, smearing the wetness that pulsed out at his touch. "I want you inside me."

Those magical silvery eyes flashed diamond bright. "You aren't still sore after last night? I don't want to hurt you."

"Please, I need you in me." Drew leaned over and kissed Ash. "Make me feel." He turned over on his stomach and got up on his knees and elbows. Ash rolled over and pulled open the drawer of the night table. Condoms and a small bottle of lube sailed in the air, landing next to Drew.

Drew closed his eyes, a throb of pleasure almost choking him. Although he'd just experienced an intense orgasm, his cock began to stiffen. "Please," he whispered over and over. "Please, touch me, love me." Making love to Ash had opened a wellspring of desire inside him that he'd bottled away, his guilt forbidding him to enjoy any pleasure.

"Oh, baby, I'm gonna love you so hard they're gonna hear you in the next building," Ash crooned to him in that slight Southern accent that never failed to drive him wild. An unashamed whimper broke from him at the touch of those strong fingers massaging the cheeks of his ass.

"More, please, more." He didn't care if he begged. He needed Ash inside him. When those cool slicked fingers brushed his hole and pressed inside, Drew almost wept with relief. "God, yes, please, now. *Now.*"

But Ash didn't listen, merely kissed down the curve of his back and continued to twist those taunting, wicked fingers inside him, brushing his gland, once, twice, three times now, until Drew saw stars and he almost screamed from both the white-hot pleasure and frustration.

"Fuck me, goddamn it."

He heard the condom packet rip, and within moments, the thick, broad head of Ash's erection prodded his entrance. Not wishing to wait another minute, he pushed back, hissing as it breached his newly opened channel.

"Baby, you all right?" Ash stopped moving, the concern in his voice evident.

"Yeah, do it." He gasped for air even as Ash slid in with care. Drew had no idea why he was so turned on, but the feel of Ash inside him gave him a high; his very skin burned with desire.

This was where he was meant to be, and no one would ever tell Drew otherwise. Ash moved then, sliding into him with long slow strokes, holding on to Drew's hips as he thrust. "Ash, harder. I'm not gonna break."

Ash leaned over him, biting his ear. "Okay, baby, you asked for it. I'm so crazy for you. I can't believe you're really here in my bed." He thrust hard, kissing him down his back. Ash snapped his hips over and over, and Drew moaned, thrashing his head back and forth, his body soaring to unimaginable heights.

Ash stroked deeper, and once again, Drew's body burned. Sweat dripped from every pore; his vision blurred. Giving himself up to this man altered him forever. He could never go back to what he was, knowing now the passion life had to offer.

"Fuck yeah." Ash let go, and Drew felt him coming as he emptied himself inside the condom. Ash shuddered, and he draped over Drew, completely spent. Drew loved the weight of Ash's strong, heavy body on top of him. To him it meant Ash trusted him, knowing he could give himself so completely and relax.

Ash pulled out with care and disposed of the condom then lay on his back with Drew tucked into his side. When he met Ash's eyes, Drew almost lost his breath at the emotion he saw shimmering in their depths. "What is it? You look almost sad, while I feel incredible." He laid his head down in that sweet space between Ash's neck and shoulder, and when Ash's arm came around him to hold him even tighter, he allowed himself a smile.

They lay together, holding one another as their breathing steadied and the world re-centered. Drew reveled in the soreness of his newly opened body, proving he lived how he wanted to for once. Because now he knew, being with Ash was truly where he was meant to be, and therefore there was no choice at all. He burrowed further into Ash's arms, comforted by their strength.

The rumble of Ash's deep voice broke the quiet. "I don't know what I've done to deserve you. You're everything good in this world, and when I'm with you, the pain gets pushed to the side. But when I'm alone, all I can think of is how I failed everyone."

"You mean Luke and Brandon?" Drew asked.

"Yes. They must hate me. That's why they never tried to find me."

In that unconscious move Drew had come to know so well, Ash rubbed the numerous scars up and down his arms. Fortunately there didn't seem to be any fresh cuts. Drew tangled his fingers in Ash's hair, forcing Ash to meet his gaze. "Why do you still do it? Hurt yourself, I mean?"

"To remind me how I've failed everyone. And to tell myself I control what I do with my body, and no one else will ever touch me again unless I want them to." His voice sounded curiously dead and flat, but younger and so very vulnerable. "I've tried to put it all behind me, all the horror that lives inside me, but it's like a leech sucking at me, and it won't let go. I thought that if I hurt myself, all my pain would fade away, but it didn't work. The pain waits for me from when I wake up in the morning, and it's still there when I close my eyes."

Ash's honesty seared him and Drew kissed his neck. "It's all right to be afraid. Everyone is afraid of something."

"I'm not afraid, Drew; I'm fucking scared to death."

And there they were. Two lost souls bobbing around in the choppy waters of their lives, desperately holding on to keep afloat. Somehow they'd found each other, and tentatively they reached out to become the other's shelter from the storm.

"Let me help you deal with it. Lean on me. Talk to me. I'm not running away." Drew rubbed his cheek against Ash's shoulder. No one would ever guess the power and confidence Ash projected was all a façade to cover up his fractured and broken mind and body. "I'm here for you; whatever it takes."

"Why, Drew? Why me? I'm not sure I'm worth the effort."

The heart wants what it wants, or else it does not care. Drew remembered that line from an Emily Dickinson poem he'd read in high school. He wanted Ash. He cared. Lying here with this man, listening to him open his heart, made him realize how much he cared for and wanted Asher Davis. He swept the hair off Ash's brow and kissed him. "I think you might be worth everything to me."

Chapter Twenty-Five

ASH BREEZED INTO his office, coffee cup in hand and a smile on his face. "Good morning, Laura. How are you today?" He stopped by her desk to pick up his messages.

"I'm well, Mr. Davis, thank you." She gave him a once-over. "You're looking happy."

He stopped to think for a moment. In the past week he and Drew had spent almost every night together, having dinner after working at the clinic or relaxing at one of their apartments. Spending his nights buried inside of Drew, having his warm, lean body wrapped around him every night was fast becoming a highly addictive habit.

"I am, Laura. Very much so, as a matter of fact." He leaned over and kissed her on the cheek. "Thank you for putting up with me all these years."

He never thought he'd see Laura speechless, but he grinned at her obvious surprise. "Is something wrong? You look shocked."

"Oh, nothing, Mr. Davis. It's nice to see you happy; that's all."

He winked at her. "It's nice to feel this way as well."

He strode into his office and sat down at his desk. The first piece of mail he opened was a large envelope from the court. A huge grin broke over his face, and he immediately picked up the phone.

"Hello?" Though he'd only left him an hour ago, Drew's sexy, sleep-roughened voice sent a pang of longing through Ash. He wanted to be back in bed, running his hands through Drew's silky curls, kissing his soft pale skin.

"Did I wake you, sleepyhead?"

"Yeah." Ash could hear him stretching and yawning over the phone. "Some crazy sex maniac kept me up all night doing unspeakable things to me."

"Oh really? Are you complaining?" Ash leaned back in his chair. The memory of Drew, naked and impaled on his cock, riding him into oblivion had him instantly hard and wanting.

"Yeah." Drew dropped his voice low until it purred in his ear. "I'm here alone in my cold bed, and I miss him."

"It sounds like you're the sex maniac." Ash laughed. "I called with some news."

"Mmm? What is it?"

"I got the papers from the court. Your divorce is final, baby. You're a free man at last."

The silence at the other end of the phone surprised Ash. He'd thought Drew would be happy or at least say something.

"Drew, are you still there?"

"Yeah. It's funny, you know. When you said it now, I have to admit, I'd almost forgotten what she looked like. I certainly don't have any great memories of Jackie. But I married her. Shouldn't I feel something—sadness, or a wish that things could've turned out differently?"

Unease gripped at Ash. Was Drew upset about their relationship? "Do you? Wish that you were still married to her, or with a woman, instead of being with me?" His heart thumped in his chest.

Drew's swift answer relieved Ash. A part of him still didn't believe Drew wanted to be with him, rather than a woman. "No. I don't want to be with her or any other woman. Or man, for that matter. I'm exactly where I want to be." His whispered voice calmed Ash's frenzied pulse. "I've never been happier in my life, thanks to you."

Ash wished he could be there with Drew to hug him and thank him for everything he'd done. He remembered so well the first time he'd seen Drew across the conference table, so pale and sad, and compared him to the sweetly sleeping man he'd left all flushed and sated in his bed. "Who would've ever thought that day we first met, six months later we'd be together celebrating your divorce. Hey." An idea popped into his head. "Let's have people over to celebrate on Saturday night. Esther is well enough to come to you now, right?"

"Yes, and it's not like I could keep her away. I think it's great. I'll call the guys and Rachel."

"Do you think Jordan will come?" Ash kept his tone neutral. Jordan flat-out refused to accept them as a couple. Rachel had confided in them that he still believed Ash somehow coerced Drew into a sexual relationship. "He treats me like I'm a predator, you know."

"If you don't want me to ask him and Keith, I won't."

Even though he tried not to show it, Ash saw how incredibly hurt Drew was over Jordan's behavior. He'd even offered to cut ties with his childhood friend, but Ash refused to allow that to happen. Knowing Drew's greatest fear was losing the people closest to him, Ash made certain to try and never alienate Jordan, not even saying a negative word against him no matter how many times the man snubbed him. Ash's only concern was for Drew.

But true to form, Drew's thoughts centered not on himself but on Ash's feelings. "I've told him I won't put up with him treating you this way. Not when I care about you so much."

"Give him time, baby. He'll come around."

"I don't want to talk about it. I'll call Keith and let him tell Jordan. If he doesn't want to come, it's his loss." His flat tone didn't fool Ash.

"Okay, okay." Ash tried to soothe him. The last thing he wanted was to upset Drew. "Let's not dwell on it. I'll take care of all the arrangements. All you need to do is show up and look gorgeous like you always do."

"That's my line. Do you know how lucky I feel to have you? I think about how empty my life was before you. I don't know if you realize how much you mean to me, Ash."

Ash swallowed the huge lump that suddenly lodged in his throat. He managed to choke out the words as a burning sensation stung his eyes. "I know. I think you may have saved my life." An overwhelming rush of emotion flooded through him like a cleansing bath. It had been weeks since he'd thought of hurting himself. The need for pain and control didn't drive his life anymore, not with Drew by his side.

At Drew's urging, he'd begun seeing a therapist. Even though he'd only had one visit, Ash could tell the doctor would be able help him. They'd discussed his driving need to punish himself for what he believed was his selfish abandonment of his foster brothers. The doctor had told him to look deep within himself and question his supposed abandonment of Luke and Brandon. Late at night, alone in his apartment, Ash could admit he'd never really had a choice at all. He'd been driven to the point where had he stayed, he would've either killed Munson or himself. Though he chose to live, Ash continued to punish himself for that choice. Slow as his progress would be, he held out hope that eventually he might forgive himself.

"I have to go now, baby. I—" Ash stopped short. "Um, have a great day, and I'll see you tonight.

He clicked off and cradled his head in his hands.

Had he almost said the *L* word? It would've been so natural and easy. What would it feel like, to be able to come home every day to Drew and tell him *I love you*? Shaking his head, he picked up the phone again, this time to call Esther. He loved talking to Drew's grandmother. She was the family he'd never had a chance to know.

He smiled as Esther picked up the phone, already talking. "Asher, sweetheart, I have that caller ID now. The kids insisted I get it after that little incident."

He did love this woman and would kill anyone who tried to hurt her. "No further problems though, right?"

"No, none at all. Mrs. Delaney and I have had a very peaceful time of it here."

"Good." All of a sudden he was uncharacteristically nervous. What if Esther wasn't as happy with Drew not being married as he thought she was? "Well, um, the reason I'm calling is that today I received Drew's final divorce papers, and we thought a small family celebration was in order." He licked his lips. "That is, if you're fine with it."

"You know, I wasn't happy when he married that woman. I knew it probably wouldn't last because she obviously only wanted to be any doctor's wife, not my grandson's wife."

Ash held his breath and listened.

"Of course no one wants to see their child divorced, but Drew is so much happier now than when he was dating or married."

"He is?" Ash smiled to himself.

"I may be old, but I'm not blind. You've played a very big part in Drew's recent happiness, I believe. Am I right?"

"We've become good friends, yes. Drew is a very special person." He tried to keep his tone as noncommittal as possible, as he had no idea what she might think. Would she be all right with Drew in a relationship with him?

"How good a friend, may I ask?"

He'd argued cases before judges who'd sent grown men out of the courtroom in tears, yet Esther's simple question made him more nervous. In his mind, he wanted Esther to know about his and Drew's relationship, yet he thought it should be up to Drew to tell his grandmother about something so important.

"Esther, you're fishing for information. Whatever you want to know, I think you should ask Drew. Now the reason I called is that Saturday night at Drew's apartment, he's having a small get-together to celebrate his divorce being final, and of course you're the first one he wanted called."

"Good. I'm so glad he can put that episode behind him and move on with his life, don't you agree?"

Still fishing. The woman was relentless. "Yes, Esther. Rachel and Mike will pick you up Saturday night."

"Hmm. Fine." Her disappointed voice had him chuckling even as he hung up the phone.

BY SATURDAY NIGHT, Drew's apartment had undergone a total transformation. Ash had his secretary arrange everything, from the food to the liquor and flowers. He wanted everything to be perfect. Distraught from all the tumult, the cat hid under the bed, his yellow eyes glowing in the dark. Domino even forgot his favorite pastime of torturing Ash by swiping at his ankles whenever he walked by.

Ash dressed casually in a stark white linen shirt, sleeves rolled up to his elbows, and crisp black pants. Last night, lying in each other's arms after making love, Drew had remarked upon his hair. *"It feels like silk. Gives me something to hold on to when you're inside me."*

A flash of green caught his eye, and he watched as Drew strolled out of the bedroom looking deliciously handsome in his pale green linen shirt and khaki pants. Ash's gaze raked hungrily over his lover's perfect face, slim hips, and the pale wedge of skin that showed at his neck where his shirt lay unbuttoned. He licked his lips, remembering how sweet all that skin tasted.

"Hi, baby." He pulled Drew against him, then bent down to capture his mouth in a bruising kiss. Drew's lips opened to his questing tongue, and as usual, Ash lost himself in the miraculous feel of their mingled breaths and slick tongues. Kissing Drew, Ash discovered, was as addicting as any drug.

"Uh, excuse us, you guys, but can you hold it off

until later?" A familiar voice broke into Ash's befuddled mind, but he didn't care and continued to place soft kisses on Drew's lips. Only the sound of a throat clearing and a muttered curse caused him to break contact with Drew's hot mouth to slant a look to the side.

He caught Keith's amused smirk, but his stomach clenched at the grimace of disgust on Jordan's face. With one final kiss, Ash pulled away from Drew but kept his arm draped over Drew's shoulder, his body tucked into Ash's side.

"Hello, you two." He extended a hand first to Keith, who took it, giving him a strong clasp and a squeeze. As Keith shook Drew's hand, Ash offered his hand to Jordan, who stared hard at him for a moment, then deliberately turned his back on him to walk over to the bar and pour himself a drink. Ash's face flamed at the purposeful insult, but he said nothing. This was Drew's night, and he wasn't about to ruin it for him.

"He'll come around. Don't worry." Rachel spoke into his ear and squeezed his arm as Drew followed after Keith and Jordan.

"Thanks. I don't care if he doesn't like me, but it hurts Drew, and I can't stand to see that happen." Ash leaned down to give her a kiss hello and clap Mike on the back.

Mike gave him a curious look. "You and D are really, um, together? Like a couple?"

Ash braced himself for more criticism from another of Drew's friends. "Yes. I hope it won't be as much of a problem for you as it is for Jordan."

Mike shrugged. "I don't care. As long as you're good to him, it doesn't matter to me. Jordan's always been overprotective of Drew and me, maybe because he's the oldest of our group. I don't know." He glanced over at Rachel. "I'm sure you'll eventually work out any problem with him. He's a pain in the ass but means well." He and Rachel excused themselves to get a drink as Esther approached.

"Asher, darling boy. Come give me a kiss."

A genuine smile broke across his face. "Hello, Esther. You're looking lovely as usual." He kissed her cheek and then her slim fingers. Tucking her little hand into the crook of his arm, he walked her across the room, over to where Drew stood, still talking to Jordan and Keith.

"I love walking arm in arm with a big, strong man. My Sy was like you, and he always made me feel so safe." She patted his arm.

"I'm honored you compare me to your late husband in any way. Drew tells me he was a wonderful man."

She nodded and squeezed his arm. "He was, yes. And you have been wonderful for Drew and those young children at the clinic." She halted their procession and faced him, placing her hand on his arm.

He tensed as her gaze fell to his bared arm. Her face blanched, and he knew she'd seen and felt the many scars that twisted over his exposed skin. He'd forgotten to roll down his shirtsleeves before everyone started to arrive for the party. Now Esther had a full view of his humiliation and self-destruction.

"My dearest child." Her lips trembled, and he noticed how white she'd become. Fearing for her health, he led her quickly to a chair and sat next to her. "Why?"

He could never tell her. It was enough he lived with the memories, but a woman like Esther didn't deserve the burden of his self-destructive behavior.

"It was long ago, before I came to New York; before I managed to make something of my life." He released a breath he wasn't aware of holding. "I've done many things I'm ashamed of and wish I could erase. I treated people like they were nothing, nobodies like me. Having Drew as a friend and you, Esther, as someone who cares for me has irrevocably changed me."

He'd never known what it meant to belong, to have someone else worry or care about him, nor had he ever thought of anyone else's feelings but his own. Being with Drew and working at the clinic had showed him his life could have purpose and that he meant something, not only to those kids he tried to help, but to Drew and Esther. He'd never thought it possible to dream of a life full of happiness, yet every day that he woke up with Drew, the dream became a reality.

Tears brimmed in her eyes. "I love you, Asher. You've become as dear and special to me as if you were my own. Promise me you'll never do anything to harm yourself again."

"I'm not good. I'm selfish, arrogant, and quick-tempered. I don't know what you see in me." He grabbed both her hands in his. "But I don't have that driving need to hurt myself anymore. I think I'm beginning to believe maybe I am not fully to blame for the past. I'm learning to find my happiness, and enjoy it." And as he spoke, he realized it was the first time he'd ever said it. But it was true. He *was* happy, and as his gaze slid over the people in the room and found Drew, warmth suffused his body and the tension within him melted away. With the uncanny sixth sense they had when the other was around, Drew caught his eye and winked. A smile crept across Ash's face.

"Does my grandson know?"

"Know what, Esther?" His concentration remained on Drew.

"That you love him. And from the looks he's giving you, I'd say the feeling is mutual."

Ash's heart dropped to his stomach. All the saliva in his throat dried up, and he tasted sawdust in his mouth. "Um, I—"

"Is this the dashing, silver-tongued lawyer I've heard so much about?" Esther, her voice full of amusement, stunned him with her perception.

"Esther." Ash sighed. "I don't know what to say to you."

"You don't have to say anything. I see it in your eyes. Only you know how you feel and what's in your heart."

What did he feel? He had no idea. He only knew

that a life without Drew in it now seemed inconceivable.

He watched her gaze settle on Drew and Jordan, a fond smile crossing her lips. “Did you know after Jordan told us all he was gay, I marched with him in the first gay pride parade he attended? I was so proud of him, standing up for himself, against all the bullies.”

Ash swallowed his hurt. “Jordan hates me. He remembers the way I used to be and the corrupted life I lived. He doesn’t trust me and thinks I’m going to hurt Drew.” He regretted so much in his life, but never more so than tonight. If only he’d behaved himself and not been the man-whore he’d been in the past, perhaps he would’ve been accepted by Drew’s best friend.

“And are you?”

As usual Esther came straight to the point. She never let him get away with anything, forcing him to face his innermost secrets. Tonight was no different except he no longer had the driving need to hide his feelings not only from her, but from himself.

“I’d hurt myself again before I’d hurt Drew. I care about him more than I’ve ever cared about anyone else.”

“I never imagined you to be a coward. You know, I’ve lost so many people I’ve loved I no longer wait for what I think is the right time or let people dictate to me what’s right or wrong. Don’t waste your time thinking.”

Ash bent down and gave her a kiss on her cheek. As a child he used to wonder about his real mother. Who she was, whether or not she had dreams for him when she was pregnant and after he was born. But now, as he soaked in Esther's love and acceptance, from the gentle touch of her hand on his to the soft, knowing look in her eyes, the past had receded far enough that it no longer mattered how his life had begun.

It only mattered where he was going and whom he'd be journeying with.

"Thank you, Esther."

He walked toward Drew.

Chapter Twenty-Six

"WHAT THE FUCK are you doing with him?" Jordan's anger pushed against him like backdraft from a fire. As long as he'd known him, Drew couldn't remember his friend exhibiting such hostility.

"I'm still not sure why you think I need to explain anything to you." His voice remained deceptively calm, but Drew's eyes narrowed in anger. "Since when have you appointed yourself my keeper?"

"Since you started making such fucking stupid decisions, man. What the hell is wrong with you lately? First you marry that cheating bitch; now you allow yourself to be taken in by some self-centered prick." Jordan ran his hand through his hair, causing the usual neatly styled arrangement to stand up on end.

Drew's temper snapped like a worn-out rope. "Enough. I don't know why you, Rachel, or Mike think you have the right to voice opinions on my choices in life. I'm not fucking four years old on the playground anymore."

"Then stop acting like it, and use your brain instead of your dick," Jordan sniped, his blue eyes icy cold. His usual cockiness had been replaced by the sneering arrogance Drew heartily detested. From childhood, Jordan had consistently believed his decisions were always best, stemming from his natural-born confidence as the oldest and therefore the leader in their group. As children, Drew had always found it easier to follow in Jordan's wake instead of asserting his own independence.

It had never mattered that much until now.

Almost desperately, Drew put a hand on Jordan's arm in an attempt to salvage the conversation and perhaps their friendship. Because he knew that no matter how important his friends were to him, if he was forced to make a choice, he'd choose Ash.

"Don't you understand? I don't want to make this choice, and I shouldn't have to. Why are you forcing me? How would you feel if I told you I didn't like Keith? Would you break up with him?" Drew watched as a look of disbelief flashed across Jordan's face.

"You actually have the nerve to compare Keith to that arrogant piece of shit? I'll bet he's never told you how he feels about you. And you're too trusting, like always. You'll never learn, will you?"

"Well, well, Jordan. Why hold back?" Ash sauntered over, and Drew winced at the harsh planes of Ash's handsome face. Where moments before he'd been relaxed and carefree, now his eyes flashed steel and his mouth had hardened to granite. "Let everyone know how you really feel about me." Glowering, he folded his arms. Drew didn't want this to descend into a shouting match between the two men.

Keith stood next to Jordan, as usual, trying to calm him down, his hand caressing the nape of Jordan's neck. This time, however, Jordan wouldn't be denied his say.

"Don't tell me not to care when I see my friend making a mistake. Especially after the last one he made." He looked around the room, pushing Keith's hand away. "Doesn't anyone else see how wrong this whole situation is?"

Drew's voice rose, uncharacteristically loud. "I've already told you my life is not yours or anyone else's to run or control. Leave my personal life alone, or leave. Period."

The room fell silent. Drew could hear Mike asking Rachel what had happened, but she shushed him. Jordan's laugh rang uneasily. "Don't be ridiculous. We're best friends. You wouldn't choose him over our friendship of thirty years."

He loved Jordan like a brother, but Drew couldn't take his pushy manipulation any longer. "It's not me choosing him. You're forcing my hand. I don't need you to fight my battles for me anymore."

"I didn't say anything when you married Jackie, even though I knew she was wrong for you, and now look where you are. Divorced after not even a year. Maybe if I'd spoken up, you wouldn't be here today, throwing a party to celebrate a failed marriage."

Rachel's gasp filled the room. If a knife flayed open his chest, Drew wouldn't have felt as much pain. He'd always known his friend's arrogance and opinionated nature didn't win him many popularity contests, but he'd thought it was done out of love. After hearing those hurtful words, Drew now questioned the very foundation of their thirty-year friendship.

"I don't owe you or anyone here explanations for what takes place in my life. Like I said. You don't like it; you know where the door is." He stood face-to-face with Jordan, watching his eyes widen with shock.

Ash's hand came down on his shoulder, heavy yet comforting. "Don't make snap judgments. Being the oldest in the group, he feels protective." Ash's hand gave a quick squeeze. "Strangely enough, I can understand that."

As the oldest and self-appointed protector of his foster brothers, Ash would understand Jordan's position. It made sense that he could relate. All Drew wanted was for his family to get along together, but Ash was his lover, and he would defend him to his friends and family.

"Are we good, Jordan? Please?" Drew didn't want to fight. For the first time since he could remember, his life seemed to be going smoothly. He had no desire to see a ripple in the water disturb his fragile peace. "Come on, man."

Keith leaned over and murmured in Jordan's ear. Whatever he said turned the tide as Jordan relaxed into Keith's embrace. "I'll accept it, but I don't have to like it. However"—he put up his hand—"I won't sabotage you, Davis. My concern is Drew. If you hurt him, disappear before I find you." He stalked off.

At that moment Peter and his wife walked in, and the tension in the room eased as they greeted his grandmother. Ash left their group to greet his friends, and Drew followed his progress across the room.

"You really care about him, don't you?"

No use in hiding the truth. Keith's question brought a smile to Drew's lips.

"Yeah. You all don't know him because you only see his public face. There's so much more to him that you can't imagine, but it isn't my story to tell."

"You're in love with him."

Drew stiffened at Keith's words. "Are you planning on giving me as hard a time as Jordan? If so, then please don't say anything else."

"No. But let me give you a piece of advice."

Drew faced him. "Yes?"

"Don't wait for the right time or a special moment, if that's what you're doing. Believe me, I know better than anyone, being a cop. I could leave one morning and never come home." For a moment wetness glimmered in his eyes. "The regrets some people live with are crushing. It may sound clichéd, but I don't ever take what I have with Jordan for granted, because I know how easily it can all disappear." With that, Keith left Drew's side and slipped his arms around Jordan's waist, kissing the top of his head.

Tonight, Drew thought.

By this time, Rachel and Mike had joined him. "I know you say you're together now, but you were never interested in men before. And, your willingness to throw away a lifetime of friendship isn't the brother I've known all my life. Since you met Ash, you're like a different person. In spite of our talk, I still don't understand." The confusion and concern in Rachel's face clouded her eyes and caused a furrow in her normally smooth brow. "And don't think I'm still not concerned about Ash's reputation. I kind of get where Jordan's coming from."

"Will you excuse us, please?" Drew took his sister's arm and steered her toward his bedroom, where he sat on the bed and indicated she should do the same. He rubbed his hands on his thighs, warming himself up for this talk. To know she'd come through her darkness, a strong secure woman, with so much love to give and receive, was all the knowledge he needed to decide his own life had been put on hold long enough.

"Look, you know we've never been ones to place a label on anyone. When you experimented in college and introduced me to your girlfriend, I didn't care. As long as you were happy."

Rachel's lip curved in a small smile. "Yeah, Samantha was fun to be with, but we never took it seriously. It was about finding our way, and sex was a part of it."

One thing Drew had been curious about. "Have you told Mike you were with a woman for a few months?"

She rolled her eyes. "Yeah. And typical man, he got

all excited and wanted to know if we'd taken any pictures. Honestly, sometimes you men are such pigs." She laughed, but the nervous winding of her necklace around her fingers indicated she still had concerns.

"Good, because you don't want secrets. Ash and I don't have secrets either. He knows me, Rach. Really knows me. I think he knows me better than I know myself."

"But when did you realize you were bisexual?" Her color rose. "You're obviously sleeping with each other, but you've never done that with a guy before. Right?" Her green eyes held his, but there was no condemnation in her regard. Merely curiosity and love.

"Look, there are things I've never spoken of because, well, it was personal to me. So it isn't that I've never been with another man; this has nothing to do with sex. It's that I couldn't be with anyone else but Ash. He's the difference here, not my sexuality. There's something about him that brings me peace. He's taken away my loneliness."

"Was it that bad?"

"Yeah." He pushed the hair away from his face. "I blamed myself for Mom and Dad's death. If I hadn't been such a baby, so afraid to be by myself, I wouldn't have needed them to come up that weekend to hold my hand and tell me everything would be all right. They died because I was afraid to live my life. And for years afterward, I let Jordan and you guys push me in whatever direction you thought was right for me, without ever questioning what I wanted."

Tears trickled down her cheeks. "I didn't mean to do it. It's only because I love you and want the best for you."

With the pad of his thumb, he swiped at her cheeks. "I know. And the one time I asserted myself I married Jackie, and look where that got me."

She sniffled but smiled through her tears. "Yeah. But, it found you Ash. You know I'm a great believer in fate. Maybe you needed that mistake to lead you in the direction you were always meant to be."

God, he loved her. Every day was such a precious gift. He couldn't imagine life without her. "I love you. And maybe you're right, but I'm still finding my way."

"Well, if you want my opinion—"

He clapped a hand over her mouth. "I know you mean well, but it's time now for me to do it my way with all the bumps and bruises that may come along with it. Do you understand?"

Before she had a chance to answer, the sound of a throat clearing broke the anticipatory silence. When he glanced toward the door, a smile broke out across his face. "Hi."

Ash leaned his long torso against the doorframe, and although to the average bystander he might seem relaxed, Drew knew better. Those broad shoulders strained, tense and tight against his shirt, while his silvery eyes glittered with repressed emotion Drew had become too familiar with. It hurt to see Ash so wary around him. Especially after all they'd shared.

"I didn't see you for a while and wondered if everything was okay." Ash's gaze settled on Rachel. "I'll leave you two." He turned to go.

"No, please." Rachel jumped up and gave Drew a quick hug. "We're finished, and I'm leaving." When she passed Ash in the doorway, she stood on her tiptoes and brushed her lips to his cheek. "He's all yours."

Rachel disappeared down the hallway, but Drew only had eyes for Ash.

It didn't come to him like a big bang, with the proverbial trumpets blaring. Ironically, the quiet intensity of it made it so much more real and potent. His chest ached, and his heart raced. Every hair on his body rose and quivered, his skin prickling at the mere thought of Ash's touch. He *longed* for this man. Never in a million years had he thought another person could turn him inside out so the absolute rawness of his feelings lay right at the surface of his skin.

And the fact that he was drawn to a man? Irrelevant. The strength of that hard body coupled with the softness of Ash's touch nearly had him whimpering out loud with repressed desire.

He loved him.

Tonight, he'd tell him. Tell this wonderfully complex man, who was brave yet fearful, honest yet still so hurt and hidden, that he loved him with all his heart.

Drew held out his hand. "I'm glad you came to find me. It's nice to have a moment of time together, without all the negative judgment surrounding me."

Ash pulled Drew into his chest, and Drew sank into the embrace, resting his chin on Ash's shoulder, while their hips and groins nestled together in a familiar position. Nothing gave him peace and contentment like being held in Ash's arms.

"Is everything all right with you and Rachel? Is she okay with us?" Ash's hands massaged Drew's back in a soothing circular motion.

He smiled against Ash's shoulder. "Yeah. She is. I think it's all going to be fine."

A brief press of lips against the top of his head and then Ash stepped away. "We should go back." His normally unruffled voice sounded ragged and harsh. "People want to talk to you."

Bemused, Drew nodded but slipped his hand into Ash's and tugged. "Together, right?"

"Yes. Of course."

They walked back into the living room, and he found himself surrounded by his friends. Peter and his wife were there, as well as Ryder Daniels and his husband, Jason Mallory. They'd brought along Connor Halstead, who, as a Legal Aid attorney, had become an invaluable resource to them in navigating the convoluted mess of the child welfare system. Connor's wife Emily had recently given birth to their first child and chose to stay home.

Drew returned to his grandmother's side and found her in an earnest conversation with Jordan. Upon his approach, Jordan's expression shuttered, returning once again to an impenetrable icy shield.

Rachel tapped a glass filled with sparkling champagne. "Quiet, everyone." She raised the glass in a toast.

"To my darling brother, Drew, whom I love with all my heart." She hugged him tight. "I hope you have your heart's desire. I love you so much."

Drew squeezed her close. "I love you, baby girl," he whispered into her hair, loving her clean, fresh scent. "I'm working on it."

He hugged her hard. After filling a flute with the golden bubbly wine, he raised his glass in a toast.

"Thank you to all who helped me through this, no matter how big or small a part you played. You must know how invaluable you've been to my psyche. Whatever's left of it."

Everyone laughed, and then he continued. "An extra-special thanks to my family, who stood by me from the beginning to now, the way families should, whether or not they agree with what I did." He raised his glass. "To family."

"To family," everyone shouted.

Drew had finished his glass of champagne when there was a loud crash, then the sound of breaking glass from the far window of the living room. Rachel and Lisa screamed while his grandmother looked about, a confused expression on her lined face.

On the floor of the living room was a large brick with a paper tied to it. Keith raced over to where the brick landed. "Drew, do you have any plastic gloves and a clear plastic bag?"

Drew ran to the kitchen and opened the cabinet doors under the sink. He always kept a supply of gloves for cleaning the litter box, so he grabbed a pair along with a plastic bag, then sprinted back to the living room and handed them to Keith. He pulled them on and slipped the note out from under the twine.

They all crowded around Keith to read over his shoulder. Drew saw the bold black letters, and his blood ran cold.

Next time the old lady won't be so lucky. Close down that faggot clinic.

They all stared at each other. Keith slid the note into the plastic bag and handed it to Drew. "Take this and call 911. Tell them what happened and that I'm here at the scene, off-duty but with my weapon." He then pulled out his service revolver and motioned everyone away from the window.

Drew made the call and returned to the living room. Keith instructed them to stay away from the window, then went downstairs to meet the police officers. Red lights flashed against his windows from the street, indicating the police cruiser had arrived. After about twenty minutes Keith came back upstairs, in full police mode.

"Drew, have you had any threats at the clinic before?" Keith had his little black notebook with him, and his laser sharp eyes never wavered from Drew's face.

"No. Never. Everyone in the neighborhood has been so supportive." There had to be something else. He remembered when his grandmother was hospitalized and the two young men who pretended to help her with gardening but shoved her around. "What about the two kids who pushed her around the night she fell ill? You know those kids in Stevie's neighborhood have hassled him about working at the clinic with me."

Keith made a note. "And we know their penchant for violence. It's a good place to start. I'll talk to them tomorrow then take Esther to the station and have her look at some pictures. I wanted to wait until she was stronger, but I think we have to move fast on this."

Drew's lips tightened. "Don't let her stay too long. She won't admit it, but she still gets tired."

Keith patted him on the shoulder. "Don't worry. She's special to me too. To all of us."

Drew smiled briefly, and then he searched the room until he found his grandmother sitting with Ash and Rachel. His heart squeezed.

His family. He'd do anything to protect them.

Chapter Twenty-Seven

"ESTHER, ARE YOU well? Would you like a drink of water?" Ash sat at her side, worry gnawing away at his stomach. Nothing could happen to her. Nothing.

"I'm fine, Asher. Really. Why is everyone hovering around me?" Her lips thinned as her eyes narrowed with irritation. "I'm sure it was some neighborhood kids. They do these things all the time. What they need is strong family guidance and a place where they can play or read."

Her naïveté was sweet, but Ash knew better. For some reason, Drew was being targeted. If it was only the brick, maybe it wouldn't have raised his warning flag, but the fact that there was a note scared him. They'd already had one close call with Esther.

"I'm sure you're right." He stood and kissed her cheek, and he and Rachel exchanged knowing looks. With a brief nod, he threaded his way around the groups of people standing about. The two police officers were taking statements from everyone and were in the process of interviewing Drew, so he joined Peter and his wife, Lisa, as they waited their turn.

"Hi, you two." He kissed Lisa's cheek. "Sorry for the extra entertainment this evening."

"Oh, Ash, what's happening? I heard that the note mentioned the clinic. Are you in any kind of danger?" Her green eyes clouded with worry, and she gripped his arm.

Even after all these years, he couldn't stand being touched, even if he knew the person as well as Lisa. He stiffened and gently shook her off, hoping he didn't offend her. "I don't really know, but yes, it's meant as some sort of intimidation against the clinic." The worry wasn't for himself. He didn't spend as much time at the clinic as Drew or Rachel did, or the kids who volunteered, making them easy targets for this kind of hate crime. The thought of something happening to Drew kicked his adrenaline into high gear. Spots danced before his eyes, his vision grayed, and a roaring sounded in his ears.

"Ash, Ash, are you all right? Here, sit down." Peter took him by the shoulder. The touch wasn't right. It wasn't Drew. Oh God, if anything happened to Drew, he knew he couldn't survive the loss. "No," he rasped out. "I need to find Drew. I need to tell him something."

An earnest-looking young police officer was still interviewing Drew, so Ash could only watch him from afar as the thoughts tumbled around in his head. When had this man become so important to him, and why?

Mr. Frank, as usual, had been right all along. Somewhere along the way, the need for human touch, to feel warmth had returned to his soul.

"Ash? What's going on?" Stevie's voice pierced through his internal musings.

"What are you guys doing here?" Ash saw not only Stevie, but also Javier hovering by his side, a fierce, protective expression on his face. "Are you two dating?" His lips tugged up in a smile.

Javier scowled. "Don't make fun, man. It's all right. We're having a good time together, right?" Javier took Stevie's hand, and Stevie blushed a bright red.

Stevie'd had a crush on the older boy for several months now, so it made Ash happy that they'd gotten together. Stevie needed a strong male protector to teach him how to stand up for himself.

"But what's going on? We were biking by and saw the cop cars." Stevie surveyed the room. "Did anyone get hurt? Is Dr. Drew okay?"

Ash patted him on the back, happy to notice that Stevie didn't seem as bony as he had a few months ago. "Everyone's fine. It's a brick thrown through the window with a threatening note attached. You remember Keith, right? He called the police to come down."

Instead of looking scared, Stevie looked thoughtful. "Is Dr. Drew gonna have to close down the clinic?"

"Why would you ask that?" It was a strange question coming from Stevie, especially since the note had mentioned that very thing. "Have you heard something, maybe out on the streets?"

All at once, Stevie's nerves seemed to get the better of him. "No, I don't know nothing."

Ash steered him over to the sofa and sat next to him. "Don't be afraid of anything. If you've heard something, anything, let me know. You should talk to Keith again."

"Now?" Stevie gulped, his wide eyes darting to where Keith stood, talking to one of the officers.

"Don't worry," Ash soothed. "I'll be right here while you talk to him."

"O-okay," Stevie stuttered.

Ash motioned over Keith, and Drew followed from behind.

"Keith, remember Stevie?" Ash took the boy by the shoulders. "He said he may have heard something on the street about the clinic."

"Sure I do. Hi, Stevie." Keith smiled, and Ash caught Stevie's eye and nodded.

"Don't be afraid. You've spoken before, and nothing bad happened to you. Tell Keith what you know."

Javier moved in next to Stevie and held his hand. "Go on, tell 'em everything you heard."

Stevie took a deep breath. "Um, well, you know the two guys who always give me trouble, right?"

Ash was only too well acquainted with those punks. "Yes."

"I heard them talking about how they didn't like having so many queers in the neighborhood now. That Dr. Drew should leave before something bad happens."

Ash's chest tightened as Keith spoke. "Did they talk about hurting anyone or doing something to the clinic?"

"No." Stevie tucked his hair behind his ear. "But they keep telling me that Dr. Drew ain't gonna be around much longer; then I won't have any friends."

Javier put his arm around Stevie's thin shoulders. "Don't you worry. I'm here, and Dr. Drew and Dr. Jordan ain't closing down the clinic, right?"

Ash's nod was emphatic. "Absolutely not. Don't you worry, Stevie. Go get something to eat, then go home, all right?"

"Okay, if you say so." Stevie let himself be led away by Javier but kept shooting troubled looks over his shoulder.

"What do you think?" Ash turned back to Keith, who put a finger up in a "just wait" gesture as he finished jotting down notes.

"I think," Keith said grimly, "the time has come for me to pay these boys a little visit and make them see the errors of their ways."

"I'll come with you." Ash jumped up from the sofa, anxious to get going and confront the bastards who had not only terrorized Stevie, but also may have hurt the people he loved.

Keith walked toward the front door with the police officers, and Rachel cleaned up the glass from the floor. Most of the guests had left after making their statements to the police, and only Drew and his friends remained, along with Esther and Rachel. Ash joined them, coming in on the tail end of an argument between Esther and Drew.

"Nana, look. I have to go. I'm sure it's those two punks who are always harassing that boy Stevie who threw the brick. If they're the ones who hurt you and are also planning something against the clinic, I need to know."

"Let the police do their job. You could get hurt." Her eyes bored holes into Ash. "Tell him, Asher. Tell him not to go."

He opened his mouth, only to be cut off by Drew. "Not you too. Are you going to try and tell me what to do?"

Ash had never seen Drew so upset. "Wait, let me talk."

"No, Ash. You're as bad as they are, trying to tell me what to do. I won't let them destroy what I worked so hard for. They're only a couple of punks. I can handle them. It's my clinic and I need to confront them and show them they can't run me out, despite their threats."

Without waiting for anyone to speak, Drew ran out of the apartment, and within minutes, Ash heard a car engine revving up, tires squealing down the street. "Damn it. I'm going after him." He remembered he didn't have his car. "I need a ride, please," he heard himself begging, and didn't care. Drew had run off, spoiling for a fight, and as hopped up and angry as he might be, Ash knew he wasn't capable of handling a physical altercation with two teenage punks.

Keith waited by the front door. He was on his phone, calling his partner, Jerry Allen, to let him know what was happening and to meet them at Stevie's apartment building. Jordan yelled out. "Come on, let's go."

Ash bent down and kissed Esther's cheek. "Don't worry. I'll make sure he comes home safe and sound."

She held him close. "Please. You children are all I have."

He hugged her, then broke away and ran after Keith and Jordan.

Chapter Twenty-Eight

DREW KNEW STEVIE'S address from the forms the boy had filled out prior to his starting work at the clinic. It didn't take him more than fifteen minutes to reach Stevie's foster home in the forbidding area in Red Hook, in one of the hulking projects. He swallowed his nerves and stormed up the path leading to the front of the apartment building. Drew figured he'd start with Stevie's foster parents, as they might know where he should start looking for the neighborhood boys.

After waiting for several minutes for them to answer the security buzzer, it became apparent no one was home, so he chose to wait in his car. It only took another five minutes of him ignoring several texts and phone calls from Ash before the two punks came swaggering up the street.

He exited the car and met them in the front of the apartment building. "You're Jimmy and Donny, right?" They looked at each other in surprise, and Drew could see right away Jimmy was the leader of the two.

"Who the fuck are you?" The boy's hands balled into fists as he strutted up to Drew.

"I'm Dr. Drew Klein. Stevie works for me."

Jimmy's sneering face grew even uglier. "Oh yeah? What's he do for you, suck your dick? Are you a fucking queer too?" The boy had several inches and about twenty pounds on Drew, and shoved his face up close in an attempt to intimidate him. "We don't need no more fags, so you need to get outta here."

Drew prayed his voice wouldn't shake when he spoke. "I'm not closing down the clinic, and we aren't going anywhere. So tough shit and get used to it, punk."

Sirens wailed in the distance. The two young men muscled their way up close to Drew, pushing him until his back pressed uncomfortably into the stairway post.

"Listen, Dr. Queer. We're telling you to get the fuck out of our hood, or we're gonna torch the place, and maybe you might still be inside." Jimmy's laugh rang out into the night like an evil carnival clown's. "Maybe we'll pay your dear old grandma another visit."

Drew's blood ran cold, and a red veil of anger descended over him. "I knew it was you two who went to her house." The thought that Nana had trusted them, and they'd almost killed her emboldened him. "You fucking bastards, you dared to put your hands on her? You almost killed her, you sons of bitches."

Drew never saw the punch coming. A hard, heavy fist connected with his cheek, and he saw stars. Though his head still reeled from the punch, the knowledge that these boys could've killed his grandmother spiked his adrenaline and he charged at the two young men.

Hitting them was like hitting a stone wall, but Drew got lucky and caught them by surprise, because he knocked the quieter one, Donny, off his feet, sending him sprawling to the ground. Jimmy, however, was a different story. He put his bullet-shaped head down and barreled into Drew, knocking his head against the stair railing. Pain lanced through Drew's skull. Woozy from the blow, Drew heard a car pull up, doors slam, then shouting from the direction of the street. He thought he heard Ash or maybe Keith, but he couldn't be sure.

With his head still spinning, he nonetheless shook it off as best he could and began to swing at the young man. He managed some good hits, but when Jimmy landed two quick punches to his stomach, Drew fell to his knees, gasping for breath.

As if in the distance, Drew heard Keith yell out, "Police, halt." Jimmy, the closest to him, muttered something to Donny. Drew lay on the ground, still holding his stomach, as blood from the gash on the back of his head dripped down his neck. Over his own heavy breathing, he heard Donny pleading with Jimmy.

"No, Jimmy, you can't. Put it away."

"Fuck them," Jimmy muttered.

Drew's vision cleared, and with horror, he saw a gun in Jimmy's hand. He heaved himself up and croaked as loud as he could. "Gun. He's got a gun."

He attempted to stand but the world spun crazily

out of focus. Shots rang out and then everything went black.

A LOUD BEEPING noise filled his head, and dull pain radiated throughout his body. His initial attempt to open his eyes failed miserably, and he groaned out loud.

"Drew, Drew. Do you hear me?"

Where was he? "Ash? Is that you?"

"Yes, baby. How do you feel?" A large, warm palm stroked his cheek. "Can you open your eyes?"

He tried again and met with success. Ash's worried face hovered over his. Drew blinked, and his vision cleared. "Oh, Drew." Ash kissed his lips and sighed. "You scared me."

"Where am I?" He sensed movement underneath him.

"On your way to the hospital to get your head checked out." Ash continued to stroke Drew's cheek. "You have a nasty cut on the back of your head, and may have a concussion."

As if to validate Ash's statement, an EMS worker appeared from behind Drew with a blood pressure kit. Ash slid back against the wall and allowed the man to take Drew's pressure. Drew winced as the man's fingers probed his head, but he had no blurring of vision or nausea, signs, he knew, of a possible concussion.

"Lie back, Doctor. You need to take it easy. We'll

be at the hospital in a few minutes, and they can check you out more thoroughly there."

Drew gave the man a faint smile. "Thanks." He turned back to Ash, who looked pale and ill.

"What happened? Did Keith arrest Jimmy and Donny? They were the ones who pushed Nana around and threw the brick through my window."

Ash nodded. "Yes, we know. But they didn't arrest them."

He tried to sit up, knowing he couldn't have heard Ash correctly, but the pain slicing through his head almost caused him to throw up.

"Lie back, please, Doctor. You have to relax and remain still." The EMS tech placed a hand on Drew's shoulder, but he ignored it, reaching for Ash.

What the hell? "How could Keith not arrest them? They're criminals." Drew's confusion grew at the sight of Ash's face, which had paled to an almost unnatural white. A sick feeling of dread crawled up his spine. "What's going on? There's something you're not telling me, isn't there?"

Ash tried to take his hand, but Drew knocked him away. "What is it? Tell me."

"They're both dead, shot by the police. But Drew, it's Keith. He was shot, and it doesn't look good."

Oh God. "No. That can't be. Keith is with Jordan. There were other police officers." Drew sat up so quickly he almost fainted from the nausea and pain. "You're lying."

"Baby, I'm so sorry. After Jimmy hit you, he fired

at the person directly in front of him. Keith had already arrived and didn't wait for his backup when he saw them attacking you. The bullet hit Keith in the neck."

"No." Drew leaned over the edge of the gurney and vomited, heaving violent spasms onto the floor of the ambulance. He stayed in that hunched position, shivering and weeping, as the tech cleaned up the floor. The EMS worker then forced him to lie back down, threatening him with a shot that would put him out unless he complied. Drew gave in, but the pain in his head and his heart remained.

Not Keith. Why? Please God. Help him. Don't let him die. All the thoughts swirled around madly through his mind as the ambulance stopped and he was off-loaded into the emergency room. He saw several news trucks on the street before he was whisked past the worried faces of Rachel, Nana, and Mike.

There was no sign of Jordan.

"Ash." He reached out a hand blindly, and Ash grabbed it, squeezing it tight.

"Yes, baby, I'm here."

"Please. Find out about Keith. I have to know."

"But I want to stay with you."

"No." His voice rang out sharper than he intended. "I'm sorry. I didn't mean to yell at you. It's only that...Keith. I need to know what's happening." His eyes searched Ash's red-rimmed ones. "Please," he whispered. "Do this for me."

Ash laid his cheek on Drew's. "I'll do anything for you, baby." After kissing his cheek, Ash left, the curtain swinging behind him.

Nurses and doctors came by to see how he was, and they sent him for an MRI. Drew knew he was getting special treatment because he was a doctor himself, but for the first time he didn't care. As soon the attending physician told him he didn't have a concussion and they'd stitched up his head wound, he brushed aside their suggestion that he stay the night for observation and made his way to the waiting room. It was there he found Rachel, Ash, Mike, and Nana, all waiting with white, strained faces.

"Nana."

"Oh, Drew, my darling baby." She broke down in tears, and he rushed to her side to gather her in his arms and hold her close. "I thought we'd lost you."

Her familiar scent and loving arms caused him to break down for a moment. He pulled away and, still hiccupping somewhat, got himself together. "I'm fine. Where's Jordan? What floor is Keith on?"

"They're operating on him now," said Ash. "Jordan is in the waiting room on the seventh floor."

"Let's go." Drew stood, and they all followed. He still held on to his grandmother. "Nana, you should go home."

"I'll not leave that boy. I called his mother to tell her what happened, and she told me that only Jesus could save her son then hung up." Fresh tears poured from her eyes. "He'll not die without me there to fight for his last breath."

She was the most amazing woman in the world. "I

love you, Nana. And Keith will fight. I know he will." He hugged her and pressed the elevator button.

Within minutes, they were on the seventh floor and found the waiting area. Jordan sat in a daze, surrounded by half a dozen police officers as well as Keith's partner, Jerry. Jordan barely acknowledged them, but Nana went and sat next to him and took him in her arms.

"Jordy's parents are away on vacation," Mike whispered in Drew's ear. "They're somewhere in Switzerland, and he's had a hell of a time getting in touch with them."

Drew simply nodded. How could this be happening? Jordan and Keith were planning on getting married next year. They'd bought a home together. The two of them had figured out the secrets of love and a happy life.

A sob wrenched out of him, and Ash put his arm around him, pulling him close.

"Sit down with me. You're still in shock yourself." He allowed Ash to lead him to a chair where he slumped down, resting his head against Ash's broad shoulder. "Rest a little, baby. It isn't going to do anyone any good if you collapse on the floor."

His head pounded, and as the time passed, he managed to close his eyes, but the nightmare of the evening reared its ugly head again and he couldn't sleep. Jordan hadn't moved once that he could tell. He sat in the chair drinking innumerable cups of coffee and stared at the door as if willing the surgeon to come through.

The hours ticked away.

Drew woke with a start. He checked his watch and saw it was early morning. He stole a glance and saw Jordan's frozen, stoic face trained upon the door, his hands still clutching a paper coffee cup. Slipping out from under Ash's arm, Drew made his way to the seat next to his best friend.

"Jordy." He put his hand on his friend's arm. Jordan flinched, his hand shaking so much, drops of cooled coffee slopped over the side.

"I know, D. But I can't take anyone touching me right now." His agonized whisper died as the door opened and the surgeon walked in. Great pools of sweat darkened his green scrubs from under his armpits to his chest. Drew took one look at his face and knew the news wasn't good. He glanced back at Ash and reached for him, finding he needed to feel the strength of his arms around him for what he knew would be crushing news.

Jordan stood. "He didn't make it, did he, David?"

Dr. David Cantor shook his head. "I'm so sorry, Jordan. We did everything we could, but the bullet caused tremendous damage and he lost so much blood…"

Jordan put his hand up and then fell to the floor on his knees. "Don't. Don't tell me the details. I can't bear to think of the pain he went through at the end, and how I wasn't there to help him or hold his hand." He threw the paper cup across the room and cried out in his pain. "Why, God? Why Keith?" He moaned, clutching himself around the waist, rocking back and forth. "It should have been me. He was too good to die. Please, no, it can't be true. I want to die too. Take me with him."

Helpless to do anything but feel his heart breaking at the sight of his friend falling to pieces, Drew clung to Ash. "Dear God, how can this be happening?" Ash's wet face rested against his own. "What now? Keith was such a good person."

"I know. He was the best."

Ash held him as he sobbed. In the background, he heard the quiet crying of Rachel and his grandmother. Pulling out of Ash's arms, he beckoned to Mike, and the two of them knelt and put their arms around their childhood friend. Jordan buried his face in Drew's chest and howled his pain, his tears soaking through Drew's shirt.

"Let me die, Drew. I'm no good without him. He's the only one who'll ever love me." Jordan laid his head in Drew's lap. "I can't live knowing he's alone and cold." His piteous weeping broke Drew's already cracked and beaten heart. "I need to hold him to keep him warm. Who's going to keep him warm now?"

"Shhh. Don't talk like that. Keith wouldn't want you to feel like that." Mike brushed away his own tears, and Rachel came to sit beside Jordan, giving him comfort.

Drew kissed Jordan's forehead. "We'll be there for you, all of us will, Jordy."

"It's not fair. Not Keith, not my life, my love.

Please, God." He grabbed on to Drew's shirt. "It's a dream, right? I'm in a bad dream, and you're all in it." Wild-eyed, he glanced around the waiting room. "Tell me it's a dream and wake me up now."

"Shhh, Jordy, we're all here for you." Drew didn't know what else to do but repeat those same ineffective words.

"It has to be a dream. He can't be dead. He can't be. We're getting married. We were going to adopt a baby." Jordan stared into Drew's eyes beseechingly. "Please, please, tell me it's not true."

Drew could only hold him and shake his head, his own tears blinding his vision. "I'm so sorry. I loved him; we all did."

Jordan's shoulders slumped. "I'm being punished because I'm a bad person. I was cruel to you and Ash. I'm sorry, Drew. I'm so sorry I said those things about Ash. I know how much you love him."

Drew stiffened, hoping Ash hadn't heard, but Ash was on the other side of the room staring out of the window, lost in a world of his own. "I haven't told him."

Jordan sat up and took him by the shoulders. His eyes were wide and almost feverish in the brightness. "Tell him, tell him tonight. You see how life is? How one minute you're alive and the next you're gone." His breath caught on a sob. "I didn't tell Keith today that I loved him. I always told him every morning, but not today. Now he'll never know."

"Oh, he knew, and he loved you so much. He told

me so tonight." Drew soothed his friend, holding him close.

"He did?" Jordan's hopeful face broke Drew's heart all over again.

"He did, and he knew how much you loved him. Your love will last forever."

"How am I going to live without his touch, without holding him at night?" Jordan broke down all over again. "I miss him so much already."

At the tap on his shoulder, Drew turned to see the deeply grieving face of Keith's partner, Jerry Allen.

"Let me take over for a while. My wife says I have broad shoulders to cry on."

Jerry sank down next to Jordan and murmured in his ear, putting his arm around him. The rest of the police force, who'd been standing around waiting, all converged upon Jordan now, showing that famous blue wall of support. The police commissioner came in, as well as the mayor. Drew had heard the police department was one big family that came through in a family's time of need, and this outpouring of support left no doubt Jordan would be taken care of.

Drew stood and found himself crushed in Ash's embrace. He let himself be wrapped up in the man's overwhelming strength, soaking in the waves of heat coming off Ash's body. "Baby, I told Mike to take your grandmother home. I called Mrs. Delaney and had her prepare a light meal and then told her to make sure she went to bed."

"You're wonderful." The events of the night caught

up with him, and Drew sagged into Ash's arms, nuzzling his strong neck. "I'm so lucky to have you."

"I'm the lucky one." Ash's hot breath tickled his ear. "And I want to take you home."

"I have so much to tell you." Drew cradled Ash's jaw in his hand and kissed his soft warm lips. "So much and it can't wait. I don't want to wait any longer."

"Let's go home, baby. But first let's make sure Jordan is okay." Ash took his hand, and they waited for the crowd of uniforms and suits to step aside. Jordan was quieter now, more resigned but no less broken. The self-confident, arrogant man had disappeared, replaced by a gray, worn-out shell.

"Jordy." Drew held out his arms, and Jordan clung to him for dear life.

"I know I've been a bastard." Jordan's voice trembled. "I can't believe he's gone, Drew. I'm never going to see him again. How am I going to go on?"

Before Drew could open his mouth, Ash spoke. "You're going to think about him every day, Jordan, and draw your strength from his goodness and his memories. And it will hurt like fucking hell for a long, long time." Ash put his arm around Jordan, and Drew stood, shocked at how easily Jordan hung onto Ash's words. "But we'll all be there for you, whenever you call, to help you through it."

Jordan grabbed on to Ash, pulling at his shirt. "I was wrong, Ash. I had no right, no right at all to try and keep you from Drew. I was arrogant, selfish, and cruel. What you have is as precious as what Keith and I have—had."

The stricken look on Jordan's face as he corrected himself almost killed Drew. It hit him then, like a fist to the stomach, that Keith was really gone forever, leaving Jordan alone.

"Jordy, I love you." Drew threw his arms around his best friend. "No matter what we've said to each other, you'll always be my brother."

"Go home, Drew. Never take life for granted." Jordan gulped, the tears rolling down his face. "I'll always love him, you know that, right? He saw through all my bullshit and arrogance, and I love him so fucking much." He shuddered and fought for control. "I need to be by myself and say my good-byes to Keith alone."

Drew could only hug him tight and kiss him, then turn to Ash who put his arms around him. With one last glance over his shoulder at his best friend standing all alone in the middle of the waiting room, he left, Ash holding him tight, giving him strength.

Chapter Twenty-Nine

IT WAS QUITE possibly the worst night of his life. Ash couldn't understand how a day that had started out so beautifully and with so much happiness had ended in such horrendous tragedy.

Drew sat strangely quiet during the cab ride to Ash's apartment. Ash had called Marly and asked her to stop by Drew's house and feed the cat. There was no chance on earth he'd let Drew go back to that apartment tonight. The memory of Keith, so vibrant and alive at the party, would be too devastating to face in the light of day. If he had his way, Drew would never go back there again.

When they reached Ash's apartment building, he helped Drew out of the cab and led him inside. Keeping his arm around Drew, Ash nodded hello to the concierge.

"Good morning, Mr. Davis."

"Good morning, Lawrence. I'm not home for anyone today, unless it is Mr. Klein's family." Drew sighed into his shoulder, the warmth of his breath gusting into

Ash's neck.

"Very good, Mr. Davis." The concierge nodded. "Terrible thing about that police officer who was killed last night."

Drew stiffened but said nothing, though Ash sensed his trembling. He had to be in shock, both from the effects of the blow to his head and the loss of his friend.

"He was a friend of mine and Dr. Klein's. A wonderful man." Ash tightened his arm around Drew feeling him tremble. "Thank you, Lawrence."

"You're welcome, sir."

Neither of them said a word during the elevator ride up, nor did they speak in the hallway as Ash unlocked his door. Ash went right to the bar, poured some vodka, then came back to the kitchen and added ice. Drew stood by the door, exactly where Ash left him. His eyes remained closed, his body slumped against the wall.

"Take a sip of this and come with me." Drew took the glass, and Ash covered his hand, helping him hold it steady to take a sip. "Easy, killer," Ash joked as Drew gulped the drink, then coughed.

"That's straight vodka." Drew sputtered and wheezed.

"That's what I drink." Ash grinned for the first time. "I thought you could use it to help you relax."

A weary smile broke over Drew's face. "The only thing I need is you."

And you have me. Forever if you want.

Although it was morning, the room remained dark;

he'd yet to draw open the curtains to let in the early pale daylight.

"I'm here for you."

Drew's face fell. "How will Jordan ever forgive me?" He wandered away from the entrance hall to enter the large living room and sat down on the sofa before the fireplace. Ash followed but remained at a distance feeling helpless. Desperate, he searched for something comforting to say to Drew who remained locked in his own private hell.

"He'll hate me and never want to see me again and I don't blame him."

"I'm sure he won't. It wasn't your fault."

Drew met his eyes unflinchingly, tears running down his face. "Of course it was. If I hadn't run off, Keith would have stayed back at my apartment and he'd still be alive. Of all the stupid, impulsive things I've ever done this is the worst."

There was no way in hell he'd allow Drew to tear himself apart over Keith's death. And while his running off to confront those two kids was foolish, Ash would never say it to Drew's face, especially in tonight's highly charged atmosphere of grief.

"Keith was a veteran cop. Every day was a risk for him. He understood that and eventually Jordan will."

"But I led him into it. It's just like what happened with my parents. If it wasn't for me—"

"Knock it off, Drew." Ash cut him off. "Stop making this about you."

Drew's eyes widened. "I never said it was."

Guilt was a horrible monster and could destroy you from within if you let it, Ash refused to allow it to consume Drew until he wound up broken and alone.

"You're equating one horrible occurrence in your life with another. Both were enormous tragedies that should never have happened. But you were only a peripheral part of it. No one knows better than I do the pain of guilt, but what I'm learning now in therapy is that you have a choice: to either control the guilt or allow it to consume you."

"Like you did."

Sitting next to Drew, Ash took the drink from him and placed it on the coffee table. "I shouldn't give you alcohol either. It's another crutch."

"When did you become so wise?" Drew leaned his head back on the sofa pillows to stare up at the ceiling.

For years Ash would come to this apartment with Mr. Frank to work and learn from him. But at the end of the evening, he'd leave to go drown his pain in a blur of meaningless sex and vodka, while Jacob Frank sat by himself in his opulent surroundings. Ash wasn't sure who was lonelier. Perhaps now he understood why Mr. Frank chose him. They both fought demons that might have killed a lesser man, each choosing to do so in vastly different ways.

I wish you love and peace in your heart.

He'd finally found both.

"Since I fell in love with you."

Drew sat up, his face pale, eyes wide and bloodshot from all the crying.

"You love me?"

"How can you doubt it? You're the best thing that's ever happened to me. The only good thing." Ash pulled him close, reinforcing what he'd already suspected; only when he had Drew in his arms could he take a deep breath. This man had become as necessary to him as air and water. Life.

Drew buried his face in Ash's neck. "I thought tonight would be the perfect time to tell you I love you. I had it all planned. Keith told me not to wait. He said to tell you as soon as possible. It's as if he had this premonition. He talked about leaving Jordan and never knowing if he'd come home or not."

Drew's tears soaked through Ash's shirt and he held him tighter. Nothing he could do or say could take away Drew's pain and it tore Ash up inside, but Drew had to know what was in his heart.

"I don't know why you love me but I'm so damn grateful. You gave me a sense of worth. A will to live. A life. And something to live for."

"It was always there inside you, Ash. Waiting for you to recognize it and embrace it. And as for loving you? You gave me your passion, your secrets and your heart. You gave me everything and took my breath away. How could I not fall in love with you forever?"

Holding one another tightly they sat in the living room and Ash counted his blessings. He played over in his mind what Mr. Frank had said to him before he died, how he needed to let go of his pain and learn to love. He hadn't understood it then, but he did now. It didn't make Ash a bad person to love Drew, even though he'd yet to see Luke and he didn't know where Brandon was. By taking on the abuse they might have suffered, he'd gained strength, a knowledge that no one would ever use him again. Loving Drew and being loved in return was a precious gift, as they'd seen tonight. A gift that in a moment in time could be snatched away, leaving behind devastation and unimaginable heartbreak.

He kissed Drew, hard and hungry, pouring into him the love he'd kept locked inside all his life. Drew twisted in his arms and Ash captured his warm mouth, slipping his tongue inside, twisting, tangling, and thrusting with Drew's until they broke apart, panting and shaking.

Drew pushed him down on the sofa and straddled him. "I love you so much it hurts. It's like I woke up and the whole world changed around me while I slept. For the first time in years, I'm alive. You did that for me." He stretched out over Ash and laced their fingers together.

While they lay there, chest to chest, belly to belly, Ash murmured in Drew's ear, "Even if I'd died tonight, it was all worth it to have had you for this short time."

"Shh." Drew still lay on top of him, his weight negligible, their hands entwined, like a lovers' knot, binding them forever. "Don't say that."

But he spoke the truth. He'd seen the ugliness of the world and lived through it but it changed him irrevocably, stealing his right to live carefree and with hope. Now Drew gave him a chance to start over again, with his work in the clinic, watching over Esther and loving Drew. And always in the back of his mind, paramount to everything, finding Luke and Brandon.

"You should lay down. You had a blow to the head and need rest yourself. Let's go."

He took Drew by the hand and they walked toward Ash's bedroom.

"I'll call my office and tell my associate to handle everything until I get back. It's going to be a long haul and Jordan will need you."

At the mention of Jordan, Drew's face fell, and the shadows chased away the light in his eyes. He stopped at the bedroom doorway. "I'm afraid he won't want to talk to me."

Ash led Drew into the bedroom and quickly stripped him of his shirt and pants. He flung back the comforter and pointed. "Lie down. There's no use in speculating so you might as well rest for the moment."

"Join me? For a little while. I know you have things to do, but I don't want to be alone right now."

And because he could never refuse Drew anything, Ash lay down next to him and took Drew into his arms, listening to him unburden his heart.

"I keep seeing Jordan, standing by himself. I've never seen him so lost." Drew laid his head on his shoulder.

It would be impossible not to feel sorry for Jordan but Ash hoped after the initial shock and sorrow, he wouldn't turn on Drew.

"It's going to be very difficult for him. Not only was he and Keith such a strong couple, Jordan's not one to let his emotions show. I've seen men like him before. They tend to hide how they really feel."

"He's always been open with us."

Ash tightened his hold on Drew, wishing he could shield him from the inevitable fallout his impulsive actions had caused. In truth, he wasn't sure Jordan and Drew would come out of this with their friendship intact.

"Try not to think about it. We'll all be there for him and right now that's what he needs."

When Drew failed to answer, Ash glanced down to see he'd fallen asleep. Satisfied, he carefully extricated himself and folded back the comforter to cover Drew. With any luck he'd sleep for several hours. Ash went into the bathroom, showered and shaved, then moving about his bedroom on silent, bare feet, got dressed in a button-down shirt and pants. Weariness flooded through him, despite the invigorating shower.

With one last look at Drew sleeping soundly, Ash left the bedroom and closed the door quietly behind him. First, before he even called his office, he called Esther's house to speak with Mrs. Delaney.

To his surprise, he heard Esther's voice on the other end of the telephone.

"Esther. Why aren't you asleep? You barely had any rest last night. I'd have thought Mrs. Delaney would insist you stay in bed."

"Asher, are you scolding me? I may be old but no

one can make me do anything I don't want to do."

That was the plain truth. "Drew is sleeping and I wanted to check on you to see how you feel."

"I feel like I've lost one of my children. Poor darling Keith. And my poor Jordan. He loved that man with everything he had. I've known him all his life and I've never seen him so settled and happy as when he was with Keith."

At the sound of her sniffling, Ash thought his heart would break. Maybe love wasn't such a good thing after all; he'd never been in as much pain as when he thought Drew had been shot and now to hear Esther cry…then he thought about the man sleeping in his bed and how Drew brought him back to life and now understood all those cheesy love songs he heard on the radio that promised love can make everything better.

"Eventually he'll learn to live with his pain. Unfortunately most of us don't get to lead the charmed life he's had up until now. No matter how he treated me, I do feel terrible."

"I know you two have had your differences, but please. Put them aside and help him through this, Asher. If not for Jordan's sake, then for Drew's and mine."

"Esther that's not fair. You know I can't say no to you."

"I know."

Ash bit back his first smile of the night at the smug tone in her voice.

"You're a good man. And with all the pain in your

life, I know you'll be able to help Jordan thorough his ordeal."

"I'll do what I can, but my main concern is Drew. I won't let Jordan bully him or make him feel guilty."

"My grandson is very lucky to have someone like you in his life."

That statement begged the question Ash had been putting off asking Esther for some time now.

"Esther can I ask you something?"

"You can ask me anything."

First checking over his shoulder to make sure Drew remained in the bedroom, Ash walked into the living room and stood by the picture window overlooking Park Avenue. As always he marveled at how far he'd come and how much he still missed Jacob Frank. More than anything he wished his benefactor could have seen the man he'd become and met Drew. The man who'd made it all possible.

"Are you really happy with the turn Drew's life has taken? I know you say that love is love and I don't doubt you care for me. But Drew and I are going to move in together, hopefully soon, which means you'll be seeing us together all the time—"

Esther cut him off.

"I see I still need to reassure you. You know, I grew up in a very small village. When I came to this country, I'd never met anyone who wasn't the same as me. Living here and meeting people from all different walks of life has made me a better person. I've seen the worst that man can do to another man, Asher, and lost my entire family, my history because of it. Do you think for one minute I'd ever dare to deny the people I love, or anyone for that matter, the right to their own happiness?"

"I wish more people thought like you."

"In time they will. Remember what I told you. Never stop hoping." Her voice softened. "You and I, Asher, we're very much alike. We've seen the worst of mankind but are lucky to have come out of the fire to the other side of the mountain."

It was true. His life had been a walk through fire before he met Drew. It had burned him, leaving scars and nothing but scorched earth behind. Only by meeting and falling in love with Drew had he learned every day was a gift never to be taken for granted. And while he'd never forget his past, learning to live with it was proof a person could come through hell and back, sometimes stronger than before.

"I don't want to disappoint him. Or you. I couldn't bear it if I did."

"The only way you could is to stop loving him. Since his parents' death, he walked through life but didn't live it. That's all changed now. Give him the strength he needs to get through this ordeal with Jordan. It won't be easy for either of them."

"Drew feels very guilty."

"I can only imagine. Those two are in for some tough times ahead. I'm afraid for their friendship."

"I'll do what I can to help Drew."

"You'll help them both because it's what's best for

Drew and you love him."

Sighing because he knew she was right, Ash hung up but not before giving her a warning. "If I find out that you haven't rested at some point today I'm going to sic Rachel on you."

"Fine," she grumbled. "Good-bye."

"Bye."

He hung up and spun around to the sound of a throat clearing. A sleepy-eyed Drew leaned against the wall.

"Was that my grandmother?"

Ash walked over to him and led him to the sofa. "Sit down, you look exhausted. Why aren't you sleeping?"

Drew shrugged. "I dunno. I guess I'm still too wound up. Was that her?"

Lacing their fingers together, Ash nodded. "I wanted to check on her to make sure she was resting but sure enough she wasn't."

Having Drew here with him now in these early morning hours made Ash realize how lonely he'd been before. Rarely able to sleep through the night, he'd often wake up well before sunrise and stare out the window, wondering where Luke and Brandon were, and if he'd ever find them.

In loving Drew, he'd found the sleep of peace.

With gentle fingers, Drew traced the scars that wound around his wrists and forearms. Since he'd confessed to Drew, Ash no longer needed to hide his damaged skin.

"I can help you with these, you know. If you want to make them less noticeable."

Did he? Ash had come to look at his scars as part of who he was; they identified him as a survivor.

"Do they bother you?"

"Only because I know the torment you went through and what made you do it."

"I have other things to think about now."

"You do?" Drew smiled and nuzzled into his neck, kissing him. "What? I have a feeling I might like it."

"I have one more call to make and then I'm all yours, how about that?" To hell with work and the office and everything else except Drew. Esther was right when she spoke of Drew and Jordan's friendship being at a crossroads.

Drew lay back on the sofa staring up at the ceiling. "I want to call Jordan later. He has no one with him; his parents are stuck in Europe and Keith's parents never accepted him."

Ash could only hope Jordan would accept Drew's call. In the heat of the moment with emotions running high, Jordan needed Drew, giving Drew a sense of false hope that things hadn't changed between them. Ash knew better. He knew how Jordan's mind worked. With the passage of time, Ash feared Jordan would come to blame Drew for Keith's death. And no matter what, Ash would stand with Drew.

"I still can't believe this happened. I feel guilty that Keith died trying to protect me." Drew's eyes glinted with wetness. "I shouldn't have gone over there myself.

Keith would still be alive if I hadn't run off to confront those fucking bastards."

"Oh, baby, come here." Ash pulled Drew to his chest. "Keith knew the risks; he took them every day when he went out there. Life is all about the choices we make and the risks we choose to take." He kissed Drew soundly. "I'll help you get through this, I promise. But first you need your rest. Now get back into bed and if you're lucky I'll join you."

Drew slipped out of his arms and kissed him. "Yes, sir. Whatever you want."

Ash followed Drew back into the bedroom. "You, baby. I only want you."

Chapter Thirty

THE FOLLOWING DAY dawned gray and gloomy as if it understood the devastation within Drew's heart. It took him until late afternoon to work up the courage to go to Jordan's home, and Drew cursed himself for being a coward. Neither Ash nor Rachel could offer him any comfort or sage words of advice. This was a road he'd have to travel alone.

With trepidation, he exited the cab and mounted the stairs to Jordan's Chelsea brownstone, practicing what he planned to say to his life-long best friend. Shit, he'd never been this nervous before and despite Ash's reassurance it would work out, Drew knew Jordan's capacity for grudge-holding and wasn't so sure.

He pressed the doorbell, and heard the chimes resonating within. Bouncing on his toes, he swallowed his nerves and plastered a smile on his face as he heard footsteps approach. The door rattled and opened. It wasn't Jordan who greeted him but Mike.

"How's Jordan?"

Mike's normally cheerful face darkened. "It's bad.

Really bad. He won't talk and won't eat. Come on in."

Drew trailed behind Mike, following him down the long hallway which he knew opened up into the large country kitchen at the back of the house. One might think it was a normal get-together, except when the entered the kitchen and Drew looked over Mike's shoulder at the farmhouse table across the room, bouquets of flowers and sympathy baskets crowded the surface.

Mike stopped and stepped aside. "Jordan. It's Drew."

"Hey, Jordan." Drew walked over to his friend who sat motionless in his chair. His usual impeccably styled blond hair lay in lank strands across his forehead and from the wrinkles in his shirt and pants, Drew would hazard a guess he'd slept in them. When Jordan met Drew's eyes, it was all he could do not to gasp out loud. In all the years he'd known Jordan he'd never seen him in such pain. His normally sharp and bright blue eyes stared back vacantly, all life drained out of them.

"Jordan?" Drew put a hand on his arm, only to have Jordan draw back, visibly flinching from the contact.

"I can't do this. I'm sorry Drew, but you shouldn't have come."

Drew staggered backward; if Jordan had hit him with his fist, he wouldn't be in as much pain. "What are you talking about? Of course I should—where else would I be?"

"It's too soon for me."

"But I love you and Keith. I want to be here to help you through it all." Drew took a tentative step back toward his best friend.

At the mention of Keith's name, Jordan shuddered and made no effort to wipe the tears streaming from his eyes. He stood so abruptly, his chair clattered backward onto the terra cotta floor.

"I don't want to hurt you, Drew. Go home." He walked out of the kitchen.

Coldness washed through him at Jordan's detached manner. In a daze, he watched Jordan's retreating back, barely registering Mike picking up the toppled chair.

"He hates me."

"What?" Mike stood in front of him. "Did you say something?"

"Did he talk about me, or say anything about me to you?" Drew leaned against the granite countertop and clasped his trembling hands together.

The guarded expression on Mike's face told Drew all he needed. "I see. I knew it. I told Ash, Jordan would blame me for Keith's death."

"Give him time. It's only been a day. He'll come around. You can't blame yourself. No one expected those guys to have a gun; that's why Keith took the risk going after them without a vest."

"I thought I'd be able to handle it on my own. You understand, don't you? They hurt my grandmother and threatened her again. I couldn't sit around and do nothing."

Jordan had stopped in the hallway by the stairs and

stood staring at the wall of photographs. He took down one Drew knew was of him and Keith on the day Keith received his detective shield. Jordan traced his fingers over the surface of the glass and Drew's heart shattered at the pain etched on Jordan's pain.

Mike squeezed his arm. "It isn't going to help Jordan or you to talk about it right now. Let him get through the next few days and then the funeral. It's barely had a chance to sink in that Keith's not coming home."

At Mike's words, Drew's eyes welled up; but he spoke the truth. Keith's presence could be felt everywhere and Drew half-expected him to show up at the front door with a smile. The enormity of Jordan's loss hit him, leaving him stunned and breathless. In one second, Jordan's whole world had been snatched from him; the shape and plane of his entire future irrevocably altered. Drew could hardly blame him for his zombie-like state.

Thinking back to his conversation with Ash the other day, Drew made a decision. "You're right. I'm not going to push him. It isn't about me, it's about helping Jordan. I'm going to step back and support him any way I can. Right now, that's being there whenever he needs me."

Mike slung an arm around his neck. "That's the best thing any of us can do."

Yet deep in his heart, Drew knew it wouldn't be as easy as he and Mike made it out to be. Drew's instincts were proven correct, when he went to give Jordan a hug goodbye and he stood there stiff and unyielding.

"Bye, Jordy. I'll see you tomorrow, okay?"

Jordan turned away. "My parents are coming in; they got a flight. I'll see you at the funeral." He walked up the stairs, his back straight and stiff.

Defeated, Drew zipped up his jacket and hurried out of Jordan's house without even saying goodbye to Mike. For close to an hour he wandered the streets of the city blindly, ignoring text messages and phone calls. He hadn't felt this lost and alone since his parents died. And though Ash had helped him see their deaths weren't his fault, it was hard not to make the correlation that once again he'd fucked up. Perhaps his family and friends would be better off if he simply disappeared.

Chilled and heartbroken, he found himself close to Ash's office and decided to pay him a visit. Ash and Jordan may not have gotten along, but Ash understood better than anyone about loss and pain. He pushed through the revolving glass doors and welcomed the enveloping warmth. The elevator whisked him up to the thirtieth floor and he entered the law office suite. A spurt of pride hit him at all Ash had made out of himself.

"Hello, Dr. Klein. Mr. Davis is in a meeting. Was he expecting you?"

Ash's secretary, Laura, gave him a smile over her pink, cats-eye glasses. Despite his bleak mood, Drew returned her smile. "No. I was in the neighborhood and hoped he might be winding down for the day and that we could go home together." He sat into one of the comfortable chairs in the reception room. "I can wait."

Laura's face softened. "I'm so sorry about your friend."

If he spoke he might cry, so Drew simply nodded and picked up a magazine to hide behind. He couldn't humiliate himself any further today. Perhaps Laura sensed his unease for she left him alone, while he pretended to read. Voices filtered from down the hallway and he recognized Ash's.

"Drew?"

He looked up to see Ash standing several feet away, a quizzical tilt to his dark brows.

"Hi. I was in the neighborhood…" The excuse sounded weak even to him.

Skepticism clouded Ash's eyes but he refrained from speaking. He shook hands with the two men standing next to him and walked them out. Drew took the time to draw several deep breaths, inexplicably nervous and stood by his chair. Maybe he should leave. This was a dumb idea.

The door opened and Ash reappeared. "Come on into my office. Laura, I don't have anything else scheduled, right?"

"No."

"Good. Hold all my calls, please." He turned to Drew, "Follow me." He walked away.

"I'm sorry. Maybe I should leave. This is your office and I'm intruding."

Ash stopped in his tracks and turned around, an incredulous look on his face. "Intruding? Are you serious?" Concern puckered his brow. "Wait. You went to see Jordan."

That flat statement cut through Drew. Ash understood.

"Yeah."

"Come here." Ash beckoned and Drew complied, finding himself taken around and held. "Was it bad?"

Drew nodded into Ash's shoulder. "He hates me."

Ash pulled him away to stare into his face. "He told you that? Even I can't imagine Jordan saying that to you."

"He didn't have to."

"Come, let's go inside." With his arm still around Drew's shoulder, Ash led him into his office and closed the door behind him. "Sit." He pointed to the comfortable leather sofa and Drew complied. Ash joined him a moment later, handing him a cup of cold water.

"Now tell me everything he said."

"That's just it, he didn't say anything. He wouldn't talk to me. I know Jordan. It's him trying to be nice because if he did talk to me he'd tell me how much he hates me for getting Keith killed." Drew gulped down the water and held the empty cup in his hand. "You can dress it up all you want, but he's right. I wish it had been me who got shot." He viciously crumpled the cup.

"I see," said Ash staring at him. "You think that would make things better?"

Drew shrugged. "It couldn't be any worse."

Ash pulled out his phone and after tapping on it, stood and got his coat from the closet. "Let's go."

"Where?"

"You'll see."

He hadn't the strength to argue and didn't much care. Drew knew the truth. He followed Ash out of the office and into the elevator where they rode in silence. When they exited the building a black car waited for them at the curb.

"Get in."

Drew scrambled into the back seat, Ash sliding in next to him, then he slammed the door shut and they took off. Ash's stony profile reminded Drew of those early days, when the two of them barely spoke and his chest hurt, thinking of a life without Ash. It would be no life at all.

But sometimes sacrifices needed to be made for others to live free. Rachel had Mike now and they'd most likely be getting married. And Ash? Drew loved him more than he thought possible but Ash deserved someone strong, a man who could be a true partner and lover. He didn't need someone who consistently hurt everyone around him.

Before he realized it, they were in Brooklyn and he recognized the route they were driving. He had no desire to come here now.

"Why are we here?"

The car pulled up in front of his grandmother's house and stopped. Ash opened the door and stepped out, waiting for him to follow. The front door to the house opened and Drew's heart sank, knowing he had to go inside, now that his grandmother knew they were there. Defeated, he scrambled out of the car and walked past Ash.

"You bastard."

He placed a smile on his face and greeted his grandmother.

"Nana, let's go inside, it's getting chilly; it's almost November."

"I know, and I'm not a hothouse flower, you know." She kissed his cheek and scanned his face. "Yes, Asher was right, come with me."

Scowling at Ash, who'd joined him on the porch, he nevertheless followed his grandmother into the warm house, to the kitchen in the back.

"Sit down."

The table was set with a coffee pot, cups and milk, and a platter of cookies.

"I'm not in the mood for a lecture or cookies, I'm afraid. I don't know what Ash told you, but—"

"He doesn't have to tell me anything. I've known you since the day you were born and seen you grow up, always taking on the pain of everyone around you."

"This is different."

"Really?" Ash slid into the chair next to him and poured himself a cup of black coffee. "Not half an hour ago you said you wished you had gotten shot and not Keith."

A spoon clattered to the table and he watched as

tears filled his grandmother's eyes.

"No, you didn't."

"Why did you say that?" He glared at Ash. "You knew how upset she'd get."

"Exactly for that reason. Because you have to know that wishing you were dead would kill your grandmother as well. It would devastate Rachel and me, and everyone else who loves you."

"I can't help it. The guilt is killing me. It's like a snake winding around me, constricting every move I make. I can't take a deep breath; it's choking me."

"Baby, come here." Ash took him in his arms and held him close. "Talk it out. Don't let it eat you up inside."

The one place he'd found his peace had been with Ash, yet even now, the pain of his guilt remained as bright and sharp as when his parents died.

"Darling, you must stop this." His grandmother put her soft hand on his. "Losing yourself in blame doesn't make the pain go away. Jordan's grief is so fresh and raw, he can't deal with his feelings about you yet. Let him bury poor Keith first."

Talking about burying Keith seemed surreal, when Drew could hear his voice and see his smiling face clearly in his mind.

"I never know the right thing to do."

"Who does, when someone dies?" Ash rubbed his hand in comforting circles. "I could blame myself for suggesting the party in the first place. Any of us could find a reason to blame ourselves. You want to know what's really to blame?"

Drew gazed up into Ash's eyes, surprised at the passionate tone of his voice. "What?"

"Illegal guns. Those kids who killed Keith couldn't have done it without access to getting an illegal handgun. Guns are much too easy to buy. They get transported across state lines and wind up in the hands of petty criminals and people with mental disorders. Background checks are sketchy at best half the time. But get the gun laws changed and the guns off the streets and the death rate, especially in poor communities, would go down."

"Intellectually I know you're right. But when I come face to face with Jordan all I want to do is beg him to forgive me."

"Let it go now. But be there for him. Love him and show him you care." His grandmother wiped her eyes. "That boy is going to need all our help to get himself through this horrible time." She fixed him with a direct stare, her expression strained. "And don't you ever, *ever* think you're a burden to us or we'd be better off without you. I've had enough loss in my life." Tears rained down her cheeks. "I can't bear anymore."

Stricken, he slipped out of Ash's arms and knelt by his grandmother's chair. "Nana, please don't cry. I'm sorry. I didn't mean to upset you."

"I don't want to hear you didn't want to upset me. I want you to promise you'll stop thinking this way. Nothing in the world means more to me than you and Rachel and Asher. Losing you children would take a piece of my heart." She took his hand and held it fiercely tight.

"I didn't mean it. I felt sorry for myself, and didn't think of the consequences."

He returned to his chair and Ash took his hand. "For years when I hurt myself I did it deliberately, without caring about myself or anyone else. Who would've cared if I died—I had only myself to think about. But, I couldn't take that final step because I didn't want to die without doing everything I could to find Luke and Brandon."

"We're going to find them. You know where Luke lives. It's only a matter of time now."

Ash smiled and Drew recalled how when they'd first met, his eyes remained a blank wall. Now they glittered with life and purpose.

"And If I had died without finding you, none of it would have mattered. I won't let you fall into the blackness I once lived in."

He kissed Ash's cheek and wrapped his arms around him. Life was so much more precious now with Ash by his side. He needed to never lose sight of everything he had and not concentrate on what he'd lost.

"I love you," he murmured into Ash's neck, inhaling his wonderful, dearly familiar smell. "As much as it hurt me thinking about what I did, being alone, without you beside me now would be far, far worse."

Regrets were merely memories of a past he couldn't change—a past he'd constantly beaten down the devil to conquer. But with Ash by his side to love and loving him, Drew was ready to fight any battle necessary.

Epilogue

One month later

"ASHER, DARLING COME here, will you?"

Ash followed Drew's grandmother into the kitchen, where the wonderful aroma of frying onions and roasting chicken enveloped him, then through to the spacious dining room, where a large table was set with beautiful china and crystal.

"Do you need help with something, Esther?" He smiled down at the tiny woman who stood before him. He'd reach into the sky and grab the moon for her if she asked. And even if she didn't ask, there was nothing Ash wouldn't do for her. No one in the world meant more to him than Esther. Except perhaps Drew.

Thinking of Drew and the way they woke up this morning sent a flush of heat through him. Their lovemaking had been extra sweet; Drew had officially moved in with him and it felt like home at last. Sometimes Ash woke up in the middle of the night and wondered if it was all a dream and had to touch Drew to make sure he lay next to him and it all wasn't a figment of his imagination. Good things didn't happen to people like him, who'd done so much wrong in their lives. But he'd take it. He no longer questioned his right to be this happy.

"I wanted you to help me set up the menorah for the candle lighting tonight." She indicated the large bronze candelabra set in the center of the dining room table.

Ash fidgeted, tugging at the cuffs of his shirt. "Uh, I've never done anything like this before. I don't know much about the holiday, if anything. We didn't learn about other religions growing up. Just that we'd go to hell if we didn't believe in what the teachers and the preachers told us."

Esther squeezed his arm. "That's why I wanted you to do this with me. You're part of our family now, Asher. That means you celebrate our holidays with us. I'm not asking you to give up what you believe in, merely join our traditions with yours."

The only tradition he knew of was hiding when his foster father was around. "I'm more than happy to celebrate Chanukah. Believe me, like I've said before, Santa never stopped by our house growing up."

"Nana, what are you up to?" Drew strolled in, a smile lighting up his face when he saw Ash. "Are you sneaking off with my guy?" He slipped his arm around Ash's waist and Ash drew him closer. When had the mere touch of this man become so important to him, he wasn't complete without him near?

Ash leaned into Drew, soaking in his warmth. "If I

were ever to leave you, this is the only place I'd go. This is home to me. I can't explain it, but—"

"Shh." Esther stood watching them, and wiped her eyes with the corner of her flowered apron. "You don't need to explain anything. What you said right now, about this being your home, means everything to me. You mean everything to me, my darling boy. I love you as if you were born to me."

He slipped his arm from around Drew's waist to enfold Esther in a hug. "I love you too."

Hopefully there would be many more years of embraces and joy with this remarkable woman. He let her go and watched her give Drew a loving kiss on the cheek.

"Now, Drew knows what to do, so you need to learn so you can do this at home together. Get the candles from the breakfront, please, Drew."

"I'm already ahead of you. I have them right here."

Drew produced two candles and a matchbook from the pocket of his pants and handed them to Esther. "Aren't we going to wait for Rachel and Mike?"

Esther shook her head as she opened the box "They're coming here for dinner, but are doing the candle lighting at his parents' house tonight." She handed the two candles to Ash.

"What do I do with these?" The thin twisted candles rolled between his fingers, their waxy lengths smooth to the touch.

"Come." Esther took him by the hand and led him to the table. "Put one on the far right side and then light this second one."

Drew struck the match and lit the wick on the candle Ash held. Their eyes met over the flame and he smiled. "Thanks."

"Light the one already in the menorah and then place this one in the middle."

Ash followed her orders obediently and soon both candles flames danced, their shadows flickering against the walls as Esther recited a prayer in Hebrew. After she finished, her eyes were wet but a smile lit up her face.

"Nana you cry every time you light the candles." Drew hugged her and handed her a tissue.

She sniffled. "I used to pray for you children to find your happiness. Now I pray that I live to see you all married and with children. I added an extra prayer for poor Jordan to find peace in his soul. The funeral for Keith was such a beautiful testament to the wonderful man he was." After tucking the tissue into her sleeve, she slipped her arm through Ash's and they stood for a moment looking at the candles.

A sense of peace stole over Ash. He truly meant it when he said this place was home to him. While he loved his apartment—even more so now that Drew lived there—memories of his former life, the pain and loneliness he'd endured for years followed him through those hallways. Having Drew there to chase away the shadows in his soul helped. Slowly, the scars on his heart had healed.

But here, nothing lived but love and acceptance. These walls sheltered him, keeping the demons of his past at bay. When he came to Esther's, he could breathe, simple as that.

Esther led them back into the homey kitchen, where once again the mouth-watering aromas of their impending dinner surrounded them. She took a bowl from the refrigerator and stirred it, then set it down on the counter next to the stove. "Come help me, while we talk."

Drew winked. "You'll get to taste everything as it's cooked. Best spot in the house."

Before he joined Esther at the stove, Ash leaned down and kissed Drew. "I love you, baby. Did I tell you that today?"

"You might have this morning. Afterward." The pale skin on Drew's neck flushed as Ash pressed a quick kiss to the rapid pulse beating at his throat.

"I'll make sure to tell you again tonight. Afterward." He smiled into Drew's pale green eyes, loving how they gleamed with desire.

"I'll hold you to it."

Esther had been busy at the stove, dropping heaping spoonfuls of a potato onion mixture into the hot oil. They smelled like heaven.

"Take the platter, sweetheart and put some paper towels on it to soak up the oil, please."

Ash followed her instructions and watched as she deftly flipped the pancakes. When they were done, she slid them onto the platter and spooned more into hot oil. It sizzled and splattered in the cast iron pan.

Ash couldn't resist taking a bite of the crunchy fried

pancakes. They were crisp on the outside, soft inside with just the right flavoring of saltiness.

"Oh Esther, these are amazing." He snuck another one, finishing it off in two delicious bites.

"Here, you try it now." She handed him the spatula and stood back. "Do you know what the story of Chanukah stands for, Asher?"

"Not really. Something about eight days is all I know." Ashamed at his ignorance, Ash concentrated on the frying pan, making sure he didn't let the pancakes burn.

"Don't be embarrassed. It's not a major religious holiday. But we love to celebrate it because it symbolizes hope and a miracle."

He slid the crusty pancakes on the second layer of paper toweling Esther had laid over the first batch, sprinkled on salt the way he'd seen her do, and waited for her to taste them.

"Delicious," she proclaimed. Taking the platter in one hand and his arm in another, she walked back to the table and sat down next to Drew. "I bring it up, Asher, because the holiday reminds me of you."

"Of me?" He let out a self-conscious laugh. "How so?"

"Because I've witnessed your struggles this past year and saw how you, with the help of my Drew, never gave up hope. Hope in yourself and in those children in the clinic. But most of all, you never gave up hope to find your brothers and now, God-willing you will." Her soft hand, mottled with age-spots came to rest upon his. "And like the oil the Maccabees found that burned for those eight nights was a miracle, so is the love you have found with my grandson."

A year ago, it would have been impossible for Ash to imagine himself sitting here, part of a family, in love with a man who not only loved him back but also changed the way he looked at life. Though guilt still tore at him and sent him into darkness, those times were less frequent now, and he found the strength to talk about them with Drew and his therapist. Holding Drew at night, having someone to whisper his fears to, who understood and loved him unconditionally, was his miracle.

"You may be right; I never thought of it that way."

With a self-satisfied smile, Esther patted his hand. The front door opened, heralding the arrival of Rachel and Mike. As she stood to greet them, she whispered to him. "I know I'm right."

THEY RETURNED HOME with enough leftovers to tide them over for a week. His grandmother made sure to give them extra potato pancakes for Ash and the apple cake he loved.

"Have you spoken to Jordan at all?" Ash pulled off his tie and unbuttoned his collar.

"I've called him several times but he's brushed me off, saying he was busy." Drew recalled how Jordan avoided him all throughout Keith's funeral. They'd all sat together, but a yawning chasm existed between the two of them. Jordan may have smiled and said all the right things to him, but Drew was no fool. It was all an act. Thirty years of friendship had given him insight into Jordan Peterson few people had and Drew no longer had any idea what he could do to set the course right again for their friendship.

"You want my advice?" Ash handed him a beer then went to the bar and poured himself vodka over ice.

Domino wound his way around Drew's legs, looking for attention and Drew gave him a treat, then joined Ash in the living room. "It's been a month now since the funeral and things haven't gotten better. Of course I do. I'm at a loss. Everyone says to wait and give him time and I understand, but I'm afraid the longer I wait the less chance we'll have to reconcile."

"Be there but don't be there for him."

Puzzled, Drew set his beer down untouched and flopped down on the sofa. "Now you're talking lawyer-speak. You need to explain for the rest of us."

Ash smirked and joined him on the sofa. "Jordan is the type who, if he thinks you're watching him, will pull away and go dark. He's one of the proudest men I've ever met and the most arrogant. He not only thinks he knows everything but hates when people try and smother him with too much attention."

"Wow," said Drew, impressed with his analysis. "You're good."

"Not really," admitted Ash. "He's a lot like me; it's

why we butt heads. We recognize each other. So give him space but keep calling to say hello, and we'll make sure to drop by at least once a week."

"You're pretty smart, aren't you?" Drew kissed his cheek and laid his head on Ash's shoulder. "I think you're right."

"I agree on both accounts." Ash set his glass down on the table. "And there's one more thing I'm right about."

"Hmm?" Drew slid down to rest his head in Ash's lap. "What?"

"That I love you."

Hearing Ash say that to him still sent a thrill though Drew. "Mmm. I concur, counselor. And might I say I'm very interested in your legal briefs." Drew rubbed his cheek against the thick bulge in Ash's pants and hearing Ash's sigh of pleasure, traced his finger down the zipper. "Maybe we should take it somewhere more comfortable and I can do a more thorough inspection."

Ash's laugh rumbled deep in his chest. "I'm more than happy to open my personal files for you."

Drew stood and pulled Ash into their bedroom, shutting the door on a very unhappy cat. "I've been dying for you all night." He pulled his sweatshirt over his head, took off his pants and boxers then climbed onto the bed, sitting crossed-legged in the center.

"Did you see Domino's face? If looks could kill I'd be dead." Ash laughed as he stripped out of his clothes. "I hope he doesn't take it out on my furniture."

"Is that all you can think about? The furniture?" Drew cocked a brow and stroked his cock. "Perhaps you aren't that interested—"

Before he had the chance to finish his sentence, Ash tackled him flat on the bed, holding him down. "Never say or think that." Ash pressed his lips to Drew's and as their tongues met in an eager slide, Drew fell into the sweetness of their kiss. Ash's mouth moved hot and hungry across his own, setting Drew's blood on fire. "You're everything to me. There could never be anyone else."

Tonight Ash's touch felt different; stronger and surer, each press and stroke of his fingers sent Drew soaring, crying out for release. Ash's declaration of love and their moving in together solidified their relationship, elevating it to a higher level.

He pulled away from Ash, and met his questioning gaze.

"I want to make love to you."

Ash stilled and sat back on his heels. "Make love to me…how?"

"Trust me?" He held out his hand, barely breathing.

"With my life." And with no hesitation, Ash placed a hand in his and Drew gently pushed him down on the bed, so he lay flat on his back. His heart squeezed at the vulnerability shining in Ash's eyes and the slight, yet visible tremors running under his skin.

"You've given so much to me these last months. I want to give you back everything and more. I love you." He straddled Ash and commenced kissing down his chest, licking at the tiny brown nipples hidden in the swirl of silky black chest hair.

"Baby, I—I don't know." He stroked the top of Drew's head.

"Shh." Drew moved down, ignoring Ash's erection and the heady smell of his desire. Instead he sat back on his heels and picked up Ash's hand, kissing each fingertip, then tracing the scars winding around Ash's wrist and arm with his tongue. "Let me kiss away your pain." He finished one arm and took the other, repeating the kisses. Ash lay quiet, his eyes half lidded, a drowsy smile of desire on his lips.

"With you I have no pain. Not anymore."

If Drew had anything to say about it Ash never would. When he watched his grandmother tell Ash the story of Chanukah, he vowed to make this night one neither would ever forget.

"Let me love you," he whispered and kissed the slick, firm tip of Ash's cock, swirling his tongue down the thick shaft. He pushed Ash's legs wide and felt him tense and shift nervously. "Shh. It's going to be fine."

Ash said nothing, but his hands clutched the sheets and Drew's heart went out to him. He dipped his head down and licked Ash's balls, inhaling his scent, loving his smell, his taste. In the silence of their bedroom Ash's harsh, uneven breathing hurt Drew's heart. Knowing Ash's continued fear and pain, Drew vowed to make this as special for Ash as it would be for him. Another first for them to share.

He licked at Ash's hole, running his tongue down the shadowed crease of his ass. Ash moaned, his head thrashing on the pillow and Drew, taking that as a sign to continue, spread the globes of Ash's ass wide and gently, almost reverently kissed his hole then licked around it, wetting it thoroughly before sliding his tongue inside.

"Ahh, fuck." Ash cried out, his heels digging into the bed.

Drew continued to lick at Ash's ass, alternating between flattening his tongue to swipe across the hole and spearing it inside. Tremors wracked Ash's body and Drew sat back, breathing heavily.

"How do you feel?"

From their talks, he knew Ash had never allowed another man inside him since those horrifying days as a teenager. Drew's only wish was to give Ash the same pleasure he unselfishly gave to Drew whenever they made love.

"Like I need to be inside you yesterday. C'mere." He held out his hand and Drew lay down next to him, fitting himself down Ash's side. Drew caught his breath only a moment before Ash rolled over trapping him beneath his body.

"What an incredible gift you've given me tonight. I didn't think I could ever enjoy anyone touching me there again. I thought he stole my ability to love, to feel. You've made me see it was only in my mind." They kissed and Drew couldn't contain his sigh of happiness as desire rolled through him. He slipped his arms around Ash.

"Kiss me again. Kiss my neck, my mouth, every part of me belongs to you."

Shards of pleasure rippled up Drew's spine as Ash licked and nibbled his way down his throat, only to return to his mouth and crush their lips together, tongues sliding and tangling. Their bodies picked up a natural rhythm and Drew felt the hard ridge of Ash's erection brush against his stomach and thigh as Ash rolled his hips.

"Now, please."

Ash continued to pepper his face with kisses, his arms braced on either side of Drew's face. "You want me, baby?"

"Yeah. I want you. All of you, naked against me. Inside me."

He and Ash had never discussed it but they were monogamous, in love and committed to each other. As far as Drew was concerned, they had no need to use condoms anymore. He also knew Ash had never gone bare before.

Ash studied him, his darkly handsome face serious. "I'd hoped you'd want to one day. This evening has been so perfect in many ways, I've never felt closer to you and I think it's the right time for us." He took the bottle of lube and slicked himself up, and Drew opened himself wide, then slid his legs over Ash's hips feeling the head of Ash's cock push inside him.

The bed creaked in a slow and steady rhythm as Ash thrust into him, awakening all Drew's desire, as always making him come alive.

"Oh, God." Every bump and vein of Ash's flesh lay naked up against his skin, raw and hot. He'd never been bare with anyone, but it could only be with Ash, who'd started out a stranger but found a way to piece together Drew's broken soul and now owned his heart. This moment would be one he'd remember forever; a new beginning for them both, wiping away the sins and heartaches of their pasts.

A fine sheen of sweat gilded their naked bodies as they moved together until Drew could no longer hold back and came with a harsh cry. Ash followed him a moment later, filling Drew deep inside with his warmth. They lay plastered together, chests heaving and breaths mingling in the cooling air. Drew loved these quiet moments after they'd both climaxed, neither of them wanting to move and break the skin to skin contact. Now they'd shared something neither ever had with another partner, sealing their already solid commitment.

He pressed his lips to Ash's shoulder, thinking back upon the night and the holiday. So many years he'd spent alone or at bars making small talk with people—strangers he never intended to see again. They weren't wasted years, at least he didn't believe them to be so. As Rachel once said, everything happens for a reason; even the mistakes you made were a pathway toward your final destination.

Ash kissed his head and after pulling out, stretched out alongside him, chest to chest, tangling their feet together under the sheet. It seemed he too had a need for nestling and holding on tonight. "What're you thinking about, baby?"

"I'm thinking about you and me." Drew brushed back the hair from Ash's forehead to gaze into his glittering, diamond-bright eyes. "And miracles."

Keep reading for a Sneak Peek of Jordan and Luke's story in After the Fire, coming Winter 2017

Chapter One

ONLY THE PAIN in his heart eclipsed the ache in his head. Bleary-eyed, Dr. Jordan Peterson lifted his head from where he sat, slumped at his kitchen table, to stare into the void of his house. Empty bottles of vodka littered the table, alongside half-full takeout Chinese food containers.

Still alone.

Each time he awakened, Jordan prayed the nightmare that played consistently in his head would cease. It played like that annoying song on the radio you heard every hour you want to forget, but can't.

"I'm sorry, Jordan, but Keith didn't make it."

How do you move on from the finality of the death of your love when you've promised him the rest of your life? After almost nine months Jordan still didn't have the answer.

The doorbell rang. Groaning with the effort it took to move his protesting body, and with his head pounding from another vicious hangover, he grabbed the bottle of aspirin siting on the countertop and popped two pills, aided by a handful of water directly from the tap. Then, swallowing his nausea, he shuffled to the front door of his town house. Jordan massaged his temples and squinted through the peephole, grimacing at the sight of his best friend, Drew, with his lover, Ash.

Jordan's chest tightened at the happiness on his friend's face as Drew kissed Ash's cheek, unaware he was being spied upon. Smothering the bitterness he'd held close to his chest toward Drew these past months, he yanked open the door to greet the two men.

"Damn, you look like shit." Ash's sharp gaze raked him up and down. "Ow." He rubbed his arm when Drew elbowed him. "Don't get mad at me, baby. You know he does. Look at him."

"Can we come in, Jordy?" Drew's kind smile only made him feel worse, not better considering the enmity Jordan carried inside.

He said nothing and pulled the front door wider for his friends, leaving them to trail behind him back through the house and into the spacious kitchen. Sunlight poured onto the terra-cotta floors and glinted off the glass-fronted maple cabinets. The kitchen was his pride and joy, and when he and Keith bought the brownstone, it had been the only room he cared about decorating. Jordan had always loved staring out of the large bay window at the garden and the sky as he relaxed with his cup of coffee in the morning, Keith beside him reading the paper. Now all he saw was an empty chair beside him.

"Did you have a party?" Drew tipped his head to the table, still cluttered with vodka bottles.

"Party of one, more likely."

Despite a throbbing head and a roiling stomach, Jordan lashed out at Ash's muttered remark.

"Shut up, Davis." He and Ash had never had the easiest of relationships; the man still irritated the hell out of Jordan no matter how happy he made Drew.

"Why, Jordan? The truth hurts?" Ash's voice, oddly enough, neither condemned nor derided him. Instead, it held an overall note of sadness, mixed with empathy that pulled Jordan up short. "You sit here, night after night, refusing our dinner invitations, as well as Rachel and Mike's, or even Esther. We know what you're doing and why."

Jordan winced. Shit. A kindhearted, sympathetic Ash Davis was almost worse than the usual sarcastic attitude he dished out to everyone. "I'm not in the mood for company; that's all."

"And I call bullshit on that. You're still mourning Keith, and I get that, but that doesn't mean you don't go on living. When your only company since he died has been a bottle of vodka, you're heading for disaster."

"Jordy." Drew entreated, bracing his hands on the kitchen island. "I'm worried about you. You've lost weight, skipped days at the hospital, and I was told that during surgery last week—"

"Are you checking up on me?" Shaking with anger he fisted his hands at his side. "What the fuck, man? You're not my goddamn keeper." Humiliation, shame, and a sense of despair tore through him as he turned away from his two friends to sit at the kitchen table. He ran his hands over the battered wood of the long farmhouse table, recalling how happy he and Keith had been to find it in the small Pennsylvania town they'd stumbled upon one Saturday. The memory of making love on top of it after lugging it up the stairs of the brownstone will forever remain etched in his mind. He gripped the edge of the table to steady himself.

For over thirty years he and Drew had been friends; the man knew him better than anyone. People might think Drew Klein a sweet and easygoing pushover of a man, but Jordan knew the core of steel within him. Drew refused to back down if he thought he could help. True to form, Drew dropped into the chair right next to him, challenging and direct.

"Jordan. Look at me."

It took an effort to tear his gaze away from the tabletop, but he inhaled a deep breath and smiled into Drew's face. "What is it?"

He didn't fool Drew. "Don't give me that fake-ass smile. I'm not checking up on you. It's common knowledge you showed up to your first surgery since Keith died and had to wait an extra hour to start because you had the shakes." Drew's mouth thinned to a hard line. "Are you crazy showing up drunk for surgery? You could lose your fucking license, for God's sake."

"I wasn't drunk. I was overtired and hadn't eaten since lunchtime the day before."

Behind him he heard Ash snort with laughter. "Are you fucking kidding me, Jordan? You can come up with a better one than that."

"Fuck off, Ash," he shot back. "I couldn't care less about your opinion."

"How about mine? Don't lie to me." Drew's stare remained unflinching, his eyes soft and knowing. "I know you're still having a hard time moving on from Keith's death, but it'll be a year soon."

"It's only been nine months. God almighty, did you expect me to forget him already?" Horrified, Jordan swept his hand across the table, sending the empty bottles and food containers crashing to the floor. "Keith and I were together for almost four years. You haven't even been with Ash a year; could you forget him so easily? Stop pressuring me to move on with my life. It's over for me. There will never be anyone else."

"So you plan on drinking yourself into an early grave, losing your job and quite possibly your friends along the way?" Drew placed a hand on his arm. "I don't think Keith would expect you to mourn him forever."

"I didn't expect to have to mourn him at all. He was supposed to be here, with me." The tears, always threatening below the surface, spilled over, coursing hot and fierce down his cheeks. It seemed he hadn't stopped crying since Keith's murder. "I can't get past it. No matter what I do, he's always there with me, and I can't let him go." All the fight and anger left him deflated like a balloon several days after a party. An ineffable weariness stole through him, and he laid his head on his arms on top of the table. "Go home, you two. Leave me alone."

Without a word, Ash found the broom and dust-pan and began to clean up the broken glass while Drew remained seated next to him at the table.

"Look, I understand what you're feeling. But destroying yourself isn't going to bring him back. We know you miss him."

"You don't understand." Jordan shook off Drew's attempt to comfort him. "I'm beginning to forget him. Not only his voice, but also the way his arms held me. The way the sound of his breathing calmed me, so I could fall asleep every night." His breath caught in his throat, and a shudder racked his body.

Jordan couldn't reveal the worst—that he could no longer recall the press of Keith's lips on his or the sweet sweep of Keith's tongue in his mouth. The warmth and smoothness of Keith's skin, once as familiar as Jordan's own, had begun fading to a cold and distant memory. Sometimes he'd sit in bed late at night and play his voicemail messages simply to hear Keith's voice. How fucking disloyal a love was he? It had only been nine months, yet Keith's touch, something he'd longed for every day of his life and sworn he'd never forget, had slipped away like fog in the summer wind. Gentle and swift, leaving no trace behind that it had ever existed.

"Shouldn't I remember? I lived with him and loved him with my life." He lifted his head to stare into Drew's eyes, seeing the sympathy and pain that had resided there since Keith had died. Hating Drew for that. He didn't want anyone feeling sorry for him, perceiving him as weak. He preferred the way Ash treated him, with stark truth and harsh reality. At least with that he could get angry and curse But when Drew treated Jordan with kid gloves, all sweet and sympathetic, he couldn't strike back.

"It has nothing to do with loyalty. It's merely the way the passage of time allows us to accept what's happened. After my parents died, I raged over not saving their voice mails." Drew's green eyes glimmered with tears. Though his parents had been gone now well over ten years, killed in a horrific car crash, Jordan knew Drew still mourned their senseless deaths. "To be able to listen to their voices might've brought me some comfort. I knew they were really gone when I couldn't hear their voices in my head anymore. But in a way, it finally allowed me to move on with my life."

Jordan watched as Ash placed his hands on Drew's shoulders, bending down to brush a quick kiss on his cheek. That was what he missed. The support, the small gestures letting him know someone loved him enough to care.

"What if I don't want to move on? Or can't?" Unbeknownst to Drew, he was part of Jordan's problem, though Jordan couldn't bring himself to tell Drew that relevant fact. It would crush Drew. He pushed himself up from the table and took the broom out of Ash's hands. "There's nothing you or anyone can do. I'm doing the best I can, so leave me alone. Go bother someone else."

"You're such a bad liar." Ash leaned his hip against the kitchen counter. "This"—his hand swept at the debris littering the floor—"is the best you can do? Day-old takeout food and empty liquor bottles? Where's the Dr. Jordan Peterson I knew—stylish, arrogant, and always in control?" Ash quirked a brow. "Even before you met Keith, you were a proud bastard. This is far, far from your best."

A knot twisted in Jordan's stomach. That was the point. He didn't want to go back to the way he'd been before. There'd been other relationships, but none had mattered. Only Keith had seen through him right from the start. No one knew how badly Jordan needed Keith to anchor him. Jordan knew he could be that proud bastard, as Ash called him, to the outside world, because he had Keith at home, loving him, flaws and all. With Keith gone, the soft part of Jordan, vulnerable and needy for comfort and love, was dying.

"Go away, both of you, and leave me alone." He continued to sweep up the floor, unwilling and unable to meet his friends' eyes. The *thunk* of the mail falling through the slot gave him the perfect excuse to leave them. As he made his way to the front door, the bell rang.

Christ, was he to get no peace today? The weekend was supposed to be for resting.

He answered the door to see his mailman on the stoop. "Hey, Bill. You have something for me?" Jordan and his mailman were on a friendly basis since Jordan had operated on the man's knee early last year with excellent results.

"Yes, Dr. Peterson. I have a certified letter you need to sign for." He held out the green card, which Jordan signed and returned. "Thanks, Doc."

"See you in a few months for your checkup." Jordan smiled at the mailman and watched him walk away, noting with a professional eye the even gait and freedom of movement of the Bill's knee as he descended the steps of the brownstone. Jordan turned away and closed the door behind him. As he scanned the letter, he saw with a sinking heart it was from Lambert and North, the financial consulting firm Keith had used to set up his accounts.

Most people hadn't known the extent of Keith's wealth. The man had truly had a Midas touch when it came to having his money make money, and he'd been intimately involved in the investment of that money. When Keith died, he left Jordan as his main beneficiary. He'd also created a trust for charities dedicated to LGBT inner city children.

Upon the reading of the will a month or so after Keith's death, Jordan learned Keith had created a foundation to prevent gun violence among the city's youth population. He'd coordinated it with the police department so that the teens would be taken to Riker's Island to see what happened to men and women who chose to get involved with crime and illegal guns. But there was much more to it. There were after-school sports programs to be set up, music lessons for kids, computers, anything to keep them off the street. Though it was mainly centered around Keith's precinct and the schools in the area, Keith had arranged for several corporate sponsors to keep the money coming, but the hope was that more private funding would flow into it once they publicized the charity.

Jordan had been named the president of the foundation and administrator of the trust, but had been putting off meeting the financial adviser since the reading of the will. He didn't have the heart or strength to get entangled in this endeavor, even if Keith had wanted him to. He was so tired of it all and wanted only for people to leave him alone.

"Who was that?" Drew asked. He and Ash both looked up from the floor, where they had recommenced cleaning. All the glass had been swept up and put in the garbage, Jordan noticed, and Drew had wiped the tile floor with some wet paper towels. He really did have some good friends, even if they came with pain-in-the-ass boyfriends.

"It was the mailman. Nothing important." Jordan knew better than to tell these two how he'd been blowing off meeting the foundation's financial adviser. Drew's own cause, the medical clinic he'd set up for abused young men and women, was his whole life, and his and Ash's dedication to it was extraordinary. They wouldn't take kindly to him dodging his responsibility. For a brief moment, shame coursed through him, and he decided he'd call to set up an appointment with the financial consultant.

"Don't think you have to babysit me. I'm going to take a shower and run some errands." He needed to refill his liquor cabinet and some prescriptions, but they didn't have to know that.

Ash shot him a hard look, disbelief apparent in his eyes while Drew merely shook his head. "Is that what you think we're doing? You're my best friend, yet I barely see you anymore." Drew's inscrutable expression unnerved Jordan. Seeing Drew so guarded and hurt, shame once again pricked Jordan's conscience. Keith had been his lover, but Drew and their other friend Mike were his brothers in every sense of the word. He'd never hidden anything from them. Until now.

The past few months had made him an expert in masking his feelings. So with a smile he hoped didn't look too fake or forced, he slapped Drew on the back, trying to lighten the mood. "You're right. And I promise to make an effort to get out more and get a handle on my life." With a small prayer of thanks, he watched as his two friends prepared to leave.

"Don't be a stranger. My grandmother misses you." Drew hugged him, whispering into his ear, "I miss you."

Guilt cramped Jordan's stomach.

"Seriously, Jordan. Come by for dinner this week. Maybe you can distract that cat from attacking my ankles every time I walk by." Ash grimaced, but his eyes crinkled with amusement.

Even Jordan laughed at Ash's running battle with Drew's cat, Domino. Seemed the cat resented Ash's place in Drew's life and took out his displeasure every chance he got.

"I can't help it if the cat has good taste, Davis." Jordan smirked and ducked Ash's friendly punch before he followed Drew out the front door.

Jordan couldn't help but notice how, when they were halfway down the block, Ash stopped, grasped Drew around the neck, and kissed him hard. They continued to walk, Ash's arm snug around Drew's shoulders to tug him close. A pain sharp and deep knifed through Jordan, and he caught his breath. There was no one left to hold him. Not anymore.

Grief-stricken and unwilling to face more loving gestures between his friends, Jordan turned his back and re-entered his house. He picked up the certified letter and opened it, scanning the brief paragraph.

Dear Dr. Peterson:

I have tried, unsuccessfully these past few months, to contact you regarding the foundation the late Keith Hart created. As you have failed to respond, I will take this as your decision not to participate in this worthwhile endeavor. Please consider this as formal notice I will be asking the other members of the board to remove you from this position, and we will begin the process of acquiring a new president of the board.

Very truly yours,
Lucas Conover, Platinum Account Services
Lambert & North, LLC

Jordan's eyes narrowed as the burn of anger rose in his face. Fucking snotty bastard. Who the hell was this Conover to talk to him like that? He'd make sure to call today for an appointment. Jordan stormed into the bathroom and opened the medicine cabinet. The bottle of pills sat there, mocking him. Jordan grabbed it, wrenched the top open, and swallowed the last two. If one was good, two were better. Antidepressant? Shit, make it more like anti-feel anything at all. The way Jordan liked it. He slammed the door and faced himself in the mirror, wincing at his too-pale skin and bloodshot, sunken eyes. Once the pills kicked in and he took a shower, he'd be good as new. The languid sense of well-being from the drugs began to seep into his body. He couldn't wait until Monday morning, when he'd come face-to-face with that little prick, Lucas Conover.

About the Author

I have always been a romantic at heart. I believe that while life is tough, there is always a happy ending around the corner, My characters have to work for it, however. Like life in NYC, nothing comes easy and that includes love.

I live in New York City with my husband and two children and hopefully soon a cat of my own. My day begins with a lot of caffeine and ends with a glass or two of red wine. I practice law but daydream of a time when I can sit by a beach somewhere and write beautiful stories of men falling in love. Although there are bound to be a few bumps along the way, a Happily Ever After is always guaranteed.

I love hearing from readers!! Find me here:

Join my newsletter for contests, exclusive sneak peeks, and giveaways

bit.ly/FelicesNewsletter

Felice's Fierce Fans:

facebook.com/groups/1449289332021166

Website:

www.felicestevens.com

Facebook:

facebook.com/felice.stevens.1

Twitter:

twitter.com/FeliceStevens1

Instagram:

instagram.com/felicestevens

Goodreads:

goodreads.com/author/show/8432880.Felice_Stevens

Other titles by Felice Stevens

Through Hell and Back Series:

A Walk Through Fire

After the Fire: Re-release coming Winter 2017

Embrace the Fire: Re-release coming Spring 2017

The Memories Series:

Memories of the Heart

One Step Further

The Greatest Gift

The Breakfast Club Series:

Beyond the Surface

Betting on Forever

Second to None

What Lies Between Us

Other:

Rescued

Learning to Love

The Arrangement